# Regency Rogues:

## Disgraceful Secrets

### CHRISTINE MERRILL

MILLS & BOON

First Published in Great Britain 2020
By Mills & Boon, an imprint of HarperCollins*Publishers*
1 London Bridge Street, London, SE1 9GF

REGENCY ROGUES: DISGRACEFUL SECRETS © 2020
Harlequin Books S.A.

*The Secrets of Wiscombe Chase* © 2016 Christine Merrill
*Lady Priscilla's Shameful Secret* © 2012 Christine Merrill

ISBN: 978-0-263-27953-5

**MIX**
Paper from
responsible sources
FSC™ C007454

Printed and bound in Spain
by CPI, Barcelona

# THE SECRETS OF
# WISCOMBE CHASE

To Kevin McElroy and Wayne White.
Congratulations from someone who knew
you when…


'Love is something eternal. The aspect may
change, but not the essence.'
—Vincent van Gogh

# Chapter One

'Miss North, would you do me the honour of accepting my hand in holy matrimony?'

Lillian North did her best to smile at the unfortunate boy kneeling before her on the parlour rug and readied herself for the only answer she would be permitted to give.

Once, she had harboured illusions about love and romance. Most young girls did. But they had been left in the nursery, along with the other spectacular fictions about fairy princesses and brave knights riding to their rescue. When she'd made her come-out, Father and Ronald had explained the way the world truly worked.

It was her job to be pretty, pleasant and biddable, and attract what offers she could from gentlemen of the *ton.* In the end, she would marry and marry well. But it would be to a man of Father's choosing and she was not to question the choice.

She had been in London for months, both this year and last. She had danced at Almack's until her slippers were near to worn through. She had smiled until her cheeks ached with it and been so agreeable that people must think her simple in the head. It felt as if she had been introduced to every eligible man in Britain. While she'd her favourites, she had not allowed herself to form an attachment to any of them. She must never forget that the final choice would not be hers.

She had done as she was told and cast the properly baited net as wide as possible. When the time was right, her father and brother would draw it in to evaluate the catch. They would throw back the unworthy and keep no more than two or three of the very best. Then, the serious negotiating would begin. In the end, she would be decked in flowers and sent up the aisle of St George's to stand at the side of a scion of the nobility. Father had assured her that he would settle for nothing less than a London cathedral and a groom that would leave other girls green at her success.

But now, all the plans and the manoeuvring of a season and a half were for naught. Without warning, she had been hauled out of town and informed that the choice had been made. She was to marry Gerald Wiscombe.

And who was he? It was as if she had cast her net and brought in a dark horse. Her metaphors were as muddled as her thoughts, but she could hardly be blamed for confusion. Mr Wiscombe was a total stranger to her. Although he was not a particularly memorable fellow, she was sure she'd have recalled meeting him, if only because he was unlike any of the men who'd courted her in London.

Lily had prayed each night that her future husband would have admirable qualities beyond wealth and station. Perhaps a love match was unrealistic. But, her future would be happier if it was, at least, founded on mutual respect. When she had taken the time to search for them, she had found good qualities in each of the men who had escorted her. Why, then, could she find nothing to recommend her father's final choice?

To begin with, Mr Wiscombe was too young to be taken seriously. He was barely into his majority, only a year or so older than her. He was not even out of university and more interested in his impending Tripos in Mathematics than wedding her. In fact, he'd refused to come to London and court her. She had been expected to go to Cambridge to see him, so that the burden of this proposal would not interrupt his studies.

It did Mr Wiscombe no credit that he augmented his youth and uninterest with a lack of fashion and an awkwardness of address. Where was the evidence of his precious education? There was no sign on his soft, round face that he was destined to be a wit or a wag. When he smiled, the gap in his front teeth made him look as simple as she felt.

Looks were not important, she reminded herself. After dancing with men old enough to sire her, she had steeled herself to ignore appearances. Brains were not necessary if one had rank or money.

But that still did not explain Gerald Wiscombe. A few short weeks ago, Father had turned up his nose at an interested baronet as being too low-born to qualify as son-in-law. But now, there was nothing more than a 'mister' rocking uneasily on his knees in the parlour of a roadside inn, awaiting the answer.

He must be quite wealthy to make up for the lack of a title. But Mr Wiscombe had not bought so much as a bottle of wine to celebrate this day, nor had he visited a tailor to impress her. The cuffs of his coat were worn and one of the unpolished buttons clung to the garment by its last thread.

'I do not have much,' he said, affirming her worst fears. 'I have no family to speak of. None at all, actually. I am the last of the Wiscombes. And the family fortune was gone a generation ago.'

'I am sorry to hear it,' she said, not so much sorry as totally perplexed.

'Of course, Wiscombe Chase is lovely.'

*A country manor?* She smiled encouragingly.

'Was lovely,' he corrected with a shrug and a frown, as though he'd meant to lie and could not quite get it to stick. 'It needs much work and the loving hand of a woman.'

Which probably meant it was a mouldering ruin and he was seeking a rich wife to repair it for him. This man was the polar opposite of the one she had been sent out to catch.

At some point, Father's agenda had changed and she had not been informed. But when was Father not hatching a plan of some kind? His schemes invariably left him better off than he had been, while those who had dealings with him always seemed surprised to be poorer and less successful. Even so, few of them would have called him swindler. Those who lost to him preferred to think of him as that dashed, lucky Mr North.

She had always been inside the invisible boundary that separated her family from the rest of the world. No matter how precarious things might seem, everything would go well for her in the end. Because she was a North.

Until today, at least.

Did her father not understand that a young lady's reputation was a fragile thing? Marriage was a permanent and nigh unbreakable contract. He could not barter her out of the family only to pull her back on some tenuous legal string, like the Bolivian emerald mine she'd seen him sell at a profit some three times already.

Worse yet, she was alone in her ignorance. Her brother, Ronald, had baulked when forced to escort her about London on the hunt for a suitable match. But he had been the one to introduce Mr Wiscombe and seemed as eager to see her married as Father did.

'Miss North?' Mr Wiscombe prompted, noticing the long and doubtful silence that had followed his offer.

She looked down at what was likely to be her future husband. He was staring up at her, mouth gaping slightly. He reminded her of a barely formed chick, unfledged, inexperienced and waiting to be fed. She feared the young *avis Wiscombe* was about to be pushed early from the nest and gobbled by waiting predators, *genus North*.

It made his next statement all the more worrying.

'I wouldn't bother you, if that's what you are afraid of.' Now he was blushing. 'We need time to get to know each other, before that. Your father has promised to buy me a commission so I might make my fortune. I will be gone for some years. When I am returned there will be enough money for the two of us to live quite well. And then…'

The mystery deepened. First off, he'd said the word *bother* with such significance that she assumed he meant something. And he assumed she understood. She supposed she did, after a fashion. He must be talking about what occurred between a husband and wife. She had no mother to explain details to her and was far too afraid and embarrassed to ask Father. If it was bothersome, she was not sure she wished to know the specifics.

But if he meant to join the army at her father's behest and be gone for several years? That was simply laughable. She doubted Gerald Wiscombe would last several minutes before the French, much less several years. Did her father mean to send this poor boy to his doom?

She did not want to believe it. While her father was somewhat less than honest, she had never known him to be brutal. But the harder she tried to reject it the more her mind filled with the icy certainty that this was precisely what Phineas North intended. If he was willing to sacrifice his own daughter like a chess piece, what hope did this poor young man have to survive until checkmate?

If that was the game, then she refused to play her part in it. It would be a lie to say that she felt affection for the man in front of her. But neither did she wish him ill. Even if she felt nothing at all, how could she live with herself if the marriage was little more than a death sentence for her husband? She would not be permitted to refuse. But perhaps if she could get Mr Wiscombe to withdraw the offer, the matter would settle itself.

Lily wet her lips. 'Are you sure that is wise?'

He was blinking at her as if he had no idea what she meant. Perhaps he was not quite right in the head.

'The army will be very dangerous.' She spoke slowly, so he could understand. When this did not seem to make an impression, she added, with additional emphasis, 'There is no guarantee that you will return in a few years with a fortune. In fact, there is no guarantee that you will return at all.'

In response, he blinked the watery grey eyes in his round face and gave her another foolish grin.

'You might be killed,' she said. Now her voice sounded testy. She did not wish to be cross with him, but he needn't be so stupid, either. She shouldn't have to spell out the trap he was walking into.

Finally, one doughy hand reached out to cover hers. 'You need not worry about that. It is a possibility, of course. But there are many others equally grim. I might fall off my horse and break my neck before we can even say the vows. Or get struck by lightning while picking flowers in the garden. Or I might survive the battle and live to a ripe old age.' He blinked again. 'You are not afraid of that, are you?'

Afraid? Why should she be afraid of such an unlikely possibility?

Now he was looking at her as though she were the

one who did not understand the gravity of the situation. Suddenly, she was sure that, all this time, he had been measuring her just as she had measured him. 'You do understand, if you are to marry me, it will be till death us do part,' he said and paused to let the words sink in. 'Although you obviously assume otherwise, my death may be a long time in coming.'

Did he think her so stupid that she did not understand the basic vows she would be taking? Or had he just insulted her, hinting that she was marrying him in the hopes that he would die? It would be too horrible, if there weren't some truth to it.

He was still blinking at her with those innocent, wet eyes. There was something hiding deep within them and it was not the eagerness of a bridegroom. The light shining there was like the sun reflected off cold iron. What he felt when he looked at her was not passion, or even affection. It was grim resolve.

His words had been a last attempt to make her prove her worth and admit that she had no desire to marry him. If she said yes to his proposal, he would assume she was as grasping and sly as the rest of her family, and meant to lure him into a marriage with the hope of imminent widowhood.

She stiffened. Any other girl would have withdrawn her hand and rejected his suit without another thought. She'd have cut him dead, had there been any chance that they would ever meet again, which they would not. If he liked his mathematics books so well, he could marry them. She would go back to the handsome, titled men of Almack's and forget him utterly. He could return to his ruin of a house. Once there, he could lick his wounds and brood upon this day with the embarrassment it deserved.

But she was not any other girl. She was the daughter of Phineas North. If she left the room after refusing Mr Wiscombe, Father would turn her back at the doorstep to hear him again. Should she manage to escape to her room, she would be locked there until she came to her senses and did as she was told. If the current plan fell through and she was able to divest herself of Gerald Wiscombe, there was no guarantee that the next choice she was offered would be any better. In fact, it could be much, much worse.

She was as trapped and doomed as the boy on his knees before her. So she looked down at him with what she hoped was an aloof, but ultimately benevolent stare. 'I am well aware of the words of the marriage ceremony, Mr Wiscombe, and have enough wit to understand their meaning. If we marry, it is for life. However long—' she gave him another probing, significant look '—or short that might be. I am also aware that it gives you the right to, as you put it earlier, bother me whenever you so choose to do so. But if you do not have the sense to be afraid of Napoleon, than why should I be afraid of marrying you?'

For a moment, everything changed and not for the better. He favoured her with the gap-toothed grin of an idiot. Then he rose to his feet. Rather than attempting to kiss her, he clasped her hand in a firm, manly shake. 'Very well. It is a bargain, then. We will be married as soon as your father can arrange for the licence.

When I return from the Peninsula, we will begin our future together.'

The poor fool. What else could she do but nod in agreement? Once he was gone, perhaps she could persuade Ronald to tell her what was really going on. But there was one thing that she already knew. If Gerald Wiscombe had chosen to make a bargain with her father, his future and fortune were decided and fate was laughing in his face.

## Chapter Two

'If you are intent on selling your commission, Wiscombe, we shall be sad to see you go. It was a fortuitous day for the British army when you first decided to take up the sword.'

'Thank you, Colonel Kincaid.' Gerry dipped his head in modest acknowledgement to the man seated at the desk. Whenever he received such compliments, he was always faintly relieved that his commanding officers had not been present on the day, seven years ago, that he'd made that decision. It had been an act of desperation, pure and simple. There had been nothing the least bit heroic about it.

'It is a shame you do not wish to continue in the service. Surely we could find a place for an officer with such a past as yours.'

The thought had crossed his mind. Even as he passed through the arched gate of the Horse Guards, he had considered asking for another posting. A few years in India would not go amiss. But after so much time away, avoiding his home felt more like cowardice than bravery.

Gerry looked Kincaid square in the eye to show that he would not be moved. 'It would be an honour to continue in service to the crown. But after seven years, it is time to trade one war for another.'

The colonel gave him the same mildly confused look that others had given him when he had phrased it so. It did not matter. Understanding was not necessary. He smiled back at the man to show that it was all in jest. 'It is a long time to be away from home. When I left, I was but newly married.' He opened the locket he carried that contained the miniature of Lillian.

The colonel smiled back and gave him a knowing wink. 'I see. There is little the army can offer that can compete with the open arms of a beautiful woman waiting eagerly for your return.'

Gerry nodded again. She had been beautiful. Likely, she still was. The position of her arms and her degree of eagerness were yet to be determined. His smile remained unwavering, as the papers were signed that severed him from the military.

From Whitehall, he went to Bond Street to find a tailor. He shuddered to think what clothing was still in the cupboards of his old room. He'd been a half-formed boy when he'd left the place to go to Portugal. Even if the coats still fit, they would be even more threadbare and out of fashion than they had been when he'd left. After Father had died, he'd had not a penny to spare on his appearance. But there was no need to spend the rest of his life in uniform, now that he had earned enough to pay for proper clothing.

His dragoon's regimentals were more than impressive enough to turn heads as he walked down the street. He heard the whispers that followed him as he passed the shops.

'Is that Wiscombe?'

'There he is.'

'Captain Wiscombe. Hero of Salamanca. Hero of Waterloo.'

Had the word of his return reached Wiscombe Chase? It must have, if strangers could recognise him on the street. What would North's reaction be when Gerry turned up to reclaim his home, after all this time?

And what would *she* think of it?

He turned his mind away from that question and ordered the new clothes sent on ahead of him. Then he turned his horse to the north and began the ride home.

Once he was clear of the city, he gave Satan his head and let the miles pass uncounted. This was how it should be, man and steed travelling light. When the beast tired, they stopped and slept rough, not bothering with an inn. When it rained, Gerry threw an oilcloth over his coat and let the water run off him in sheets. Later, the sun returned and dried them, filling his nostrils with the smell of steaming wool and horse.

Kincaid had been right. He would miss this. But the whole point in buying a commission had been to gain the money to save the house and secure his future. He'd succeeded in that some years past. After Vitoria, there had been more than enough money to clear his debts, fix the roof and have a tidy sum left to invest.

He could have gone home then. But he had not. Even after Boney was sent to Elba, he had dawdled. The little Frenchman's escape had come as a relief, for it meant a few more months during which he could delay the inevitable.

Now that the last shot had been fired and Napoleon was off to St Helena, he was out of excuses. It was time to return to his first responsibility.

And there, on the horizon, was the stone marker that indicated the beginning of the Wiscombe family land. His land, he amended. There had been no family living when he had taken up the sword. If there had been anyone left, the cowardly boy he had been would have appealed to them for help and avoided the next seven years of his own life.

Gerry shrugged at the thought and the horse under him sensed his unease and gave a faint shift of his own.

He stroked the great black neck and they continued on the road that wound through the dense wood surrounding the house. The wild, untamed nature of the property was more beautiful than any formal garden. Beautiful, but useless. Dense woodland was bordered on one side by rills and streams too small to navigate by boat and on the other by granite tors and bogs that made coach travel impossible.

His life might have been easier had his ancestors settled in a place capable of sustaining crops, cattle or industry. The land around Wiscombe Chase was fit for nothing but hunting. Since he did not intend to ever take another life, animal or human, it might be better to sell the lot to a sportsman who could appreciate it.

But after all the blood he had shed to keep it, he could not bring himself to entertain the idea. Some men at his side had fought for king and country. Others hated the French tyrant more than they loved their own cause. Still others wanted money or glory.

He had fought for his birthright. This ten square miles of wood and moor was his own country to defend and rule. It generated not a penny of income. If he was honest, he did not even like the draughty and impractical manor that had drained away the Wiscombe fortune. But, by God, it was his, to the last rock.

As if to confirm the wisdom of his decision, he saw a shift in the leaves on the left side of the road. He reined in and warned Satan to be still. A twig cracked and he held his breath, waiting. The stag stepped into the road, watching him as intently as he watched it. The spread of the antlers was broader than he remembered and the muzzle had more grey in it. But the left shoulder had the same scrape from his father's bullet, so very long ago.

'Hello, old friend,' he whispered.

The deer gave a single snort, then tossed his head and disappeared into the trees.

In response, Gerry's heart leapt with joy at the rightness of being home. Though he'd fought against it since the day he'd left, he belonged here. He spurred the horse to clear the last stand of trees and the house came into sight.

It had been near to ruin when he'd left. But now the heavy brown stone was clean and the roof sported new grey slate. The windows sparkled bright in the growing dusk. And every last one of them was lit.

Perhaps they had filled the house to the rafters with friends to welcome him home. He could not help the ironic smile this idea brought. He'd had no friends at all when he'd left England. To the best of his knowledge, that had not changed in his absence.

It likely meant that he was interrupting someone else's party. He felt the same unholy glee that sometimes took him when charging on to the battlefield. It had never been the carnage that attracted him. It was the clarity that came when one knew life might end at any moment. Other fears paled in comparison, especially the fear of one's own mistakes. He had learned to act before he was acted upon. After years of being life's pawn, he had become the force of chaos that acted upon others.

He smiled. If ever there was an opposing army deserving of chaotic upset, it was the North family.

He cantered the last half mile, coming to an easy stop at the front door. The footman who came forward to take the horse did not know him. But then, in '08, he had not been able to afford a servant at the door, much less the livery that this boy wore.

His butler had no such problems with recognition. The door opened and the expression on the man's normally impassive face changed to surprise. 'Master

Gerald?' Those words were smothered with a quick
clearing of the throat and 'Begging your pardon, Captain Wiscombe.' But underneath the reserve, he was
near to grinning, and so proud of his master that he
looked ready to pop his waistcoat buttons.

Gerry had no reason for reserve with the man who
had comforted him on the night his father had died.
'Aston.' He reached forward and offered a brief, manly
embrace, clasping the fellow's shoulder and patting him
once on the back. 'It is good to be home.'

'And to have you home as well, sir. We have followed your exploits in the newspapers. It was very
exciting.'

So they had heard of him here. Of course they had.
Who had not? All the same, he was glad to have worn
his uniform so that he might reinforce the image of
returned war hero. Even after days in the saddle, the
short jacket and shiny boots were more than a little
impressive. And the sword at his side was proof that
he was no idle fop in feathers and braid.

Aston looked past him. 'Are you unaccompanied?
Where is the luggage?'

'Arriving later. I had it sent, direct from London.' He
smiled at the old servant. 'I did not wish to wait for it.'

The man nodded back, taking his haste for a compliment. 'We are all glad that you did not.'

Was that true above stairs as well as below? He
sincerely doubted it. 'Where is she?' he said softly,
looking past the butler. 'Not waiting at the door for
my return, I see.'

'Come into the house, Captain.' The man was still

grinning over the new rank. 'While you refresh yourself, I will find Mrs Wiscombe.'

'Aston? Who was at the door, just now?'

It seemed the summons was not necessary. Lillian was standing on the main staircase. She looked as beautiful as he remembered and as enigmatic. He felt the same tightening in his throat that had come upon him the day they'd met. This time, he fought against it. While it might be fashionable to moon over another man's wife, it did not do to be so affected by one's own.

He straightened to parade-perfect attention, then looked up at her. 'No one in particular. Merely your husband, madam.'

Her head snapped up to see him. Her face shuttled through a half-dozen expressions, trying to settle on the one that could both express her emotions and welcome him properly. He was pretty sure that none of what he saw resembled gratitude or joy. But before any of it could truly register, she gave up and her eyes rolled back as her knees began to fold under her.

'Bugger.' He lunged forward, putting his battlefield reflexes to good use, and caught her before she could reach the ground. The woman in his arms was heavier than she'd appeared at the altar. Hardly a surprise. He had changed, as well. But she was not too heavy. Had he found her in Portugal, he'd have described her to his mates as a 'tidy armful'.

'The bench, Captain.' The butler gestured to a place beside the stairs.

'The sitting room,' Gerry corrected.

'I will send for madam's maid with the hartshorn.'

'Nonsense,' Gerry announced, carrying his wife through the open sitting-room doors to a divan by the fire. 'She just needs to get the blood back to her head.' He settled Lillian on the sofa and sat at the opposite end, taking her feet into his lap to elevate them.

The feel of her dainty slippers against his thighs did more to redirect his blood flow than hers. He snatched a pillow from behind him and slipped it beneath them to give her more height and him a chance to regain his sanity.

Her eyelids fluttered, the long lashes revealing flashes of eyes as soft and brown as a doe's. It must have been God's own joke to give such an innocent face to a woman like Lillian North.

He smiled to hide his thoughts. 'There. See? It is working already. Fetch her a ratafia, or some other restorative.' Damn it all, he could use a stiff brandy himself. But he needed a clear head if he was to stand against the Norths, so he asked for nothing.

His wife was fully awake now. When she realised her position, she hurriedly pulled up her feet and righted herself, swaying slightly on the cushion beside him as she tried to regain her poise.

'Easy,' he cautioned. 'Do not rush or you will become dizzy again.'

'You startled me,' she said, rubbing her temple as if her head ached. More likely, it was to shield her face so she did not have to look him in the eye.

So she was startled. How unfortunate. Even though she had not expected to see him again after their wedding breakfast, she must have heard of him in these past years. It had probably vexed her and her family to find him so stubbornly hard to kill.

The butler signalled the footman, who stepped forward with a glass. Gerry pressed it into her hand.

She drank deeply, as though desperate for anything that gave her an excuse not to talk.

'So it shocked you to unconsciousness to see me again,' he prompted, enjoying her discomfort.

'I was aware that you had returned to England. But if you had notified us of your impending arrival, the house might have been prepared for you.' She had the nerve to sound annoyed with him.

He smiled all the wider. 'In my time away, I've learned to value the element of surprise.'

'I must tell the servants to air out your room.' She set aside her glass and made to stand up.

'No need.' He grinned at her and took her hand, pulling her none too gently back to the seat next to him. 'They saw my arrival and are most likely doing so without your instruction. I am sure they would not expect you to leave my side so soon after our reunion. We have been apart for ages. We have much to discuss.'

She looked so miserable at the thought of their impending talk that he almost pitied her. Then he remembered that she had earned any misery a hundredfold for the way she had treated him.

Before they could begin, they were interrupted by voices in the hallway. A man and boy were coming towards the sitting room in animated conversation about the quality of the trout they had caught for tonight's dinner.

In truth, it was the younger one that did most of the talking. The man with him answered in annoyed monosyllables before shouting, 'Aston! What would it take for a man to get a drink before dinner? And what the devil is all the ruckus about? The rest of the party is not yet back from their hunt, but servants are running around as if the house is on fire.'

Lillian's eyes widened and she looked ready to call out a warning.

Gerry laid a hand on her arm to silence her. Then he spoke in a voice that carried easily to the hall. 'You have but to ask the lord of the manor, Ronald North. Or have you been playing that role yourself, in my absence?' He'd meant it to sound joking, but it came out as an accusation. Gerry softened the words with his most innocuous smile, as his wife's brother appeared suddenly in the doorway and braced a hand against the frame as if to steady himself.

'Wiscombe.' Though his voice had been clear and jovial a moment before, now Ronald seemed winded. He looked even more shocked than his sister had been.

Gerry took care to hide the malice he felt behind a wide-eyed, innocent look. 'What a surprise to come home and find you still in my house.'

'Surprise?' The man stammered over the word, still trying to decide what his reaction should be.

'Well, not really,' Gerry added, his grin broadening. 'Of course I expected to find you here. I gave you permission to live here in my absence. But there appears to be a house party in residence. Is it to honour my return? You must have heard of my homecoming and gathered my friends to welcome me.'

'Of course.' Ronald leapt for the lifeline he'd been offered, clinging to it for all he was worth. 'When we heard that you had survived Waterloo…' He gave a capacious wave of his hand to encompass the frenzied celebration that his success had caused. From one who had no right to set the comings and goings of the household it was more than a little presumptuous.

'It was a dashed piece of good luck that I am here at all,' Gerry answered him, with a pleased nod. 'I've been within ames ace of coming home in a box so many times over the years that I quite lost count.'

'How did you manage to survive?' By his tone, Ronald North was annoyed that he had done so.

Gerry shrugged. 'I suspect it was the prayers of my lovely wife that did it. There always seemed to be an angel who could grab me by the collar and pull me back from the brink.' He gave a deliberately expansive wave of his hand and jostled the glass Lillian had been holding, sending a splash of her drink on to the rug.

'I suspect so.' Ronald was staring at him intently as if wondering whether he might still be the lucky idiot they wanted him to be. Gerry smiled back, doing his best to look harmless. Let him think what he liked. Better yet, let him think what Gerry meant him to.

'But Waterloo is several months passed,' Gerry continued. 'Do not say you have been rejoicing all this time without me. Judging by the red in your nose, the cellar must be quite empty by now.' The same years that had toughened Gerry had softened his wife's brother. The chestnut hair he shared with his sister had lost its lustre. His waist had thickened and his face was bloated from over-indulgence. In school, Ronald had been a handsome fellow with an easy manner and enough blunt in his pocket to ensure his popularity. But now it was hard to see his brother-in-law as anything other than the dissolute wastrel he had been even then.

'You need not fear that the house is dry,' Ronald said, matching his tone to Gerald's. 'Your cellar is excellent, Wiscombe. I know, for I stocked it myself. And the guests that are here for your arrival?' He gave another flourish of his hand. 'The cream of London society, dear boy. The very pinnacle.'

'The pinnacle? Then they are likely strangers to me.' He'd been a young nobody when he'd left for Portugal, well beneath the notice of the *ton*. It had flattered him that Ronald North might think him a fit match for his beautiful sister. He had been a fool. He gave Ronald another empty-headed smile to prove nothing had changed. 'But I am sure we will get on well. The chaps in my regiment said as long as I was paying for the wine I was very good company.'

He felt his wife tense next to him as she recognised the sarcasm that her brother had missed. Even at their first meeting, she had been better at reading him than either of the other Norths. It was a shame that her character was not equal to her intelligence.

'You will meet the guests over dinner,' Ronald said, smiling back. Apparently, he was also oblivious to the fact that it was not his place to be issuing such assurances to the man who owned the house.

'I must change the seating at the table,' Lily added, trying to escape him again.

Gerry pulled her down again. 'Aston will have told the housekeeper by now. Mrs Fitz is quite capable of rearranging a few chairs.' He gave her a smile that would have terrified her, had she known him better.

Perhaps she did know him. He felt another tremor in the muslin-draped leg resting against his. He dropped a hand on to her twitching knee in an overly familiar gesture of comfort and she stilled. But it was not a sign of calm so much as the terrified immobility of a rabbit before a hawk.

For now, he ignored her and her brother as well, staring towards the hall. 'Never mind them. There is but one person here I truly wish to meet.' He raised his finger to point towards the shadow hovering in the doorway behind Ronald North. 'Come forth. Let me get a look at you.'

The boy stepped forward from around Ronald's legs and walked into the room. He looked at Gerry with none of the nervous suspicion of the two adults in the room. But what reason would he have to fear this stranger? Especially since he had been eavesdropping on the conversation and must be aware who he was about to meet.

Gerry saw the lightning-fast glance that passed between the siblings as the boy stepped forward and they sought the words to cover this situation in a single shared look.

Once again he had the element of surprise. He pressed his advantage and sprang the ambush before they could speak. 'As if I could not discover with my own eyes who this must be. Come forward, boy. Meet your father, returned from the wars.'

## Chapter Three

Lily was going to faint again. She could see the black dots gathering before her eyes as Stewart stepped forward towards Captain Wiscombe's outstretched hand. Now, of all times, she must not lose her senses. The dizziness came from holding one's breath and denying oneself of air. It was a bad habit of hers and she must learn to break it if she did not want to appear frail and unworthy to her heroic spouse. She forced herself to take the breath that would clear her head. The resulting gasp was loud enough to be heard by the entire room.

Stewart started like a rabbit. But Captain Wiscombe ignored it, even though he must have felt the couch shake with her quaking knees.

She had nothing to fear in this meeting, or so she'd been telling herself for most of the past seven years. Before he had left her, Mr Wiscombe had been kindness itself. He had been gentle with her, considerate of her feelings and almost as frightened of the idea of marriage to her as she'd been of his chances in the army. The Gerald Wiscombe she remembered had been more likely to be harmed than to cause harm to another. She would explain to Gerald what had happened. He would understand and arrange a quiet separation.

But it was foolish to think of the man beside her as the same person who had left. He had not just been transformed by experience. He had been transmuted into another being. There was nothing left of the pudgy, scholarly boy who had stammered out a proposal to her. The soft brown hair had burned blond in sunlight and wind had given it a casual wave. In contrast, the skin of his face had darkened and the features had sharpened to a hawk nose and cleft chin. The grey eyes set beneath his furrowed brow were bright and as hard as flint.

He was still wearing the dashing red coat of a dragoon, with gold at shoulder and sleeve. And somewhere, there had to be a sword. By the resolute look on this man's face, it had seen good use. If he decided to punish those who had wronged him...

'Stewart, isn't it?' His words stopped her breath again. He knew her son's name without being told. 'That was my father's name, as well.' He favoured the boy with the same harmless smile he had used on Ronald. But there was an ironic note in the statement that was hidden so deeply she could not be sure that it existed outside her imagination.

Stewart swallowed nervously. Then he smiled back and nodded.

Now the captain was touching her boy, taking him by the shoulders and turning him side to side to give him a thorough examination. She tensed, waiting for his reaction. 'You look very much like your mother.'

Was that meant to be ironic, as well? Or was it only she who noticed the way it focused attention on the lack of similarity between the boy and the Wiscombe family?

Why was he, of all people, not surprised to see this child? While the rest of the world might think it quite normal that she had a son, she must now face the one man in the world who would have questions.

And yet, he was not asking them. He was pretending to be simple and pleasant Gerald Wiscombe, and behaving as if he had expected this meeting all along. He had known the name of her boy because someone had told him. But who? How much had he been told? And how much of what he thought he knew was the actual truth of the situation?

Now he was questioning the boy in languages and receiving the sort of indifferent responses one could expect from a very young child who enjoyed the countryside more than the classroom.

When he had tried and failed to answer yet another simple question put to him in Latin, Stewart's limited patience evaporated. 'I am much better at mathematics than at Latin. Mama says that you are, too. Would you like to hear me do my sums?'

For the first time since he'd arrived, Captain Wiscombe's composure failed him. He might have known of Stewart's existence. But clearly he had not prepared himself to face a living, breathing child who was eager to give him the hero's welcome he deserved. His overly bright smile disappeared, as did the bitterness it hid. Stripped of his armour, she caught a glimpse of the awkward boy who had proposed to her, trapped in a social situation he was ill-equipped to manage.

Then the facade returned and he clapped the boy on the shoulder. 'Your sums. Well. Another time, perhaps. Now run along back to the schoolroom and leave the adults to their talk. I am sure you have a nurse or a governess about who is supposed to give you your dinner.'

Stewart hesitated, staring at the captain with a hunger that could not be filled by his dinner tray. But Wiscombe saw none of it, or at least pretended he did not. Now that he'd made his acknowledgement, his interest in the child had disappeared as quickly as it had arisen.

Her son shot a hopeful look in her direction, as if pleading on her part might earn him a reprieve.

She gave him a single warning shake of her head and a slight tilt of her chin towards the stairs. Captain Wiscombe was right. Until they had spoken in private, Stewart was better off taking tea in the nursery.

Once the boy was gone, her husband turned his attention to Ronald. 'I expect you have somewhere to be, as well.'

'Not really,' her brother replied with a bland smile. Now that he'd had time to recover from the shock of seeing Wiscombe, her brother's sangfroid had returned.

'Might I suggest you find somewhere?' Her husband was smiling, as well. But there was a glint in his eyes that promised mayhem if his orders were not obeyed immediately. Then he softened to harmlessness again and threw an arm around her, hauling her into his lap.

'After seven years away, it is not unreasonable that I wish to be alone with my wife.'

The sudden feeling of his arms tightening under her breasts and the rock-hard thighs beneath her bottom sucked the wind from her lungs and she was seeing spots again. *Breathe*, she reminded herself. *Just breathe.*

When she'd mastered her panic, she found her foolish brother was smiling in agreement as if he expected Captain Wiscombe was seeking immediate privacy so he might mount his wife in a common room. Could he not see that the gullible young man they'd roped into this union had returned as a dreadnought?

'Then I will leave the two of you alone,' Ronald said with a wink to Captain Wiscombe, treating her as though she were not even in the room with them. 'Do not worry, Lily. I will see to the dinner arrangements and tell the guests of the captain's arrival.' Then he disappeared, shutting the door behind him, totally unaware of the storm about to break when her husband gave vent to his true feelings.

'Yes, Ronald. Go and see to your guests. Inform them of my presence. I hope you remember to tell them enough about me so they can pretend that we share an acquaintance.' Now that he was gone, her husband made no effort to hide his scorn for her brother. She could feel his muscles tensing like a great cat gathering before the spring. Then he shifted, dumping her back out of his lap and on to the cushion at his side.

Lily moved as well, sliding to the far end of the small couch to put as much distance between them as possible. Never mind breathing, it was impossible to think when he was touching her. Even when he was not, she could feel an aura of virile energy emanating from him, raising the hairs on her skin.

Or perhaps he was simply angry. She rushed to fill the silence before the fear of him could suck the breath from her lungs again. 'If company is not to your liking, we will send them away immediately.'

'But that would be most rude,' he replied in a soft, mocking tone. 'And above all things, I would not want to be thought rude. Tell me, wife, who are my guests? I do not like being the last one to know what is going on in my own home.'

'Mr and Mrs Carstairs…' she began hesitantly.

'And they are…?' He made a coaxing gesture with his hand.

'A businessman from London, and his wife.'

'What is his trade?'

'I believe he is an ironmonger.'

'A wealthy one, I presume.'

She cleared her throat. 'I believe so.'

'Who else, then?'

'The Burkes and the Wilsons, also of London.'

'And also cits?'

'Yes, Captain.' How quickly she had fallen into the role of loyal subordinate. But there was something about the man that commanded respect, even in a private setting such as this one.

'Others?'

'Sir Chauncey d'Art and his friend, Miss Fellowes.' She hoped he did not wish her to speculate on the nature of the friendship. Though she had provided two rooms for the couple it was likely that only one of them was getting use.

'Is that all?'

'No, Captain.' She wet her lips. 'We are entertaining your neighbour, the Earl of Greywall.' He was the last person she wished her husband to meet. All the more reason that they should clear the house as quickly as possible.

'Greywall.' There was another moment of blank vulnerability before his smile returned and he counted on his fingers. 'If we add you, your father and brother, there are twelve.' The smile became a lopsided grin. 'Now that I am here, there shall be thirteen at dinner. I expect it will be quite unlucky for somebody.'

Lily threw caution to the winds and reached to touch his arm, adding a smile warm enough to melt butter. If she used her imagination and all the talent she had inherited from Father, perhaps she might persuade him that she was glad to see him home and had not been dreading this moment for most of the time he'd been gone. 'Unlucky? Surely not. We are all fortunate to have you here.'

For a moment, it actually seemed to work. He softened and looked ready to cover her hand with his. Then he remembered that she was nothing more than a fraud and pulled away with a frustrated sigh. 'Really, madam. If you must lie to me, try not to be so transparent about it. The facts are these—your father and brother tricked me into marriage with you for their own ends and never intended for me to return. In giving me that commission, they thought they were sending me to my death. And you—'

'I'm sorry.' She blurted out the words before he could finish his sentence. 'Despite what you think of me, I am glad that you are safe.' She was relieved, at least. For years, she had been too afraid to pray for his return. But that was not the same as wishing him ill. Just as he had said in jest, she'd prayed for his safety each night.

'Are you?' His expression hardened. 'Then you are more foolish than I thought. After I am satisfied that you've paid for what they have done to me, I mean to put you and your family out in the street. The guests, as well. And your precious Stewart will be the first to go.'

She was feeling light-headed again, images impending of exile and humiliation swirling in her mind. But this time, she was not alone in her suffering. She had to be strong for Stewart. She took another deep breath and cast down her eyes to assure him she was beaten. 'It is within your right.'

He laughed. 'What? You are not going to plead for your safety? I would have thought, at least, you would have a word of defence for our darling boy. Are you not going to beg me? Tell me I am hard-hearted to turn the product of our love off the property he is heir to. Why, when I think of that one night of passion we shared...'

'Stop!' She could not bear his mocking a moment longer.

'Do you remember it differently?' he said, innocently. 'It has been so long. Perhaps I am mistaken. If so, tell me the truth of it now.'

She could not speak. Her tongue was frozen in her mouth, unwilling to speak the truth.

'Talk!'

If this was what he brought to the battlefield, it explained his success. His command was stronger than the fear that kept her silent. 'We shared no night,' she said, choking out the words. 'Only a brief ceremony, the breakfast and two separate rooms at the inn. We did not lie together. The next morning, you were gone.'

He nodded. 'I promised I would not come to you until we knew each other better. To be gone so soon and with no guarantee of a future…it did not seem fair to either of us.' For a moment, he sounded almost wistful for the innocents they had been.

Then his voice hardened. 'When I think of how it was, in those first months… I carried a miniature of you, everywhere I went. I kissed it each night at bed and before battles for luck. I was pure as a monk, waiting for the moment when I might come back to you. I wrote you dozens of letters. There was not a single response.'

She had been too upset to write. At first, she had been angry at him for being so foolish as to fall for the plan, going to what was likely certain doom. She was ashamed of herself as well, for obeying her father when she had known what they were doing was wrong. Later, she had been ashamed for other reasons and angry at him for leaving her alone and defenceless.

He did not notice her discomfiture and went on. 'When a commanding officer came to me, less than a year later, with the good news of the birth of my son?'

He laughed at this, as though it were a ribald joke in a brothel. 'I did not have to feign surprise. We all went to a cantina, where I had to pay for the wine so they might drink my health, and to the health of my good wife and heir.'

He had known, almost from the first. It explained why his letters to her had stopped. 'When you stopped writing…I thought you had died.' Would he believe that she had cried over him? Probably not. But she had.

'That news was the making of my career,' he added. 'When a soldier has no reason to fear death, it leads to the sort of recklessness that makes heroes. Or corpses,' he added. 'I do not like to think of the men under my command who lacked the damnable luck of their leader.'

She'd felt bad enough knowing that he might lose his life because of Father's scheming. But to think that others had been affected and that she was in some way responsible for their fates made her guilt even heavier. 'I am sorry,' she said again.

'So you keep saying,' he said with a mocking smile. 'Tell me now. The truth, for once. Were you with child when we married? Was that the reason that your father rushed to unite us?'

'No!' There was much wrong between them, but she did not want to claim a fault that was not hers. Then she saw the change in his expression and knew that it would have been kinder had she lied.

'So you admit to cuckolding me.' He shook his head again. 'Were you really so sure I would die that you did not think I might return to see the consequences of your infidelity?'

The answer to that was very nearly yes. But it was so much more complicated than that. How could she even begin to explain? Having to talk about it at all was bringing on one of her headaches. She rubbed her temple and tried to concentrate. 'At first, I did not know what to do. I barely understood what was happening to me, much less what to do about it. The longer I did nothing, the easier it became to go on as I had started.'

'How well does it work for you now?' he asked, staring at her as though she had confirmed his low opinion of her. 'And do not apologise to me again. There is no apologising for what you have done.'

There was an explanation. But it had been years since that night. What proof could she offer him that she spoke true? She took a breath and squared her shoulders. 'At least the waiting is finally over. You will do what you will do. I do not have to imagine what that might be. My only request—'

'You have no right to request anything of me.' Once again, she heard the command in the voice and understood how the boy she had married had become a hero.

'I will do so, all the same. My son is not at fault. If there is kindness in your heart at all, do not let the punishment fall on him.'

'You mean, on your bastard?'

She had been foolish to hope for better. 'My son,' she repeated softly. 'If you cannot mete out both shares of the punishment to me, then give me time to tell him the truth before he hears it from another.'

'He does not know?' For a moment, his anger was replaced by surprise.

'No one knows,' she said. 'A few people closest to me might guess. But no one is sure, other than you and me.'

'Not even...' He was wondering about Stewart's father.

He had been so drunk that night she doubted he even remembered what he had done. She shook her head. 'No one knows. And Stewart is far too young to understand. All his life, he has been fed on stories of the heroic father he has never met. To find that it is a lie... It will come as a shock.' This was not true. It would be utterly devastating to him.

'His heroic father,' the captain said with bitterness. 'And who is that man? I wish to congratulate him and make him aware of his responsibility. Or are your affairs so numerous that you cannot fix on a single name?'

She did not think he had the power to hurt her with mere words, but the question stung like a slap to the face. 'There was but one man and one night. I could point to it on a calendar, if you wish.' Not that she needed a paper record. The date and time, down to the minute, had been burned into her memory. The clock in the hall had been striking twelve as her life was ruined.

She shook her head, which was still ringing. 'I will not tell you his name. Nor will I tell Stewart. You are the only father he has ever known. He had been learning to read by following the news of your battles. His first toy was a wooden sword. He has entire battalions of tin soldiers and sets them to fighting each other at every opportunity. His only ambition is to grow to be as brave as you have been.'

'That is no doing of mine,' he insisted. But there was a gruffness in his voice that hinted at emotions other than anger. And then the brief flicker of sympathy vanished. 'You should not have lied to him.'

'Nor could I have told him the truth.' It was an awful enough story to carry on her own. She had no desire to taint the boy's life with it. 'I told him a partial truth at least. You are brave and worthy of his admiration. If he meant to create an idol, he could do much worse than you.'

'Do not think to flatter me,' the captain said. 'It will not work.'

But neither did it seem to be doing her any harm. This time, he had been the one to look away, as though her praise made him uncomfortable. 'It is not flattery if the statement is truth.'

'I didn't return to this house seeking your approval,' he snapped. The tenuous connection she'd created was gone. His gaze locked on hers again as his suspicion returned.

'I know that,' she said quickly. 'You owe me nothing and you need nothing from me.' But she could not believe it was in his nature to be cruel, even to an enemy. And certainly not to a child.

Suddenly, his look held speculation. 'On the contrary. I owe you much. I vowed before God to protect you. I do not like to break my word.' His voice did not sound kind. But neither was it as sharp as it had been.

Had she said something to change his mind? What had it been? She grasped at the opportunity. 'I made promises to you, as well,' she said, softly. 'And I have broken them. You deserved to find a virtuous wife waiting for your return. I failed you. I have failed Stewart, as well. If you could help me in any way...'

It had been too much to ask. He'd flinched at the mention of the boy's name.

She tried another way. 'If, once you have decided my fate, you could at least allow me enough time to speak to him, to try to tell him the truth gently, before...' Before they were turned out of the house, as he had threatened before. It was no less than she deserved. The only consolation she might find in it was that her brother and father would follow her in banishment. After seven years, this charade would finally be at an end.

Captain Wiscombe did not answer. He was staring at her in a way that made her even more nervous than before. His eyes held the same curious intensity that her father's sometimes did when he found a pigeon ripe for plucking.

Since she had no choice in the matter, she stood his scrutiny in mute embarrassment.

At last, he spoke. 'There is another possibility.'

She fought down the urge to agree without waiting for an explanation. Sometimes, she suspected she was far too obedient for her own good. It was quite possible that what he planned for her might be even worse than the humiliation she would experience when the truth about Stewart was revealed.

'You said I needed nothing from you.' His hand reached out to her, his fingers brushing her cheek. 'That is not precisely true.'

She could not help it. She shuddered. Part of it was

nerves. But there was something else, something about the look in his eyes that raised other, more pleasant feelings in her. She was being touched by the dashing hero whose exploits she had followed for years. In person, he was even more handsome than she had imagined him. And he wanted her help. 'What do you wish from me?'

He smiled. 'What does any man wish from the woman he has married? Loyalty, my dear. Thus far, you have given me every reason to doubt that I have yours.'

Loyalty? That was disappointingly mundane. But it was also easily accomplished. According to *The Times*, Captain Gerald Wiscombe inspired devotion in all who knew him. She would much rather obey him than her less-than-honourable father. She dipped her head in consent. 'Despite appearances, you have my complete allegiance, sir. Let me prove it to you.'

'You will have to,' he said, 'if you wish to remain in the house even one more night.'

'Anything you want, I will get for you,' she said. 'What do you require?'

He was still looking at her with an intensity that sent chills down her spine. 'What do I want? Satisfaction. Reparation. Revenge. I have done my duty, in service of my king. I have seen things that no man should see and done things I would never have thought myself capable of. But I survived, madam. Though your father and brother thought they were sending me to my death, I survived. Now I mean to make them pay for what they have done. Are you with me, or against me?'

'With you, of course,' she replied without hesitation. Hadn't this been exactly what she had longed for? Someone to come and make her family regret its selfishness? It would be her pleasure to help him.

'You answered very quickly. It is as if you didn't think about it at all.' He nodded in mocking approval. 'Do you expect me to believe you without question?'

'You are my husband,' she said. 'By the laws of man and church, I must answer to you in all things. My father and brother have no say in the matter.'

'Just as you no longer have a say in what will happen to my son,' he said, with a wicked smile. 'The fact that you bore him does not give you the right to decide his future. You are but a woman and I am the head of the house.'

'Your son?' Her heart stuttered eagerly. Did he mean to claim the boy?

'You have declared him so,' the captain reminded her. 'If you did not wish me to have power over him, you should have told the truth.'

'What do you mean to do with him?' she said, suddenly afraid.

He fixed her with an insincere smile. 'If you do as I say? Nothing so terrible. When we have cleared this house of your family and their accompanying friends, I will find a school for the boy. He will start as soon as it can be arranged and will remain there over summer and for holidays as well. He will be perfectly safe, fed, clothed and cared for. But he will no longer live in my house, pretending to be my blood. Until the time comes for him to go, you will keep him out of my sight. I do not wish to be reminded of his presence.'

She had known that school was in Stewart's future, but not for a few years, at least. He was still so young. This was not education, it was banishment. Stewart would be crushed when he realised that the father he worshipped could not bear the sight of him. And when he was gone, she would lose the only unsullied love she had ever known.

He had noticed her silence. 'It will not be so different from my own childhood,' he said, with a shrug. 'My father sent me to Eton when I was eight. I stayed between terms when he was away from the house. I grew to prefer it to home.'

'Stewart is much younger than that,' she said in a whisper.

He gave her a pitying look. 'Surely you did not expect that we would remain together as a happy family.'

'Of course not,' she lied. But he was the hero of Salamanca. She had been hoping for a miracle.

'Well, then you understand that I am being more generous than most men in this position.'

She nodded, for it was true. But she did not care. She needed more than this. Boarding school was an improvement over the immediate exile he had been threatening less than an hour ago. If he was given time to get to know the boy, she must trust that his mood would soften even more.

'Will you stand with me, or against me?' he said.

'With you, of course,' she said, eager for the chance to prove her worth to him. 'I am yours to command.'

'Very good,' he said with a nod. 'I am glad we have an understanding.'

He stood and walked towards the door. Then he stopped and turned back to her again, placing his index finger against his chin as though there was some point they had forgotten to discuss. Then he smiled, as if the idea had suddenly come back to him. 'We have not yet discussed what is to become of you, after all is settled.'

'Me?' The word came out in a squeak, like a mouse that had just been caught in a trap.

'There is more to being a wife then parroting "yes" each time I ask a question. I expect you to share my bed, as well.' He'd added it in an offhand manner, as though it was a minor consideration, hardly worth mentioning. 'You will submit to me whenever I request it. I will use you as I please, when I please. If I tire of you, I will abide no fussing or tears. Under no circumstances will you be taking admirers of your own. I said I wanted loyalty, my dear, and in the bedroom it will be absolute.'

His eyes narrowed in satisfaction at her look of shock. 'The alternative is that I turn you from the house this very day. There will be no time for niceties. You will leave with your whelp and the clothes on your back, and the devil take you both.'

The fear of that was clearer and more immediate than anything that might happen in the captain's bed. She gave a hesitant nod.

He nodded back at her, the old, harmless smile returning. 'Very good. I knew we could come to an understanding, if we had a few moments alone to talk.'

She fought against another shiver. If she thought about it, she would realise that this meeting had gone better than she could have hoped. Stewart would be safe. She would be rid of her family. And as long as he had a use for her, she might keep her place as lady of the house. It was not the stuff of fairy tales, but it never had been.

More importantly, this was Gerald Wiscombe ordering her to his bed. If she searched, she might still find traces of the gentle, awkward boy who had postponed the consummation of their marriage to spare her feelings. At the very least, he was an officer and a gentleman, not some uncaring brute. If she did what he asked of her, he would not hurt her just for the sport of seeing her suffer.

He was also the hero of Salamanca.

Half the women in England swooned at the mention of his name. In their midnight fantasies, they offered themselves to the gallant and heroic Captain Wiscombe, thanking him for his service with their bodies.

Would it surprise him to discover that his wife was no different? That she felt a dark thrill at his command to submit to his desires? If he had meant it as a punishment, he would be just as likely to reject her again, should she seem too eager for his attention.

She stood so that she might look him in the eye and pretend that it did not matter to her if he wanted her or not.

Then, as if to prove just how false her bravery was, he pulled her forward into his arms and kissed her hard upon the lips.

It was over just as quickly. But fantasy paled in comparison. He had told her with a single kiss that he was her lord and master and she had responded as if she longed to be ruled by him. When he released her, she fell back into the cushions of the divan, weak from the sudden loss of control over her body and her future. Before she could comment, he rose, walked out of the room and left her alone.

# *Chapter Four*

In Belgium, when they'd all thought the war was over, there had been far too much time to drink and reminisce with other officers. Gerry had noticed a certain arrogance on the part of the infantry commanders towards their counterparts in the cavalry. Given any excuse, they would insist that fighting from horseback was not real fighting at all.

To be above the action and looking down upon it was, in their opinion, to cheat. Not only did it give the rider a tactical advantage, but it removed the need to face the enemy eye to eye. Bravery, to an infantryman, was to see all of the common thoughts and emotions that rendered one man equal to another reflected in an enemy's face, and to attack in spite of them.

Today he wondered if there might be truth in that. When he'd imagined himself coming home, it had been in a metaphorical galloping charge. It would be the work of an instant to vanquish the interlopers who had claimed his home. He would take special pleasure in seeing his wife wailing and gnashing her teeth as he put her out and slammed the door in her face.

In his imagination, it was always raining the kind of cold drizzle that one got in the north. It added an extra air of pitifulness to her entreaties and those of the rat-faced whelp clinging to her skirts.

The actual meeting had been quite different. Evidence still proved she was a cheating whore. But he'd thought she would make some effort to deny the obvious. Perhaps she would try to hide the child. At the very least, she would have some tragic story to explain it.

Instead, she had offered complete surrender before he could strike a metaphorical blow. Even worse, she had displayed her greatest weakness. She wished to protect her son even if it meant sacrificing herself. She had not even resorted to the weapon all women seemed to use against men. Not a single tear had been shed as she'd awaited his judgement.

These were not the actions of a worthy opponent. She was behaving like a martyr. Even worse, the boy showed no mark of his mother's perfidy. Because of Lillian's lies, the child seemed illogically eager to see him. To send him away would be like kicking a puppy because it had wagged its tail.

After the interview, he'd felt dirtied by more than the grime of travel. There was no fault in expecting fidelity and no villainy in being angry when one did not receive it. There was no sin in demanding that one's wife behave like a wife, in bed and out, if she wished to remain under one's roof. But if all that was true, then why did staring into those sad brown eyes make him feel like a lecherous cad?

And what had the kiss meant to either of them? Compared to his plans to take her to bed, it had seemed almost chaste. But at the end of it, she had been shaking in his arms and he had been left unsettled, ready to saddle his horse and go before closer contact with her made him forget her unfaithfulness.

He would feel better after a drink and a wash. But apparently, that was too much to ask. 'Aston! Mrs Fitz!' He roared for the servants in his best battlefield voice and was satisfied to hear doors opening and closing up and down the guest-room corridors. His unwanted visitors had learned the master of the house was home and was not happy.

The servants appeared, out of breath and in unison, before he had to call a second time.

He pointed to the door to his room. 'What is the meaning of this?' There was a shiny brass lock on the door of the master bedroom, where none had been before.

'Oh. Oh, sir. I mean, Captain, I am so sorry.' His poor housekeeper was devastated that their first meeting after his return was because of an error in her management. 'When the maid aired the room and lit the fire, she locked it after. It is always locked. The mistress's room, as well.'

'I see that.' He had tried the door just down the hall from his, thinking he could enter his own room through the connecting door. He had been blocked there, as well. 'Am I expected to break down the be-nighted doors to gain admittance, then?'

'No, sir.' Aston was fishing on his ring for a key. He turned it in the lock and then placed it in his master's hand. Gerry's single glance down the hall to his wife's room had the servant relinquishing that key as well.

'We meant no insult by it,' Mrs Fitz said hurriedly.

'Of course you did not. But what is the purpose of such security?'

Aston cleared his throat. 'There are frequent guests here. Strangers to the house sometimes wander down the wrong hallway and disturb the peace. Mrs Wiscombe thought it better that the family rooms be locked when not in use.'

'Yours especially, Captain Wiscombe,' Mrs Fitz said, as though it was somehow a point of pride. 'She was adamant that no matter how full the house, your room was to be kept empty and ready for your return.'

'As it should be,' he said. The housekeeper gave his wife far too much credit for simple common sense. 'Before I left, I gave the Norths permission to use the house as their own. But it is not as if we are running some roadside hostel with rooms to let.'

There was an uncomfortable silence from the two servants at his side.

'I said, my home is not an inn.' His voice was rising again, as was his temper.

Aston cringed. 'Of course not, Captain Wiscombe.' Then why did he sound doubtful?

'But?' Gerry gave a coaxing twitch of his fingers and waited for the rest of the story.

'The Misters North entertain here. Frequently,' Mrs Fitz said, with a little sniff of disapproval.

'There are often large house parties,' Aston supplied. 'Guests come from the city for hunting and cards.'

'Friends of the family?' Gerry suggested.

'The Earl of Greywall is usually among the party. But the rest…' Aston looked uncomfortable. 'Very few guests are invited twice.'

'I see.' In truth, he did not. Why would Ronald and his father bring crowds of strangers to such a remote location? And why was Greywall here? He knew he was not welcome and he had a perfectly good residence only a few miles away.

He considered. 'Is the earl in residence now?'

'Yes, sir.'

*Damn.* When he was alive, Gerry's father had loathed the peer who could not seem to limit himself to the game on his own side of the property line. After he'd died, Greywall had not waited for the body to cool before he'd begun to pester Gerry to sell house and land for less than they were worth. The crass insensitivity of his offers had convinced Gerry that anything, including a sudden marriage and military career, would be preferable to giving in to Greywall's demands.

His stubbornness had netted nothing if the earl had caged a permanent invitation to house and grounds. It was about to be rescinded, of course. But it would have to be done carefully. Even peers one did not like demanded special handling in situations like this. He sighed. 'Then I suspect I will meet him and the rest over dinner.'

'Very good, sir. Do you require assistance in changing? A shave, perhaps?'

'As long as my bag and kit are waiting, I can manage on my own,' he said, although the thought of the master dressing without help clearly appalled his poor butler. He gave them both an encouraging smile. No matter what had occurred in his absence, the staff was not at fault. 'It is good to be home,' he added.

They smiled back, and Mrs Fitz bobbed a curtsy. 'And to see you again, safe and well, sir. If you need anything...'

'I will ring,' he assured her and gave a brief nod of thanks to dismiss them. Then he opened the door and entered his room.

For a moment, he paused on the threshold, confused. Before his sudden marriage and equally sudden departure, he'd never felt at home in the master suite. He had gone from the nursery to school, returning only on news of his father's death. For most of his life this had not been his space at all, but his father's.

He'd felt woefully out of place during the few months he'd been master of the house. Days had been spent in his father's study trying to decipher the bookkeeping and poring over stacks of unpaid bills. Nights had been marked with uneasy sleep in his father's bed, too embarrassed to admit that he missed his cot in the nursery. How was one expected to get any rest, surrounded by so many judgemental eyes?

His father had been a mediocre parent, but an avid sportsman. The bedroom, like so many other rooms in the house, was full of his trophies. Gerry did not mind the pelts, so much. He would even admit to a childish fascination for the rugs of tiger and bearskin in the billiard room. But what was the point of decorating the room in which one slept with the heads of animals one had killed? Stags stared moodily down from the walls. Foxes sat on the mantel, watching him with beady glass eyes. Antlers and boar tusks jutted from the wall behind the bed as though they might, at any moment, fall to impale the sleeper.

Gerry had proved in countless battles that he was no coward. When the killing was done, he'd treated the dead with as much respect as he was able. He had hoped for the same, should his luck fail him and circumstances be reversed. A gentleman should not gloat on the lives he'd taken, especially not at bedtime.

His father had not shared the sentiment. Of course, to the best of Gerry's knowledge, his father had never killed a man, much less dozens of them. The stuffed heads had been nothing more than decorations to him. But to Gerry, they would be reminders of other soulless eyes, judging him as he tried to sleep. It was with trepidation that he opened the door tonight, prepared for the distasteful sights within.

He stood on the threshold, confused.

Today, as he'd walked through the house, he'd noted the subtle changes that had been made to the decorating. The overt masculinity had been retained. There could be no doubt that he was in a hunting lodge and not a London town house. But the stained and faded silks had been removed from the walls and replaced. Paint had been freshened. Furniture had been reupholstered and rearranged. Though most of the trophies remained where he remembered them, they had at least been dusted. One could entertain both ladies and gentlemen here, without fear of embarrassment.

But no room he'd seen so far had been so totally transformed as his own bedroom. The dusty velvet chairs had been replaced with benches and stools covered in saddle leather. The heavy green baize on the walls had been exchanged for a cream-coloured, watered silk. The hangings over the bed were no longer maroon brocade. They were now a blue sarsenet shot through with silver. To stare up at the canopy would be like staring into a night sky full of stars.

The table at the side of the bed held the two volumes of the *Théorie Analytique des Probabilités* and a fine wooden version of Roget's new slide rule. He'd heard about the advances in mathematics since he'd been away and had been eager to return to his books. If he wished, he could take up his studies this very night.

Best of all, he could do it without the distractions of dozens of glass eyes. All evidence of his father's skill as a hunter had been removed. The walls were decorated with watercolour landscapes. He stepped closer to admire the work and started in surprise.

He knew the place in the picture. He had been there himself. It was Talavera de la Reina in Spain. But the picture was of the sleepy village and not the backdrop for battle. The next was of the Nive flowing through France. And here was Waterloo. Beautiful places all, not that he'd had the time to enjoy the scenery when he was there. But this was how he wanted to think of them. The land had healed. The blood he had shed was not muddying the dust. It had soaked into the ground and left only grass and wildflowers as memorial to the dead.

As he admired the work, he felt relaxed and at peace, as though he had finally come home. This was *his* room, totally and completely. If he had written his wishes out and sent them ahead, he could not have been more pleased with the results. The years of sacrifice had been rewarded with a haven of tranquillity. He could leave the war behind and become the man he had once intended to be.

This must have been Lillian's doing. No mere servant would have dared to take such liberties. Hadn't Mrs Fitz said it had been his wife's orders to keep the place locked until his return? But how had she known what he would like? How had she managed this without consulting him?

Most importantly, why had she done it?

## Chapter Five

'The diamonds, or the pearls, madam?' The maid was holding one earring to each ear, so Lily could judge the effect in her dressing table mirror.

She frowned back at her own reflection. She wished to look her best for the captain's first night at home. Despite their current difficulties, she could not help the wistful desire that he might admire her looks and perhaps even comment on them. When he'd proposed she had been a foolish young girl, so supremely confident in her ability to enthral him that she hadn't even bothered to try. She certainly wouldn't have needed jewels to enhance her appearance. But now that he could compare her to half the señoritas and mademoiselles of Europe she was obsessing over each detail in an effort to win his praise.

And what message did it send to wear jewellery that he had not bought for her? The diamonds had been a gift from Father for her last birthday. But suppose he suspected they'd come from a lover? It would be better to wear the pearls she'd inherited from her mother. She'd been wearing them on the day the captain had proposed.

Would he remember them? Even if he did not, they were modest enough that he could not accuse her of profligate spending or accepting gifts from strangers. She pointed to the pearl drops and the maid affixed them and brought out the matching necklace.

On her left hand, she wore the simple gold ring that had belonged to his mother. When they'd married, he'd had nothing else to offer her but the ring and the house. His fortunes had improved since then. She was not sure how much money he had sent back from Portugal, but his banker in London had assured her that any bills she submitted would be paid without question. She hoped he was a rich man. He deserved to live comfortably after sacrificing a third of his life to the army.

But she had done nothing to earn a share of his wealth and had done her best not to abuse his generosity. She had taken very little from the accounts for frivolities, preferring to make sparing use of the allowance that had been provided for her. One of the first lessons learned as a member of the North family was to keep back a portion of any success for the moment when things went wrong and a quick escape was necessary. To that end, she had a tightly rolled pile of bank notes hidden in her dresser that not even her father was aware of.

The gown she was wearing had been one of her rare purchases, a London design that had arrived not two weeks ago. The pearls did not suit it at all, but they would have to do.

There was a knock on the bedroom door and her brother entered without waiting for her welcome.

She did not bother to turn to him, frowning at his reflection. 'Such rude behaviour is why my door is almost always locked.'

'Surely you have nothing to worry about, with your husband in the next room.' Ronald was smiling back at her, as if he thought the prospect of rescue was unlikely, even if she needed it.

'You have more to fear from Captain Wiscombe than I do,' she said, amazed that he would joke about such a thing.

'The day will never come when I can't out-think Gerry Wiscombe.' Ronald's arrogance was undimmed by recent events. 'Nothing he said to you today after I left the room will make me believe otherwise.'

This was probably his way of requesting a report of her conversation with the captain. She ignored it, turning her attention back to her maid so that they might finish her toilette.

Ronald made no move to leave her, leaning against the wall by the door and staring as she made Jenny re-pin her braids and fuss over the ribbons at her shoulders until it was plain to everyone in the room that she was stalling. At last, she gave up and dismissed the maid, remaining silent until the door was shut and she could hear the girl's retreating footsteps at the far end of the hall.

'Well?' her brother said, arms folded over his chest. 'What did he say to you?'

She stared back at him, expressionless. 'If the words were meant for you, he'd have spoken them in your presence.'

'Ho-ho,' Ronald responded with an ugly smirk. 'You mean to side with him in this?'

She blinked innocently. 'Was that not the intention, when you and Father gave me to him?'

'I doubt Father expected that the day would come when you would throw your own flesh and blood to the wolves to save yourself.'

'Throw you to the wolves?' She laughed. 'If Captain Wiscombe has a problem with you or Father, I will have no say in it.'

'But what about your son?'

'What of him?' she said. Ronald had always been the least subtle of the Norths, trying to force information from her rather than waiting for it to be revealed. She turned back to the mirror, giving full attention to her appearance and none to his simmering anger.

'Gerry did not seem overly surprised by his presence.'

'Why should he be? We are married. There is a child.' Ronald had hinted his suspicions before. Now was not the time to confirm them.

'Your child was born nearly ten months after your husband left for the army.'

'You exaggerate,' she said, adding a touch more powder to her cheeks. She shouldn't have bothered. The addition took her from perfection to unhealthy pallor.

'When Stewart's next birthday arrives, even a man as stupid as Gerry Wiscombe will count out the months and have questions for you.'

She turned to glare at him. 'My husband is no fool.'

At this, her brother laughed out loud. 'So sorry to offend you, little sister. If that is what you wish, I will try not to think of him as the poor gull who I tricked into marrying you.'

'You tricked him?' Now she was the one who doubted.

'I told him you had seen him from afar. That it was practically a love match and that all it would take to win one of the most celebrated beauties of the Season was a show of courage on his part and an offer. He asked for your hand. Then, dutifully as a child, he ran off to war to impress you.'

'That is how you remember it?' Perhaps Gerald had shown a different face to her family than he had to her. Though his proposal had been gallant enough, she'd got no sense that he was dazzled by her beauty. He'd been a man with a plan. Marriage to her had been little more than a point of intersection between his goals and those of her father.

Her brother was still smiling at the memory. 'I had never met a fellow so easily persuaded or so quick to act against his own best interests as Gerry Wiscombe the day he proposed to you. It was a pity he had nothing more to offer than the house. If there had been money in his purse, I'd have got it all in one hand of cards.'

'It does not matter who he was when he left England,' Lily said, disgusted. 'The man who returned is different from the boy you remember.'

'So you claim,' he said with a sceptical nod. 'But when we spoke today he was the same amiable dolt I went to school with.'

'His successes on the Peninsula were not those of a halfwit. If you'd read the accounts of the battles...'

Ronald held up a hand to stop her. 'Your obsession with the war has always been most unladylike. Now that Napoleon is imprisoned, I wish to hear no more of it. Even your brave captain admitted that it was luck that saw him safely home. That seems far more likely than a magical transformation into a man of action. Just an hour ago, he was smiling over nothing and all but upsetting your wine glass.'

'It is an act,' she said and immediately wondered if she had already broken her vow of loyalty to her husband by giving him away. But his bravery and tactical acumen were hardly a secret to one who bothered to read the papers. 'Even if he was not shamming this afternoon, you must realise that he plans to take control of his estate. Your games with Father must end.'

'Must they?' Ronald gave her an innocent stare. 'I see no reason that they cannot continue, once we have taken the time to convince Gerry of their usefulness.'

'You mean to convince a man of honour to run what is little more than a crooked gaming hell?'

Her brother clucked his tongue at her. 'Such a way to describe your own home. This is not a professional establishment. It is merely a resort for those from the city who like sport, good wine and deep play.'

'Call it what you will,' she said. 'It is not, and never has been, your house. Now that the master has returned, things will be different.'

'Yes, they will,' Ronald agreed. 'Once Gerry has settled his account with us...'

'Settled with you?'

'The upkeep on such a large place is extensive. The slates. The curtains. The wine in the cellar...'

'You do not mean to charge him for wine that he has not even tasted. And though he gave you permission to live here, he did not ask you to fix up the house.'

Ronald held his hands palms up in an innocent shrug. 'I am sure he did not intend for us to live with rain pouring through the holes in the roof. Something needed to be done. How much blunt does he have, do you think?'

'Even if I knew, I would not tell you.' However much he had, her brother would see to it that the captain owed him double. If a direct appeal for funds failed, Ronald would win it at cards or billiards, or through any other weakness that could be discovered and exploited. Before he knew it, her husband would have empty pockets and the struggles of the past few years would be for naught. That was the way the Norths did business.

Ronald smiled. 'We might be persuaded to forget his debt, as we did for Greywall. The chance to meet the famous Captain Wiscombe will bring even more people up from London. I am sure he must have friends recently retired from service who would enjoy a chance to share our hospitality. We simply have to persuade him.'

'You will never convince him to do such a thing,' she said, praying that it was true.

'Perhaps not. But I will not have to. You are so very good with men, little sister,' he said, touching her shoulder.

She shrugged off his hand. 'I will not help you hurt him.'

'You did once, Lillian.' He patted her shoulder again.

'And I regret it,' she said. She had been young and foolish, and there had been no choice. It would not happen again.

'Regret?' Ronald laughed. 'You are a North, Lillian. That is not an emotion we are capable of. The time will come when blood will tell and you will come around to our way of thinking again.'

'Never,' she said.

'We shall see. But now I must go to my own room to dress. I will see you at dinner.' He smiled. 'Remember to look your best for Gerry. If he is a happy and contented husband, it will be that much easier to bring him into the fold. And once we are assured of his help, we will be even better off than before.'

As it usually was at Wiscombe Chase, dinner was a motley affair. Guests were either tired from the hunt, well on the way to inebriation, or both. Today, most of them still wore their fox-hunting pinks, having gone from the stable to the brandy decanter without bothering to change for dinner.

At the centre of the table, as it so often was, there was venison. When she'd first arrived here, Lily had liked the meat. She had to admit that Cook prepared it well. The haunch was crisp at the end and rare and tender in the middle. The ragout was savoury, with thick chunks of vegetables from the kitchen garden. The pies were surrounded by a crust that flaked and melted in the mouth like butter.

But venison today meant that yesterday another stag had been shot and butchered. The supply of them seemed endless, as did the stream of guests that came to hunt them. Was it too much to ask that, just once, a hunt would end in failure? Perhaps then the word would spread that the Chase was no longer a prime destination to slaughter God's creatures.

Of course, if there were no more deer, they would just switch to quail. A brace of them had been served in aspic as the first course. At tomorrow's breakfast, there would be Stewart's fresh fish. A starving person might have praised the Lord for such abundance, but Lily had come to dread meals when requesting vegetables had begun to feel like an act of defiance.

At the head of the table, Captain Wiscombe stared down the length at the plates and gave a single nod of approval. His eye turned to the guests and the approbation vanished. And then he looked at her. Did she see the slightest scornful curl of his lip?

He must think her totally without manners to have arranged the table with no thought to precedence. But she could hardly be blamed for the tangled mess that these dinners had become. Attempts to arrange the ladies according to rank before entry to the dining room were met with failure, as none of them seemed to understand their place. If she resorted to name cards beside their plates, they simply rearranged them and sat according to who wished to speak to whom. The men were even worse, with businessmen bullying lords to take the place next to the earl.

With the addition of Captain Wiscombe, things were even more out of balance than usual. The ladies at either side of him were the youngest of the four. Miss Fellowes, who had pulled her chair so close that she was brushing his right sleeve with her arm, was not even married. Mrs Carstairs hung on his left, laughing too loudly at everything that he said, as though polite dinner conversation were a music-hall comedy.

Her father and brother had packed themselves into the middle of the table on either side and chatted animatedly with the guests who lacked the spirit to fight for a better chair.

On her end of the table, the earl took her right, as he always did. He remained oblivious to the insult of the cit at his other side, as long as he was supplied with plenty of wine and an opportunity to ogle her décolletage.

The space between them was punctuated by silence. He had long ago learned that if he attempted to speak to her, she would not respond. But even if she did not look in his direction, she could still feel his eyes upon her like a snail trail on her skin. She took a deep sip of her wine to combat the headache that came with pretending indifference to it.

On her left was Sir Chauncey, staring dejectedly up the table at Miss Fellowes as though watching his romantic hopes disappearing over the horizon. Tonight she made a half-hearted effort to engage him in conversation, to take his mind from the sight of his lover flirting with her husband. But eventually she tired of his monosyllabic responses and let their end of the table return to silence.

Then she looked towards the head of the table as well and hoped that the captain would not catch her studying him. Who would have thought that a shy boy could turn into such a magnificent creature? Even when at ease, he still had the air of command that she had noticed in the sitting room earlier. He did not stare, nor did his eyes dart from face to face. Yet he seemed aware of each action taken and each word spoken up and down the table.

While he took care that this observation of his guests did not seem ill-mannered, the women surrounding him did not bother with niceties. They stared openly at the way the candlelight shone gold off the waves in his hair and the shadows accented the sharp planes of his cheeks. When he smiled, and he did so often, they could not contain audible sighs of admiration. Fox hunting might have held their attention this afternoon. But if such a fine male specimen showed even a hint of interest, the women of the party would be doing any future sporting inside the house with the captain.

The feeling this aroused in her was unfamiliar, but she assumed it must be jealousy. It explained the urge she had to pry the two women away from him and claim the place at his side. When she'd imagined his homecoming, it had not been at all like this.

For one thing, he was even more splendid to look at then she'd dreamed. She had pictured him as growing taller, leaner and more mature, an older version of the ordinary boy who had left her. She had not expected the blond god lounging at the head of the table tonight.

She stared, fascinated, as he rolled the stem of his wine glass between his fingers. Was it a sign of irritation? Boredom? Or was it simply a habit? It did not matter what it meant to him. To her, it hinted that the hands that had been brutal on the battlefield were gentle enough to hold a wine glass, or a woman.

Miss Fellowes was watching his hands, as well. And there was another difference. In Lily's fantasies, there had been no competition for his attention. Nor had he stated plainly, during their first conversation, that he might desire others and that she was to have no say in the matter.

She should have spent less time on dreams and focused on the harsh realities. He had no reason to like her, much less love her. Even in the best marriages, male fidelity was not guaranteed or expected.

Her father had no such trepidations. He was smiling up the table as if Christmas had arrived in September. A dragoon in dress uniform was just what the table needed to convince a band of foolish cits that they were dining with the upper class. The splendid red jacket hugging his shoulders had an excessive amount of gold braid covering it. Despite the time spent on horseback, the breeches beneath it were still snowy white and tight enough to display the muscles of a superlative horseman. Though the captain's excuse was that his clothing would arrive in a day or two, the full uniform made him into just the sort of prize that would have guests swarming to the Chase to meet him.

Her father stood, raising his glass. 'May I offer a toast to our host and thanks for his safe return?'

Lily tried to contain her flinch. No, he might not. If a toast was to be made, especially so early in the meal, her husband should be the one to offer it. Even while attempting courtesy, her father was rudely overstepping his place.

Gerald accepted it with a smile and only the slightest narrowing of his eyes, to show his annoyance.

As she feared they would, the guests responded not with a polite, 'Hear, hear', but with raucous laughter and applause. The toast itself resulted in several spills on the linen and a cracked glass from Mr Wilson. Greywall, who always drank twice as much as the other guests, needed to have his glass refilled before he could participate. He drained it rather than sipping and gestured for the footman to leave the bottle. He turned to smile at her, lifting his glass in a private salute, and Lily could feel the slight pain in her head turning to a full megrim, tightening about her temples like an iron band.

From halfway down the table, Mr Burke began to regale them with a tale of the day's hunt. Conversation on all sides ground to a halt, except for the interjection of needless details by Mr Wilson and a brief argument between the two over whether the wind was easterly or from the west when the dogs first caught the scent.

At the head of the table, her husband was silent.

His eyes were on his guests, but the knife in his hand was slicing the meat on his plate with mathematical precision.

When, at last, the poor vixen had been run to ground and her gory dispatch applauded, the table turned to Captain Wiscombe for his reaction.

He responded with a smile. Then, very deliberately, he set down his knife and fork and pushed his plate of venison away as if he'd lost all appetite.

Mr Burke stared at him in surprise. 'Do not tell me, Captain, that you do not enjoy hunting.'

'Not so much that I would wish to kill the animal a second time, during the meal,' he said, continuing to smile.

'Surely a little blood does not bother you, Wiscombe,' Greywall said. He forked up a large bite of rare meat and waved it before him as if to goad his host.

'A little blood?' He considered for a moment. 'It depends on whom it belongs to. I am more bothered by a small amount of mine than a large amount of another fellow's. And that of a fox?' He shrugged. 'If it does not come into my home to provoke me, then I see no reason to run through its home with a pack of dogs, waving my gun.'

'Did you see very much blood, when you were in Portugal?' This question came from Mrs Carstairs, who seemed to find nothing unladylike in broaching such a topic at the table.

The others at the table leaned in expectantly.

Lily held her breath.

'See blood? Yes. Yes, I did. But, unlike a fox hunter,

I did not intentionally rub it on my face to mark my first kill.' His smile dimmed and his distant expression made her wonder if he still saw carnage when he closed his eyes at night.

Mrs Carstairs was as oblivious to the slight as she was to the small fleck of blood left on her cheek from her first hunt. 'I am sure you have stories that are far more interesting than Mr Burke's. Was stalking Napoleon and his men so different from hunting dumb beasts?'

He thought for a moment. 'I wonder if, in a table somewhere in France, there is a man being asked the same thing about hunting me?' He offered nothing more than that, staring at her with a fixed smile until she looked away and changed the subject.

When dinner had ended, her father stopped her before she could escape to her room to ease the pain in her head. 'Lillian, a moment, please.'

For a moment, she considered pretending she had not heard him, as she usually did when he spoke to her. She had learned, years ago, that there was little point in conversing if she could not believe anything he might say. But if they did not talk here, he would follow her to her room, just as Ronald had done. A conversation in the hallway would be shorter and less painful. She rubbed her temple. 'What do you want?'

'I have not yet got the chance to speak to your husband about the future of our endeavours here. And I was wondering if you—'

She cut him off. 'It will not be necessary. There is

no future for them.' Then she glanced about her to remind him that they were on the main floor where anyone might overhear them.

'No future?' He seemed surprised. 'It has taken years to get things running just as they are. We cannot stop now.'

'On the contrary. What you are doing is wrong. You should stop it immediately.'

Her father was looking at her as Stewart had, when she'd explained that nice little boys did not pull Kitty's tail. 'Wrong? The guests enjoy their visits here. In fact, they leave as happy as they arrive.'

'But poorer,' she reminded him.

'But they do not mind it,' he argued. 'If they do not, then I fail to see why you do.'

'The fact that they do not mind it does not make it right,' she said. She was using her patient, mothering voice. But she did not feel at all patient. She should not have to teach decency to this man. He should have been the one who taught it to her. The imaginary metal band that circled her head was tightening with each word.

'Right and wrong are nebulous things, Lillian. If no one is hurt, has a wrong truly been done?'

'How would you know that no one has been hurt?' she snapped. 'Have you ever asked them? Have you thought, for even a moment, about anyone other than yourself?' She was getting angry. If she was not careful, people would notice. And then everything would be worse and not better. She took several slow, deep breaths and felt the pain in her head lessen somewhat.

Other than to stare at her in shocked silence, her father did nothing. And that was just as expected.

When she'd calmed herself enough to continue, she said, 'What happens will be Captain Wiscombe's decision, because it is his house. He is an honourable man and he will want no part in the humbug you have created.'

Her father favoured her with a childishly eager smile. 'Then you must make an effort to persuade him.'

'I?' she said, shaking her head in amazement at his stubbornness. 'After all that has happened in this house, you come to me for help to keep things as they are?'

Now his expression turned to one of puzzlement. 'Of course I do. Who else could better help me persuade the captain?'

The pain in her head was near to unbearable. If she did not go to her room soon, the servants would have to carry her there. 'Even if I wanted to help you, what makes you think he would listen to me?'

Now it was her father's turn to speak to her as if she were an ignorant child. 'Because he dotes on you, my dear.'

'He certainly does not.' If anything, the opposite was true. She'd had years to develop an infatuation with her own husband. But his affection grew more unattainable with each passing minute. 'He hates me,' she said and the ache in her head seemed to move to her heart.

'Nonsense. He adored you when he offered. I saw the look in his eyes after you'd accepted him. It was as if the crown jewels had fallen out of a tree and landed in his lap. I am sure nothing has changed.'

He was telling her what she wanted to hear, to win her to her side. But then, her father had always been good at making people believe in the impossible, even as he ignored the obvious. She must not be swayed by him. 'Everything has changed, Father. *Everything.*'

He smiled. 'Then you must change them back. Captain Wiscombe might have prevailed against Napoleon's army. But you, Lillian, are a North. The poor man does not stand a chance.'

## Chapter Six

Gerry had begun to envy his wife her megrim.

Lillian had claimed illness and disappeared immediately after the meal, forcing the female guests to settle in the parlour with only a footman for company. The elder North and the earl had joined them, seeking a quiet game of cards by the fire.

The other men were proving themselves to be as annoying after dinner as they had been at the table. At Ronald's suggestion, the six of them remaining had retired with their port to the billiard room.

Either Lillian had not completed her redecorating, or she had given up on trying to make this room look like anything other than what it was. The tiny game room retained the utter lack of charm that had been so evident in the home of his youth. Hunting trophies still lined its upper walls, staring down at them as they played. Their glassy eyes glittered in the smoke from too many pipes and cigars.

Gerry leaned against the wall under a moth-eaten

roe, sipping a brandy and watching as Lillian's brother toyed with his third opponent of the night. It was clear from the way he played that no one had bothered to take care of the slight warp that existed in the surface of the table, nor had they taken the time to properly iron the baize covering before the game began. The small wrinkles that still marred its surface would make play difficult.

The problems were near invisible to the naked eye, especially in a smoky room. But Gerry had found his ball trapped by the table's deficiencies often enough when learning the game from a competitive father who showed no mercy. When he'd whined about the unfairness of it, his father announced that a man who played a game without assessing the risks deserved what he got.

The elder Wiscombe would have got along well with the Norths. Tonight, Ronald was using the same philosophy to remove money from his guests. Poor Carstairs had just lined up a shot he had no hopes of making. Before he attempted it, he paused to chalk his cue by grinding it into the plaster of the ceiling like the barbaric cit that he was.

Gerry gritted his teeth into a smile and retracted his sympathy for the man. Then, without a word he offered Carstairs the cube of white chalk that sat on the table's edge. He would have to come back in daylight to assess the damage to the ceiling. Judging by the current company, there were likely years' worth of marks left by men that had no sense of how to deport themselves outside of a public billiard hall.

For now, he would enjoy the surprised look on

Carstairs's face as his ball rolled just short of its mark and stopped.

Ronald's response was to pot two balls in one stroke and finish the match.

'Game to me,' he said with a smile.

'You are a damned lucky fellow,' Carstairs said, wiping his brow and reaching for a pad and pencil to write a marker of his debt.

'Very lucky,' Ronald said, feigning modesty. 'But I will allow that I have some skill in the game.'

'You must play me next,' Gerry said, finishing his drink in one gulp and giving the broad smile that he knew made him look like a simpleton. 'I have not played in ages. There was no time for games in Wellington's army.'

'Well, then. This should be interesting for both of us.' Ronald's smile was positively wolfish as he chalked his cue.

Gerry turned to the rack and chose a mace instead. The old club-headed sticks were horribly out of fashion. But he was as good with one as he was with a cue and they overcame the deficiencies of the table quite nicely.

Ronald arched an eyebrow in surprise and replaced his cue, as well. 'My, but it has been a while since you played.'

'When Father taught me, it was with wooden balls so lopsided there was no telling where they would go, even at the best times.' As if demonstrating, he swung the mace wide, nearly knocking a drink from the hand of Wilson, who was standing too close to him.

'You'll find that the new ivory balls work much better,' Ronald said, setting up his first shot and tapping the red ball with his white one.

'I expect so,' Gerry said and deliberately missed, sending his cue ball bouncing off the padded rail. Then he looked up and smiled. 'But we have not set a wager yet.' He brought the mace up so quickly it set the oil lamps above the table to swaying.

Ronald sent Gerry's cue ball rolling into a pocket. 'Nor have we set the points. Play to six?'

An easy thing for him to say, when he was already up by four. Gerry smiled broadly again. 'Excellent. And let us make it interesting. Fifty quid?'

'Fif...' The wind was escaping from Ronald like gas from a balloon. 'I do not have so much ready money.'

'Fifty from me, then,' Gerry said. 'And if I win, you may forgive the debts of the men who have played so far. That should call it even.'

'If you really think that is wise,' Ronald said, pityingly.

Gerry grinned and nodded like a fool. Then, with a single stroke, he sunk all three balls with a cannon, to the calls of 'Capital shot' and 'Huzzah for the captain!'

'And how many is that, again? I cannot remember.' Gerry counted points on his fingers.

'Ten,' said Ronald, his smile disappearing. 'Game to you, sir.'

'It is all a matter of geometry, dear fellow. Back in the day, I was quite good at mathematics. The markers, if you please.' Gerry held out his hand for the IOUs and his brother-in-law handed them over with a frown.

Gerry tore them in half with a single decisive motion

and dropped the pieces on to the table beside him. Then he yawned. 'And now, I think it is time that I retire.'

'You must not,' Carstairs said. 'The night is just beginning.' By the slur in his voice, the night had gone on far too long already.

'I have been away from home and wife for seven years,' Gerry said. 'She will not want me lingering with the gentlemen until dawn.'

'A lovely woman she is,' Burke announced. 'And a shame that she has been alone so long.'

Gerry felt the hair at the back of his neck prickling as if it could rise like the ruff of an angry dog. How many other men had noticed Lillian's beauty and made drunken comments over the billiard table about her sleeping alone? And what sort of man was Ronald North for showing not a hint of disapproval?

'Those days are now past,' Gerry said and gave Burke a look that brought a mumbled assurance that no disrespect was intended.

He nodded and looked past the man at Ronald. 'I am home for good.' Then he stared into his brother-in-law's eyes to be sure the idiot noticed that there was a wolf beneath the sheepskin. 'I will be with her, until death us do part. Just as I am sure you intended when you introduced us.' Then he quit the room, ignoring the low curse behind him.

## Chapter Seven

Once upstairs, Lily put on her best nightgown and allowed the maid to put a ribbon in her braided hair. By the smile on Jenny's face, she could guess that the girl was imagining the fond reunion to come.

The ribbon was superfluous. She doubted it would matter to Captain Wiscombe how she looked. Despite what her father and brother believed, Gerald's reasons for lying with her had nothing to do with romance. He was merely staking a claim of ownership.

Would that her own motivations were as clear. She could tell herself that going to his bed tonight was nothing more than an attempt to be the loyal wife he'd deserved from the first. It would have been much easier to believe, if both her father and brother had not reminded her that she was a North and therefore an expert manipulator. Was she being her usual, obedient self and doing what Gerald wanted her to do? Or was she following her family's instructions and doing what might make him do what she wished at some later date?

Or was this about nothing more than her fascination with Captain Gerald Wiscombe, late of the Fifth Dragoons? Her only experience with what went on in the bedroom had left her with no desire to repeat the act. But after years of reading about his exploits, the thought of Captain Gerald Wiscombe made her heart flutter in anticipation.

There was fluttering in other places, as well. Her husband was not some paper idol. He was here and all too real. And tonight, she would finally be his bride. Suddenly, it felt like her chaste cotton night rail was made of butterfly wings. Each shift of cloth on skin reminded her of just how bare she would be when he removed it.

For a moment, memories from the past clawed at her mind like a rat in a cage. The headache, which had eased during the quiet hours since dinner, began to return.

She took a slow breath to clear her head. The past was the past. Tonight would be different. There would be no fear or guilt since the man involved was her husband. Not only that, the man she had married was a romantic daydream come to life. There was not a braver or more honourable man in all of England than Gerald Wiscombe and there were few men as handsome.

If only he didn't hate her...

After what seemed like hours of silence, she heard the hall door of the room beside hers open and close. There was no second voice, or any other indication that he'd summoned a servant to help him prepare for bed. In fact, there was no sound at all. Had he forgotten about her already and gone to sleep?

It would be better to face her fears and seek him out than to lie awake in her bed, waiting for a summons that might never come. It took a few more minutes to steel her nerve before she tiptoed across the floor of her room to the connecting door and opened it, just a crack.

'Come.' It was a command. The first of many, she suspected. As a good wife ought, she obeyed it.

Perhaps the wine at dinner had mellowed him. Except for his boots, he was still dressed and stretched full length upon his bed, staring at the canopy above him. Compared to the scowls of the afternoon and the guarded smiles of dinner, he looked at peace with himself and the world.

It would be a shame to ruin that for either of them. She had the sudden, craven desire to retreat.

'I thought you had a headache,' he said without looking in her direction.

'It is better,' she lied. Now that she was in his room, it was coming back again.

'Then do not hang about the doorway. If you are coming in, come in.' He did not finish with the suggestion that she should do it or go away, but it was implied.

So forward she went, into the room, shutting the door behind her. *A different man*, she reminded herself. *A different room.* Or it might as well have been. She had made sure that nothing remained of the old master bedroom but her memories.

He turned away from her to stare at one of the pictures on the wall, giving it far more attention than a simple landscape deserved. Were the details in some way wrong? Most likely they were and he was making a note to have the thing removed and replaced.

The one thing he did not seem interested in was her. She had not expected him to spring upon her like a wild beast and force her on to her back. But neither had she expected uninterest. She felt like a fool standing here in her simple gown and her sad little hair ribbon. He did not want her. Now that they were alone, there was no reason for him to pretend otherwise.

He sighed as if her presence in the room was an interruption and looked back to her, then gestured absently to the side of his bed closest to her own door. When she did not move, he prompted, 'Get in.' Then he sat up and untied his neckcloth without bothering to see if she complied.

Before he could ask again, she pulled back the coverlet and climbed between the sheets, resisting the urge to pull them up so she might hide under the blankets. It was not as if there was anything to see, should he decide to look. Her gown was buttoned to the throat. But it proved one thing to both of them. She was not planning to bend him to her will through seduction. If she'd intended that, she would have done a better job of preparing for it.

Her husband sat on the edge of the bed, his back still to her. When he pulled his shirt over his head, she got her first look at a man's naked back. She could not help it. She gasped.

'Eh?' He turned with a half enquiring, half annoyed look.

'The scar.' She pointed.

His face softened, then he laughed. 'It is not a very heroic story, I'm afraid. A screaming Frenchman was galloping down upon me from behind. On seeing that my attention was elsewhere, my friend, MacKenzie of the Scots Greys, shot him in the back. It was too late to stop the full charge. He did not run me through as he'd planned. But the damned frog dragged the blade down my back as he fell and cut my coat to ribbons. It was some time before we were able to dress the wound, which was hardly deep enough to care about. I stripped off what was left of my shirt, and Mac poured a measure of his usquebaugh on my back and a wee dram into me. Then I sewed up my jacket and slept on my stomach for a week.'

'That is all?' she said, surprised.

He nodded. 'If it bothers you, then I suspect you will be even more disturbed when you see the rest of me.'

She had been thinking just such a thing when trying to imagine him naked.

He laughed again and gave a lascivious waggle of his eyebrows to show that he had been talking of other scars, but knew full well what she'd been thinking.

She shrank a little farther under the covers. The papers had said nothing of such things. They'd left her to imagine entire scenarios based on the phrase *heroic charge.* 'Were you injured often?'

He gave a non-committal shrug as he pulled off his stockings and threw them towards the wardrobe. 'As much as anyone, I'm sure. But not as much as those who did not come home.' Then he stood, turned to face her and displayed his chest. There was another cut across his upper arm, but it was clear from the wide scar that this had been deeper than the one across his back. And lower, just above his waist, was a puckered puncture.

He pointed. 'This is the one that should have done for me. A hole in the guts is a damned ugly way to die. But it managed to miss my vitals and come right out the other side. Of course, you won't see that until I take off my breeches.'

'But you recovered,' she said with a sigh of relief.

'I was feverish, of course. But I fought it off and was back in the saddle in a month and a half. The surgeon said it was a miracle. I assume I should be thanking you for your prayers for my safety.' He said the last with an ironic twist of his lips.

For all she knew, it was exactly how he had survived. Would he believe her, should she tell him so? 'I prayed fervently for your good health each night for seven years.' When she saw the answering glare, she added a smile as ironic as his had been. It seemed to satisfy him more than her sincerity.

'And now you have got your wish.' He undid the buttons on his breeches, dropped them to the floor and kicked them out of the way as he pulled back the bedcovers and climbed in beside her.

She had known for some time that it would not be the soft dumpling of a boy who came to her, should her wedding night ever occur. But she had not been prepared for Gerald Wiscombe in the flesh. Even flaccid he was a formidable specimen. His lack of embarrassment at his own nakedness made him all the more intimidating.

Despite the scars, he was also blessedly intact. She'd seen more than her share of veterans of the Peninsula walking the halls of the Chase on wooden legs and crutches, or with empty coat sleeves pinned up to keep them out of the way. But whether from luck or answered prayers, her captain had returned with two strong arms and two good legs.

Now that she could see all of him, she'd noted the tracery of smaller scars that accompanied the major wounds. This was a man who viewed injury as mere inconvenience, should it stand in the way of what he wished to achieve. Once he had begun, resisting would be futile.

For a moment, the old fears returned and she shrank back even farther towards the edge of the bed, glancing towards the door of her room.

He made no effort to reach for her. 'You may leave if you wish. I have no intention of holding a wife by force, especially you.' Then he rolled on to his stomach. 'Or you might make yourself useful and rub the knots out of my shoulders. After three days in the saddle I am as stiff as an unsoaped harness.'

'H-how would I do that?' It was an unexpected request. But it would be less frightening to do than to be done to.

'It will not be difficult. Begin by putting your hands about my throat and pretending that you wish to choke the life out of me.' He laughed into the pillow.

She could not see his face. But by the tone of his voice he seemed to be honestly amused by the idea that she might want to hurt him. At least he trusted her

enough to turn his back to her while naked and defenceless. She responded to his trust with her own and pulled
her legs up under her to kneel at his side. Then she
placed her hands on his shoulders and began to knead.

It was easy to see why he'd wanted her help. The
muscles beneath her fingers were as hard and unyield-
ing as bags of sand. Or perhaps that was normal. She
had never touched so much bare male skin in her life.
As she worked over them, she felt the flesh begin to
soften and relax.

Her own tension was easing, as well. The warmth of
his body and the rhythmic kneading of her own hands
worked as a soporific. The last of the pain in her head
diminished to a dull throb, then disappeared.

It was replaced by hesitant pleasure. She liked touching him. There was something very comforting about
the feel of his warm flesh beneath her hands, as if he
could transfer his bravery to her through the skin. She
wanted to curl up next to him, to press her cheek into his
shoulder and stay there until the world felt right again.

In response to her massage, her husband grunted in
satisfaction. 'You are almost as good at this as an army
leech. Of course, he used horse liniment.'

In spite of herself, she smiled. Then she dug her
fingers more deeply into the space beneath his shoulder blades. 'I am sure we can find something better
than camphor and turpentine to use in the bedroom.
My maid has a recipe for a balm made with beeswax
and peppermint...'

He was laughing again, his shoulders shaking with
mirth. Then he gave a lurch and rolled, catching her

wrists and pulling her off balance and on to her back.
'By all means, we must render me sweet-smelling if
we are to share a bed.'

The sudden change in position left her breathless
and light-headed. But this time it was a good feeling,
more like floating than fainting. There was something
about his smile, so close above her, that kept her from
being afraid. She answered him with a hesitant nod.

He leaned on his elbows so that he might look down
into her eyes. 'You are a comely wench, Lily Wiscombe.' He ran a fingertip along the line of her jaw.
Then his smile was coming closer and his lips met hers.

*Wiscombe.*

She was not a North any more. She was a Wiscombe. One of two. Soon, two would become one. If
it was anything like this kiss, she had nothing to fear.
His mouth was open and his lips moved slowly against
hers. Very gently, she reached out with the tip of her
tongue to taste the crooked smile and the tiny imper-
fections that made him so fascinating to look at.

In response, his body stirred. His arms tightened
around her. Their breath mingled in a sigh.

'He mounted his horse in the night at the door,
'And sat with his face to the crupper.'

The song, bawdy and off-key, came like a nightmare
interrupting a dream. Mr Carstairs was in his cups, and
walking down the corridor of the family wing at the
worst possible time.

Her mind immediately flew to the hall door of her

own room. She replayed the memory of locking it after her maid left. She'd set the key upon the dresser, just as she did every night. She was safe.

But that room had never been the problem. This was the room that was dangerous. It might look different, but underneath the paint and paper it was the same. And the doors here were not locked as they ought to be. Anyone might enter from the hall. Her head was pounding now as she waited for the sound of a hand testing the handle.

Her husband pulled away from her, staring at the door. 'What the devil...?'

'Some scoundrel has cut off the head of my horse,
'While I was engaged with the bottle...'

The song was even louder now, even closer. But she was not alone this time. And it was not just her husband come too late to save her from dishonour. Her hero, Captain Wiscombe, was finally here and bristling with righteous anger.

Suddenly, her fear of the drunk in the hallway seemed overblown. She touched her husband's bare arm. 'It is nothing,' she said, praying that was true. 'If we ignore him, he will go away.' She would lie awake the rest of the night fearing that he, or someone else, would return. But as long as Captain Wiscombe was here, she would be safe.

'Which went gluggity, gluggity, glug.'

All the same, she could not seem to control her body's response. She was trembling, quite out of character with the foolishness of the song. *Please let him go*, she entreated silently. *Please.* The day had been hard enough without this.

'Enough.' Wiscombe pushed away from her and swung his legs out of the bed, reaching for his breeches.

'It is nothing,' she repeated, if only to convince herself.

'It damn well is not. It is Carstairs. The man is a bloody nuisance,' he said, throwing a shirt over his head and pulling boots over his bare feet. 'Despite what may have been condoned in my absence, my home is not a tavern and my bedroom is not a music hall. I mean to put a stop to it.' Then he was through the door and it slammed behind him.

''Tis strange headless horses should trot,
'But to drink with their tails is a—'

The song came to an abrupt end and the silence was profound. She waited, breath held, to see what would happen next.

The minutes had stretched out into an hour and still nothing happened. The singing did not continue, but neither did Captain Wiscombe return. Had he locked the door when he'd gone? She stared across the room, at the door handle, watching for movement.

She debated the sense of slinking back to her own room so that she might safely lock herself inside. Then it occurred to her that, should someone look for her, this was the one place they would not search. Even if they suspected that she was here, they would not dare enter the bedroom of a decorated soldier. She was safer in Wiscombe's room than she had been in her own.

The thought was strangely comforting. She was in her husband's bed, where she belonged. She eased back into the pillows and pulled the coverlet up. Then she closed her eyes to rest them until her husband returned.

## Chapter Eight

When Lily woke the next morning, it was in her own bed. She lay perfectly still for a moment, trying to dredge up the memory of the previous evening. Had she roused sufficiently to get herself here, or had she fled? If so, had it been before or after her husband's return?

She searched both her body and her mind for any trace of disturbance that could explain this situation. She was a sound sleeper, particularly after a megrim when she had been stressed to the point of exhaustion. But if Captain Wiscombe had returned to bed her, she'd hoped she would have some memory of it.

It appeared that he had returned to find her sleeping and carried her to her own bed without waking her. She had a vague recollection of arms lifting her up and a sigh of soft breath at her temple. It seemed he had chosen to prolong this part of his homecoming for another night, at least.

She rang for her maid. As usual, she selected a day gown that was both simple and sensible. Her father sometimes accused her of dressing no better than an innkeeper's wife. When he did, she invariably told him that since he insisted on housing strangers in her home, she saw no reason to behave as if she were entertaining friends.

But this morning, when she went down to breakfast, she would be greeted not just by her father's friends, but by the critical eye of her husband. She rejected the first gown and chose a snow-white muslin with a wide border of violets embroidered about the hem. There were purple ribbons at her waist and she requested that Jenny thread more of them through her curls. When they were finished, she looked as fresh as a spring morning.

Before he'd arrived, she'd imagined what it might be like if the past between them did not exist. Suppose they had never married and she was meeting Captain Gerald Wiscombe for the first time at a ball or garden party. This was the way she would want to look if she wished to capture the attention of the hero of Salamanca.

Against all reason, her stomach filled with hopeful butterflies. Things had seemed different last night. Though he had refused to discuss the war while at table, he'd been willing to tell her about his injuries. While she had been touching him, he'd been happy and content, as had she. Perhaps this kernel of trust might grow to be something more.

Would he notice a difference in her look or manner when she arrived at the breakfast table? If he did, he did not say. There was no indication that he approved, other than a slight raise of his eyebrow as he examined her over his coffee cup. When he smiled, it was the same false grin he had been using at supper. Whatever truce they'd achieved while together in the bedroom did not extend to the other rooms of the house. 'Good morning, my dear.' His voice was just as dispassionate as his expression.

She could answer in kind. But if she wished for a change, there was no point playing games with him. She gave him her warmest smile and curtsied. 'Good morning, Captain Wiscombe.'

'I trust you slept well?'

Was he asking because he had put her to bed, or was it nothing more than polite conversation? 'Yes, thank you.'

'I suspect it was difficult because of the noise in the hall.' This was said to no one in particular, as if he meant to call the perpetrator to task over it.

'That was Carstairs,' her father announced, as though there were nothing particularly strange about drunken serenades. 'We really must teach the man a new song.'

'Or teach him to sing the current one correctly,' Ronald added. 'He cannot seem to hit the high note, for all the times he tries. I see he is sleeping late this morning.'

'Perhaps feeling the ill effects of the bottle,' Mr Burke added.

'He is not sleeping late,' Mrs Carstairs announced. 'At least he is not doing so in our room. He was not there at all last night.'

All assembled shifted in their chairs, trying to pretend that they were not hearing accusations of infidelity over breakfast.

The offended wife's gaze swept down the table, searching for signs of guilt. 'Miss Fellowes is not present, either.'

Mrs Burke made sympathetic noises of disapproval.

'Neither is Sir Chauncey,' her father supplied. 'Perhaps Miss Fellowes is with him.'

'What would they be doing together so early in the morning?' Mrs Wilson's smile was positively evil.

'I am sure they are both in their own rooms where they belong,' Lily said, trying to stop the rampant speculation. 'And Mr Carstairs...' Really. She had no idea. 'Perhaps Mr Carstairs is hunting.'

'If he is, he must be told to leave the old stag for me,' Greywall announced to no one in particular. 'That fellow is mine.'

'I do not think that is the game he is after,' said Mrs Burke with a sniff. 'More likely he has caught a young doe.'

Mrs Carstairs hissed through her teeth and pushed away from the table as if preparing a physical response to the insult.

Before Lily was forced to intervene, there was a shriek from the hall and the sound of breaking glass. The residents of the breakfast room hurried to the doorway, eager to see what fresh scandal was brewing.

All except Captain Wiscombe. He merely helped himself to more fish and refilled his coffee. She left him to it and followed the others into the hall.

Once there she found something far more interesting than the gossip over last night's serenade. Mr Carstairs was standing in the hall, sporting a blackened eye and naked as a jay except for the silk runner he had seized from a nearby side table. Sally, one of the younger and more impressionable parlourmaids, was collapsed in a dead faint, surrounded by the sherry glasses she had been retrieving from the parlour.

'I had no intention...' stuttered Mr Carstairs. 'I awoke in a horse trough in the stables. But my clothes... I do not know... And there was a black stallion snapping at my...' He gripped the table runner even tighter over his unmentionables.

'Was the trough not full, then?' Wiscombe said innocently. He stood at the back of the group, coffee cup still in hand. 'Poor Satan must be starving. I will go and speak to his groom.' He passed his drink to an approaching footman and walked past the shivering Carstairs as though he did not see him, muttering to himself about the need to set in a decent supply of oats and mash.

Since Mr Carstairs had been just outside their door before the singing stopped, Lily suspected that her husband knew perfectly well about the condition of the horse trough, the source of Carstairs's black eye and the location of the gentleman's clothes. But if he did not wish to speak of them, neither did she.

She pushed through the knot of guests blocking her way and went directly to the maid, who needed more help than her embarrassed guest. She positioned herself so that Sally would be spared from witnessing more nakedness if she woke. Then she called for a footman to bring a glass of water and spirits of ammonia.

Behind her, in the doorway to the breakfast room, Mrs Burke could no longer contain herself. Her stern disapproval of moments earlier dissolved and she let loose with a braying guffaw worthy of Satan the stallion. Mr Burke joined her, as did the earl. Mrs Carstairs answered them with a torrent of words that no lady should know.

Phineas North made a desperate attempt to reestablish a semblance of decorum and tried to shoo the ladies back towards the table. But no amount of gesticulating and tut-tutting sympathy from her father could quell the general mirth at the poor man's misfortune. With a moan, Mr Carstairs fled for the stairs, the table runner fluttering behind him.

Mr and Mrs Carstairs left later that day, citing urgent business in London. Gerry smiled to himself as he watched from his bedroom window and saw the carriage disappearing around the last bend of the drive. He had been successful in removing the first two interlopers. The rest would follow soon enough.

A single punch to the eye had been enough to stop the singing. But Gerry had not wanted the man sleeping off the liquor on the floor of the hall, only to awake unabashed and resume the song. He'd deemed it best to provide a lesson that could not be unlearned. He had thought about the matter for less than a minute before his own infernal sense of humour had taken hold. It had ended with him carrying the man like a sack of grain out to the stables, stripping him of his garments and leaving him.

He had not intended to abandon his wife. It had just taken more time than he'd planned to settle with the drunk in the hall. He'd meant to return to Lily with an amusing story to tell. When he'd left, she'd been shaking beneath the covers like a half-drowned puppy. He'd felt almost sorry for her.

Before the interruption, things had been going better than he'd expected. He'd had a damned fine reason for his foul temper yesterday afternoon. But the satisfaction of besting North at billiards had improved his mood. Retiring to that most suitable of bedchambers to have his shoulders caressed by a ministering angel had left him as tame as a kitten. To finish the night with his needs satisfied and his head pillowed on a soft breast would have made a fine end to a difficult day.

Then Carstairs had come and ruined everything. He'd lost his temper and the lady had lost her nerve.

By the time he'd got back to his room Lily had been fast asleep, curled into a ball beneath the blankets as if she feared attack. It had been an impulse to carry her to her room and put her to bed properly. There, she had settled in her own place with a happy sigh and continued sleeping.

What was he to make of her strange behaviour? When he'd imagined his return to Wiscombe Chase, he had assumed his wife was as conniving and crooked as the rest of her family. She would come up with a dozen unlikely stories for the condition of his house and the child presented as his heir. Perhaps she would try to seduce him into forgiving her. He would allow her to attempt it, at least for a time. She might be faithless, but she was every bit as beautiful as she had been on the day he'd married her. Back then, he'd been too embarrassed by his own inexperience to take what was his by right. Despite himself, he still wanted her. He would not miss the opportunity again.

But she was not the scheming jade he'd expected. Her dress was modest, her manner apologetic and obedient. At dinner she'd remained polite but aloof from the dinner guests. He wondered if she had feigned illness to escape them. When she'd come to his room, there had been no sign of the chronic headache that had been described to him by her brother.

Instead, she had been concerned and sympathetic to his injuries, old and new. She had talked of beeswax and peppermint, hinting at massages to come. And she had returned the kiss he'd given her.

She had been cautious of him, but not frightened. She had not shown fear until they'd been interrupted by the man wandering outside in the hall. But why? Carstairs had been no threat at all. He was just a jolly drunkard who could be tricked by his own weakness. It served him right for treating his hostess's hospitality with the same contempt he had for the billiard-room ceiling.

This morning, it pleased him that Lily had needed no instruction to hold her tongue. She'd taken her cue from his indifference and pretended there was no logical explanation for the naked man in her hall. But he suspected she had been amused by it. Had he seen a faint flicker of a smile on her lips as she'd rushed to help the maid?

She approved. Her approval should have meant nothing to him after all this time. But it did.

But he had far more approval in this house than he really wanted. He frowned down at the paper on the writing desk that sat under the bedroom windows. When he'd returned to his room after breakfast, he'd found it on the rug in front of the door, as if it had been slipped beneath to lie in his path as he entered.

The rectangle of parchment was folded once, the crease bisecting the writing with a razor-sharp line. Opening it revealed the multiplication table copied out in ink. It would have been an exaggeration to call the writing neat. There were smudges and blots, and a few grains of sand still clinging to the drying ink. But it was hard for a small hand to manage a pen. At that age he'd been using pencil, or chalk and slate.

This was clearly an attempt to impress him. And damn it all, he did not want to be impressed. He wanted to forget the one doing the writing so he might enjoy his new life at home. He wanted to clear the house of undesirables and stare into Lily's soulful brown eyes and pretend that she had never betrayed him. That would be impossible with a child underfoot, trying to get his attention.

He crumpled the paper and turned to throw it in the grate. Then, something stopped him. Too much work had gone into the preparation of this gift. While he did not want it, he would feel guilty if he destroyed it. Perhaps the child's mother would wish to see proof of the boy's educational success. He smoothed it flat again and tucked it between the pages of the *Théorie Analytique* where it would be out of sight until he was ready to deal with it.

He smiled down at the books. They were just the sort of gift he appreciated. How had she known he would want them? For that matter, how had she known to do any of this? Did she have some ingrained talent for homemaking and hospitality, to turn his detested childhood home into such a welcoming place?

Now that he'd got a look at it in daylight, he was even more eager than he had been to evict the guests, so he might enjoy his home in peace. The old heap of stone was comfortably familiar, yet so very different from the way he remembered it. It had been a sad house when he'd left it. Generations of neglect had worn on it, making it seem not just old, but tired of spirit. Even on the best days, there had been an odour of rank greenery and loam about the place, as if in a few more years the forest would reclaim the land and leave nothing for the last of the Wiscombes.

Now, even standing by the open windows, the air seemed fresh and cool. Lily and her horrid family deserved some credit for chasing out the dampness, fixing the roof and giving it all a wash and a coat of paint.

Then he reminded himself that if the other Norths were involved, the spaces outside his bedroom had not been done for his benefit. There was a plot in progress and he was tired of feeling as if he'd wandered in on the last act of the play. It was time for Lillian to prove her loyalty and tell him what had been going on here.

To find his answers, he left his room and took the stairs down to the wing that was the ladies' side of the house. There was no such thing, really. But his family had traditionally split itself along the line created by the centre hall. The billiard room, the library and the trophy room were to the left. The breakfast room, the morning room and the conservatory were to the right. Generations of Wiscombes had found that, if one wished to, one could avoid one's wife most of the day, except for dinner and the bedroom. A man's life could be largely unchanged by marriage if he had the sense to stay on his own side of the hall.

In his youth, Gerry's father had limited himself to half the house, even after his wife had passed. While Gerry kept the memory of his mother alive by haunting the spaces that had been hers, Father had treated the right side of the house and the son in it as if they no longer existed.

If the current lady of the house truly wished to avoid her houseguests, she must have fallen in with Wiscombe tradition and retreated to the wing not littered with empty wine bottles and dead deer. As Gerry turned down the right hallway a young face peeked out from behind the curtains in the hall, then disappeared again.

It was the boy. It explained the feeling he'd had all morning that he was being watched. The sounds of scrabbling and rustling that he'd heard while touring the ground floor earlier had not been mice in the wainscoting. It had been but a single pest, following behind, waiting for an invitation to come closer and discuss the gift.

When he was young, Gerry had tried such tricks on his own father and had been consistently rebuffed. The elder Wiscombe had had little use for anyone not old enough to take up a weapon and follow him into the field for a hunt. But at least Gerry had been the actual heir. It was annoying that this little whelp who had no claim of blood thought he was entitled to attention.

He did his best to ignore it. But now that he had recognised it, the sound of shifting feet on the hall rug behind him was maddening. At last, to no one in particular, he said, 'Go away.'

There was a sniffle in response.

Children's tears were even more annoying than women's. Especially when they were someone else's children and none of his concern. But it was not the child's fault that he was a bastard. It would be unfair to treat him too harshly. 'And well done on the mathematics,' he added, without turning around.

The sniffling stopped. There was a sigh, then the shuffling receded down the hallway.

Very good. He had no time to deal with a single mouse when the whole house was full of rats. He continued down the hall. Gerry checked the morning room, and music room, and salon, but found them vacant. This left him with the biggest folly of his foolish house: the conservatory.

Father had claimed that no true Wiscombe cared a fig about plants, on a plate or in a pot. So it had been the first space to fail after his mother had died. With its cracked panes and overgrown tangles of ivy and ferns it had sat for years like a cancer in healthy flesh, letting the noxious wildness into the rest of the house, as if the woods themselves had come to take revenge for the continual disturbance of the wildlife.

But when he entered today, he was struck by the fresh smell of lemons on the two dwarf trees that flanked the entrance and the sweet spice of geraniums and gillyflowers in pots by the windows. Sunlight streamed through the glass roof and walls, which were both clean and unbroken. The beams shining though the green glass panes that decorated the walls cast a mottled pattern on the veined marble floor that resembled a carpet of fallen leaves.

In the midst of it was the fairest flower in the house: his Lily. She had not yet noticed him enter, so he used the opportunity to observe her. Did she know that the midday sun behind her shone through the muslin gown to reveal far more of her figure than he had seen last night while they were in bed? A thin layer of gauze and a few embroidered flowers were all that stood between him and the paradise of her high, full breasts, round hips and shapely legs.

Seven years' bitter experience separated him and the naive child he'd been when he'd married her. Yet, when he looked at her he felt the same tightening in throat and groin that he'd experienced on the day he'd met her. He'd known that they were not making a love match, despite what her father claimed. What would a beauty like her want with a nothing like him? But perhaps, if he returned to her with a chest full of medals and a full purse, she would look at him with something other than frustration and disappointment. What a fool he had been.

As if she had heard his thoughts, she looked up at him now and gave a little gasp of shock. She dropped the bamboo-handled paintbrush she had been holding and it rolled across the floor to stop at his boot toe.

He stared down at it in surprise. Just now, he'd been too preoccupied by her figure to notice the easel she worked at and the watercolours on the glass-topped table beside her. It should not have surprised him. All ladies had hobbies and this one was not uncommon. But it had never occurred to him that *his* wife would have interests, other than spending his money and making him miserable with her infidelity.

Without a word, he picked up the brush and went forward into the room to give it back to her.

'Thank you, Captain Wiscombe.' She gave a nervous curtsy and cast her eyes downward, as though not quite sure how to respond to his sudden appearance.

His mind was equally unsettled by her demure response. 'You paint?' It was good that he had not been trying to impress her. He'd never have done it with such a fatuous remark.

She shrugged, embarrassed. 'Watercolours, mostly.' When pressed to make conversation, she seemed just as awkward as he felt.

He glanced down at a tall stack of books and newspapers beside the paints. A closer look revealed them to be a mix of atlases, gazetteers and histories of Spain,

France and Portugal, along with several old copies of *The Times*. 'And these?'

'Inspiration,' she said and almost knocked over her water glass as she tried to hide the clipping on the top of the stack.

He was faster, holding her wrist with one hand and snatching up the paper with the other. He scanned the text, reading a few lines aloud. '"And notable for their valour in the charge was the troop led by Captain Gerald Wiscombe…"' He put the paper back on the table and smiled at her. 'You find me inspiring?'

She shrugged again, blushing. 'I followed the news of the war. It would have been foolish not to. And while flowers are lovely, one can only draw so many of them before it becomes tiring.'

A feeble excuse from someone who was obviously enamoured of the dashing hero the newspapers had made him out to be. He'd met such women before. He could set them to giggling and blushing with a single smile. An invitation to hear a few of his tamer war stories would end with them sitting indecently close, his arm draped about soft shoulders in reassurance as sweet lips offered rewards for his bravery.

He looked at the woman before him, *his woman*, and stifled recollections of his romantic past with an embarrassed cough. He released her hand. 'And what is your current project?' He glanced at the work in progress. 'Mont-Saint-Jean?' He could not keep the surprise from his voice.

'It is only a copy.' She pointed to the open book beside her paints.

Perhaps it was. But the style of rendering was familiar. 'You did the paintings in my room?'

'It seemed like a sensible place to put them,' she said. 'At least until something better could be found to decorate the walls. I hesitated to choose permanent ornaments without your input. I will remove them, if you like.'

'No,' he said hurriedly. 'Your work is surprisingly accurate for someone who has never visited those places.' He glanced back at the picture in the book. 'See here?' He pointed. 'You've changed the angle of the light and captured the colour of it in a way this pencil sketch did not. And in the pictures in my room you've found the wild beauty of the countryside and omitted the chaos and blood that we left. It is how I want to remember the places I've been. The pictures are perfect just where they are.'

'Perfect,' she repeated, surprised.

'I like them well, as I do the rest of the decoration. Is that also your doing?'

She gave another shrug. 'I merely chose the things I imagined a man such as Captain Wiscombe might appreciate, after reading accounts of your bravery.' Her gaze dropped even farther, as if she were fascinated with the toes of her own slippers. 'You were quite famous, you know.'

'I did nothing that other soldiers wouldn't have done in my place.' If she would giggle or flirt, he might be able to respond in kind. But the earnestness of her praise embarrassed him. While in the thick of the action, he'd never intended to be a hero.

'On the contrary, the papers said Captain Wiscombe showed singular bravery, charging ahead when others retreated.' Now that she'd admitted to her preoccupation with his career, she gathered the nerve to look up at him with wide-eyed awe.

'You talk of this Wiscombe fellow as if he is some sort of paragon that a lady might swoon over and not standing here in front of you.' He looked at her, waiting for her to laugh at the hyperbole.

Instead, the blush in her cheeks turned scarlet. She could not seem to utter a syllable in response. This was no common infatuation that might be appeased with a single kiss on the cheek. She might have stood yesterday's criticism with cool grace. But today, she was suffering an agony of mortification over gentle mockery.

Had she really created an ideal of him in her mind and doted on it, just as he'd hoped she would? If so, it was too late. Her loyalty was worth nothing if she'd only found it after she'd betrayed him. But staring at the half-finished picture on the easel, he felt the anger beginning to drain out of him, just as it did when he entered his room the previous evening. He looked away.

'Whatever the reason for your painting,' he said gruffly, 'you've done well by it. And the bedroom you've prepared for me is quite the nicest I have been in. It suits me. Do not change a thing about it and hang as many pictures there as you care to paint.'

'Very well, Captain.' With her assent, she seemed to stifle her more tender feelings with the unquestioning obedience he'd requested yesterday.

She must not give up so easily. 'We will admire

them together tonight,' he reminded her, flashing his most devilish grin. It was unfair to toy with her, but he could not resist.

'Yes, Captain.' This time, the breathlessness in her voice stole his own, as did the thought of this beautiful creature in his bed. It would be just as he dreamed of, after all. Once he'd chased the last of the guests from the house, they would be able to explore their passions in private.

And then he reminded himself that she and her family had been instrumental in gathering the people he must now evict. While they might have stopped the leaks in the roof, they'd let Greywall into the house, allowing the one thing he'd hoped to avoid by accepting wife and commission.

While his wife's devotion to him was flattering, it was a new thing compared to the loyalty she'd shown to her conniving father and brother. Though Lily was beautiful, sometimes poison could be hidden in a pretty bottle. He should have better sense than to drink it.

'I did not come here to speak of my war record, or your feelings about it,' he said, crushing the fragile rapport between them. 'I want you to tell me what is really going on in this house.'

'What, exactly, do you wish to know about?' He watched the blush fade from her cheeks, revealing the cool, distant woman who presided over his dinner table. Her question was not an evasion so much as a request for clarification.

He gave it to her. 'What are your father and brother doing in my house, and who are these guests they have invited here? And what does it have to do with their initial eagerness that I marry you?'

To his surprise, she looked almost relieved that he had asked. 'My father makes regular trips to London, where he has ingratiated himself into the sorts of circles where there is too much ready money and very little standing in society. When he has found three or four fellows who seem interested in changing one for the other, he invites them to a house party.'

'You cannot buy rank,' Gerry said with a shake of his head.

'You did,' she pointed out. 'Father often opines that it would be better if society worked as the military did. There would be room enough at the pinnacle if it were easier for men of vision to pay their way up to being gentlemen.'

'Perhaps so,' he acknowledged. 'But that is not the way of things.'

'But suppose there was an opportunity to dine in intimacy with a member of the peerage. A friendship there might result in other invitations and a chance to move in more august circles once one returned to London.'

'Greywall,' Gerry said with a frown.

'An earl could be kept like the bear in the Tower of London,' she agreed.

'As if my neighbour was ever of real benefit to anyone,' Gerry said sceptically. 'And what does your father gain by this far-fetched altruism?' It was a question he should have asked himself when offered a beautiful wife and a commission. 'Does he charge admission?'

'That would be too obvious.' She waved the hand that held the brush as if painting the truth in the air. 'The gentlemen who visit are better at making money than friends.'

'They are drunken louts,' Gerry agreed.

'It makes them susceptible to offers that appear friendly, especially when they include a chance to make even more money. After a few days spent bagging partridges and chasing foxes, and a few nights drinking good wine, they are offered an opportunity that cannot fail to profit. My father thinks of them as investors.'

'Investors,' Gerry repeated. 'In what?'

'I believe the current offering is the breeding of Russian sables,' Lily responded with a sigh.

'That is the most ridiculous thing I have ever heard.'

'So you would think. But it has worked several times before. The first time, he bought an actual pair of the animals to bolster the plan.'

'The first time?' he said, amazed.

'It seems the sable farm is doomed to failure. The first pair escaped into the woods and have been—' she gave an embarrassed cough '—fornicating with martins and not each other.'

'If he has no sables, how can he convince anyone of the viability of this plan?'

She gave a small shrug. 'Does a Londoner know what a sable looks like before it has been made into a coat collar? A stoat dyed black will do just as well.' Now she was smiling. 'Ronald got a rather nasty bite during that process. Apparently, stoats do not enjoy being dipped.'

'Is that your brother's sole part in the scheme, the painting of weasels?'

She shook her head. 'My father is a man of big ideas. My brother less so. He enjoys cards and billiards. Any game of chance, really. He invariably wins. That is why Greywall is here. At this point, I believe we own more of his estate than he does himself.'

*We.* Had she even noticed she'd said it? Possibly not. But it annoyed him that as she'd explained her family's plans, she'd grown more animated and the colour had returned to her cheeks. 'That explains your father and brother,' he said. 'The guests and the earl, as well. But what is your part in all this?'

Her smile disappeared. 'Recently? I am hostess. Nothing more than that. I make sure the house is maintained. I avoid the guests as much as I am able. I do not approve of what is happening here. Really, I do not.' The protest was adamant, but it came far too late in the conversation.

'But that is, as you say, recently. What was your part before?'

'To be pretty and biddable,' she said, her eyes falling. 'To marry where I was told and not ask questions.'

'You were bait for me,' he clarified.

'To make the plan work, they needed the earl. He is your neighbour.'

'And he has coveted this house since my father was alive,' Gerry added.

'He wants the stag that has been roaming your land for ages.'

Gerry nodded. 'My father called him Rex. King of the forest. I saw him in the woods as I arrived.'

'Wanting a thing is different from getting it,' she replied.

'I am aware of that.' He looked at her and thought of his own marriage and what that first decision had gained and lost him over the years.

'They wanted you so they might get the house. They needed the house to trap the earl. The earl attends these parties to reclaim his markers from my brother.'

'And his presence attracts your father's investors from London,' he finished.

'As will yours, if they are allowed to continue,' she whispered, glancing at the door as if she feared to be overheard. 'My brother thinks he will convince you that you owe them for the improvements made on the house. If that does not work, he will find some other way to trick you out of your money. Father assumes I will help them because I am a North. And the Norths always look after their own.'

She looked so dejected at the thought that his common sense fled, just as it had on the day he'd met her. 'Then it is a good thing you are not a North,' he reminded her, taking the paintbrush from her hand. 'You are a Wiscombe now.' Then he tipped her chin up so that he might kiss her.

In Portugal, he'd often regretted that he had not come to her on their very first night as man and wife. He should have claimed her as his own immediately. But kissing her today, the remorse faded. Without having known others, how would he have recognised the sweetness of her kisses? Her mouth opened to him with the slightest coaxing. As he drank deeply from it, her body settled against his, ready to submit.

His hands were resting on the bare flesh at the base of her neck and he felt the pulse beating against the tips of his thumbs grow faster. He squeezed her shoulders in encouragement before smoothing his palms over and down her back, pressing her breasts and belly hard against his chest. At last, he reached the flare of her hips and her rounded bottom. He first cupped and then kneaded the flesh until she was squirming against his budding erection, gasping in eagerness.

He would have her here, naked as Eve in the Garden of Eden. He could imagine trapping her against the windows, his palms pressed flat to the cool glass. The scent of lemons would mingle with her musk as he thrust. And her cries...

Her cries would alert the household. He did not give a damn for any of the people here. But it would be more enjoyable to act out this particular fantasy once he had divested the Chase of the excess inhabitants.

He tightened his hands to fists, digging his nails into his palms to distract him from the temptation of her body. Then he moved his hands back to her shoulders and gently pushed her away. It pleased him to see that she looked as disappointed as he felt by the end of their play. But it was not nearly as nice as it would be when they had time to continue.

He cleared his throat and smiled. 'As I said before, tonight we will have time to discuss the pictures that are hanging in my room.'

'Yes, Captain Wiscombe,' she said with a dazed smile.

'And we will discuss your concerns about the future, as well. But do not worry, Mrs Wiscombe.' He added a slight emphasis to the surname, so she might remember it. 'Since there are but two of us Wiscombes, we must stick together.'

'Three.' The child's voice came from the doorway, breaking his mood like a stone through window glass. 'There are three Wiscombes, Papa. Do not forget me.'

He had, damn it all. Just for a moment, he had forgotten the boy. But his memory had returned and ruined everything. He shot a wordless glare at the woman before him. Then he turned, pushed past the child and was gone.

# *Chapter Nine*

No matter what he intended, Gerry was far too quick to play the fool for this family. A few daubs of paint, a doe-eyed glance and a pair of soft lips and he had been ready to forget the obvious, until it had intruded on him and demanded his attention.

He must not be swayed by appearances. The woman he'd married was as crafty as Eve, just like the rest of her family. But if she was to be any use to him outside the bedroom, it would be easy enough to prove. He crossed the length of the house to his study, pulled the chequebook from the desk drawer and wrote a hurried draft. Then he went in search of his brother-in-law.

'Ronald North.' He found him in the billiard room and greeted him with the same joviality he had on the previous night.

'Wiscombe.' The memory of the previous night's game must have been fresh in his mind, for he did not bother to be pleasant.

'Practising for a rematch?' Gerry said, picking up

a ball from the table to spoil the shot. 'I would think, after years of chasing Rex about the wood, you would know that it is very hard to beat a native habitué of the Chase at any game played here.'

'It was never my intention to best you,' Ronald said, with a smile. 'There is no reason we need to be at odds. We are family now, after all.'

'By marriage,' Gerry reminded him. 'And while I am grateful for the help you provided with the house and lands, I suspect you must be growing tired of the place and eager to get back to wherever it was you came from.' He pulled the cheque from his pocket and held it out to his wife's brother. 'This should cover the cost of repairs made to the house and the commission your father bought. I have added an expression of my gratitude for your help, as well.'

The look of shock on Ronald's face was most satisfying. It was clear that he would not have thought to ask for this much, had he carried through with his original plan. Now, he was torn between pocketing the money and looking for the catch hidden within the offer.

'There should be enough here to find a place of your own, if you do not already have one,' Gerry added. 'Dear Lily and I are eager to begin a private honeymoon, now that I am returned.'

Ronald withdrew his hand. 'You and Lily and Stewart, you mean.'

And there was the boy again, in the way even when he was not here. 'We are speaking of you at the moment,' Gerry reminded him, dragging the conversation back to where it belonged. 'I suspect it will be very dull for you, once your friends are gone. Unless you wish to spend your future evenings playing Spillikins with us.'

Ronald laughed. 'No guests and nursery games? Are you going to tell me you had no time for cards in the army?'

'I am as skilled at them as I am at billiards,' he admitted. 'But I do not like them overmuch, since the time I was forced to challenge an acquaintance for cheating at the table.'

'A rather extreme reaction for what was probably a mistake on your part,' Ronald said, watching him closely.

'On the contrary, it was the other fellow's mistake.' He smiled, baring his teeth. 'He didn't have an opportunity to make another.'

'And what does this story have to do with anything?' Ronald asked, impatient.

'It is merely to inform you of the future of Wiscombe Chase,' Gerry said. 'No guests. No cards. No hunting either, for that matter. Nothing but peace and quiet from here onwards.' He held out the cheque again.

Ronald took it from him, ripped it in half and handed it back to him. 'Do not insult me, sir.'

Gerry grinned back at him. 'If you find this insulting, you have much to learn, Ronald. Let me know when you have found a place to settle. We will need the direction so we can forward the mail.'

'I do not think Papa likes me very much.'

After the captain had left them, Lily had struggled to calm her racing heart. It was not just the touch of her husband's hands that left her feeling naked and exposed. She thought he'd uncovered everything about her, from the reason for their marriage to her devoted reading of his war exploits. Then Stewart had come into the room and reminded them both that there were some secrets still remaining.

Even though the captain was no longer in sight, her son was staring back down the hall, hoping he'd return. It had been foolish of her to feed the child on tales of the hero of Salamanca. Had she honestly thought that an outpouring of devotion from the boy would result in answering love from the man?

Of course she had. It was different for women. She had not wanted a child, either. At one time, she'd even planned to send him away, never to be spoken of again. But once he'd arrived she could not manage to do it. He was harmless and blameless and he needed her. More importantly, he was blood of her blood, closer to her than her father and brother would ever be. Stewart was the only person in the house, perhaps the only one in the world, who truly loved her without boundary or question.

Now she came forward to take him by the hand, leading him away from the doorway to their favourite place, a bench by the window that was all but hidden by large ferns.

'Papa does not like you?' She put her hand in the middle of his back and felt the trembling that was a first indicator of tears. It would be even worse for them both if the captain realised that he had been burdened with what some might call an overly sensitive child.

She rubbed his shoulders, soothing him until the tremor passed and he was calm again. 'I think it is too soon to make such judgements against him,' she lied. 'He has been home but a day. You barely know each other.'

'Before, in the hall, he told me to go away,' Stewart said.

'And so you followed him into the conservatory?' Lily could not help but smile.

'I did not know he would be here,' Stewart argued.

'But he thought you disobeyed him,' Lily said gently. 'That might be the reason he seemed angry.' One of the reasons, at least.

'He was kissing you.' Now militant anger was banishing the doubt.

Here was another thing she had not thought to prepare him for. 'Yes. And he will do so again. At least, I hope he will. I quite like it when the captain kisses me.' Finally, there was a bit of honesty in the conversation.

'Do you like it better than when I kiss you?' Worry was creeping back into the boy's voice.

'It is a very different thing when you kiss me. I like your kisses, as well.' She turned to him, held out her arms and was rewarded with a wet kiss on the cheek. She kissed him back on the top of the head and smiled down at him so he might see nothing had changed between them.

Stewart frowned back, unimpressed. 'Well, I do not like it when he kisses you. If anyone must go away, it should be him. At least he could stay away from the conservatory. That is our place. He can have the stables. He likes horses. I do not.'

This was another problem that she had not dared mention to the cavalryman. The only time they had tried to put him in the saddle, they'd found Stewart a mare so placid it should have been no more dangerous than riding the parlour sofa. And yet she had dumped him into the first hedge and broken his collarbone. Stewart did not like horses and, as far as anyone could tell, the feeling was mutual.

'It does not matter if you like horses or not,' she said, hoping it was true. 'I suspect he would rather you not ride at all than that you do so simply to hunt foxes. He seemed most disapproving of that activity at dinner last night.'

The boy brightened a little.

'And we cannot send Captain Wiscombe away,' she added. 'This is his house and he is quite eager to stay in it, after so long away.' But her husband was far less eager to share the house with the child at her side. How could she ever explain it to Stewart in a way that did not break his heart?

She gave him an encouraging smile. 'But for now, you must do your best to be patient with the captain. I am afraid he does not know very much about the likes and dislikes of little boys.'

Stewart frowned. 'He should know more than you. He used to be one.'

That was true enough. But it did not sound as though his childhood had been a happy one. 'When he was young, things were very different. The captain's father was very strict and sent him off to school at a very young age. He was not allowed home, even for holidays.'

'But he would not do that to me, would he?' he asked in a frightened whisper. By the look on Stewart's face, he could not imagine a worse fate than the one that might very well be his immediate future.

'Of course not.' Perhaps she was not a North. No member of family had ever been as unconvincing a liar as she was now.

Despite her efforts to hide it, Stewart had glimpsed the truth. 'But if he wanted to, you would not let him,' he said and stared up at her, desperate for reassurance.

If her husband insisted, what choice would she have but to obey? How would she survive when he was gone? What meaning would life have if she regained the love and trust of her husband by sacrificing the child who had loved her without question from his first breath?

'Of course not.' She kissed him on the top of the head so that he could not see the fear in her eyes. 'Do not worry about the captain, or anything else. I will take care of him and you.' She would find a way to make this work. She had to. 'But for now, do not cling to his heels. Give him time to recover from his travels. I am sure everything will work out for the best.'

She must have grown more convincing with practice. Her son nodded to her and gave her a small smile and another hug.

She smoothed his hair. 'Now back to the nursery with you. It is almost time for lessons and you do not want to keep Miss Fisher waiting.'

When he had gone, her brother stepped forward from the other side of the fern. 'Everything will work out for the best?' He applauded her with a series of slow claps and an ironic smile. 'A touching performance, Lillian.'

'It was not a performance,' she whispered, glancing towards the hall to make sure her son had not heard.

He laughed. 'It was made up of whole cloth to keep your son from crying.'

She walked across the room to shut the doors so there would be no further interruptions. 'He is just a little boy. What would you have me do?'

'You could tell him that his position here is even more precarious than yours.'

'What good would that do, other than to frighten him?'

'At least it would be honest. You should have told him the truth from the first. You should not have raised him to idolise a man who is not his father.'

'When did you become a champion for the truth?' she snapped.

'When did you become so good at lying to yourself?' he countered. 'You are pretending that it will be possible to resolve the problem of Stewart with time and patience.'

'Stewart is not the problem,' she said, closing her eyes so she would not have to see the smile on Ronald's face.

'Of course not,' he said, suddenly gentle. 'Gerry Wiscombe is. If he'd had the decency to die as expected, we would not be in this mess.'

'You mustn't say such a thing.' She opened her eyes again to stare past him, at the door.

'Do not lie and say you never thought it yourself.' Ronald moved in front of her so she could not avoid his gaze. 'Admit it. Life would be easier for Stewart if your husband was dead.'

It would. But she would die herself before she said so. 'I will not choose between my husband and son. And if you and Father have plans for Captain Wiscombe, you should not be wishing him dead.'

'We had plans,' Ronald said, almost too sweetly. 'But just now, he caught me in the hall, grinned like an idiot and, without so much as blinking, offered me ten thousand pounds for the repairs done on the house. Then he asked me where our future home might be, now that we would no longer be able to entertain here.'

'Did you take the money?' she said, hoping that, just once, her brother would do the sensible thing and admit defeat.

'Of course not. We can make ten times that if we stay here. But how did he know to bribe me? Did you tell him of my plans?'

She said nothing, for it was clear he knew the answer.

Her brother nodded, as if he had expected her silence. 'It is clear that we cannot trust you to be loyal to your family, even though it is in your best interest. So, dear sister, I will make it easier for you.' There was something dangerous in his offer of help, like the warning hiss of a snake before the strike.

'What do you mean to do?'

He smiled again, and waved a warning finger. 'If I tell you, Lillian, you will pass the information on to Gerry, just as you did before. You've done enough tattling, so I must give you a reason to stop. If you offer him so much as a word of warning that something is afoot, I will track down young Stewart and tell him everything that you have not.'

'You would not dare.' But, of course he would. After a lifetime watching her brother take advantage of others, there was not a doubt in her mind that he would hurt a child to further his ends.

'If you wish to test me, talk to your husband. Ask the heroic Captain Wiscombe to protect the boy from me and see what that gains you. He cannot stand the sight of the child. He might even applaud my effort to clarify Stewart's position here.'

'He would never be so cruel,' she said.

'Put him ahead of your family again and we shall see. Or do what you should have done from the first. Hold your tongue and trust that we will take care of you, just as we always have.'

## *Chapter Ten*

With the absence of the Carstairs, the upstarts at his luncheon table had each moved a seat closer to the head of the table. Against all decorum, Miss Fellowes still held the spot on his left, while Mrs Wilson had taken the right. While the married lady seemed more interested in the wild boar and mushroom pie on her plate, Gerry was beginning to worry that Miss Fellowes intended to make a meal of him. He'd noticed several accidental touches of his sleeve at the beginning of the meal. Now that they were finishing, he felt the gentle pressure of a knee against his own.

He shifted to the right to evade her and stared down the dining table at his wife. If possible, she was even lovelier than she'd been in the conservatory. There was still a pleasant flush in her cheeks from the kisses he had given her. And though her throat was bare of ornament, he could not seem to tear his eyes away from it. He wanted to touch his tongue to the faint pulse beating there, to make it race as he seduced her. If he was not careful, he would give himself over to her, body and soul, as he'd been ready to do this morning.

At least, until her son had interrupted them and brought him crashing back to earth. How had he managed to forget about the one obstacle in their marriage that was all but insurmountable? Even if he managed to rid the house of the child, there was the question of inheritance. He must see if it were possible, at this late date, to deny parentage of the boy, if only to protect any real offspring they might have. The longer he waited, the worse it was likely to be for all concerned.

Laws being what they were, it might be easier to disown a legitimate child than cast off his wife. Now that he was here, and could look into her huge brown eyes...

It was lust. That or stupidity. When he held her, he forgot to be sensible. Her obvious attraction to him made it even more difficult to control himself. And her willingness to share her family's secrets left him with the illogical hope that there might be no more lies between them.

The stunned look on Ronald's face when he'd offered to buy him off had done much to justify the hardship he'd endured to get the money. Ronald would live to regret that he'd refused that offer. The alternative methods of ridding himself of the Norths were far less pleasant than bribery. And with Lillian's continued help he would be one jump ahead of her brother at every turn.

'Will you be joining us in the sitting room this afternoon, Captain Wiscombe?' Miss Fellowes batted her eyes and closed the distance between them again.

'The gentlemen have declared the day too wet for a hunt. And last night we ladies missed your company.'

From the end of the table, Sir Chauncey noticed the attention Gerry was receiving from his light o' love and shot him an icy glare.

Apparently, the insolent puppy did not realise the insult he had given, bringing a whore to a house party. Gerry ignored him and awarded her his most empty-headed smile. 'Of course, Miss Fellowes. My wife will be joining us, as well. She is fully recovered from last night's headache.'

Lily's mouth had already been open to refuse, but she read the look in his eyes and closed it slowly, forcing a smile. 'Of course, Captain. I am looking forward to it.'

'I imagine you are,' he replied. But something was wrong. The skin about her lips was white with tension and her brow was furrowed. Perhaps her megrims were genuine. If so, she must learn to ignore them. Tonight, he would speak to her about the need to be socially available, in case he needed her help. If she did not like the people her father entertained, she must see that avoiding them and hiding in her room had done nothing to reduce their numbers. The way to conquer adversity, or a gaggle of unwanted house guests, was to meet it head on.

After the last of them had finished their meal, they adjoined to the sitting room and the ladies requested a table be set up so they might play loo.

'Captain Wiscombe,' Mrs Burke called, 'you must

open your purse wider for your poor wife. She refuses to bet with more than sixpence. If there is so little in the pot, it is hardly worth playing.'

There were mutters of agreement from the other ladies, and another longing look in his direction from Miss Fellowes. Lily frowned at her cards, but said nothing.

Gerry ignored her and the Fellowes woman, and gave Mrs Burke a sympathetic smile. 'I am afraid there is nothing to be done about that, madam. Lillian is far too sensible to listen to me on a subject as important as money. I cannot seem to hang on to that from one day to the next.'

'Then you must come talk to Mr North,' Mr Wilson called from the middle of the discussion on the other side of the room. 'He is the sort of brilliant businessman who can turn one pound into ten in the blink of an eye.'

'Or ten pounds into one,' Greywall added. Ronald North leaned across the card table and filled his glass before he could speak again.

'I will be careful not to close my eyes if he is near my purse,' Gerry said.

The elder North gave a merry laugh as though the comment did not bother him in the least. 'You have nothing to fear from me, Captain. I would not encourage others to invest in some of my riskier endeavours. It would pain me greatly if anyone incurred a loss while following my advice.'

'What sort of investment might that be?' Apparently, Mr Burke was the sort of man who could not tell the difference between a warning and a welcome. Nor could he recognise the obvious trap being set for him.

'My current venture is far too likely to end in failure,' Mr North demurred. 'Of course, the odds might improve if I was able to raise enough capital to do the job correctly...'

'Tell us more,' Wilson encouraged.

'Yes, Phineas. Tell us more.' By the sound of it, the earl had said his line so many times that he'd lost the ability to sound sincere. Ronald refilled his glass again to keep him quiet as North continued his pitch.

'As you can see from the magnificent pelts that are displayed in the trophy room, the land surrounding this house is teeming with wildlife. Beaver, badger and otter all but walk into the traps set for them. But suppose it were possible to catch fur-bearing animals and breed them? We might be hip-deep in skins before the winter season. Tailors and hat makers in the city would take as many as we could supply.'

'You mean to breed beavers?' Miss Fellowes was staring at him with wide eyes.

Mr North shook his head. 'They are fine animals, of course. But if one could find a flock of Russian sables...'

'Are they measured by the flock?' Gerry interrupted.

'I have no idea,' North said, then continued. 'If I could acquire a pair of sables, house them, feed them and encourage them to mate...'

Miss Fellowes giggled.

'But where would you get Russian sables?' Gerry asked.

'From Russia,' Ronald snapped, staring at him as if trying to gauge whether he was the stupidest man in the room, or the most devious.

'I have already imported the first pair,' Mr North admitted.

'Let us see these wondrous animals, immediately,' Gerry said with a smile that should have put Ronald on guard.

'I do not know if that is wise,' his father-in-law said with a worried smile. 'They are very delicate creatures. Any disturbance can interfere with their breeding.'

'But it is daytime.' Gerry reminded him. 'Surely they breed at night like good Christians.'

Miss Fellowes giggled again.

'Perhaps. But in daylight, they are rather excitable,' North said. 'And prone to biting.'

On the other side of the room, Ronald flinched. Lily held her cards up to her mouth, probably to disguise her smile.

'Perhaps it will help if I speak to them in Russian,' Gerry said. 'I know a few words. I will tell them that we mean no harm.'

'But we do mean harm, if we wish to make coats out of them.' Mr Wilson glanced out at the rain and looked longingly back at the card table.

'Then I will be forced to lie,' Gerry said cheerfully. 'Let us go out to the stables at once. If they are going to make us all rich, I must see these little foreigners immediately.'

At the mention of riches, Wilson changed his mind and called for hat and umbrella. Even Sir Chauncey set aside his jealousy and agreed that a little fresh air would be an excellent idea.

They set off a short time later, stumbling through the mud towards the cluster of wire-mesh cages standing at the back of the stables. 'Are these they?' Gerry asked, pointing to the two forlorn animals housed there.

North beamed. 'The pride of the Urals. My supplier assures me that they can have up to a dozen kittens a year. It would be better if there were more pairs, of course. It strengthens the bloodline.'

Without waiting for further explanation, Gerry unlatched the door and thrust his gloved hands in, dodging needle-sharp teeth to grab the animals by their necks. Then he pulled them from the cages and held them out, one in each hand, so all could see. 'Say hello to the fellows, Mr Sable. We are all eager to meet you. And Madam Sable, as well.'

Then he gave a dramatic pause. 'What ho, Madam? What have we here?' He held the animals out to Wilson. 'Do you see what I think I see, sir? Surely I am not mistaken.'

Wilson leaned forward and then back again as the animal hissed. 'I do not think it likes to be examined, Captain.'

'None of us does,' Gerry replied with a smile.

'Let me see.' Miss Fellowes stepped forward.

'This is not...' Gerry stopped himself. He had been ready to say that it was not a sight for a lady. But since the caution did not apply to Miss Fellowes, it hardly mattered.

The woman in question saw what he had and turned away with a giggle.

'What the devil are we looking at?' Ronald said, angry that he did not see the source of the mirth.

Gerry turned to North, the stoats wriggling in his hands. 'You are right, sir, when you say the investment is a risky one. The person who sold these animals to you has sent you two stallions and no mares.'

'Males?' The shock on Ronald's face at this revelation was quickly turning to anger.

North had an entirely different reaction. 'Two males.' He laughed. 'Well spotted, Captain. There is no cheating a man with such sharp eyes.' He laughed again and patted his belly, as if he'd just eaten a full meal and been well satisfied. 'Would that I'd had your perspicacity. It seems I have been duped by a wily trader.'

And there was the secret of North's success. Even caught in the act, he was so good-humoured about it that one wanted to believe he was not at fault. 'I recommend that you write to Russia immediately and take the supplier to task over this,' Gerry said, feigning earnestness.

'I will indeed,' North agreed.

'Males,' Ronald repeated.

Lily, who had skirted the edge of the crowd as they'd approached the cage, was nowhere to be seen. But Gerry thought, from somewhere on the other side of the stables, he heard a peal of feminine laughter.

\* \* \*

On the way back to the house, North hung back from the rest of the party and Gerry lagged, as well. They waited until the rest were well out of earshot before either of them spoke.

'Ronald underestimates you,' North said, the half-smile never leaving his face.

'At his peril,' Gerry agreed. 'To save us both further embarrassment, I will not denounce you publically. But I trust I will hear no more about turning my home into a sable farm.'

'There is always the ruby mine in Brazil,' he said wistfully.

'Brazil is known for emeralds, not rubies,' Gerry pointed out.

'All the more reason to invest in the rubies,' North replied. 'When we find them, they will be twice the value of emeralds.'

'And if you do not find them?'

'Mining for gems is a dangerous and difficult thing, under the best circumstances.'

'But even if the investors are left empty-handed, I suspect you will still come away with a tidy profit.'

'There is no reason for me to bear the whole cost of a failure,' North said. 'The whole point of having investors is to minimise liability, should something go wrong.'

'I would hope that it is a way to share profits, as well,' Gerry said. 'Should I examine the schemes you have backed since taking residence here, I would bet not a one of them succeeded. But despite all these failures, you are able to fill the wine cellars and entertain.'

'Perhaps I am merely unlucky,' North admitted. 'But I have managed to make the best of my failures.'

'Perhaps you auction seats at my dinner table as though you were trading horseflesh at Tattersalls,' Gerry announced. 'And while you peddle weasels dipped in boot black, your son sharps at billiards and cheats at cards.'

'The people who come here deserve what they get,' North said. 'They are trying to find a route to wealth and status that does not involve hard work. We both know that is not the way the world turns.'

'Did I deserve what was coming to me when you tried to swindle me out of my house?'

North paused to look him up and down. 'When I found you, you were an impoverished student with a ruin of a manor. Now you are a rich man and respected by all in Britain for your heroism. The house is still yours, as is my only daughter.'

'I could just as easily have died penniless,' Gerry said.

'But you did not,' North reminded him, smiling.

Gerry stared back in amazement. The man was truly a master manipulator. North was looking at him with the grin of a proud father, doting on a son's success.

Gerry offered no smile of gratitude in return. 'You are trying to persuade me that the last seven years has been a boon and not a hardship. Do I need to remove my shirt and show you the battle scars?'

'If you do, I will show you a mirror, so that you

might see the positive changes the army has wrought in you.'

Arguing with the man was like trying to hold an eel. 'I admit I have changed. But it was not necessary for me to join the army to do so. There is no telling what might have been, if you'd just let me alone.'

North snorted. 'I will tell you exactly what you'd have done. You'd have ended up a Cambridge mathematics tutor married to some parson's pinch-faced daughter.'

'I would never...' But it was an accurate assessment of the future he'd planned for himself, before Phineas North had stepped in and upended his life.

'Eventually, you'd have been forced to sell this house to Greywall. I know for a fact that he wanted it. And I know you refused.'

'Because he hounded my father into the grave trying to get it,' Gerry admitted. 'I did not particularly like my father. But I like the earl even less.'

'He is a rather unlikeable fellow,' North admitted.

'But I did not need to go to war to keep the house out of his hands. If all you wished was the use of it, I could have just as easily rented it to you. Or sold it to you, for that matter.'

'I could never have afforded to bid against an earl for the purchase of this place. It was cheaper to buy a commission than a house,' North said, beaming. 'So I gave you an opportunity. You used it as an honourable man would and made a success of yourself.'

'But you could not have known the outcome,' Gerry insisted.

'I beg to differ,' North said. 'To do what I do, one must be a good judge of character. While I am sorry to admit that both of my children doubted your chances of survival, I knew from the first that you would return to us. Today, you proved that you are the sort of fellow who sees stoats when others see sables.'

'I had Lily's help with that,' Gerry admitted.

'My darling girl.' North's smile broadened. 'Such a daughter is a father's proudest achievement. A jewel as pure as diamond and more valuable to me than all the emeralds in Brazil. I am glad to have found a man worthy of her. Even without her warning, you'd have seen my sables for what they were. You, Captain Wiscombe, are a man of vision. You see a move ahead of the other fellow and behave accordingly.'

Then why did he have such difficulty reading his own wife? 'If that were true, I would not have listened to you in the first place.'

'On the contrary. Even as you agreed to my offer, you knew it was too good to be true. I read it in your eyes. But you wanted Lily and you wanted a chance to prove your worth to yourself, and to her. So you weighed the risks and said yes.'

It was true. He had known that something was not right about the marriage. But the benefits of the commission had outweighed any potential problems.

'You must admit, now that it is over, it has turned out splendidly. You are home safe to your beautiful wife and adoring son. What more could you want?'

*He did not know.*

When Lily had insisted that no one knew the true

origins of Stewart, he had assumed that she was lying. But by the look on North's face, he honestly believed Stewart to be legitimate and that his daughter was a faithful wife. It would be a bitter enlightenment when the truth came out, but it could wait until after he and his son had been extracted from the house.

Gerry cleared his throat and forced himself to answer. 'What more could I want? There is one more thing I want and I will have it with or without your agreement. I want a quiet and empty house. I will have no more parties like this one in my future. There will be no more breeding of sables and no mining for rubies, emeralds or any other non-existent stones. If you attempt this scheme or any other, I will stop you. And the next time I will not bother to be subtle about it.'

'Very well.' North sighed.

'You may tell your son that I will permit him to play billiards, as long as the table is properly maintained. But if I discover he is cheating at cards, he will think fondly of the days when the worst he'd experienced was a bite from an angry stoat.'

North nodded in approval. 'It is a shame we cannot convince you to join in the fun. As a mathematician you could have a natural talent for calculating odds and angles.'

'I am not sure that is the compliment that you mean it to be,' Gerry said.

'Take it for what it is worth,' North said, with a wave of his hand. 'But know that, if we were to do it all over again, I would gladly give my daughter's hand to such a man as you.'

'To get my house,' Gerry finished for him.

North shook his head and gave Gerry a sad smile. 'Because her heart was never in these little games of mine. Her disapproval has only hardened with the passing of time. She will hardly speak to me any more. Since you would rather risk your life in service of the crown than cheat your fellow man, she will be much happier with you than with me.'

The affirmation had touched Gerry's heart and his mind was crowding with ordinary responses about being a worthy husband for the man's precious daughter.

Then he remembered that none of the Norths were to be trusted. Phineas's fine words about his daughter did not explain a bastard son and years gone by without so much as a note. 'Do not worry about Lily. For now, think of your own future, and accept that, wherever it might lead you, it will not be Wiscombe Chase.'

## Chapter Eleven

By the time they arrived back at the house, Gerry was feeling well and truly pleased with himself. North was not such a bad fellow, once he'd been persuaded to move on. The guests seemed to have lost interest in cards and were either seeking naps in their rooms or by the fire in the sitting room. While Ronald North was still somewhere causing trouble, things were not the muddle they had been just two days before.

But it seemed he had lost his wife again. Lily had left the house with them when they'd set off to visit the sables. But she had disappeared before the matter was settled. It seemed she was available only when necessary, there one minute, gone the next. Would she be more accessible after the others were gone, or would it be like living with a spirit who had to be conjured and bound each time he wanted her?

Perhaps she had gone back to the conservatory. The afternoon light was not nearly as good as that in the morning. But when he turned towards the ladies' wing, he came face to face with her noxious little boy who was, as usual, roaming the house and ready to spoil his mood.

Stewart stood frozen in the middle of the hallway like a marble statue.

Gerry stared, waiting for him to move.

He made no effort to do so. 'Mama said I was not to follow you about.'

Gerry continued to stare. 'You mother is an intelligent woman. You should listen to her.'

'I am not following you,' Stewart said. 'I am in front of you.'

The boy had a point. While he'd met officers that thought they could lead from the rear, it was much harder to follow from the front. 'Do you have lessons to do?'

'Already done,' the boy said, giving no quarter.

'Perhaps you need a nap,' Gerry suggested.

The boy shook his head. 'Adults take naps. Because they are old. Do you need a nap?'

'Perhaps I do.' But it had not been his intention to take it alone.

'You should do that, then,' the boy said and turned to walk into the conservatory.

Gerry sighed. If Lily was in the conservatory, there was little hope of privacy, short of grabbing the little beast by the collar and hauling him back to the nursery. Such an act would not endear him to the boy's mother. In truth, he would have little respect for himself after. He had learned from his own father how it felt to be punished for the sin of existing. He would not inflict that on another.

All the more reason that Stewart should be sent away to school. Since he was young, he would adjust quickly to his new surroundings. He would find friends, teachers and the company of good books. When he was old enough to understand, Gerry could explain that it was nothing personal. He would be provided with an education, an allowance and a trade. But there could be no future for him here.

Today, he could have the conservatory, if he wanted it, and the company of his mother.

He sighed and made his way to his side of the house and the trophy room, thinking it might be nice to pass some time in the small library beyond it. If there was any room that the current guests had no interest in, it was probably the one that held books. In truth, the library had got little use when the Wiscombes had been the sole occupants of the house. His father had made sure that the room that displayed the majority of the heads and horns held pride of place before the rest of the rooms on the main floor.

What his father had viewed as a convenience, Gerry considered an obstacle to progress. It seemed impossible to get so much as a cup of tea on the gentlemen's side of the house without walking by the trophy room door or passing through it to get to the opposite hall.

But today, there was reason to pause. Apparently, he had been wrong about the location of his wife. The sound of a woman singing drifted through the open doorway. He stopped to listen.

'I would love you all the day.
'Ev'ry night would kiss and play,
'If with me you'd fondly stray,
'Over the hills and far away.'

The tune was the same as the song they sang in that old comedy about the recruiting officer, telling men to leave their brats and wives and take the king's shilling. But these words were a hundred times sweeter and he let himself be wooed by them.

From now forward, if he ever had to wander the hills, they would be close to home, not far away. He'd stay with the woman who loved him. He stepped through the door to declare himself. 'I'm here, darling. And come to collect, if that song is an offer.'

'Captain Wiscombe?' The singing stopped. Miss Fellowes appeared from behind the torso of a steinbock that Father had dragged back from an excursion to the Alps.

His smile froze in place. 'Miss Fellowes. My apologies. I thought...' Stuff what he thought. With the look she was giving him he was forgiven for the mistake. He strode towards the door on the opposite wall that led to the library.

'Don't go.' She hurried across the room to stand between him and his goal. 'I have hardly got the chance to talk to you, even though you are my host.'

'I have been home but a day,' he reminded her. 'I've barely spoken to my own wife yet, much less talked to...' He'd been about to say 'unwelcome guests' and barely caught himself in time. 'I was just looking for

Lillian.' He turned to retreat the way he'd come so he might continue to do so.

She countered to stand before him again, blocking the way to the door. 'I was so excited when I heard we would be coming to your home. But I had no idea that we would actually meet the great man himself.'

'It was a surprise to me, as well,' he said, looking longingly past her at escape.

'And for a chance to hear the tales of your exploits…' She clasped her hands in rapture.

'They are hardly stories that I would tell a lady,' he said, although there was much doubt as to how much of a lady this woman was.

'I am sure the accounts in the newspapers do not do them justice.' She pressed her clasped hands under her chest and sighed. The amount of bosom this displayed at the neckline of her gown was too impressive to be anything but a calculated move.

But for a moment the cheap trick worked. He was distracted.

'You deserve to be rewarded for your bravery,' she said, stepping closer.

'No reward is necessary,' he replied automatically, dragging his eyes back from her breasts to her face and taking a step back into the room.

'The gratitude of a grateful nation is hardly enough.' She beamed at him, more pleased than offended by his attention and took a step to close the distance between them.

'It is more than enough for me.'

'The Regent made Wellington a peer,' she argued.

'I am no Wellington.' He took another step away.

'Only one of his most courageous horsemen,' she said, coming even closer.

'I don't need…' He was backing hurriedly towards the library door now and glanced behind him to be sure of the direction.

'But, I insist.' In that moment of inattention, she pounced.

He was growing soft from inactivity. On the battlefield, his reflexes had been faster and he'd have been smart enough to keep his eye on the enemy. He certainly hadn't displayed any of the foresight that Phineas North had credited him with.

But a single kiss from a pretty woman was hardly a matter of life and death. She was a comely thing and her eagerness hinted at rewards far beyond a quick tussle in a common room. Perhaps, if circumstances had been different…

There was a crash from the doorway to the hall.

He broke from the Fellowes woman and looked up to discover the cause. His own wife stood frozen in the doorway. A broken vase was at her feet and a bouquet of camellias was scattered beside it.

The Fellowes jade looked up as well and gave her a flushed and triumphant smile.

In response, Lily made a sound that was almost a whimper and muttered her pardon. Then she bent to scoop up the flowers and stuffed them, stems and blossoms awry, back into the vase. Water ran through the cracks in it, staining her gown. She dumped the mess on to the hall table only to see it totter on its bro-

ken base and almost fall twice more before she could
steady it enough to let go and escape down the hall
towards the stairs.

The lock to Lily's room turned with a satisfying
click, sealing her away from the mortification awaiting
her in the rest of the house. For a moment, she leaned
her forehead against the silk-covered door panel, as if
it were as possible to draw strength and comfort from
the wood beneath.

How could she have been so stupid?

She had known in her heart that her husband had
not been faithful to her while he was gone. After seven
years apart, there was no chance that he'd return as the
same awkward innocent. He had been tricked into the
marriage and there had been no guarantee that he'd
live to return. She could hardly fault him for a lack
of fidelity.

But she'd chosen to imagine that once he'd returned
home, if he forgave her at all, he'd want only her. He
had thought her beautiful, once. For him, she'd worked
hard to maintain an illusion of youth that was becoming increasingly hard to cling to. She did not deserve
to see him turning to younger, prettier women within
a day of his arrival.

When had she become so foolish? He had told her
on the very first day that this was not to be the case.
But then, he had said, *if I tire of you.* Could it really
have happened so soon? It did not matter. There was
no sense in being hurt. He would do as he pleased and
she had no say in it.

Before they'd married, she'd been sensible. She'd understood that her life was out of her control. But while he'd been gone, she'd convinced herself that if she was pretty and biddable, eventually she would get what she wanted, as a matter of course. He would come back, sweeping into her life like a rescuing knight. He would forgive her trespasses, banish her troubles and they would live together, happily ever after in the home she'd prepared for him.

Perhaps she had been imagining Lochinvar. Captain Gerald Wiscombe was no romantic hero who would give her her dreams. He was a man. Therefore he was just as uncaring, cruel and faithless as all the others.

The worst of it was, she had embarrassed herself by showing that she cared. When she'd caught him in a tryst she should have had the sense to withdraw quietly. Instead, she'd called attention, fumbling with that vase and drawing out the retreat. Now she was hiding in her room in a sodden gown, too humiliated to have a maid see her crying.

It was nearly as bad as the worst night of her life. Then, she'd lain shivering in her bed, unwilling to call for help. She had told no one. When she'd realised that she was with child, it was easier to stay silent than to admit that she had been so foolish as to leave her door unlocked in a houseful of drunken men.

But brooding on the past did not change the fact that she was cold and wet right now, and had likely ruined her favourite day gown. Tugging at the bodice would rip the muslin and make matters even worse. She straightened, stepped away from the door and stretched her arms to the middle of her back. Then she clawed helplessly at the tiny mother-of-pearl buttons, only to stomp her foot in frustration when she could not manage them. And now the tears were falling faster.

'Let me help.'

Captain Wiscombe had followed her to her room and she had been so upset she had not even heard him enter through the connecting door. 'I do not need help,' she lied, refusing to turn and face him so that he might see her tears. 'Not from you. Not from anyone.'

'I disagree.' His voice was surprisingly gentle, as were the hands on her back, undoing the buttons of her gown. Once it was open he lifted it over her head and she watched out of the corner of her eye as he walked across the room to drape it over the door of the wardrobe. Then he returned and undid her petticoat so she could step out of it.

Now she was standing in nothing but stays and shift, and shivering from reasons other than cold. 'You can go back to Miss Fellowes now,' she said, crossing her arms over her chest.

'I would rather not.'

'Then why were you kissing her?' It was childish to ask such questions. She should at least have the sense to pretend it had never happened.

'She was kissing me,' he said.

'It is near to the same thing.'

'I beg to differ,' he said. 'There is the matter of consent to be considered.'

'I suppose she forced herself upon you,' Lily said sceptically.

'It was a surprise attack,' he replied.

'Well, whatever it was, you do not need to explain it away,' she said. 'It does not matter to me what you do.'

'Then why are you crying?'

'I am not.' She swallowed hard, trying to stop.

The hands on her back went to her waist and he turned her around to face him. His fingertips brushed her wet check to prove her a liar.

She squeezed her eyes shut tight, trying to stop the flow of tears, but felt them still sneaking out and wetting her lashes. But if she did not look at him, at least she did not have to see the pity in his eyes. 'I was startled. That is all.' Then she added, 'I thought you had better taste.'

He chuckled. 'The next time, I shall find someone worthy of your approval.'

'The next time…' Before she could argue that she had no intention of passing judgements on his inamorata, his lips touched hers. Then they were gone again.

'I meant, the next time it will be you,' he said with a smile. 'I was looking for you. I heard singing and I thought, perhaps…' He paused. 'Do you sing?'

She frowned. 'Would you like me to?'

Now he looked like his embarrassed younger self. 'I don't require it of you, if that's what you're asking. But I still know very little about you and what you do for pleasure.'

'I can sing, but I seldom have reason to,' she said.

'That is a shame.' A curl had come loose from its pin and he twisted it around his finger before brushing it off her face. 'While I cannot assure you that my return will have you singing for joy, I can promise that there will be no more tears over the kind of foolishness you witnessed just now in the trophy room. Now that I am finally home, I have no wish to take up with another. Let us put the past behind us. As long as you are loyal to me, I shall be loyal to only you.'

It sounded suspiciously like he was forgiving her for having Stewart. There was a nagging doubt at the back of her mind arguing that, since she had not been at fault, there was really no reason for forgiveness. But her heart leapt at the chance for a fresh start with the man she had adored from afar.

She nodded.

'Very good,' he said, the confidence returning to his smile.

Was that settled, then? If he had nothing further to say, would he leave her and go back downstairs? Suddenly, it seemed urgent that he did not. 'Why were you looking for me?' she blurted into the awkward silence.

'To give you this,' he said and kissed her again.

'Oh,' she said with a sigh. She could not help it. She was leaning into him, her mouth open, as if he had touched a sweet to her tongue, only to pull it away. She wanted more.

'But now that I have you half out of your clothes and behind a locked door, I have an even better idea,' he said, pushing the strap of her chemise to the side so he might place another kiss on the bare skin of her shoulder.

He meant *the act*. Now that the time had finally come, she didn't dare refuse. But it was broad daylight.

He would see the marks that childbirth had left on her body and be disappointed. Worse yet, he would see if she was afraid, or if it hurt. God forbid, what if she did not like it at all? What if it was as bad as the last time? Everything would be so much easier to hide under the covers and after dark.

'I do not think…' she said, before another kiss stopped her words. Dear Lord, but it was good. She had never known how lonely she had been until he'd kissed her. It was as if a part of her that had been missing was restored.

'That's right,' he said into her ear. 'Do not think. Just feel.' He was undoing the laces at the back of her stays with short, efficient jerks of his fingers. Now he was lifting the garment out of the way, dropping it to the floor with one hand as her breast dropped into the palm of his other hand like falling fruit. His thumb was rubbing back and forth across the nipple, making it stand proud beneath the thin cloth of her shift.

His head dipped and he took the other one into his mouth, sucking till the wet linen clung to her body. She could feel the slight unevenness of his front teeth, rough against her, teasing but not marking. How much better would it be if her breasts were bare? And suppose he buried his face deep between her legs?

At the thought, she let out a strange, hiccupping gasp, which made him stop and smile up at her expectantly.

She shook her head, unsure of what response was expected.

He nodded in satisfaction as if he understood her

without words. Then he straightened and she opened her mouth to receive another kiss.

When his lips touched hers, she was reborn. It was as if she had spent years under water, only to burst to the surface and take her first clean breath. His kiss was life for her. They belonged together, the two of them connected by breath and taste and murmured words. The thought glowed in her brain, warmed her heart and heated her blood until a tingling rush seemed to chase through her limbs and settle in a dangerous hum of arousal between her legs. Was he feeling this, as well? Or were men always inflamed, as they seemed to be?

As if to show her, his arms tightened about her, his hand spreading over the small of her back to stroke downwards, pressing her close. Then he pulled his lips away just long enough to sigh, 'Lily,' against the shell of her ear, taking a breath as though he were inhaling a flower.

'Captain Wiscombe.'

He laughed. 'Gerald. Or Gerry.' Then he cupped her bottom and lifted her, perching her on the back of a nearby bench so her knees spread and her feet dangled. He stepped between them and pushed the hem of her chemise up to her waist.

Her physical balance was as precarious as her spirit, shifting between terror and elation as the inevitable end of this journey approached. She closed her eyes. The past was the past. When the moment came, she could let herself fall and trust that he would catch her.

She was rocking on the edge of her seat and the

heads of the studs that held the upholstery in its place were making ridges on the backs of her legs. From now on, when she looked at this bench, she would blush and remember the strange and primal feel of the metal branding her thighs.

He knew what she was thinking. She could see it in his smile. And now he meant to take her, not silently in a bed in the dark tonight, but right here, standing up in the daytime. His hand moved to his trousers, undoing buttons.

'Gerry,' she said on a gasp.

'Lily,' he challenged, dropping the flap of his pants and touching his body to hers, as gentle as a kiss.

For a moment, he stared down, transfixed by the sight of their bodies together. Then he slipped a hand between them and ran a fingertip along her slit, spreading the moisture from back to front.

The bottom dropped out of her world as suddenly as if the chair had been pulled out from under her. What was this feeling? Nothing in her life had prepared her for it. He pushed into her and it was even better. The slide of flesh against flesh: large, smooth and rock-hard against soft, wet, throbbing.

She gripped his forearms to steady herself as he withdrew and stroked again. This was not frightening. This was right, just as the time before had been wrong. She had promised herself to this man for this very purpose, for ever until death. But what heaven that came after could ever compare to what was happening right now?

'Gerry.' She loved the sound of his name and the

taste of him on her tongue. She kissed his funny, crooked smile. She kissed the cleft in his chin and the stubble that was coming in on his throat. A moment ago, she had been afraid to do more than tug at his sleeve. But now, she dug her fingers into the side of his waist, trying to pull him closer. She was clinging to him, lost in the feel of his arms about her.

Another spasm of pleasure shook her, leaving her hungry for the movement. Without thinking, she pumped her legs as if she was on a garden swing, trying to go higher. And higher. When he answered her movements with faster, deeper thrusts, she slid her thighs up his body to his waist and locked her feet at the small of his back to hold him. Then she pumped and thrust, eager to meet each stroke, letting the speed build until she broke through the clouds, soaring like she had wings. This time, when she cried out his name it was from the explosion of joy at being so touched by such a man.

He answered with an equally explosive curse. A joyful swearing, if such a thing was even possible. His mouth was pressed to the skin of her throat like a wild animal ready to rip the life out of her. Instead, it was as if a lion had taken her, frightened her to the core and then playfully licked to show how utterly he possessed her.

She took in a great gasp of air and giggled. There was a man inside her, a thing she had hoped never to feel again, for it meant she was helpless, trapped. But this was different. This was happiness and freedom, and when she looked into his face she saw the surprisingly sweet boy who had proposed to her, hidden inside the conquering hero.

She pushed playfully against his arm. But when he made to step away and part from her, she locked her legs just as tightly around his body to settle her opening at the root of his sex.

'Why, Mrs Wiscombe,' he said with a sigh of pleasure, 'I think you are one of those women.'

'What women are those?' She frowned back at him.

'The sort that appear all helpless only to try to ensnare a man into an erotic adventure in the middle of the afternoon.'

She remembered Miss Fellowes in the hall and tried to pull away from him in earnest. 'I am no such thing. If that is what you are seeking, you can go right back down the stairs to that…that…'

'Only a madman would trade his fondest dream for such common coin.'

'Your fondest dream?' she asked, surprised.

'To take you hard and fast until you screamed my name,' he said, seeming quite satisfied with himself. He reached to the neckline of her chemise and gave a sudden tug, ripping the fabric to expose her breasts. He palmed one of them, rolling the nipple between his fingers. 'And I've a good mind to do it again.'

'Perhaps, on the bed,' she suggested.

'Oh, no, love. I mean to christen each piece of furniture in this room and the next.' He pushed the scraps of her shift to the side, tracing a line from throat to navel. 'Did I not say that I meant to have you any way I could think of and as often as I like?'

The words that had frightened her yesterday now made her dizzy with excitement. 'Even in the afternoon, Gerald?' she said, pretending to be shocked.

'Especially in the afternoon, Lillian,' he said, undoing his neckcloth and smiling.

## Chapter Twelve

When Lily returned to the hall the following morning, the maids had replaced the broken vase with a fresh one. She pulled a flower from the arrangement, twirled it in her fingers and smiled. The blooms were open wider this morning than they had been when she'd brought them in from the garden. She was like the flowers. It had been winter for so long. But now Gerry was here, it was full summer and she had bloomed.

As he had promised, by the time they retired to the bed, they were far too tired to make love there. They had lain, dozing in each other's arms. Just before sleep had taken them, he had whispered that this was just the beginning.

They'd woken, still tired to the bone and aching in strange places. She'd rubbed his back. He'd offered to return the favour and slipped his hand between her legs. An hour later and half a house away from him, and she was still laughing.

'We missed you at supper, Lillian.'

Her smile faltered. She replaced the flower in the vase and turned to face her brother. 'It was the headache again. I did not feel well enough to come down.'

'Nor did the captain,' her brother said with a dry smile. He reached out and touched her cheek. 'You look well enough this morning. Almost too healthy, one might say.' By the look in his eyes, he knew exactly what she had been doing, to the last prurient detail.

She stepped back, out of his reach. 'Is it possible to be too healthy?'

'Yes. If it causes you to think only of yourself and forget those around you. How is Stewart this morning?'

She could not answer the question. She had not seen him since yesterday. She had not said good-night to him. Nor had she visited with him at breakfast. In the course of a few hours, she had forgotten all about him and neglected her responsibilities as a mother. Her newfound happiness evaporated as fast as it had arrived.

Her brother nodded, reading the answer in her expression. 'I warned you yesterday that disloyalty on your part might lead to unfortunate revelations.'

'You do not need to drag him into this,' she said. 'I said nothing more to Gerald about your plans.'

'Nothing more.' Ronald frowned at her. 'Which means that you did as much damage as you could before I could speak to you.'

'You are putting me in an impossible position,' she said, holding her hands out to him in supplication. 'He is my husband. I cannot refuse him and I should not deceive him. If you wish to keep secrets from him, then do not include me in your plans.'

Now Ronald smiled again. 'My thoughts exactly.' Then he said nothing. The silence was more ominous than his threats had been, for it meant that there was something in the works to settle with Gerry and there was no way to warn him about it.

Ronald made a little shooing gesture. 'Do not stand there gawping at me, Lillian. You told me not to speak. I am giving you what you asked for. Now go to your little boy and explain your everlasting devotion to a man who could never want him.'

She did as he suggested and hurried to the nursery so she might prove her brother wrong. Balancing her husband and her child would be difficult, for a time. But it was nothing that all the other wives and mothers did not do. It might be unfamiliar to her, but it would not take long to learn.

She would begin by reassuring Stewart that the captain's return had changed nothing between them. He must not think he was being replaced in her heart by a man who did not love or understand him.

And surely that misunderstanding was a temporary thing. Two days at home had done much to dissipate her husband's anger over what had happened in his absence. In a week, or perhaps two, they could revisit the subject of Stewart's future and she would persuade Captain Wiscombe to relent.

*Gerald.*

She sighed. After last night, he was Gerald. Or

Gerry, as he wished to be called. She smiled. She would very much enjoy changing his mind.

When she arrived at the nursery, Miss Fisher, the governess, met her at the door.

'How is he?' Lily whispered.

'We had a difficult night,' the servant admitted. 'He asked about you.' There was no judgement in her voice, but Lily felt it all the same.

'I am here now,' she said, smoothing her skirt and hurrying into the room.

Stewart was still at the breakfast table, poking a toast soldier into his egg as if he wished to drown it. He glared up at her.

She ignored his mood and stepped forward to kiss him on the cheek. 'Good morning, darling. Did you sleep well?'

'No,' Stewart said and went back to stabbing his egg.

'I am sorry that I did not come to kiss you goodnight,' she said, and smiled. 'You will have to take two kisses from me this morning.'

'You were with him,' Stewart accused, not looking up.

'He is...' She had been about to say, *your father.* Was there any point in adding to the lies? 'The captain has been away for a very long time. I must spend some time with him, even if it means that I cannot come to you as often as I did.'

'When he sends me to school, you won't have to see me at all.' He crushed his toast against the plate.

'Stewart.' How could she comfort him when his worst fear was exactly what Gerald planned for him?

'Stewart.' She knelt down beside his chair and put her arms around him. 'I know you are afraid that things are changing. But I am your mother and I love you more with each day that passes. And I would never make you go anywhere that you do not want to go.' Her throat tightened with what felt like the beginning of tears. She pulled him close so he could not see the wetness on her lashes and held until she felt the resistance leave his body and he hugged her back.

When she pulled away, she could smile again. 'Tell Miss Fisher there will be no lessons today. To make up for last night, I will spend extra time with you this morning. You are my boy. My miracle. Nothing will change that.'

'Papa will,' Stewart said, still not smiling. 'He will change everything.'

## Chapter Thirteen

A duel.

When he'd returned to his room after a delightful
night in his wife's bed, Gerry had noticed the letter
slipped under his bedroom door, and assumed it was
another note from the boy. He'd sat down on the trunk
of clothes that had been delivered from London, opened
it and scanned the note in his hand. Then he'd read
it again, more slowly, sure that it had to be a badly
worded joke.

*Captain Wiscombe,*
*Yesterday afternoon, I witnessed you kissing Miss*
*Fellowes in the trophy room. For the offence to*
*my honour, and the honour of the lady in ques-*
*tion, I challenge you to meet me, tomorrow morn-*
*ing, at dawn. My second, Mr Ronald North…*

Aha. It was serious. And there was the true instigator of the thing. Ronald had convinced the Fellowes

woman that a meeting would be welcome. Then he had put the baronet up to taking action. And Gerry could think of no man in England who was less capable of action than Chauncey d'Art.

A man of violence would have stormed into the trophy room and stopped the kiss. He would have issued the challenge face to face, perhaps after a sharp punch to the offender's jaw. At the very least, he would have put the lady's honour ahead of his own in this pathetic letter.

Sir Chauncey was an utter failure at being a man. And now Gerry was going to have to shoot him, which would ruin his perfect morning. Where was he to find a second? He did not even have a valet, much less a local friend who would want to end a seven-year separation by getting up before dawn and loading a pistol.

He crumpled the paper and tossed it aside, undoing the latches on the trunk and searching for clean linen and a coat suitable for another man's funeral.

Of course, he must not let it come to that. Gerry hated duelling almost as much as he did hunting. It was not that he was incapable of either, or doubted his inevitable success. He simply did not see the sport in killing just to prove his manhood. There were times when diplomacy was a better answer than war. The fact that he had no experience with peace did not mean he could not wage it.

Once properly washed, shaved and dressed, he walked down the hall to the guest wing and rapped sharply on the door of Sir Chauncey's bedroom. Then he entered without waiting for an invitation.

The poor man sat on the edge of the bed. At Gerry's interruption, he stood unsteadily, hand clutching the bedpost for support. He was wearing the same rumpled clothes he'd had on the previous afternoon and appeared to have been drinking, or crying. Or both. He gestured at the door with his free hand. 'You cannot...'

'It is my house,' Gerry said. 'I think I can.'

Sir Chauncey tried again. 'You are not to see me until the duel. It is bad luck.'

'I believe you are thinking of brides and grooms and weddings,' Gerry said as patiently as possible, shutting the door behind him to prevent Ronald North from appearing out of nowhere to offer help where none was needed. 'Since an effort should be made to reconcile differences before resorting to violence, there is no reason we should not talk.' He pulled a chair from the fireside and placed it next to the bed, then gestured for the baronet to sit again.

Sir Chauncey sank back on the mattress as obedient as a dog. 'We cannot settle this by talking. You have humiliated me by seducing my fiancée.'

Gerry sighed. 'I do not know which part of that statement is more ludicrous. First, I was not the instigator. She set upon me in the trophy room. Secondly, there was no seduction. I managed to escape before I was as mounted as the rest of the animals in there. Thirdly, she is not your fiancée, she is your mistress. It is you who should be apologising to me for bringing her to my house.'

'I know what I saw.' Sir Chauncey raised an accusing finger. It trembled slightly, spoiling the effect.

Gerry grinned. 'You saw it, did you? Then unless you ran like a frightened girl, you saw my wife interrupt the kiss seconds after it began. I went to comfort her and spent the rest of the day in her bed, apologising.' Not in bed, precisely. But there was a limit to honesty and that crossed it.

'I know the two of you were in the trophy room. I saw you both enter. And later, she was not at dinner,' he said petulantly.

'Who else was missing?' Gerry asked.

'Ronald North was late,' he admitted in a sullen voice.

'And I suppose he was the one that alerted you to this supposed tryst and suggested the duel,' Gerry said.

There was a flicker of clarity on the baronet's face, before it settled back to belligerence. 'Someone must pay for this slight to my honour.'

'Do you mean to shoot Ronald North, once you have finished with me? I will not allow that, either.'

'What would you have me do?' said Sir Chauncey, annoyed.

Gerry leaned forward to speak confidentially. 'Let me tell you how this will end, if we continue on the course you have set. If we fight, I will kill you. Then I will have to flee the country to escape the scandal.'

Sir Chauncey went white at the mention of his probable fate.

Gerry ignored it. 'I would not enjoy it, of course.'

'Killing me?'

'No. Fleeing the country.' Gerry sighed. 'I cannot abide travel, I am thoroughly tired of the Continent. I am just beginning to enjoy my home and do not want to leave it.' The truth of that statement was almost as big a surprise as the letter of challenge. He enjoyed his house. He enjoyed his wife. Only a few things stood between him and a perfect life.

He looked back at Sir Chauncey, annoyed.

'I might win,' Sir Chauncey said, hopefully.

Gerry shook his head. 'That might be what Ronald was hoping, when he orchestrated this fiasco. But it is an impossibility. I might simply wound you, which will hurt very much. And with even the smallest wound, there is the risk of sepsis, protracted suffering and death. If a single thread from your shirt is driven into your body by the ball and not removed?' He released a puff of air and gestured to express the escaping soul.

Sir Chauncey went even paler.

Gerry nodded in sympathy. 'I would not want you to suffer. More likely, I will kill you quickly and flee. Then Ronald will keep both my house and your mistress. You may not have noticed, but the Norths are very good at separating people from their valuables.' Then he smiled and shrugged, as if to say, *Family. What are we to do with them?*

At this, Sir Chauncey looked depressed. 'There is no hope for me, then.'

Gerry patted him on the back. 'Of course there is, my dear man. First, you must accept my apology for any pain or dishonour I've caused you. And I am sorry, truly. Once we are settled, I suggest you call for your carriage, immediately. Tell Ronald that you have seen through his devious plan and want no part in it. Then leave.' It took an effort not to smile at his own suggestion. 'Take Miss Fellowes with you. And tell her that if there is any more nonsense you will end your arrangement with her.'

'Will that work, do you think?' Sir Chauncey brightened.

Gerry leaned forward and clapped him on the shoulder. 'Damn it, man. Of course it will work. You are a baronet, not some nobody. If she prefers another to you, then leave her at the first inn you pass and make her fend for herself. There are dozens of women who are just as pretty and will not have their heads turned by the first redcoat they see.' He stood to go.

Sir Chauncey stood as well and took his hand. 'You are right, Captain. I must assert myself.'

'You must and you will, Sir Chauncey. I have every confidence in you. And, if I do not see you before you go, farewell, Sir Chauncey.'

*'Au revoir,'* Sir Chauncey said.

'Farewell,' Gerry said, more firmly, and let himself out of the room. Then he went to tell Mrs Fitz that there would be two less at supper.

Lily walked quickly down the hall on the main floor, stopping in the open trophy room door to clap her hands. After a moment's pause to listen for Stewart's faint answering clap, she moved down the hall to the billiard room. Since the remaining guests were out for a morning hunt and her husband was still resting in his room, she had promised Stewart the run of the house and a spirited game of hide-and-seek. But the boy knew the house so well that without the help of clapped clues, it was impossible to find him.

She opened the billiard room door suddenly, hoping to catch him unawares. Her cry of 'Ha!' was premature. The room was dark and empty. Back to the trophy room, and the library beyond it.

She moved quickly through the cases of stuffed birds and over the bearskins on the floor, trying to ignore the glass eyes staring down from the walls. Even after seven years, the room made her uncomfortable. Perhaps, when the guests were gone, Gerry would banish the last of the animals and find a better use for the space they occupied.

But today she could hear Stewart's voice from the adjoining library. He was speaking to someone, answering questions pitched too low to carry to the next room. Could it be Gerry? She smiled in anticipation. If her husband would just take the time to talk to the boy, he might see there would be no harm in Stewart's remaining at the Chase.

She opened the door to surprise them and her smile faded.

'And how old are you now, boy?' The Earl of Greywall was lounging against a library table, his hand resting on Stewart's shoulder.

For a moment, she was too shocked to say anything at all. She took great pains to keep her son away from the guests and made sure that he had no part in the schemes of his grandfather and uncle. He was so good at staying out of sight that many of the visitors had come and gone totally unaware that a little boy had shared the house with them.

She'd made it especially clear that he was not to bother the earl, informing the boy that he was a very important man with no time for children. It gave the peer far too much credit, but Stewart had been convinced. But now he had been trapped, just as she was. The headache which had been gone for nearly two days returned with a vengeance.

Greywall looked up at her and smiled, his question forgotten. 'Your son, I presume?'

'And Captain Wiscombe's,' she replied, pulling Stewart away from the earl and to her side.

'We were just talking.' The earl's smile became a leer. 'Since you refuse to speak at dinner, I must find others to converse with.'

'Children are better seen than heard,' she said, hoping that Stewart understood the warning. Then she took a few carefully controlled breaths and forced herself to do something she'd not done in ages. She smiled at the Earl of Greywall. 'And I must make an effort to be better company.' Her stomach churned at the thought. But for the moment, nothing was more important than getting Stewart out of the room and away from this man.

'Perhaps, if I ask the captain, he will allow the boy to join us for a hunt.'

'I do not like hunting,' the boy said and Lily felt the muscles under her fingers go rigid.

'Nonsense,' responded the earl. 'You are old enough, I am sure. Tell me, boy, when were you born?'

'I will decide when he is old enough to hunt,' Lily snapped, before Stewart could answer, pulling him closer. 'Or his father, the captain, shall.'

'Mama, you are holding me too tight,' he whispered, squirming to get away from her.

'Yes, Lillian,' the earl said. 'Let the boy go. You cannot protect him for ever.' He was smiling at Stewart again, leaning close enough to him that Lily could smell the brandy mingling with his foul breath. She had to go. If she did not leave immediately, she would be sick. But she could not leave without her son.

The earl leaned even closer and reached out a hand. 'And he is a fine, handsome lad. Just like his father.'

'Thank you.' Gerry was standing in the doorway, his hand resting on the frame. He stared at the three of them, face expressionless, though she was sure his eyes missed no detail.

Without bothering to explain, she seized Stewart by the arm and pulled him from the room, hurrying him through the trophy room and down the hall without looking back.

## Chapter Fourteen

~~~~~~~~~~~~~~~~~~~~~~~

'The party is somewhat diminished tonight,' Gerry said, nodding at the empty places up and down the supper table.

Lily gazed back at him, forcing her expression into a placid smile. She had not spoken to her husband since he had discovered her in the library with the earl. In the silence of her bedroom, she'd gone through the conversation again and again, trying to decide what her husband might have seen or heard. What had he read into the few shared words? They had been ordinary enough.

But Gerry was perceptive, almost too sharp for his own good. The empty chairs at the table tonight were proof of that. They had both been too busy to notice the departure of the Wilsons yesterday. After seeing the dyed stoats that might have been their future, they had waited only long enough for the skies to clear before setting off for London.

Today, the baronet and his Cyprian had set off as

well. She was sure that it was Gerry's doing, but she was almost afraid to ask how he had managed it. Perhaps he would evict Greywall as well, without requiring an explanation for the afternoon's exchange. Then the Burkes would go and they would have the house to themselves.

'We are no less jovial for the smaller numbers,' her father said with a smile, reminding her that ridding themselves of the guests would not be enough to set her free.

'It will give us the opportunity to better know our host,' said Mrs Burke, obviously pleased that a lack of competition had finally gained her a seat near the head of the table.

'Yes, it will. I find I am most eager to speak with him,' Greywall said and Lily reached for her wine to hide her apprehension.

'You flatter me, madam,' Gerry replied to Mrs Burke. The earl's lips barely moved as he spoke and the sound of his voice did not carry to the others at the table. It was meant just for her, as a reminder that their talk in the library had been innocent in comparison with the one he could have with Gerry.

She must make sure that it did not happen. Her husband was in an excellent mood this evening. She would do her best to keep him so and to keep him away from the peer.

Or perhaps Mrs Burke would do the job for her. She was too close to him, batting her lashes and behaving as Miss Fellowes had done before her sudden departure. It would have annoyed her had Gerry not shot her a look that hinted the hero of Salamanca wished to be rescued from his own dinner table.

She would ignore Mrs Burke, and the earl, as well. She smiled at him, as if his words were polite dinner conversation and not threat. Then she went back to her meal. Only a few more days, she assured herself. He would be gone and he would not be coming back.

'Flatter you. Captain?' The conversation at the other end of the table continued and Mrs Burke was as loud as the earl was quiet. 'It is nothing but truth. I've often said to Mr Burke that it would be fascinating to speak to a great hero like Captain Wiscombe.' She planted a meaty hand on Gerry's arm and gave an affectionate squeeze. Her own husband, who sat on Gerry's opposite side, seemed surprised to be included in the discussion and offered an ambivalent nod.

Gerry shook his head. 'I am no storyteller, madam. But I look forward to a quiet evening in the company of you and your husband. I would not mind a few hands of cards after dinner, if any of you are so disposed.' He was using the same cheerfully innocuous tone he'd employed since he'd returned. As usual, there was an iron resolve behind it that put Lily on her guard.

'My God, yes,' the earl said, draining his glass again and looking up the table. 'It is about time that someone with money in their pockets joins us. I am tired of losing. Let it be Wiscombe's turn.'

'Yes,' Ronald said. 'By all means, join us.' He was almost salivating at the prospect of a game.

Which meant that her brother would attempt to cheat him as he had everyone else who played. The warnings she had given him had done no good. She glared at her father, willing him to understand the danger that such a game might create.

'Are you sure you might not prefer billiards?' her father suggested. But he was putting none of his usual effort into guiding the conversation to suit his ends. Perhaps, in the end, he cared no more for Ronald than he did for her.

'No,' Gerry said firmly. 'Tonight it must be cards. I am feeling lucky. We will all play cards.' He stared down the table to her and raised his glass in a private salute.

After the stress of the afternoon, she longed to retire to her room and avoid the impending doom. But the glance Gerry had given her was as clear as a verbal command. She was to attend him and the guests. She answered with a barely perceptible nod.

When dinner was finished, they retired to the sitting room and pushed two tables together so all seven of them could play. Lily held her breath as Gerry took his seat opposite her brother at the card table for a round of Trade and Barter. With the speed of play and a chance to force cards when other players drew from one's hand, there were numerous opportunities to cheat. And though the earl and the Burkes had full glasses, Gerry had refused another drink after dinner. Her husband would be far too clear-headed to fall for her brother's usual tricks.

The game began simply enough, with Gerry shuffling and dealing out three cards to each of the players. After a round of spirited play, Mrs Burke took the pot with three tens. The next two hands were equally free of mischief. But such games always began innocently. It did not do to have the guests losing on the very first go. It was only when the deal turned to her brother that things would begin to go wrong.

One did not last long in the North family if one was not able, on some rudimentary level, to count cards as a game was played. By the time Ronald had finished dealing, Lily could see that there were now five aces in play.

If her husband noticed the fact, there was no indication of it. Unless she was to count the slight lift of his eyebrow as the hand was played out to Ronald's obvious success. When the deal returned to her husband, she watched as he deftly palmed the second ace of hearts and dropped it to the floor at her brother's feet. Play continued as it had, with the addition of a slight frown on her brother's face as he realised that the card he needed was no longer in the deck.

When the hands were revealed, Mr Burke was the one to take the pot. And the next as well, when he was the dealer. It appeared to Lily that her husband went out of his way to lose, when he could control the play at all. He was displaying an ineptitude that would have had any in her family gloating at their inevitable success.

But there had been the matter of that ace. And now the deal had returned to her brother. When he had finished, his hand had four cards, not three, and he was careless in disguising the fact. When cards were exchanged, he retrieved the ace he'd dealt to Father, forced an unwanted deuce on the earl and slipped the spare card he'd drawn back up his sleeve. Then he knocked on the table to stop play and displayed his three aces, reaching for the pot.

'Damnable good luck you have, North,' Mr Burke said, mopping his forehead with a handkerchief.

'He makes his own luck,' Gerry said, 'because he cheats at cards.' The pronouncement was delivered in the same tone he might have used had he been remarking on the weather.

There was an audible gasp from the people at the table. All except for Lily, since she could not even manage to pretend surprise.

'I beg your pardon?' Though his voice was calm, Ronald's face was white with rage.

Gerry held a hand to his ear. 'Was that an apology? If so, it was not very convincing.'

'It is no such thing. I have nothing to apologise for.' Her brother pushed back his chair as if a few inches of distance would be enough to escape the allegation.

Gerry reached beneath the table and grabbed the fifth ace, dropping it in the centre for all to see.

At this, Mr Burke tossed his cards on the table in disgust. Even the impervious Greywall let out a curse.

'You cannot prove that was mine,' Ronald said, trying to salvage the situation.

'Perhaps not.' Gerry grabbed her brother by the wrist and forced his hand, palm up, on the table, revealing the king of clubs that was hidden in his shirt cuff. 'But this did not appear by magic.' Then he flipped up the remaining cards in the deck and fanned them to show the tidy stack of face cards arranged at the bottom. 'And I think it unlikely that this is a coincidence.'

'I am sure this is just an innocent mistake,' her father said, offering a smile so benevolent that the look in Mr Burke's eyes changed from suspicion to confusion.

'Unfortunately, no.' Gerry was unmoved. 'There is nothing innocent about what is happening here.'

'Of course there isn't,' Ronald announced. 'It is clear that Captain Wiscombe wishes to defame me and has created evidence where none existed. The person to make such accusations often does it to conceal their own guilt.'

Lily balled her fists under the table to prevent herself from speaking. It was bad enough that Ronald had been caught. He'd made it worse by arguing. Now that he'd accused Gerry of dishonour, the end was inevitable.

There was a dangerous pause before her husband spoke. 'Ronald North, you have been defrauding the visitors to my house. Since you are my wife's brother, I will ignore the aspersions on my character. But I demand you apologise to my guests and make immediate recompense for any money you have taken from Mr Burke.' He paused, as if the next words pained him. 'And Lord Greywall also.'

Lily held her breath and prayed that Ronald might display, if not honour, than at least common sense. His position was hopeless. He must give in.

'There is nothing to apologise for. If it is not you, then someone else has played a prank on me.' He glared at the people around the table, waiting for someone to come to his defence.

It was hopeless. He lacked their father's charm. When he was cornered he could not turn the opinion of the room back to his favour.

Gerry sighed. 'No one is tricking you. You are the trickster. If you do not care to admit it, then I must teach you some manners. We will begin with the correct way to issue a challenge. It is done thusly—face-to-face and eye to eye, not with a letter slipped under a door. Ronald North, you have insulted me and cheated the guests in my home. Apologise now or meet me on the field of honour to take your punishment.'

# *Chapter Fifteen*

The room was in uproar. Mrs Burke was shrieking and her husband pushed away from the table so fast he upset it, sending the cards spilling to the floor. The elder North was entreating for reason and calm. The earl simply laughed. The sound was long and bitter, and punctuated by demands for more drink.

Ronald North was swearing under his breath. By the look in his eyes, he would be only too happy to shoot Gerry right now, if only for the chance to make up for his ruined evening.

Gerry smiled back at him. It was another proof that the man did not think through his actions, or he'd have realised what a mistake he'd made. Everyone in the room should have had the sense to see this moment coming. Instead, they were demonstrating their stupidity with this display of shock and horror. He felt almost sorry for them.

Almost. But not quite.

The one voice he did not hear was his wife's. When he turned to look for her, she was already gone. While he had not expected her to share his feelings of triumph, he had hoped that she would at least remain long enough to act surprised by the turn of events, as her father was. Ronald had to be punished. If she did not want her reputation to be tainted with his bad behaviour, she needed to be seen at her husband's side.

Now Mrs Burke was asking about her. Gerry muttered something about a megrim and overwrought nerves, then offered to summon the woman's maid so that she might be escorted to her room, as well. It gave him reason to quit the sitting room and leave the chaos behind him to locate Lily.

Her sudden absence filled him with an unease that he'd not experienced since the war. Things had been going better than he could have imagined. The previous afternoon, her devastation on witnessing a single kiss had assured him that no matter what had gone before, he now held her heart in the palm of his hand. Then she had demonstrated her devotion in the sweetest possible way. His body tightened at the memory.

But that was yesterday. What with the nonsense over Sir Chauncey, he'd had no time to tell her of his plans for her brother. Despite the fact that the man was a bounder, he was still blood to her. She'd deserved some kind of warning about how the evening might end.

And he had yet to enquire about the curious scene he'd interrupted in the library. The Greywall he knew cared for nothing but hunting and wine. This sudden interest in his wife's son could not be good. Perhaps he had guessed the boy's illegitimacy and meant to blackmail Lily into extending his invitation.

It had been a spontaneous act of chivalry to step in and claim the boy as his own. Now he would have to explain to Lily that there had been no change in his plans for the boy's future. It was much easier to lie to Greywall than to lie to himself. The boy was not his and there was no way to forget that.

When he reached his bedroom, she was waiting for him, wearing the same prim gown she'd worn on the first night. Her face had no trace of powder and her red-brown hair was down, tied back from her face with a ribbon. His heart caught in his chest. How could he ever be worthy of such a beauty?

Perhaps she was thinking the same thing. The smile she wore was the same cold and distant look she used on her unwelcome guests. Perhaps the previous night's affection had been an act and she was more of a North than he wanted to believe. Or perhaps he had created this distance himself.

He returned her cold smile with a warm one and sat on the edge of the bed to pull off his boots. If the current displeasure related to what had just occurred in the sitting room, it would be better to get it out in the open immediately. 'Well, it looks like I shall have to shoot your brother.'

From behind him, there was silence.

He cursed himself for his ham-handedness. Trying to make a joke out of a life-and-death matter might have worked on the battlefield, where all men behaved as if they were one step from the grave, but it was foolhardy of him to try such cruel tactics on his wife.

He was one breath from apologising when she replied, 'Someone was going to do it eventually.'

Her response seemed just as flip as his greeting and showed no sympathy for the difficult position he was in. 'He was cheating at cards,' Gerry repeated the obvious. 'I caught him in the act.'

'Of course you did,' Lily answered. 'He is not nearly as good at it as he thinks.'

'I could not just let it stand,' he said, pulling off his neckcloth and walking to the wardrobe to remove the rest of his clothes. He could feel her eyes boring holes in his back, but did not turn. What would the world think if it learned that the hero of Salamanca was afraid to look his own wife in the face?

'Will the duel be tomorrow? Or will there be more time?' she asked.

'At least a day, I think. There are formalities. We must choose seconds, a location and weapons.' When he had nothing left to remove but his shirt, he turned to look at her, braced for whatever storm of emotion might come.

'Being honourable is surprisingly complicated,' she said, the corner of her mouth lifting in an ironic grimace.

'Not really.' He frowned. She was carrying it too far if she thought that the honour of his household was a joking matter. 'It is not the least bit complicated. Most men understand that it is wrong to cheat at cards, sharp at billiards or trick men out of their houses so they might use the land to swindle others.'

'We Norths do not know any other way. But I will

take you at your word.' Now the irony turned to bitter sarcasm.

'You are a North now, are you?' he said, hands on hips.

'I am a Wiscombe,' she said. 'Or at least I thought I was.'

'I am sorry that I did not give you warning of what I meant to do,' he said, suddenly not the least bit sorry. 'But it had to be done.'

'I know,' she all but shouted back at him. 'And it does not matter to me what you do to him. Kill him, for all I care. We will all be better off.'

He shook his head in disgust. 'Kill him? Duelling and going to war is no different from shooting animals to you, is it? Do you have no feelings at all, that you would turn on your own kin and ask me to butcher them?'

'Do you want me to prefer them to you?' she said, equally disgusted. 'Just what is it that you want from me?'

What did he want from her? 'I expect you to show some natural, human feeling towards your own blood.'

'Natural?' She gasped. 'And what does that mean to you? In my family, it is natural for a woman's blood to sell her to a stranger to gain a house.' She took another ragged inhalation. 'And then to forget all about her, so she might be raped by a drunkard without so much as a by your leave.' Now she was struggling for breath, clutching at her temples as if only her hands pressing against them kept her skull from splitting in two.

Perhaps there was no air in the room, for he could

not seem to breathe, either. Rape. Why had he not suspected this? It explained her unreasonable fears, the panic and the megrims that were no mere sham to avoid responsibility.

He should have demanded answers when he'd first heard of the child. Instead, he'd believed the worst and never bothered to look for the truth. Nor had it occurred to him that she might have been even more trapped by this marriage than he had been. She'd been expected to marry the nothing that he had been, a man so unworthy that he had not even bothered to speak to her before he'd proposed. Then he'd abandoned her to her fate, assuming that she would be safe until he returned.

He had been wasting time on trivialities. The only problem in this house that mattered was right here in front of him. And he'd ignored it.

He sat down beside her, seized her by the wrists and prised her hands away from her face. She was sobbing with fear and pain, so he rubbed her temples himself, urging her to lean forward until their foreheads touched, waiting for her to relax. 'It will be all right. Breathe, Lily. Just breathe.' He kept his own breath slow and steady to guide her back to composure.

It was working. She soothed at the sound of his voice and copied his breathing. The furrows in her brow began to relax and her head lolled against his shoulder. 'Thank you,' she whispered, pressing her face into his throat like a child in need of comfort. 'I am sorry to be so emotional. I know there was nothing else you could do. It is just…'

'You did nothing wrong. Ever. It was I.' He turned

his face to kiss her. But even as he did it, he knew that he was that stranger she'd dreaded when she spoke of being sold. For much of the past seven years, she had kept a secret from him. His homecoming must have been a cause of fear, not a hope of salvation. Today, that would end.

He released her hands and wrapped his arms about her, nuzzling her hair. 'Tell me what happened while I was gone.' His mouth was pressed close to her ear, so he spoke in little more than a whisper.

'I thought that was obvious. I lay with another man and he left me with child.' Her brittle laugh was muffled by the linen of his shirt. 'Of course, as you said about Miss Fellowes, there is the matter of consent to consider.'

He had all but joked about being unable to fight off that woman's unwanted attentions. But Lily did not have the advantage of size and strength. She had been helpless.

'Who was he?'

She gasped and tried to pull away. 'You're hurting me.'

He cursed himself. He had been imagining what he would do when he'd found the bastard. Without thinking, he'd tightened his grip on her. Lily, of all people, deserved the gentleness she had never been offered. He forced himself to relax, rubbing the centre of her back in a way that calmed them both. 'No one will ever hurt you again. I will see to it. Now tell me what happened.'

'There is really nothing to tell,' she said. But he could feel her tremble as she gathered the nerve to speak. 'I used to spend the evenings with my father's guests, acting as a true hostess. One night, a man mistook common courtesy for something more.' Her breath caught in her throat and he put his hand on her heart, breathing with her until she could regain control.

Then he said, 'He followed you to your room?'

She shook her head. 'It was worse than that. As an honoured guest, Father gave him the master bedroom. I did not think it would matter. The other bedrooms were full and he had to stay somewhere. I locked the connecting door. But the key was in his dresser. And he assumed...'

At the first hitch in her breathing, he kissed her until she was calm again. 'He forced his way into your room.'

'Worse than that,' she whispered. 'He carried me back here. To your bed. And the animals on the walls... So many eyes...' She was crying in earnest, reliving the details.

It had been horrible enough to sleep here under the best of circumstances. But at the thought of her in his father's old room, he was gripped by the sick terror that had taken him on the night before his first battle. 'And after that, you changed the locks and the decoration,' he finished for her.

She nodded into his shoulder. 'I pushed the wardrobe in front of the connecting door until he was gone. Then I had the servants remove everything from the room and burn it.'

Apparently, she'd enjoyed that one small act of rebellion, for he felt her laugh. 'They thought I was very strange. So I told them you had not liked the room and had requested the changes.'

'Good for you,' he said, laughing in response. 'It was abominable.' The thought of using it as a bridal chamber had been one of the reasons he'd postponed his own wedding night. In the end, he'd spared her nothing.

'I had the locks changed and left the room empty for a time, claiming that I could not decide what to do with it. But then I read of your successes in the newspapers. I decided to make a space that would be worthy of you, should you ever return to me.'

She sounded so hopeful at this imagined homecoming that he felt even worse for his recent behaviour.

'As I told you before, it was just the one time,' she was assuring him, as if she still feared he still meant to blame her for what had happened. 'I learned not to be so trusting. I limited my time with the guests. It was better to appear cold than to risk another incident.'

'And your headaches?' he said.

'Sometimes the guests are too much for me to bear. My head hurts and I become short of breath. If I go to my room to rest, I am better in no time.'

'You are a prisoner in your own home,' he said, outraged. 'You should not have to hide behind a locked door to get any peace.'

'It is not so bad,' she said hurriedly. 'It is a very nice house. And I have Stewart to care for.'

There was the boy again, a continual reminder of what had happened to her. Something must be done. But for now, it was time to put the blame for the problem back where it belonged. 'And who is Stewart's father?'

She eyed him warily. 'If I tell you, what do you mean to do?'

'I will make him pay for what he did to you. When I am finished with him, he will have no life left in his body to prey upon another innocent.'

'Before or after you fight my brother?' she said with a sigh.

It must seem that he could not solve a problem without shedding blood. He took her hand, squeezing it and pressing it to his lips. 'I will not have you blaming yourself for a thing that was not your fault. The man responsible will be brought to justice, one way or another. First, I will clear our house of guests, including your family, who should have protected you in my absence.' All her father's fine words about caring for his precious girl had had been nothing more than another trick. 'Once that is done, I will see to your attacker.'

She gave an emphatic shake of her head. 'You are too late for that. He is already dead. There is nothing to be done.'

She had spoken too quickly. But what reason would she have to lie, now that he knew the worst? 'There must be something,' he said. 'I cannot just leave this...' All the accolades and medals he'd earned meant nothing if he could not manage to care for his own wife. He was worthless and unworthy, just as his father had said.

'You have done enough just by coming home safe,' she said, lifting her head and giving him a tear-stained smile. 'It means we have a future together. But the past is the past. It is over. Leave it,' she whispered, touching his arm. 'For me.'

At that slight pressure of her hand, he felt himself break. He gathered her to him again and gave her the homecoming kiss he'd imagined when first he'd left her. She was right. The time apart did not matter. There was only now and what would come.

And if he could have this moment, it was more than enough. He could live and die on the taste of her mouth, the scrape of her tongue on his teeth and the feel of her cheek against his. 'Ask for the world and I shall get it for you,' he said.

'Not the world,' she whispered back. 'Just your trust.' She hesitated. 'And perhaps, one day, your love?'

'My trust is yours, as it always should have been.' He could not promise more than that. He'd wasted years of his life, hating the faithless seductress he was sure he'd married. But he had been wrong. The woman before him was a blameless stranger. How could he know what he truly felt for her, other than a driving need to undo his mistakes and make things right?

He kissed her again and reached to undo the buttons on her gown. He felt her tense. Yesterday, they had been in her room. But even after stripping this room to the plaster and swearing that the past did not matter, there were memories in this place that still needed to be banished. 'You can trust me,' he said and felt her force herself to relax.

He quickly pulled his own shirt over his head and cast it to the floor, making sure he was naked and vulnerable before asking the same of her. Then he placed her hands on the little pearl buttons, kissing her fingers for encouragement.

Slowly, she undid them and his eyes followed the widening vee of bare skin down to its point just above her navel. He traced the same path with his tongue, kissing her throat, nuzzling the insides of her breasts and finally resting his cheek against her stomach, dipping his tongue into her navel, licking and swirling.

She released a shuddering sigh and arched her back, as her hands caught in his hair, pressing him tighter to her. But she made no move to guide him lower.

The last time, he had been selfish. He had been so eager for her that he'd taken more than he'd given. The only other man who had touched her had been even worse. And now she had no experience to know what it was that she so clearly wanted.

He smiled against her stomach. Then very slowly, he raised the hem of her gown to bare her for his kiss. He slid his tongue down the rise of her belly.

She tensed again, still unsure.

He halted the progress of his kisses and stroked the delta of hair with his fingertips until she spread her trembling thighs to receive his hand. She stilled with a sigh as he eased his fingers into her wet, welcoming body. She wanted him there, inside her, as if she were more comfortable with his pleasure than she was with her own.

The response was tempting, but it was not what he wanted from her. Before she could object, he dipped his head and spread her even wider, replacing his hand with his mouth.

Her body went rigid and she answered the penetration of his tongue with a primal moan. At first, it seemed she might fight against him. But then the pleasure proved too great and she raised her hips as if offering herself to him.

He accepted the gift, steadied her with his hands and feasted, delving as deeply as he could into her to mimic his fingers. But still it was not the response from her that he sought. So he withdrew and left a lingering trail of kisses until he reached the little bead of flesh that would destroy the last of her resistance.

For a moment, her breathing stopped and he almost released her, fearing it was another attack of panic. Then, she gasped in amazement, and clutched at his hair to encourage him. She was sobbing now, sweet, happy whimpers that came faster and faster with each movement of his tongue.

His body answered, growing, ready and desperate to be consumed by her. He put his own needs from his mind, focusing on the sound of her cries until they stopped. Started again. Stopped. And released in a long, satisfied sigh.

He pulled away from her and lay back on the bed, achingly hard, closed his eyes and tried to think of anything but the taste on his tongue and the smell of musk. This was his gift to her. It was all he needed. When he opened them again, she was leaning over him.

He did not have to ask if he had pleased her. Her false smile was gone and had been replaced by one so real that her very soul seemed to shine out at him from behind her eyes. He smiled back.

Without a word, she stripped the gown over her head and dropped it beside his shirt. She was kneeling at his side, a glorious topography of soft curves, hills and valleys that he longed to explore.

But he had promised himself that her pleasure was foremost. He dragged his gaze back to her face. Her hair had come undone from its tie and framed her face in wild sherry-coloured waves. He wanted to bury his face in it and lose himself in her body.

Her eyes strayed lower, admiring his obvious need for her. Then her smile widened and she turned to straddle him, her hands on his shoulders, her damp thighs squeezing his hips.

'You don't have to,' he said, his voice breaking like a green boy's.

'Even after yesterday, you don't want to bother me?' she said, teasing his body with a rock of her hips.

'I don't want to demand more than you wish to give,' he said, trying not to think. 'I want to pleasure you.'

'Then let me have my way,' she said, touching him, stroking him and, finally, easing her body down to cover him.

## Chapter Sixteen

The next morning, Lily took breakfast in her room to avoid an embarrassing meeting with her guests who, unless they were even more stupid than they appeared, must have finally come to realise that the Norths had been playing them for fools. Perhaps she was a coward for not taking her share of the responsibility for what had been going on. She had been the hostess when it happened. But Gerry had uncovered her brother's cheating. It was only fair that he help with consoling the victims.

She smiled. Gerry would not mind if she did not come down at all. Last night, he had gone from commanding hero to willing slave, pleasuring her until she couldn't think. Then she'd turned the tables and ridden him, watching triumphant as he lost control because of her. She'd had no idea that something that had once seemed so horrible could be so wonderful if it was shared with the right person.

More importantly, she had finally told him enough of the truth so he knew that she would never willingly be unfaithful to him. Perhaps it had been her imagination, but after her revelation, the suspicious shadows behind his eyes had gone and a measure of his old innocence had returned. Last night he had been a bridegroom and she had finally been a bride.

It was the beginning of the fresh start that they needed. Perhaps he did not yet love her. But when the last of the guests had departed, her love for him, and Stewart's as well, would be enough to open the last seals on his heart.

Between them, they would make sure he forgot all about vengeance for previous wrongs, or dredging up the details of an incident she wanted to forget. It did not really matter if it was for her sake or to salve his own injured pride. There would be too many risks involved in seeking justice at this late date. Some people were above the law.

Even if anyone believed her story. It was more likely that revealing the truth would end with her own humiliation, while her attacker remained untouched. Challenging such a man might end with gaol or a hangman's noose for the husband who sought to defend her honour. It simply was not worth the risk.

But there were other, more immediate problems to deal with. She had just set up her easel in the conservatory for her morning hour of painting when her brother arrived. Her father was close at his heels, scanning the hall for eavesdroppers before shutting the glass double doors behind him.

'Good morning,' she said, not looking up from her work.

'Good?' Ronald gave a derisive snort. 'Do you not understand what happened last night?'

'I was there, Ronald. Gerry caught you cheating at cards and called you out.'

'"Gerry" is it now?' Ronald's voice was growing shrill. 'He threatened to kill me and you spent another night in his bed.'

'Ronald!' her father said sharply as if he were settling a fight between children. 'Your sister's marriage is none of your affair. And I warned you to be careful with Wiscombe,' he added. 'No matter what he pretends, he is not the naive young man whom we sent to war.' Then he smiled at Lily. 'The way he handled the sable farm was really quite masterful.'

'It was,' she said, surprised that she could agree with him, even on such a small thing.

'I am so glad that you both approve of him,' Ronald snapped. 'But what is to be done about the duel?'

'Done about it?' Lily said. 'What can be done? In this case, I do not think a simple apology will be enough. Perhaps you should do as he asked. If you were to reimburse the guests and throw yourself on his mercy…'

'Me? I will not abase myself to that interloper.'

'He is not actually an interloper,' she said, putting the paint box aside. 'He is the owner of the house.'

'And you are his wife,' her father reminded her with a gentle smile. 'Perhaps if you were to intercede for your brother, we might avoid an unfortunate incident.'

'Perhaps if Ronald had learned to deal from the bottom of the deck instead of hiding cards in his sleeve, he might not have got caught.'

'You were always better at it than he,' her father agreed.

'That is in no way a compliment,' she said, remembering that he was part of the problem and turning away from him.

'It is not my technique that needs improvement,' Ronald announced. 'It has never been a problem before.'

'You have not gambled against Gerald Wiscombe before,' Lily said, trying not to smile in triumph.

'Unless we are to count the first gamble that got us the house,' her father said with a knowing nod. 'Though it took some time, he won that back from us, as well. Then there was the matter of the sables. And I heard he bested you at billiards the first night he was home.'

Lily raised her eyebrows, impressed. Ronald was as good at billiards as he was abysmal at cards.

'Well, he will not win this time,' Ronald said.

'He has won already,' their father said with a shake of his head. 'No matter what we might do, I suspect that word of this will get out in London and the same game will not work again. It might be best to decamp quietly and begin again elsewhere.'

'Your best suggestion is that we run away?' Ronald stared at his father, outraged.

Lily nodded. 'I doubt he will follow you, as long as you do not involve him in future ventures, or try to abuse your connection to him.'

Faced with the only logical choice, Ronald ignored

it. 'Nonsense. You must go to him, Lily, and convince him to retract the challenge.'

'I?' She laughed. 'What makes you think I have any control over his actions?'

He responded with a knowing grin. 'You have more control over *Gerry* than you realise. I saw the look on his face yesterday morning. And today, as well. Now that you are sharing his bed, you can lead the man about by the nether parts if you wish to.'

Years of carefully maintained calm broke in an instant and she slapped him hard across the cheek. She would not let him make the best part of her marriage sound like something vile and sinful. 'Do not speak to me that way ever again. Even if I could control him, I do not wish to. Especially not for your sake, Ronald. I warned you from the moment he arrived not to underestimate him. You ignored me and made this muddle. I will not turn my marriage into another North family fraud to help you out of it.'

'Now, children—' her father was giving them the benevolent smile that worked so well on people who didn't know him '—do not fight over this. I am sure Lily would be willing to put in a good word for you with her husband. But you must ask more nicely than that.'

'I will not,' she said, glaring at her brother.

'You had better,' Ronald countered. 'Or I will have the talk with your son that you did not have the nerve to.'

Her anger turned to ice-cold rage. 'If you do, I will shoot you myself.'

'Lillian!' Her father looked more hurt than shocked. 'Do not talk that way to your brother.' He turned to Ronald. 'And what is this nonsense about speaking to Stewart? What does he have to do with any of this?'

'Now that her husband has returned, your precious Lillian pretends to be a devoted wife. But Stewart is proof that she was not always so pure. If she can use her wiles to convince her husband not to throw the little bastard out in the cold, then she can spare some influence for the rest of the family.'

'Lily?' Her normally glib father could manage nothing more than her name. He was staring at her as if he expected her to deny everything so they might all go back to ignoring the past.

'Do not dare pretend you did not know,' she said, furious that he could not manage one small moment of honesty, now that the subject had been broached.

Her father gave a confused shake of his head, refusing to believe. 'I am not pretending. I do not understand. What Ronald is claiming...' He shook his head again. 'I refuse to believe that you would do such a thing.'

'That I...' It was too much. She had to get away from them and the poison they spewed, using her, ignoring her pain and then coming to her for help when things went wrong. 'The duel will go on as planned. I will do nothing to stop it.' She stared at her brother in disgust. 'Why would I help someone who thinks so little of me and is eager to tell my son that the father he worships is not his?'

Then she turned to her father. 'And you, who knows

everything that goes on in this house. Do not lie to me like you do to the guests. You put that monster in the room beside mine. I locked the door, but you gave him the key. You sold my honour twice, as if it was no more important than your imaginary ruby mine.'

For a moment, there was no sign of understanding on his face. But then the truth hit him like a lightning strike. 'My dear.' His voice was unsteady and his hands trembled as he reached out to comfort her, as if it were not years too late for that. Or did he expect her to comfort him? 'I did not know. I swear on your mother's soul, I did not know.'

Her vision was blurring, as it sometimes did when she forgot to breathe. Or perhaps it was just the tears. She slapped his hands away, took a deep breath and was relieved to feel her head clearing as the fear receded and anger returned. 'Then I do not know who I hate more, the man who took advantage of me, or the one who did not even notice it happened.' She pushed past them both, slamming through the glass doors and out into the hall.

By the time she arrived at her room, her breath was coming in desperate pants. Once she turned the key in the lock, it began to slow to normal. She planted her shoulders square against the wood, adding the weight of her body to the bolt. She was safe, she repeated the word in her mind. *Safe*.

But why had she run? There had been no physical threat. Just a few sad truths and some harsh words.

Now that they had been spoken, there was no power left in them.

Gerry was right. She'd used the lock for comfort. She had thought she was locking others out. But if there was nothing on the other side of the door, she had been locking herself in.

'Lily.'

She jumped. Her husband stood in the connecting doorway, staring at her with concern. One look at her face and he was across the room, pulling her into his arms. 'What has happened?'

'Nothing,' she said, breathless. 'Nothing.'

'Liar,' he said, pulling her away from the door. But he did not question her further, simply held her, his cheek pressed to her temple, offering his strength to her.

As if by magic, the contact banished the beginning of her headache. She sighed.

'Hmmm?' He asked all his questions with a single noise.

'Better,' she admitted. And then added, 'I was speaking with my father and brother. They upset me.'

'Command me and I will make it right,' he whispered.

She shook her head. 'That is what they wish for me to do. They were badgering me to make you call off the duel. But I will not do it. I will not instruct you, nor will I blame you for your decision,' she added.

'As you wish,' he said. 'But it is not unusual for them to involve you in their plans. Does it always upset you so?'

'This time it was different,' she admitted. 'We talked about the past. My brother taunted me with Stewart's illegitimacy. And my father…' She swallowed, trying to gain control. 'My father did not know what had happened to me.'

'You have never talked to him about this?' he asked and held her even closer.

She shook her head. 'All this time, I have hated him for letting it happen to me. And for pretending that there were no problems, letting it go on and on. I was even afraid…' She choked back a sob and took another breath. 'I thought he might have planned the whole thing.'

Gerry swore.

'I blamed him for what happened. But he did not even know,' she repeated, still baffled.

'We have spoken about you,' Gerry said. 'Perhaps he is misguided about some things. But he loves you and would never intentionally hurt you.'

'Do not be a fool.' She must not forget that her husband was one of the many gulls that her father had tricked. 'He used me to trap you and it is pure luck that things turned out as well as they did.'

'He persuaded me otherwise,' Gerry said, sounding almost as bewildered as she felt by this statement. 'I do not think he would have arranged the marriage if he had not thought we'd make a decent match.'

'He is a liar and a thief,' she said, exasperated.

'But he is also your father.' Gerry shook his head. 'He can lie about many things. But there was something…' He shrugged. 'I have not told you much of my own father, have I?'

'I know that he was a hunter,' she said, thinking of the awful heads that filled the house.

'But I was not,' Gerry said with a smile. 'I was a grave disappointment to him. He thought me soft and rather useless.'

'Then I hope he can look down from heaven and see how wrong he was,' she said, indignant.

He laughed. 'I doubt he would be satisfied. I have killed more than my share of men. But I still do not kill animals. Even now, I do not see the point of it.'

'How odd,' she said, for it was.

'But your father seems to have a very high opinion of me, despite my spoiling his plans. That may change, of course, since I mean to shoot your brother.'

Was he still trying to gauge her opinion on the duel? She was still not sure she had one. 'I doubt it,' she said. 'Just now, when he was encouraging me to talk you out of it, he spoke well of you. Mostly, he is not happy with Ronald for being stupid enough to be caught.'

'Fathers and sons,' Gerry said, shaking his head. 'There are expectations between us that can be difficult to fulfil. But daughters are a different matter entirely. When we talked after the sable incident, he told me repeatedly that he would not have promised you to me if he had not thought that we would make a good match. He described you as a jewel.'

'He said no such things to me,' she said, trying not to let the bitterness show. But when had he had the chance? She'd been so angry about what had happened that she'd hardly spoken to him since Stewart was born, even though they shared a house.

'When he chose a husband for you, he went out of his way to find you a man that was in no way like himself or your brother,' Gerry said. 'Despite what occurred, I think he hoped to give you a future very like the one you will have with me.'

'Then what happened…'

'It was never his plan, if that's what you feared.'

'But it was still his fault,' she insisted.

'True,' Gerry agreed. But there was a silence after that which made her wonder if he thought more than he said.

'Do you expect me to forgive him, just because he was not actively trying to hurt me?'

She'd meant to be sarcastic, but there was something in his expression that said that was exactly what he wished.

'After all your talk of loyalty, I cannot believe you would take his side in this.' She pulled away.

'There are no sides,' he said. It was exactly the opposite of what he'd said when he'd arrived. 'I would hope that you will forgive him and me, as well. I should not have married you and left you alone. I was as much at fault as he was. I was not here when you needed me.'

'I never blamed you.' She had been too busy worrying about what would happen when he returned.

'Then I have much to be thankful for,' he said, kissing her hair. 'And whatever you feel for him, your father will not be living under this roof much longer. Before he goes, I will speak to him about this and see that you have the apology that you seek.'

## Chapter Seventeen

⦿───⦿◦⦿───⦿

The Burkes had fled before supper.

Lily could hardly blame them. It must have been a shock to discover that they were not so much friends as a source of income to their hosts. That said, she suspected they must have been rather stupid to have not noticed it earlier. To most guests, even the most charming venue grew tiresome after a week of continual losses at cards and billiards. But the current group had lasted almost a fortnight before Gerry had arrived to destroy their illusions.

'I suspect it was my charming personality that drove them away,' her husband said, as they walked from the house just before dawn. The previous night's supper had been a quiet affair, eaten in their rooms, followed by an early bedtime so that he might be rested for the morning.

'Now that you have returned, it is more interesting than usual,' she admitted. 'We do not usually have naked men running through the hall or intimate examinations of small animals.'

'Or so many challenges, I hope,' he added. 'Two in a week is high, even for me.'

'Two?' She looked at him in surprise.

'Did I forget to tell you about Sir Chauncey?' He waved a hand. 'Later, perhaps. It was another unsuccessful scheme of your brother's.'

'My family did not have unsuccessful schemes until you arrived,' she said, secretly rather proud.

'Well, let us hope their string of bad luck continues.' He turned grave for a moment. 'But on the off chance it should not, I would rather that you not be here to witness it. A duel is no place for a lady.' Gerry gave her a stern look, as though that would be enough to scare her away at this point in the proceedings.

'You are quite right, Captain Wiscombe,' she said with a cross frown. 'We are only halfway to the clearing where this farce is to take place and the wet grass has ruined my best boots. Even if I turn back now, they are quite beyond repair. I might as well continue.'

He laughed. 'You are a surprisingly cold-blooded creature, Mrs Wiscombe.' He gave her a sidelong glance. 'In these circumstances, at least.'

She could not help it. She blushed. Then she touched his arm. 'If you mean to do this without a second, then someone must be there to call for a surgeon, should my brother be lucky enough to wound you.'

He gave the hand on his arm a gentle pat. 'If the earl means to stand for your brother, your father would have to accompany me. That hardly seemed appropriate. And I doubt a surgeon will be necessary. But thank you for your concern.'

Surely someone would need medical attention. Unless he did not intend to shoot Ronald. Or perhaps he meant to do such a thorough job of it that there would be no point in getting a doctor. But if Gerry were hurt, who would be there to protect him from her brother? And who would protect her from the earl? She shivered.

He glanced at her, then slipped his greatcoat from his shoulders and wrapped it around her. 'It will be warmer once the sun is full up.'

'Not as warm as it was last summer. The heat then was quite oppressive.'

'Then I am lucky to have missed it.'

They were talking about the weather. How banal. What if she lost him, after less than a week together? 'Gerald,' she said, wetting her lips.

'Lillian?' He was still smiling, mocking her serious tone.

'Please be careful,' she said, releasing a sigh.

'Still not going to plead for Ronald's life?' he said. Then he grew serious. 'After today, there is a chance that you will be sharing a bed with the man who murdered your brother.'

She thought for a moment, searching her mind for the distress that ought to be there at such a time. It saddened her that she could not find it. 'I knew that it might come to this some day. It is unfair to both of us that you are the one he will meet. But what are you to do, really? What he was doing is wrong. If he refuses to stop cheating, he must be stopped by someone else. I trust that you will be as merciful as possible in your punishment of him.'

He nodded, satisfied with her answer. 'And if, as you said before, he gets off a lucky shot?'

'You must not let that happen,' she said, surprising herself with the vehemence and lack of hesitation.

'Well, well,' he said, smiling. 'I have my answer.'

'But be wary. You already know that he cheats,' she reminded him. 'Should an opportunity present itself, he will try to trick you. You must remember that my family has no honour, even in circumstances that demand it by their very nature.'

He stopped walking and stared at her. 'There is one in your family that is honourable. I am lucky to have married her.'

'Thank you.' They stared at each other for a moment in silence. But Lily had the strangest feeling that they were still talking and that something very important had been said. Then he turned and tucked her hand into the crook of his arm and walked with her the rest of the way to the duelling site.

It was one of her favourite spots in the woods, a clearing where the bluebells in spring grew so thick that it was like walking on a scented cloud. Would it be spoiled for her next year by the blood that would be shed today?

'Wait here,' he said, directing her to an oak at the side of the clearing that was well out of the way of danger. 'I will call when it is safe for you to come forward.' Then he went to join the other two men.

Her brother and the earl were already there, pacing out the ground and checking the position of the sun. Even this early in the morning, Greywall was the worse for drink. But drunk or sober, he would be no help should Ronald try any underhanded tricks. Ronald cast a look in her direction that was as dark as her own mood. *Traitor.* He did not need to speak the words for her to see what he was thinking.

Good. Let him know which side she had chosen. It was surprising that it had taken him so long to understand.

After stumbling through a brief set of instructions, Greywall held out the pistol case so the men might choose their weapons. Ronald selected first, in a desperate grab that was not quite according to protocol.

Gerald took the remaining pistol and examined it briefly, then fired at the grass at his feet. There was a loud click and a brief flash, but no report.

This was what came of having no second. She had a mind to run to them and to demand that they put a stop to this immediately.

But Gerald did not seem overly bothered. He held it up again, cocking the hammer and running the ramrod down the barrel. Then he smiled. 'I see what the problem is. It has been incorrectly loaded. You had best check yours as well, North. We want no mistakes.' Then he took powder, patch and ball, readying the weapon with a few efficient movements and another tap of the rod.

He cocked the hammer again and looked expectantly at Ronald. 'All better.'

Her brother looked decidedly pale, for it was clear that his first plan had not worked.

Greywall was too drunk to notice what was occurring. But he knew his part well enough to position the men back to back and order them to pace off the space. Then he informed them that, on the count of three, they must raise their guns and fire.

'One.' The sound was ponderous in the quiet morning air. Lily held her breath.

'Two.' It had been only a second, but the time was going so slowly, it felt as if her lungs were going to burst. But while Gerald stood rock-still, her brother's hand twitched and began to swing upwards, into position.

He meant to shoot early and catch his opponent unprepared. She had known him to be dangerous when cornered, but to see such a despicable act and to be helpless was maddening.

'Thr...'

Her own scream mingled with the final count, as she saw her brother's pistol fully up, his finger tightening on the trigger.

But Gerald was even faster, his weapon discharging in time with her brother's.

The reports of the two weapons were so close that they might have been a single shot. They were followed by a man's curse and the sharp smell of gunpowder. She turned to her husband in terror, only to see him wiping casually at a bloody spot on his cheek.

She rushed to him, weak with relief, and threw her arms about him, searching in her sleeve for her handkerchief, wet it with her tears, and dabbed at the wound.

He grinned at her. 'Only grazed. I've had worse than this shaving without a mirror. Here now. Calm yourself, woman. This is no way for a soldier's wife to behave.' Now that it was over, he looked more embarrassed than hurt.

She reluctantly pulled away from him, and made an effort to compose herself. 'Yes, Captain Wiscombe.'

'And what about me?' her brother said, voice sharp with indignation. When she turned to look, Ronald was holding his mangled right hand in his left, the pistol dropped and forgotten on the grass next to a spatter of blood. 'Damn you, Wiscombe. Damn you to hell. Look what you have done.'

'Ruined your livelihood, I should think,' her husband drawled, uninterested. 'If you are lucky enough to regain the use of that hand, it will be some time before you can deal cards with any effectiveness. I suspect the dexterity needed to hide aces and deal from the bottom is gone for good.'

'You bastard!' Ronald made a lunge in her husband's direction, ready to grab him by the throat. The sudden movement sent another spatter of blood from his injured hand and what was apparently a fresh wave of pain as well. Ronald's next curse ended in a whimper and he went back to cradling the mess that had once been his dominant hand. 'Lily, help me.'

Lily stepped forward briskly. 'Do not be an infant, Ronald. Here.' She reached up to snatch his neckcloth from around his throat, wrapping it several times around the injury tight enough so the bleeding slowed to seepage. 'Now go back to the house and get Mrs Fitz to bandage it properly.'

'Send for a surgeon,' he moaned.

Lily sniffed in disgust. 'To what end? The ball went clean through and the housekeeper can set broken fingers and stitch as well as a doctor.'

'I need laudanum,' he moaned.

'You need to reflect on your injury and thank the Lord that Captain Wiscombe did not shoot you in your black heart. You truly deserved it.'

'Lily?' Even though he was older, the pain had reduced her brother to little more than a spoiled child who expected his sister to nurse him and make all things right.

'Go!' she said, holding up a finger towards the carriage that had brought her brother and his second the short distance from the house. 'Before I tell my husband to challenge you again for misloading his weapon. If you meant to kill him, than you should be happy that he did not end your life on principle.'

Her brother gave her an injured look, limping towards the carriage, as if the slight wound he'd received had carried to his leg. Greywall put a conciliatory hand on his shoulder, then got a better look at the blood staining his coat sleeve and fainted dead away.

Or perhaps he had passed out from intoxication. Either way, it did Lily good to see him face down in the wet grass. She turned away, back to her husband, offering him a composed smile as he held out his arm to escort her.

'There,' he said. 'Did I not tell you that it would work out for the best?'

'I did not doubt you,' she assured him. 'All the same,

it is a relief that it is over and that you were able to handle it so efficiently.'

He gave a modest bow at her compliment. 'I have dealt with worse, you know.'

'But I have never been forced to stand by, helpless, and watch you do it,' she said.

'And I knew from the first that your brother was no real threat.'

'Not a threat?' She stared at him in surprise. 'He is a liar and a cheat. I am his own sister and I have no idea what he might be capable of if backed into a corner.'

'As I said before, I have seen worse.' He gave her a pitying look. 'I am sorry to say it, my dear, but your brother is a coward. While he may think himself a dangerous man willing to do anything to save his own skin, he has never killed anything more ferocious than a doe. He attempted to trick me, just as you said he would. But his attempts were obvious and easy to predict. And half-hearted, as well.'

'I suppose you'd have done better,' she said, surprised.

'If I'd wanted my opponent dead?' Gerry thought for only a moment. 'I'd have dispensed with the nonsense and shot him point-blank before the duel started. Then I'd have sworn my second to secrecy and we'd have come back to the house with the corpse. Or I might have arranged a hunting accident. It would not have been as satisfying as seeing his face as I shot him, but it would have done the job.'

'Cold-blooded murder?'

Her husband shrugged. 'It is fortunate for all of us

that I am an honourable man. But I also know what it truly means to fight for one's life. I have equal skill at killing men with sword or pistol. On several unfortunate occasions I used my bare hands. The people who speak of cold-blooded action as the greatest sin do not know what awful things can happen in the heat of the moment.'

For the first time since he'd been home, she saw the signs of tiredness and strain on his face. She had not expected him to be the young man who had left her. But he had aged a lifetime in seven years. 'There will be no more of either, once we have the house to ourselves.'

'My wife will paint me landscapes of Waterloo and I shall not slaughter so much as a rabbit ever again.' He sighed. 'It will be paradise, my dear.'

'For me, as well.' For a moment, she imagined the quiet evenings and the freedom of unlocked doors. Then an image of Stewart playing on the hearth rug in the sitting room flitted across her mind. There had to be some way to persuade her husband to relent on his plans to send the boy away. But that discussion could wait until bedtime, when he was in the most receptive mood possible.

Gerry sighed, contented. 'I am well pleased that today went as it did. I settled your brother with a minimum of bloodshed. Your father and I have come to an understanding without the need for firearms.'

'And the guests have all run back to London,' she said with a smile.

'All but Greywall,' he reminded her.

'The earl?' For a moment, she had actually managed to forget him. Then the memory of the previous day rushed back. With it came the beginnings of a headache.

'He was bothering you yesterday,' Gerry said, matter-of-fact. 'And the boy,' he added.

'He suspects,' she said. It was a massive understatement of the situation. But it was all the explanation she meant to give. 'Thank you for acknowledging Stewart.'

'I'd have said anything to put the fellow off you,' Gerry said hurriedly, as if he wished to crush any hope she might have that he was softening. 'And what goes on in this house is no business of his, no matter how often he tries to make it so.'

Her chest tightened, imagining what he might have said. 'Has he been making trouble?'

Gerry nodded. 'Since long before you arrived here. He was lurking about the property even before Father died, hoping that our diminished fortunes would be a reason to sell. When Father refused, he tried to hunt our land without permission and had to be escorted to the property line like a common poacher.' Gerry shook his head. 'The man is repellent. I will take great pleasure from sending him away again as soon as I am able.'

*Not now.* At this prolonged talk of Greywall, she could feel the beginning of another attack. This time she fought against it, focusing on the memory of her husband's hands on her face and body and his own steady breathing. When she was sure she was calm enough to speak, she said, 'I do not think it is wise to antagonise him. He may be an old drunkard, but he is still a very powerful man.'

'Do not worry. I will handle the matter as discreetly as possible.' But as he said it, he smirked, as if the prospect of doing just the opposite were actually the plan.

An altercation between the two of them would be a disaster. It was not just a matter of the secrets that would be revealed, it was Gerry's likely response to them. They were so close to having the peaceful future that they wanted. She did not want to dredge up the past again and she certainly could not stand another duel.

'Let me,' she said suddenly.

'Let you what?' he asked, surprised.

'I would like to be the one to send the earl away.' He looked doubtful, so she said, 'You have promised me often enough that I can have anything I want. After seven years of his company, I would like to tell him what I think of him and send him home.'

'Won't the conflict with a guest be upsetting to you?' he said, frowning. 'I will not be responsible for causing a megrim by letting you deal with something that should be my responsibility.'

She forced a laugh, even as she felt the growing cluster of pain behind her eyes. 'Do not worry yourself that the man who could not even watch the morning's duel without fainting will cause an upset in me. He is old and harmless and I am quite capable of sending him packing.' As long as her son stayed in the nursery, well out of the way.

Gerry was still staring at her, as if he could not quite understand what he was hearing. But at last he said, 'Very well. If that is what you want, I see no real harm in sharing the fun of turfing out the guests. But if he gives you any trouble...'

'I will get you immediately,' she said, forcing a smile and kissing him on the cheek.

They parted when they arrived at the house. Lily went to her bedroom, Gerry presumed. But he went immediately to the back of the house to find Mrs Fitz. He did not bother to ring, but went down the stairs to the kitchen dining room, where he found both her and Aston, taking their coffee before beginning their day.

They looked up at him in surprise and answered in unison, 'Captain?' before preparing to stand.

He held up a hand, indicating that they remain seated. 'Just a question and then you may return to your breakfasts. Does the household keep lists of the guests that have been here?'

Mrs Fitz nodded. 'It is easier to keep track of the preferences of repeat visitors if some record is kept.' She frowned. 'There have not been many of those. But still.'

'Very sensible of you.' He gave her an approving smile. 'And how far back might those lists go? All the way back to the time I left?' He raised an encouraging eyebrow.

'I should think so, sir.' The woman frowned. 'I would have to go through my old diaries. But they are in the still room.' She rose again, ready to get them.

He waved her back to her seat. 'The matter is not urgent.' It had waited seven years. Another day would not matter. 'Later, when you are not too busy, could you compile me a list, complete with the names of any servants?'

'Of course, Captain.'

He thought for a moment. 'And include the bedrooms they occupied.'

She looked flustered. 'Is some item missing? Because then you would be right to include the servants. I doubt that any of the guests...' She stopped, perhaps remembering the character of the people that the Norths entertained.

'No,' he insisted. 'Nothing missing.' Not exactly. 'I just wish to know the details of what has been going on in the house in my absence.'

One detail in particular.

Mrs Fitz nodded obediently. 'Of course, sir. I will see to it today and you shall have the completed list by breakfast tomorrow.'

'Very good.' By then, the rest of the guests would be packing and he would have as much time as he needed to ferret out the one thing on which his wife had been curiously reticent. If she had lied, he would find out the reason for it. There would be no punishment for it, of course. She had suffered enough.

There was but one who truly deserved to pay for the incident. And if that man still took breath, he would not be doing so for long.

# Chapter Eighteen

After returning from the duel, Lily spent more than her usual amount of time on her toilette before seeking out the earl. Perhaps if she waited long enough, something might occur that would make this meeting unnecessary.

Of course, she had been waiting and hoping for years already. So far, no miracle had come to dislodge the man from her house. If she waited any longer, Gerry would handle it himself, just as he had the rest of the guests. It was a potential disaster that could not be allowed.

Her maid had chosen a white-muslin day gown with a faint red stripe. After considering for a moment, Lily chose a red spencer that closed with a row of gold frogs. She had bought it specifically because it reminded her of her husband's uniform. She smiled at her reflection in the cheval glass. If one was to meet the enemy on the battlefield, then it did not hurt to be smartly attired. Though it seemed excessive for daytime, she let the maid decorate her dressed hair with a single coq feather that reminded her of the plume on a helmet. Then she left her room and went to the main floor to seek out her nemesis.

The house already had the too-quiet, empty feel that it got when the guests were gone. Without half a dozen noisy idiots in residence to distract her, the sound of her slippers echoing on the parquetry was unnerving. But the sort of person who was frightened of the sound of her own footsteps would never survive her talk with Greywall.

She stopped dead in the hall, listening to the sound of her own breathing to be sure it was steady and slow. Then she changed her pace, skipping like a child for a few steps and enjoying the syncopated reverberations it created. She was Lillian Wiscombe, wife of the hero of Salamanca. This was her house. She could walk, skip or even run through the halls if she wished to. And she did not have to put up with unwanted guests.

She found the earl in the trophy room, staring up at the mounted head of a stag as if he coveted it. When he looked down at her, his face held the same expression.

'Lord Greywall,' she said.

'Lillian,' he said with a wolfish smile.

'I did not give you permission to use my name,' she said, trying to ignore the nervous hitch in her pulse when she looked at him.

'Surely, after all these years, there is no reason for us to be formal.'

'On the contrary,' she said. 'I thought I've made it clear that I have no desire to talk to you at all, much less to be informal.'

He smiled sadly. 'That is a shame. Now that the house is nearly empty, I hoped there would be reason to know you better.' It would be impossible to call the look he was giving her anything but a leer.

'I already know you better than I care to,' she said. 'And the house will be even emptier soon. My husband wants you to leave.'

'He has not said so,' the earl said, feigning innocence.

'Because I requested that he allow me to speak to you. I wish you gone, as well.'

He clutched at his heart as though her words wounded him. 'You would send me away after all we have meant to each other?'

'You mean nothing to me,' she said, feeling her throat tightening again. She swallowed and waited for it to relax.

'But you are one of my fondest memories,' he said. 'The night we spent together, during that first house party…'

The air seemed to rush out of the room and her head filled with the buzzing that preceded the worst of her megrims. 'You remember.'

'Of course. Have I ever said that I'd forgotten it?'

He had not. He had not mentioned it until those hints the other day. But then, in all these years, she'd taken great care to never be alone with him. 'I thought, perhaps, you were so inebriated that you did not realise what you had done. But if you remember it so well, the least you could do is apologise for it.'

'What about that night do I have to be sorry for?'

he said, seeming honestly surprised. 'It was a pleasant interlude. I am surprised that we did not repeat it. Your husband was away for a long time. You must have been very lonely.'

'A pleasant interlude?' For the first time when facing him, her anger banished the fear. 'Perhaps you enjoyed it. But I remember being assaulted by a stinking drunk.' She was not shouting, but it felt as if she were. Her voice had no trace of the ridiculous breathiness it got when she was forced to speak to him. And her head was almost clear.

'If it was so awful, then why didn't you complain to someone?' He gave her an annoyingly triumphant smile.

'You should consider yourself fortunate that I haven't,' she said. 'It would not have gone well for you if I'd come forward with the truth.'

'Gone well for me?' At this, the earl laughed. 'My dear lady, when one reaches a certain rank it is exceptionally difficult for things to go any way but well. You would accuse me, I would call you a lying whore and that would be that.'

It was exactly the threat she had expected seven years ago, when she had decided to stay silent.

'It will be even worse if you intend to defame me now,' he said.

'In what way?'

'Now that the good captain has exposed your father and brother for the cheats they are, they cannot afford to have me go to the law.'

'Is that what you think?' she said, taking measured breaths as she waited for him to finish.

'If you accuse me, I will tell everyone that you are from a family of criminals and that you were nothing more than a part of the entertainment.'

'An entertainer.' His threats were foul. But they were nothing but words. *Inhale. Exhale. Inhale.*

'I paid well for the use of you, my dear. Your family has done irreparable damage to my fortunes over the years. It will take more than one night to equal the money they took.'

'What is between my father, my brother and you is none of my affair,' she said. 'My husband and I want no part of it.'

'And what about the boy?'

'What of him?' Her bravery was a sham. She could feel the blood rushing from her head, as her vision narrowed to a tunnel.

'He is mine, of course.'

'He is *mine*,' she said, and felt her strength returning. Stewart was hers and she would fight for him. 'He is mine. And the captain's,' she added. 'He told you so.'

'He might not know the truth, my dear. But we do.'

She ignored the tremor of unease that went through her, taking care to keep her voice calm. 'I was not sure what you knew. You have said nothing about that, either.'

'I had no desire to. It is not as if I wanted to acknowledge him. I was quite happy with things as they were.'

'I suppose you were,' she agreed. Perhaps if he had

been a less repellent specimen, she might have demanded he pay to educate the child he had fathered, instead of hiding the boy from him.

'But if you have suddenly decided to put me out, you are forcing my hand. I suggest you take a more cooperative attitude in regard to my stay here and my attentions to you. If you do not, I will go to the law and tell my tale. Your father and brother will go to gaol, where they belong. And then I will go to Wiscombe and tell him the truth about his son.' He was sneering at her as if he expected immediate capitulation.

Something inside of her snapped. The last of the headache was gone, burst like a bubble, leaving a dangerous clarity behind. 'Those are your plans, are they?'

He gave a nod.

'Then let me answer your threats. Do what you will to my father and brother. If they do not have the skill to evade the law, they are no longer worthy of the North name. And as for Stewart? I made Gerald aware of the issues with his parentage the day of his return.'

'You told him?' By the shocked look on his face, the earl had obviously not expected this response. 'Why?'

She smiled. 'Because I tell my husband everything. Almost everything, that is. I told him that my attacker was dead because I feared what might happen if he learned that you still resided under his roof.' Her smile widened. 'He threatened violence. But there are only so many duels he can fight in a single week. Though he did handle the one this morning with no real effort. I had not expected there would be so much blood...'

The earl went pale. Although he did not mind the

blood of animals, humans were another matter entirely. He rallied. 'He would not dare touch me. I am a peer.'

'He is very protective of me,' she said. 'And Stewart, as well.' That was nothing more than wishful thinking, but she said it anyway before returning to the truth. 'Just this morning, he was telling me of his exploits in the war. Did you know he is capable of killing a man with his hands?'

'But that was a Frenchman,' the earl said, his voice quavering.

'He shot my brother over a card game,' she explained. 'And he was barely annoyed about that. Can you imagine what he might be like if his anger was aroused?'

'Ronald North deserved worse than he got,' Greywall insisted.

'Just as you do. I begged him to be merciful to my brother, but I have no such soft feelings for you. One word from me and there will be no safe place in England for you.'

'He would hang for attacking an earl,' Greywall said.

'If he got caught, he would,' she agreed. 'But if you threaten me or my son, I doubt he would care. I suspect he would act first and face the consequences after. That is why I kept your secret. I do not want to see my husband risk arrest for avenging my attack. But if he finds out what you did, I doubt I would be able to stop him.'

'You would not dare tell him,' he said. But he didn't sound as sure as he had.

'And neither should you. You have nothing to hold

over me, my lord. If you tell your secret, he will end you.' Her smile turned into a grin. 'Do not think you can leverage me into becoming your mistress or make me abide your odious presence for one day longer. My husband will be putting you out of the house tomorrow and I have no intention of coming within ten yards of you ever again. If you do not like it, go ahead. Do your worst. It will not matter which of us reveals the truth, you will be the one to face the consequences.'

## Chapter Nineteen

The breakfast table was almost empty. Gerry smiled into his coffee, imagining how much better it would be when the last three guests were gone. As soon as they were, he would insist that Mrs Wiscombe move down the table to sit at his side instead of languishing at the far end. With her little red coat and a feather tucked behind one ear, she made such a fetching little soldier that when she joined them, he'd offered her a salute.

She'd responded with a cool smile of her own and a slight nod to tell him that her mission had been successfully accomplished.

There was a rattle of cutlery and a low curse as Ronald North struggled to cut his kipper with his left hand. Even with an improved bandaging and a few stiff drinks before breakfast, he was obviously in a great deal of pain.

Gerry ignored the grumbling and smiled left and right to the North gentlemen on either side of him. 'Well, my friends, now that the party is ending, have you given any thought to your future plans?'

'I plan to find some food that I can actually eat,' Ronald said, throwing his knife aside.

'It is fortunate that drinking only takes a single hand,' Gerry said, still smiling. 'You can do that anywhere. But your other favourite activities will be lacking here, now that we have no plans to entertain. Amongst the family, there is little point in playing cards for anything dearer than buttons. I am declaring a moratorium on billiards until I can procure a new table. And there will be no more hunting.'

'No hunting?' The elder North looked shocked at the idea. 'But Wiscombe Chase is a hunting lodge.'

'Perhaps the next generation will wish to take up a weapon and stalk game, but I have no interest in it,' Gerry replied.

'Does Stewart like to hunt, Lillian?' Ronald pushed his plate aside and stared down the table at his sister.

Confronted with the last hurdle to their happiness, his wife flushed as scarlet as her coat and did not answer. But neither did she appear to be suffering from shortness of breath or headache that such an attack would have caused only a few days before.

No matter what Ronald was up to, Gerry refused to be drawn into a discussion at the breakfast table that might upset her newfound equilibrium. 'That matter can be established at a later time.'

She shot him a smile and a look of such hope that he prayed she had not misinterpreted the statement as anything other than an effort to silence her brother. It was immaterial to him whether Stewart hunted or not.

Whichever choice he made, it would not be exercised on Wiscombe lands.

'But no hunting,' North said, still amazed. 'Surely an exception will be made for your neighbour, the earl.'

What the devil was North attempting now? There was no way that the earl would be allowed to return once he'd been evicted from the house.

'Yes, indeed, Captain,' the earl said. 'Your wife has explained to me your desire for privacy. Though you wish the house to yourself, you cannot mean to close the grounds to me, as well. I have been hunting them so long, I feel as if they are my own.' There was no humility in the smile that accompanied this outrageous request. Only the annoying assumption that, since his ancestors had been given a title, he should be allowed to be where he was not welcome.

As she usually was at the table, Lily remained silent. But her eyes smouldered with irritation at the suggestion that the earl might still be wandering the land.

Gerry offered him a sympathetic shrug. 'Alas, my lord, I mean to stand firm on this. No hunting. None by anyone.'

'Well, we are not gone yet,' North said with a smile. 'We will pack tonight and be gone tomorrow. But there is still time to hunt today.'

The earl brightened. 'One last hunt, Wiscombe. And then I will leave you. Now that the cits are not here scaring the game with their common behaviour, I might finally get a shot at that champion stag of yours.'

'I am sure that the London accents were the only

things standing between you and old Rex,' Gerry said, not bothering with an idiot's grin to put the man at ease.

North ignored his sarcasm. 'An intimate hunt. It is such a wonderful idea that I am amazed we have not done it before. I will accompany you, Lord Greywall.' Now North was the one grinning. As usual, his was harmless, affable and extremely persuasive. 'It is ages since I have been out in the fresh air.'

'You are so rarely out in the woods—you have no idea what trails the stag might use,' Ronald said, irritably.

'Then we shall take Wiscombe with us,' North said, with one of his most convincing smiles. 'He will be an even better guide than you because it is his land. He must know it better than any man in England.' His smile dimmed. 'At least, I should hope so.' He gave Gerry a doubtful look. 'But if it has been too long, or if you and your horse are not in fit condition for a few jumps...'

Was the man actually challenging him to prove his worth as horseman? Gerry was pushing back from the table automatically before his brain reminded him that, with his father-in-law, nothing was so clear-cut that it could be understood on first hearing. Had Ronald's comment really been a sign of his contrary nature, of a part of some carefully prepared script?

'I suppose I could accompany you,' Gerry said, slowly, looking from one face to the next, trying to find the trap.

'I thought you said you did not enjoy hunting.' Greywall was equally suspicious.

Gerry shrugged. 'Not usually. But Ronald is in no condition to go, with only one hand to hold the gun.'

At this, Ronald glared up the table at him like the petulant child he was.

'And Lord Greywall should not be forced to take to the woods alone if he is truly interested in sport,' North said. 'He would not be able to drag such a huge stag alone.'

'Surely a footman or two could be spared,' Gerry said, looking at him even more suspiciously. Perhaps after seeing what had happened to his son, North wished to get him into the woods and put a bullet in his back, on purpose, by mistake.

If so, he would be disappointed. Once they were clear of the house, and of Lily, North and Greywall could attack. He would defend himself to the death, if necessary. At least the matter would be settled today. He refused to spend his life looking over his shoulder, waiting to be shot.

'Footmen were good enough for those London commoners. But surely, since it is Lord Greywall, you should be our guide,' North insisted.

'Oh, ho. I had forgotten that this was for the benefit of Lord Greywall,' Gerry said, unable to contain his sarcasm. 'Of course, you are right. A peer cannot be sent out in the company of servants.'

'If you do not wish to take me today, perhaps another time…' The earl was deliberately forgetting that there would be no more visits.

'Since this will be your last hunt here, I wish you all the luck you deserve.'

Lily had spoken. It was such an odd occurrence at the table that all the men looked up in surprise.

'As my husband said, we are having no more hunting parties.' Her eyes were as wide and innocent as a true North. But there was no accompanying smile. 'I am sorry, my lord. Despite your desire to return as a valued neighbour, you will not be roaming our land like a stray dog. Once you leave Wiscombe Chase tomorrow, you will not be coming back. And today, my husband will accompany you to make sure you know the boundaries of the property so there will be no accidental incursion.'

'But what if I cannot manage to take the stag?' The earl was still trying to gain a reprieve.

'You have been trying for years,' Lily reminded him. 'I think it is time to admit that the poor animal has beaten you.'

'I will never admit that,' the earl said, glaring at her so venomously that Gerry felt the hairs on his neck rising in protective anger.

'Then I am sorry you cannot accept the fact that there are some things on this property that you just… can't…have.' The expression on her face as she stared back at him was totally unfamiliar. Gerry had never seen her approach conflict with anything more than panic and pain. But this morning she was clear-headed and angry. The look in her eyes said, no matter what others in the room might say, she would not be moved.

'We will discuss it when I return,' the earl said. 'Perhaps a payment…'

'There will be no discussion. The discussion is over.

I am decided. No amount of money will change my mind.'

Was it his influence that had changed her so? He'd have liked to have taken the credit, but he doubted it. Perhaps he had sparked something in her. But whatever burned now was too bright to be attributed to his doing. He offered an encouraging smile and another subservient salute, but she did not even look in his direction. It left him feeling as if he'd caught something far beyond his power to hold.

This new strength was all her. And it was magnificent. She was holding the earl's gaze with no sign of submission. In the end, he was the one to look away. 'Captain Wiscombe, can you not control your wife?'

'Apparently not, my lord,' Gerry answered.

'Then I will have to take the stag today.' He pointed to North and Gerry. 'The two of you will help me. Tonight the haunch will be served at dinner, and the head and horns will go back with me to Greywall tomorrow.'

*If that is what will get you to leave*, thought Gerry. They would be chasing after the impossible. Rex, as he always had, would slip away into the moors, hiding where no man could follow. Orion himself could not trap the beast. Then he smiled and said aloud, 'Of course. I have been tracking old Rex since I was a boy and know all his favourite places. Unless he has changed his direction, I will lead you right to him.' But Greywall be damned, he would make sure that it was done from the windward side so Rex caught their scent and left nothing but tracks in the mud.

'The sooner we start the better.' The earl pushed his

plate aside and rose from the table. 'Have the servants load the weapons and we will go.' Then he was gone to check his guns and saddle his horse.

Gerry lingered at the table a moment longer, since his wife remained at her place, smiling and sipping her chocolate. She looked up at him, her huge dark eyes shaded by long lashes. 'Do you wish a kiss for luck in today's hunt?' The words were weighted with strange and dangerous emotions, and he was thankful that none of them seemed to be directed at him.

'If you wish to give me one,' he said, cautiously.

She stood and put her arms around him, delivering a kiss that left him dazed. Several days had given his sweet and innocent wife a surprising amount of skill. Then she released him, staring up with a strange half-smile. 'Good luck to you, my captain. Share none of it with the earl. And if you care for me at all, do not let him shoot that stag.'

'I had no idea that you cared about the poor beast,' he said, in surprise.

'My only wish it that Greywall returns to his home empty handed and unsatisfied. Do that for me and I will be the most grateful of wives.' She batted her lashes again.

'Very well, my lady.' He smiled back at her.

## Chapter Twenty

'I have never gone so far from the house, when hunting with Ronald,' the earl said, glancing around him at the thinning trees. Gerry had led their little party nearly three miles already, until they approached the tor that marked the little strip of moor at the back of the property.

'That might explain your lack of success,' Gerry said, urging Satan up a narrow path through the rocks. 'If Rex has been hiding from you, this is the place he would choose.' He offered up a silent apology to the beast for sharing that knowledge at all.

Though he had no intention of disappointing Lily, the challenge of hunting without finding anything was more difficult than he'd thought. Especially since Rex seemed as interested in stalking them as the earl was in shooting him.

The stag was keeping pace with them, walking silently at their flank and awarding Gerry an occasional glimpse of hoof or tail before disappearing into the trees again. Gerry pretended to ignore him and made no move to alert the other hunters. Eventually, Rex would bore with the game and go back to his home on the moor. Since Greywall was either too drunk or too foolish to notice what was not directly in front of him, he would likely never realise how close he came to success.

'I told you that the presence of the captain would make a difference,' North called from the rear. 'Magnificent country,' he added, directing this to Gerry.

Gerry grunted in return. As far as he could tell, it was magnificently useless. Beautiful, of course. But not the sort of place they wanted to be caught in after dark. Without a clear view of the terrain and a stout stick to test the ground, the risk of ending up knee deep in a bog far outweighed the pleasure of a moonlit walk.

'Is this still your property?' They were as far away from the Greywall lands as it was possible to be. It was plain that, without a guide, the earl might never find his way home.

And what a tempting idea that was. But not necessary. One more day and the man would be gone for good, even if Gerry had to pack the bags and carry them himself. 'Do you doubt my knowledge of the property lines?'

At this, the earl laughed and Gerry could hear the rattling and sloshing of the flask as the man took a drink. 'You sound very like your father. He had an obsession with borders and boundaries, as I remember.'

It was not a reminder he welcomed. Today, his father was already uncomfortably close. Gerry had had no desire to soil his new hacking jacket, so he'd had

Mrs Fitz hunt up some leather breeches and an old poacher's coat. Both still stank of the old man's to-bacco. 'You should be grateful that I know the land as well as he did.' He reined in his horse and held a hand up to call for silence. Then he pointed towards the last stand of trees before the moor. There was a flash of russet, just out of rifle range before Rex disappeared deeper into the wood.

'I'll be damned,' said the earl, fumbling for his gun.

'Quite possibly,' North agreed. 'But you might have your stag before then.'

The voice behind him raised the hairs on the back of Gerry's neck. If North was an enemy, he had made the worst mistake of his life by allowing the man to follow him. Best to change the order of things. Gerry dismounted. 'From here, we go on foot. Keep your gun at the ready, Greywall. I will circle and try to flush him towards you.'

He made a wide circuit of the trees, going halfway up into the granite boulders before stopping to check the wind. From here, the breeze would carry his scent straight to the stag. That alone would be enough to urge a younger and less intelligent animal towards North and the earl. But Rex would know better. He had been both smart and lucky enough to outlast Gerry's father. It was hard to believe that, even with help, the earl could succeed in taking him.

Or perhaps Rex's reign had finally come to an end. Gerry had not even reached the back of the copse be-fore he heard the crack of a rifle and the triumphant shout of the earl. He turned and picked his way back to where he'd left his two companions.

'I hit him,' the earl exclaimed when he came into sight. 'And on the first shot. He is mine for sure.'

'An excellent shot,' North announced. 'The animal broke cover and, even uphill and into the sun, Greywall got him.'

Gerry glanced around him, relieved when he could not find so much as a drop of blood to indicate the bullet had found its target. 'Then where is the body?'

'It was not a clean death,' the earl said. 'But a killing shot, certainly. Let us run him down.' He turned to get back on his horse.

'Which direction did he turn?'

The earl pointed towards the moor.

Gerry held up a hand to stay him. 'The ground on the moor is too unstable to take the horses. One will turn an ankle for certain and we will be walking back.'

'Then we must track the deer on foot,' the earl announced, dismounting unsteadily and heading towards the bog.

The last thing Gerry wanted was to lead a drunkard on a jaunt across unstable ground. 'It is dangerous to stray too far from the forest, if you do not know the territory,' he said.

'There is nothing to fear,' the earl announced. 'We will only go as far as the body of the stag.

'He got off a good shot,' North agreed, then added to the earl, 'The poor fellow will be bleeding. He will not make it far and will leave a clear trail for you to follow.'

'All the same, it is better to be prepared.' Gerry

turned back to his saddle to get his stick, a knife and a stout length of rope. They would be necessary in the event that he needed to drag the animal back. But more likely, the slight delay in equipping himself would give the quarry a fighting chance to run for his life.

'You are taking too long,' the earl opined. 'We must get to him while there is still light.'

'If the shot was as good as you say, we do not need to rush.'

'You selfish bastard. My last hunt and you expect me to be frightened of a bit of wet grass. I will go ahead. Follow when you are ready.'

'That is most unwise, my lord.' There were a hundred things he might have said about the differing weight of man and deer, and the superior knowledge that even a frightened animal had of the dangerous terrain of the moor. The whole area was full of feather-beds and shifters. Patches of moss or gorse that looked solid might drag an unsuspecting hunter to a watery death. But he barely had time for the brief phrase he'd shouted at Greywall's retreating back. The earl was so eager for his stag that he was already up the tor and disappearing over it.

'Be careful,' North called cheerfully, getting down off his horse. 'I am certain the earl will take care,' North said, to reassure him.

'He is just as likely to get himself killed,' Gerry replied, cursing quietly as he dug in his saddle bag.

'We all must go some time.' The words were accompanied by the chick of a cocked pistol. 'May I see your empty hands, Captain Wiscombe?'

Gerry cursed himself for being distracted and for not bringing the pistol that would have been in this very bag had he been in Portugal and not his own back garden. He turned to display his empty hands to his father-in-law.

'Very good.' North was as cheerful as ever. He gestured with the gun. 'Could you step away from your rifle as well? Take a seat on that rock.'

'Do you mean to shoot me sitting down?' Gerry asked. 'It would be just as easy to do it standing.'

'Shoot you?' for a moment, North seemed puzzled. 'I merely wish a few moments of uninterrupted conversation.'

'You can get that just as easily without pointing a pistol at me,' Gerry suggested, then walked slowly towards the indicated seat. In his mind, he calculated the steps to his gun and the cover of the woods. He did not want to shoot both of his wife's family in the same day. But neither did he want to die with a ball in him, when success was so close.

From the moor, there was an echoing cry for help.

Without thinking, Gerry turned and took a step in the direction of the tor.

'Stop!'

He froze again, remembering the gun. 'The earl is hurt. We must go to him. You have my word that we will settle what is between us once he is safely off the moor.'

'Sit down, Wiscombe. There is nothing between us that needs settling,' North said, still smiling. 'The only problem I have with you is your predictable desire for heroic action.'

'Some of the bogs are deep,' Gerry reminded him. 'This is not one of your little games that hurts no one. He may be drowning.' When North made no move to put away the pistol, he added, 'We must help him before it is too late.'

To add weight to his logic, there was another call for help, followed by a man's scream of terror.

Instead of being moved to action, North leaned against the nearest tree. 'If we are lucky, it is too late already.'

'Damn it, man. Let me go to him.' He did not like the earl, but neither did he want to drag the man's body back from what should have been his final hunt.

'A little while longer, I think,' North said. 'I feared we would have to wait through the night to do this properly. But things are progressing nicely.'

'I should never have let him go ahead.'

'And he should never have raped my daughter,' North said, with no change in his demeanour.

'He...' Now that the truth was before him, it made perfect sense. Lily's silence at dinner and the headaches after the meal. She'd been trying to be a perfect hostess while sharing a table with her attacker. 'She said he was dead.'

'She lied,' North said. 'I suspect she was worried about what would happen if you learned the truth. One cannot just shoot a peer, Captain Wiscombe.'

But he would have done it. He would not have been able to help himself. 'She should not be the one trying to protect me,' Gerry said, his guilt returning.

'But she is trying, all the same. She does not want to risk losing you,' North said. 'She loves you.'

'She loves the hero of Salamanca,' Gerry corrected.

'She deserves a hero,' her father agreed. 'She's seen damn few of them in her life. The North men have been chronic disappointments. As her father...' He shook his head. 'If I'd only known, the matter would have been settled long before you got here. But I swear to God, I thought the child was yours. And that our estrangement...' And now, his voice broke. 'I gave the earl the master bedroom. I thought to flatter him. All this time she has been thinking I was a pandering villain and not just a trusting fool.'

'I told her that it could not have been intentional,' Gerry said.

North nodded. 'I am nowhere near the perfect father, but I would never allow anyone to hurt her. Since that has already happened, something needed to be done.'

'And the gun?' Gerry pointed at the pistol the man still held.

'There was going to be a hunting accident of some sort,' North said. 'But a habitual inebriate drowning in a bog will be much easier to explain at an inquest than a bullet in the back. If need be, you can swear that you were held at gunpoint and prevented from aiding the man until it was too late. In the eyes of the law, you are an innocent victim.'

'And the earl?' There had been no sound from the moors since that last unearthly scream.

'He got what he deserved,' North said, putting the gun aside. 'Time will tell if the Lord blesses you with a daughter, Wiscombe. If he does, you will find there are no limits to what you would do to keep her safe. And if you fail?' He shook his head. 'For your sake, I hope you do not.'

'But we cannot just let him drown,' Gerry said, knowing that they most certainly could. Hadn't he just told his wife that a convenient hunting accident would be easy to arrange?

'You've already made an effort to keep him from harm.' North's smile had returned. 'I distinctly heard you tell him that it was dangerous. Yet he went on ahead because he wanted that damned deer.'

That was true enough.

'It is a shame I could not be there to watch him suffer,' North said, with a sigh. 'But as my daughter pointed out at breakfast, we cannot always have what we want. I think it has been long enough now. Let us go and see what we can find of him.'

Gerry put the supplies he'd collected back in the saddle bag and led the way, walking a skittish Satan over the tor and out on to the moor itself. There they found the blood trail from the stag, just as the earl had expected. But the red drops were sparse and the tracks gave no indication that the stag was weak on his feet. The even hoofprints were mirrored by the boot prints of a man.

They followed the marks barely a quarter mile before they discovered the earl. The clear trail ended suddenly, devolving into a muddy mess of hoofmarks and the claw-like troughs of a man's hands searching for purchase. Gerry tapped at the ground in front of him and found the place where it gave way to bog, watching the carpet of moss that covered the muck sway and ripple as he poked at it.

Then he took out his rope and tied one end of it to the saddle before slowly lowering himself into the hidden water. A few minutes searching beneath the surface and he was able to grasp a coat sleeve and tie the other end of the rope around the corpse. Then he climbed back on to the path and urged his horse back to drag the earl to the surface.

They stared down at the dead man.

'As I told you before, people who I invite here deserve what they get,' North said.

The late Earl of Greywall stared up at the sky with a blank look of surprise, his forehead marked by the bloody print of a single cloven hoof.

## Chapter Twenty-One

It was taking too long.

Lily had never been interested in the hunts that were held almost daily at her home. But she could not help but be aware of the pattern they followed. Even the longest of them was over before dusk. It gave the participants time to wash, or more often to drink before dinner.

But tonight, the sun was almost fully set before she heard the sound of the men returning. She'd been waiting in the sitting room for some word of their progress and rushed towards the hall in time to hear the unusual request that a footman locate my lord's valet immediately.

'There has been an accident.'

The words sent a chill through her. It was some comfort that her husband had been the one speaking.

And now her father said, 'He would not listen to reason. He was following that damn stag and he would not stop, even when the animal ran on to the moor.'

From the third member of the party, she heard nothing. If he were really hurt, she'd have expected swearing or complaints, or at least a demand for strong drink. The total silence was ominous.

She pushed her way through the knot of servants gathering in the doorway to see a body wrapped in oilcloth slung over the saddle of the earl's horse.

A hunting accident.

But Gerry did not know. He would have had no reason to take action against the earl.

At the moment, she could not enquire even if she wanted to. Gerry was in a quiet conversation with the white-faced valet, who was then stuffed into a coach to make the short ride to Greywall to get others who would come back to take the earl home. Until they arrived, Wiscombe servants were gathering to find a properly respectful place for the body of a peer.

Lily turned to Mrs Fitz to request a cold supper be laid for family and any servants of the earl that might be coming, and tried to decide if her current calm was an accurate reflection of her mood, or merely the shock that accompanied sudden death. In either case, it was more ladylike than joy.

She started forward, trying to get a better look at the body.

'Lillian.' Her father took her arm to lead her away.

'I need to know,' she whispered.

'He is dead. There is no question of that. Come away.' She tried to pretend that she had not seen the nod that passed between him and her husband that seemed to confirm her fears. 'Let us go back to the sitting room. There is nothing that can be done for him.'

She shut the sitting-room doors behind him, her calm disappearing. 'That is not what matters to me. I need to know which of you shot him.'

Her father let one inappropriate laugh escape before he regained his own composure. 'What you mean to ask is, *What happened?*'

'Tell me,' she said, clutching his hand. 'Tell me that Gerald did not do something foolish on my account. Because I could not bear it.'

'The earl tracked a wounded stag on to the moors. We were not there to see his death. It appears the beast attacked him, either before or after he fell into a bog. The combination of the attack and the water...' Her father shook his head.

It really had been an accident. She sat, rather too quickly, on the sofa. But since the sudden bout of weakness was not followed by fainting, headaches or shortness of breath, it was likely a perfectly normal reaction.

'And what of the deer?'

'The deer?'

'Rex,' she said. 'The stag. I assume that was the animal he was chasing. What became of him?'

'A small wound. He's survived worse. Greywall was convinced that he was dying, of course. But circumstances proved him wrong.'

It was a relief. 'And you and Gerald.'

'Wet and tired. Nothing more.'

There was more to it than that, she was sure. It was all too perfectly convenient. Perhaps it would be best not to ask. But she could not help herself. 'When did you realise it was him?'

'When you told me, yesterday. There could be only one man you were speaking of.' He sat down beside her and took her hand. 'I did not know. If I had, there would have been a day like this one before Stewart was born.'

'It is better this way,' she said.

'But now that I have learned the truth? I hope the years of silence that have been between us is punishment enough.'

Even with the earl gone, there was still so much to forgive. 'Your little schemes were never easy for me,' she admitted. 'This problem with earl was simply the worst consequence of them.'

'I know, my dear.' He patted her hand.

'Are they finally over?'

'For you, at least,' he assured her. 'Ronald and I will be gone after supper. There are some markers that need to be cashed in before the rest of Greywall's creditors arrive.'

'And then, where will you go?'

He shrugged. 'I cannot tell. But we will not be returning here. We will send for our things when we are settled and tell you our direction.'

'You're leaving me?' For years, she had wished to be free of him and Ronald, and the life that they'd created for her. Now that it was here, she was not ready.

'I am sure, if you need me, I will not be difficult to find.' Then he smiled. 'But it may be easier for you if you do not look too hard.'

'You do not mean to change,' she said, sadly.

'Not in all things,' he said. 'I still believe that most people get what they deserve in life. But you did not deserve what happened to you and I am sorry for it. Now that your husband has come home to you, I will have no more worries about your happiness or safety. At least not as long as your brother and I keep our business clear of you.'

She leaned forward and kissed him on the cheek, still not sure how she felt. 'I think I will miss you,' she said.

'For that, I am glad.' He returned her kiss. 'And now, my dear, let us tend to the removal of the last thorn in your side. The earl is going home and will not return.'

## *Chapter Twenty-Two*

It had not even been a week since her husband's return, but it felt as if an eternity of time had passed. She had not thought that a day would ever come where coming to her husband's room at night would be as natural as going to her own bed.

It would take some time to get used to the fact that her father and brother were gone. And possibly even more to assure herself that the earl would not reappear and refuse to leave without his trophy. But as long as she could have Gerry here, her love for him would ease the sting of partings and fears of the past.

'At last, we have the house to ourselves.' Gerry was grinning at her again, grey eyes sparkling and displaying those slightly uneven teeth that made him look like a mischievous little boy. But the way he patted the mattress at his side had nothing to do with innocence.

She thought of the reason that the house was empty and shivered. 'I am not sure it is entirely appropriate to feel happy after what has happened.'

'You are not actually mourning Greywall, after what he did to you.'

'How do you know...?' After she had taken such care that he not learn the truth.

'Your father explained the situation, while Greywall was having his accident. The man might be slow to realise some things, but once he is aware of the problem, he is quick to solve it.'

'While he was having an accident?' she repeated.

'He did not want my heroic instincts to overcome common sense and lead me to rescue Greywall before justice had been done.'

'Then it was not an accident,' she said.

'It was more of an accident than many things that have happened to people who cross the Norths,' he said. 'I doubt even your silver-tongued father can persuade a stag to attack on cue. The man also fell into the bog of his own accord. If I was slow to help?' He shrugged. 'It was because your father pulled a pistol on me and explained the need for circumspection.'

'He drowned the earl,' she said.

'Certainly not. He gave Greywall an opportunity. It is not his fault that the man was foolish enough to act on it.'

'You sound very like a North,' she said, unsure whether she liked the sensation of *déjà vu* the comment engendered.

'That was why we decided it was for the best that your father and brother leave as soon as possible. I will allow one such accident on my property since the man was deserving. But I do not mean for it to become a habit.'

'You wanted peace,' she said.

'And now I have it.'

'And no more death.'

He shrugged. 'Some things cannot be helped. It was quite possible that he was gone before I could have reached him. The man was drunk after breakfast and made no effort to see to his own safety. And Rex did not grow to be as old as he is without having tricks of his own. They may look gentle, but deer can be dangerous when wounded.'

'And I did want the stag to survive,' she said. She much preferred Rex to the earl.

'Despite it all, your father is not the scoundrel that your brother is,' Gerry said, and then added, 'I am sorry that I had to shoot him.'

'No, you're not,' Lily corrected.

He laughed in the firelight. 'You're right. I'm not. But I am glad that I did not have to shoot your father as well. Nor any of the guests. Not even the one who deserved it most.'

'Let us not speak of him again,' she said, leaning close to kiss him.

'Never,' he agreed. 'But with the lot of them gone, our house is almost back to normal.'

'Almost,' she said, suddenly remembering what was still let to settle.

'I must find a school for your son, of course. The one my father sent me to is a good distance away. But it is certainly rigorous enough to prepare him for Cambridge. I will write tomorrow to see if any of my old schoolmasters remain and if they would consider taking a first-year student in the middle of a term.'

He was droning on about the distant future. Those details were not the least bit important right now. 'He is a bit young to start, is he not…?' she began carefully. 'He is not quite seven.'

'He will adjust,' Gerry said, frowning.

'But will I?' She marshalled her fears and took a steadying breath. 'We have never been apart. And once he has started school, I will not see him for months at a time.'

'More than months,' he reminded her, oblivious to her pain. 'He will be spending his holidays there. If the school cannot house him, perhaps there are some farms in the area that have room for a boarder.'

'Farms?' she said, her voice turning shrill. 'Next you will have him working for his keep like a common labourer.'

'Certainly not,' he said, surprised at her reaction. 'He will be raised as a gentleman. You will be able to write him any time you like to assure yourself of his progress,' he added, as an afterthought.

'He is barely able to read a letter at his age,' she snapped.

'The schoolmasters will read to him. And the other boys.'

'No!' The word came out as a shout that surprised them both. Her plan had been to coax and cajole. She'd meant to use her feminine wiles, to be biddable and agreeable as she always was. But despite how much had changed since his return, it was clear that his plans for Stewart had not changed at all.

'In a year or so, it might be easier for him,' she said in a calmer voice.

'Perhaps it might.' He gave her a stern look. 'But we will have to make do with the plan as it is.'

She rolled closer to him, so their thighs touched, placing her hands flat against his chest so she might feel the beat of his heart. 'I had hoped, now that you know more about the circumstances of his birth, that you might reconsider the severity of your future plans.'

'They are not severe,' he replied, covering her hands with his in an effort to calm her. 'They are sensible. If we are ever to put the incident behind us, we cannot have the boy running about the house, always in sight and underfoot.'

'The incident?' she said in what she hoped was a warning tone. She had been calm too long and it had availed her nothing.

'It is not healthy for you to brood upon it,' he answered, with surprising gentleness. 'I have seen how it upsets you when you are reminded of it.'

'I do not brood upon it,' she insisted. 'In fact, I managed quite well, despite seeing my attacker almost every day at meals.'

'You had occasional spells,' he reminded her. 'And nightly headaches.

'Sometimes the fear did get the better of me,' she said, annoyed that he was right.

'You will be even better now that Greywall is gone. And once we have sent the boy away...'

'Stewart,' she said. 'His name is Stewart.' It was one thing to want justice and quite another to think that the past could be erased if one did not look at it.

'Once Stewart has gone to school,' he corrected, 'it will be even easier.' He squeezed her hands again and slipped his arms around her, ready to pull her close and end the discussion with a kiss.

She took another breath and said firmly, 'It will not.' Then she pushed away from him and sat up.

He reached for her, as surprised by her rejection as by her words.

'The spells and headaches are all but gone, now that you are here,' she said. 'Knowing that you understand and forgive me, and having support, was all I really needed to heal.' He must see that she had changed. Everything was different now. Only her love for Stewart was unchanged. 'I was able to stand up to the earl myself this morning, with no trouble at all. He'd have left as planned, even without your and Father's arranged accident.'

'That is good to know,' he said, obviously surprised. 'But even if he'd left, he would not really be gone. His son would remain.'

'Stewart is not his son,' she said. 'He is mine. To his dying breath, the earl did not know him, or claim him.'

'Perhaps not,' Gerry admitted. 'But that does not change how he came to be in my house.' The inflection was subtle, meant to remind her that while the house belonged to him, the child never would.

'But nothing that happened here was Stewart's fault. It is not fair to punish him for what his father did.'

'I am not punishing him,' Gerry insisted.

'Then you are punishing me,' she said. That was what this would be, whether he knew it or not.

'I am not punishing you. I am trying to spare you pain.' If he thought that was true, it showed how little he knew her.

'But he does not cause me any pain. There are nothing but sweet memories when I think of him.' She touched his arm, to assure him that she was fine.

'That makes no sense,' Gerry said.

'You cannot understand,' she said 'You are not a mother. Even though I hated his father, Stewart is as much a part of me as my own heart. To take him away would be like ripping that organ out of my chest.'

'You are right,' he said. 'I do not understand, because it does not make sense. To have him here would be a continual reminder to me of what happened.'

'A continual reminder to you,' she said and felt her own anger rising again. 'That is what this is really about. Your fine words about sparing me pain are nothing more than that. The truth is this: your pride is wounded. You do not want to think that, even unwilling, I was ever with another man.'

'I do not blame you,' he said quickly. 'I blame myself.'

'Do you not see?' She shook her head. 'Blaming anyone other than the earl is quite pointless. My father did not plan for it to happen. I could not have stopped it and neither could you. We were both little more than children when it occurred . And Stewart is the most innocent of all.'

'That may be true,' Gerry allowed. 'But you ask too much of me if you expect me to take him into my home and treat him as my own son.'

'And you ask too much of me, if you want me to give him up,' she said. A rush of fear came with the words. But for the first time in for ever, there was no light-headedness, or blinding pain. The truth terrified her, but it was a relief to face it. 'I want to make you happy and be the loyal wife you want. But I cannot do that at Stewart's expense.'

'But you are my wife.' Faced with her sudden insurrection, Gerry did not sound so much angry as bewildered.

'And I promised to obey you in all things,' she agreed. 'I have discovered that I cannot keep my promise to you.'

Now he was the one acting as if the wind had been knocked from his sails. It took some time before he was able to answer at all. 'What are we to do?'

It was the first time he had asked for her opinion. It might have pleased her had she an answer that would bring them both happiness.

'I do not see an answer, other than separation. I will go and take Stewart with me. It will spare you from having to be reminded of what happened,' she said, trying to keep the bitterness from her voice.

'I will not give you money to maintain your own household, if that's what you are after,' he said, showing a trace of the anger she had seen on the day he'd arrived.

'You will not need to,' she said. 'I have enough saved

from the allowance you gave me that the two of us can live comfortably for quite some time.' If that failed, there was always her father. He was barely out of her life. Was it a sign of strength or weakness if she was to go back to him so soon?

'How very sensible of you to see to your own future,' he said in a dry tone. 'Now what am I to do with my mine, if I have a wife who refuses to live with me?'

'There might be a way to gain an annulment, even after all this time,' she said. 'If you can prove fraud.'

'There was nothing havey-cavey about it,' he said indignantly. 'The licence was legal and the banns were read.'

She sighed. 'My family specialises in making crooked things seem straight. How hard can it be to do the reverse? And a legal separation would net you nothing. It would not allow you to marry again.'

'Or you,' he reminded her.

'I have no intention of seeking another husband.' Even the thought of replacing Gerry made her heart ache.

He gave her a sardonic leer. 'Have I ruined you for all other men?'

'In a way,' she said. 'I love you. I expect I will continue to do so, even if we are apart. If I cannot be with you, then I will be happier alone.'

Apparently, she'd said a thing he could not joke his way out of, for he was silent again. Though it hurt that her declaration was not immediately followed by one from him, saying the words aloud had given her a freedom she'd never felt before. She loved him. He knew. If she had nothing else, she gained that.

But now, she must set him free. 'There is only one other alternative I can give you.'

'And what is that?' He was smiling as if he expected her to announce that she'd changed her mind and agreed with his initial plan, after all.

'If Stewart and I were to die, it would leave you free to marry and start again.'

'No.' The denial was quick and adamant.

'Not in truth. But it is far easier to arrange for two people to disappear permanently and appear dead than to navigate the courts to end a marriage.'

'You would have me live a lie, just so you could keep that child.' The bitterness in his voice as he said it proved to her that there would be no declaration of devotion forthcoming. His feelings for her were strong, but ultimately they were as selfish as her family's had been.

'When I give my heart, I do not ever take it back. It is true of my love for you,' she said, touching his cheek. 'But I love Stewart as well. Even if I could send him away, his existence will always be a barrier between us, whether you admit it or not.'

'Very well, then.' He rolled away from her. 'The sooner the better. You will leave in the morning and take the boy with you. Once you have found a place to settle, I will send your things on after you. And there will be no nonsense about faked deaths or rigged annulments. When you realise your mistake and come crawling back to me, we will settle things as I planned and that will be that.'

He stood for a moment, as if looking for a door to slam. And then he realised where they were and pointed at her. 'Remove yourself from my room, madam. You are no longer welcome here.'

'Yes, Captain,' she said and went back to her own room. The tears did not begin until she heard it lock behind her.

# Chapter Twenty-Three

Here was the last of the Wiscombes.

Gerry stared at the star-shot canopy of his bed and tried to accept the thing he had been trying to prevent. He'd got a wife and a fortune. He'd survived Waterloo to come home and father a child. He had spent a third of his life trying to stop the inevitable decay of house and name. And he had failed.

Now, Lily would take the child and go. Despite what he'd said about her seeing the error of her ways and returning to him, once she left his home he knew he would not get her back.

Eventually, he would give up on the past. There would be embarrassing legal ramblings as he tried to decide if it was even possible to dissolve this union. If the true parentage of the boy was revealed, it might be better off for him. Even the unacknowledged son of an earl might do quite well for himself, should Greywall's family be bullied into helping on the sly.

Lily would be utterly ruined by his efforts to be free. In the eyes of society, it would be better if she really died rather than feigning it. There would be no acceptance or forgiveness for her, even though nothing that had happened was her fault.

He would try to make it easy for her. Even if she did not wish or expect it, he would see that she lived comfortably and wanted for nothing. But if she left him, she would live and die alone. No honourable man would want a woman who had been cast off by her husband, even if it was at her own request. She was probably right that the best way to deal with things was a faked death and a new start for both of them.

Damn it all, he did not want another man to want her. She was his. She belonged at his side. When he'd left for the war, he'd been a foolish, infatuated child. When that had faded, he'd thought to hate her. But even as he tried, she'd haunted his dreams. If he'd lain with another, it was always while thinking of her. Would it hurt her, as she'd hurt him? Would her kisses be sweeter? Would her body be more lush? What would it be like when he finally returned home to her?

What was it like? It was like taking another sword in the side: red-hot burning agony. That wound had healed, but this one never would. He had found the perfect woman: loyal, loving, stalwart in adversity and beautiful inside and out. He'd held the other half of his own soul in his arms. After that, no other woman could ever satisfy him.

And now, just as he'd feared, she was leaving him for another man. What sweet irony it was that his rival was a waist-high toy soldier who hated horses. He was not wealthy or powerful. The circumstances of his birth did not matter. While she might claim to love Gerry with her whole heart, she would walk through fire for her son, sacrificing herself without a second thought.

He could not cast her off without destroying her. He could not replace her without destroying himself. Which meant there was no choice for him but do nothing at all to end the marriage and accept the fact that he was the last true Wiscombe.

Lily was standing over his bed, her hand clutching her key to the connecting door.

He felt a rush of foolish hope. She had reconsidered. She had found some solution he had not thought of that could satisfy her conscience and was returning to his bed. He held out his arms in welcome.

Then the hope faded. Her face ghostly pale in the moonlight. She was trembling. But not from cold, for she was fully dressed with a shawl about her shoulders.

He sat up, instantly alert. 'What is the matter?'

'Stewart,' she said in a tear-choked whisper. 'He is missing. Miss Fisher cannot find him anywhere. Nor can I. We searched the house from top to bottom. I looked in all his favourite hiding places.' Her trembling increased with the first shaking sobs.

'I am sure it is nothing,' he said. 'The boy is always wandering about. I have seen it myself.'

'In daylight, perhaps. But never at night.' She shook her head, trying to deny the obvious. 'He is outside. In the dark. You know the dangers of these woods. There are animals. Cliffs. Bogs.'

'He would not get as far as the moor without a

horse,' he said. But that was hardly a reassurance to a worried mother.

She held out her hands in supplication. 'I know that you hate him…'

'Not hate, precisely,' he said, stunned at the unworthiness of his feelings towards a harmless little boy.

She ignored his denial and continued. 'Please, Captain Wiscombe, I have no one else to turn to.'

He swung his legs out of bed and pulled on his breeches, shrugging a coat over his nightshirt and tucking in the tails. 'You were right to come to me.' He was her husband. Who else would she go to in a time of desperate need? That she turned to him as a last resort pricked at his conscience. Even worse, he had become Captain Wiscombe again. Not her husband, but some near-fictional hero no more real than a news clipping.

If the hero of Salamanca was who she needed, that was who she would have. 'Wake the servants and have them search the house again. He may have slipped by you as you looked. I will search the grounds and you will see that it is nothing.' That was just as likely to be a lie as truth. He had grown up in this house and could name any number of things that a small child might wander into at night that were either dangerous or deadly.

But it did no good to alarm the child's mother, or to brood on them himself. He gave her an overly confident smile. 'I expect I will be back in an hour or less, hauling the little fellow by the ear.'

'Thank you.' Lily launched herself at him, pressing her body to his. 'Thank you, so.'

She was clinging to him as if he were hope and salvation and instinctively his arms went around her, to protect her. He had failed her once by leaving her alone and at risk. He had failed her again when he could not overcome his foolish pride and see that he had asked too much of her. He would not fail her twice in one night. But her present need did not entitle him to hold her now.

Carefully, he set her aside. 'I will take care of everything. Wait for me here. I will be back in no time.'

She sat down on the edge of his bed, pressing herself back into the headboard and hugging his pillow to her.

He felt her arms still around him. It was as if no time had passed and they had just met. His body ached for her. His heart craved her approval. And he knew he would ride to the end of the earth, if necessary, to see her smile again. He left her there and wasted no time, taking the back stairs to the servants' quarters at a trot. Once there, he walked down the hall, rapping on doors as he went. As a line of heads poked into the hall, he issued terse instructions to Aston and the footmen for a systematic search of the house. Then he lit a lantern and proceeded out through the kitchen doors, towards the stables.

He doubted that the boy could have got far. But he could cover the ground faster on horseback. God forbid, if he should have to return with an injured child, speed might be of the essence.

Or perhaps he would not have to look far at all. As he approached his stallion's stall, Gerry could hear

Satan raging over something. The sharp cries of an angry horse tore the stillness of the night, punctuated by iron-shod hooves slamming at the back wall of a stall, as though the occupant meant to kick it down.

He quickened his pace, yanking the door wide open and holding his light high so that he might see. There, at the back of the dimly lit enclosure, was Stewart, huddled in the corner, arms over his face waiting for the inevitable.

Gerry hung the lantern on a nail in the wall and stepped forward, grabbing a bridle in one hand and swinging the crook of his other arm over the rising and falling neck. He pushed with his full weight into the shoulder, sending a steady string of curses into the pointed black ear. In response the animal backed away from the boy and ceased his plunging. When Gerry felt he was calm enough, he fastened the harness and looped the reins over a ring in the wall.

Then he turned his attention to the boy, grabbing him by the collar of his coat and lifting him bodily from the stall. 'What the devil was the meaning of that?' he shouted into the small white face before him.

He had used a tone that had terrified more than a few grown men. But the child dangling in front of him glared back and said, in a cold, clear voice, 'You cannot talk to me in that way. You are not my father.'

Gerry set him on his feet with a thump and reached for the lantern, holding it up to get a better look at the boy. He was dirty and trembling, but uninjured. But the look in his eyes was more than fear. Gerry had seen that mix of anger, betrayal and despair in the face of his enemies, just before the end. He had not let it stay his hand then and he showed no sympathy now. 'I will talk to you any way I choose, especially when you do something so foolish as to frighten your mother by running off in the middle of the night. Now what in blazes makes you think I am not your father?'

'Uncle Ronald told me, before he left. He said my father was a drunkard and a wastrel. He was a bad man and I would be a bad man, too.' The boy gave a sniff and his shoulders shuddered. But he did not cry. He was staring up at Gerry, as if waiting to be corrected. 'Uncle Ronald said Mama was ashamed to have me and that was why she lied. And that is why you hate me and want to send me away.'

It was not all true. But it was true enough that he could not just deny it. Even if he did, the child would never be free of the doubt. 'Why did you come here, instead of to me or your mother?'

'If Mama lied to me before,' he said, 'she would lie to me again. And you do not want me.'

'But why here?' Gerry repeated, more gently.

The boy's voice dropped to a whisper.

'Uncle Ronald said that no son of yours could be afraid of horses. And I am. So that would mean...' There was a long, dangerous pause. 'But maybe, if I could learn not to be afraid...'

'So you decided to lose your fear in the middle of the night, with a horse that has killed almost as many men as I have?' He shook his head in disbelief. 'Do you know what might have happened if I had not come along when I did?'

'He… He would have killed me.' The boy was whispering again. 'Because he knows I don't belong here.'

'He would have killed you because he has been trained to kick and bite at anything in front of him,' Gerry corrected. 'Satan is no ordinary horse. A dragoon's mount must be as ferocious as he is. Fearless of the carnage around him, the smell of blood and the beasts like himself dying on every side. He is ready to kick, bite and trample the enemy, if called to do so. He would have made short work of you, had I not come along.'

And thank God he had. If he had decided to search on foot, he'd have never found the boy. The next morning, the stable boys would have discovered the broken, bloody body at the feet of the stallion. That thought had him more frightened than he'd been since Waterloo.

'If he is just a mean horse, then it is not me.'

'It is not you,' Gerry agreed. 'And a love of horses is not something that appears magically in the blood. I did not always like them. When I was your age, I preferred to hide in the conservatory and pretend I was hunting tigers.' He thought for a moment. 'Of course, I do not like hunting either.' But he'd thought, perhaps if he tried hard enough, he could change.

'You hid in the conservatory? That is what I do. Does that mean I am yours after all?' Stewart was staring at him with such desperate hope that the lie was almost out of Gerry's mouth before he could stop it. Was this how it had been for poor Lily? When faced with an innocent child who had no share of blame in all that had happened, where was the virtue in honesty?

At last, he shook his head. 'Your father was a bad man. But so is your Uncle Ronald for telling you something your mother did not wish you to know.'

The first tears were streaking through the muck on the boy's cheeks. 'Who was he? And why didn't she tell me? How can I be someone else's, if she is married to you?'

What was he to say to this? The more questions he answered, the more there would be. He thought for a moment. 'It was something that happens sometimes, when a man is very bad and a woman is very beautiful. It happened because I was not here to stop it. It hurt your mother and frightened her badly. I suspect she didn't tell anyone, not even you, because she was still frightened, even after all this time.'

'She needn't be,' Stewart said, a little of his spirit returning. 'I was here to protect her.'

'You did a good job,' Gerry agreed. 'But now that will be my job.'

'And that's why you will send me to school,' Stewart finished for him. 'Because Mama does not need me, now that you are here.'

'Your mother still needs you,' he admitted. 'She told me so. But I think she might need me as well. Perhaps it would be better if we remain together, so that your mother can be safe and happy.' When one considered it, it was the only logical answer.

For the first time that evening, Stewart smiled. And then, the smile faded. 'But I am not your son.'

'Not by blood, perhaps.' The truth was forming in his head, even as he spoke. 'On the day we met, you told me that you like mathematics.'

The boy nodded, confused.

'You have not learned about them yet. But in mathematics, there is a thing called a proof. You can use a series of facts to prove another.'

The boy nodded again, trying to understand.

'If you are your mother's son, and I am your mother's husband, then I am your father. *Quod erat demonstrandum.*' His professors at Cambridge would have been appalled at the faulty logic. But the boy seemed satisfied with it. And much to his surprise, Gerry felt better than he had in days.

He stared down at the child again. 'Now that we have settled that, I trust that there will be no more trips to the stables to prove your worth under the hooves of my horse.'

The boy shook his head.

'And I suppose you are still afraid.' He didn't wait for an answer. The boy's fear was still obvious.

'To come here was not very sensible.' Then he grinned. 'But your mother will tell you that it was not very sensible for me to join the army. She thought I was going to die.'

'But you were a hero,' Stewart said, his eyes round.

'I was lucky. Just as you were tonight.'

'Wiscombes are lucky,' Stewart said.

'That they are,' Gerry agreed. 'Now stand out of the way.' He gestured the boy out into the aisle and led the horse out of the stall. Then he mounted the bare back.

When he looked down, the boy had plastered himself to the wall. He leaned over and held out an arm. 'Come here.'

Hesitantly, Stewart stepped forward into his reach and Gerry pulled him up to sit in front of him on the horse. 'You are perfectly safe, as long as I am here. Now let us go back to the house and set your mother's mind at rest.'

## Chapter Twenty-Four

Lily stood alone in the hall, her face pressed against the window glass. Gerald was naïve if he thought that she would wait in the comfort of his bed while her son was God knew where. The house was awake. Every candle had been lit. And the servants had found nothing, just as she'd known they would.

Stewart was out there, somewhere. It was dark. So very dark. How could he see to avoid the hazards? Boars. Bears. Packs of wild dogs. All the creatures that roamed the forest at night could see better in the dark than a boy, even if he had taken a lantern. They could run faster as well.

But there were other things just as bad. If he was not found, someone would have to check the cistern. And the well. 'God,' she murmured aloud. 'Do not let it be that.'

Then she saw a distant light approaching the house. It was swinging with a strange gait and seemed too high to be held by a walking man.

It was a man on a horse. She tugged the door

open and shouted into the night, 'Gerry! Did you find him?'

The horse galloped the last few yards to stop easily in front of her. Gerry smiled down at her. 'I told you not to worry.' Then he opened his coat to reveal her darling boy, astride a horse and nestled close to her husband.

She held out her arms and Gerry lowered him to the ground. And for a moment she was too relieved to speak. She could do nothing but hug him tight to her, until he squirmed in embarrassment. Then she let him go long enough to scold. 'Do not ever do that to me again, running away in the middle of the night, frightening the life out of the whole household.'

'I won't, Mama. I promise. And Papa says that tomorrow he will buy me a pony.'

'You are right you won't, young man. You will not be able to…' Then, her mind began to decipher what he was saying. His papa? A pony? He had arrived home in Gerry's arms and on a horse. But that had to be from necessity.

She looked to her husband for the answer and he gave her one of his infuriatingly charming, lopsided grins, paired with half a shrug. And under it all ran a childish descant about how ponies were small and safe and gentle and no different from big dogs. And who was silly enough to be afraid of a big dog?

The spots began to appear before her eyes again. And as the world swayed, she heard the command to 'Breathe, Lillian.' As she obeyed, his hands caught her under the arms and lifted her to her feet.

'Miss…'

'Fisher, Captain.' Aston supplied the name, *sotto voce.*

'Miss Fisher. Wash this boy. He has been playing in the stables and smells like a pony himself. I do not mind. But others might.'

'Yes, Captain.'

'And I am sorry for the inconvenience to you all, as is young Stewart. He will tell you so in the morning. Perhaps a glass of warm milk will help him back to sleep.'

'Of course, Captain.' Mrs Fitz was there and ready.

'And the rest of you? Back to sleep. Breakfast will be late tomorrow, since we will all be celebrating the quiet of an empty house.'

The staff gave a murmur of approval and one of the maids yawned and then giggled.

'Night, Mama.'

Lily felt a tug on her skirt and a kiss on her hand, but by the time she turned to look Stewart was inside the house and halfway up the stairs. The servants were dispersing as well. By the time she'd caught her breath and regained her wits, she was alone on the steps with her husband, who was still grinning.

'What happened?'

His smile faded. 'He knows. Ronald told him before he left.'

She had thought that the night could not be worse. Her breath was gone again as she imagined her son's shock and his anger at her betrayal.

'Breathe.' This time, it was not a command. Just a gentle whisper against her temple. He was not simply holding her up. He was cradling her against him, swaying slightly as if they were dancing. 'I explained things to him as best I could. There will be more questions, of course.'

'I must go to him.' She started to pull away.

He pulled her back. 'Not tonight. He is settled now. Halfway back to bed, I should think. I thought diversionary tactics would serve better than a full account of how he came to be.'

'A diversion?' She smiled. 'The pony.'

'Exactly. There will be time enough tomorrow to talk about the past. I will help, if I can.'

'Tomorrow?' She had thought they would be packed and gone by evening.

He leaned away so she could see his smile, which was gentle. 'He and I discussed matters between us. We decided it might be best for you if we all lived together. Then we might both love and care for you without the inconvenience of distance.'

'But... Love... Are you sure?' Perhaps he cared for her. But much as she wanted it, the three of them living together sounded like an uneasy truce, at best.

'You said before that I hated Stewart. He said the same.' He was still smiling, but now his grey eyes looked sad. 'It is foolish to hate a small child who has done nothing more to me than exist.' He thought for a moment. 'I hate his father, of course. Both for who he was and for what he did to you. But the boy has done nothing in his life to deserve such a parent.'

'All I wanted was for him to have a father he could admire,' she admitted. 'That was why I lied.'

'Not all of us can have a hero.' Gerry said. 'My father was a harsh man. I cannot say I liked him, or agreed with his hobbies. But neither would I say that I was better off without him. I am not as perfect as the man you were hoping for. But your son needs a father. I can be that for him.'

'I never doubted it,' she replied. But these sounded like rationalisations of a difficult situation. 'But some day, you will want children of your own.'

'Many,' he agreed. 'And soon.'

'If you acknowledge Stewart, he will stand in their way to inheritance.'

'What I want does not really matter. There is no way of knowing how many children we might have,' he reminded her. 'For all we know, there might be none. But there is no entail on the property. All could share equally.'

It was the sort of solution she'd longed for since the moment Stewart had been born. But now that it was here, it was all too sudden. If it was but a ploy to keep her, it would not be enough to secure Stewart's future. 'I would like nothing better than that we could all be together as a family,' she said, touching his cheek. 'But why now? What has changed that you would allow it?'

'Just now, I pulled your son from Satan's stall. He risked death from a beast that terrified him, trying to prove his worth to himself and to me.' And now, the brave Captain Wiscombe had to stop to swallow his emotion. 'I will not let that happen again. The boy was born here, and he stays here.' He hugged her roughly to him, as if the contact would give him the strength to master himself.

She hugged him back, for it was clear that he had finally seen Stewart for who he was and not just a horrible mistake. 'You will not regret this. Once you have got to know him, you will find he is so very much like you that he could be your own.'

'Like me?' He laughed.

'He is like you on the day you proposed. Sweet and earnest. Ready to conquer the world, with no thought to what might go wrong. You were a hero in the making, Captain Wiscombe. It just took time for your true character to be revealed.' She smiled and kissed him on the cheek to show him how dear he was to her.

'As I remember it, you were convinced that I was a fool and marching to my death,' he said, nuzzling her hair.

'You proved me wrong,' she reminded him.

'As you did me, about young Stewart. And for your information, the boy is more like you. Smart. Stubborn. Fearless.'

'And utterly devoted to you,' she added.

'Most important, he is a part of you. Since I love you to the last fibre of your being, I will love and honour your child, and make him my own.' The kiss that followed was long and slow, and soothed the last of her worries about the future.

'And I love you, Gerry Wiscombe,' she said with a sigh. 'More each day since the moment I met you.'

He was smiling again. 'I've dreamed of you saying those words almost as long.'

'My father and brother said you married me because you were smitten with me. I did not believe them. You had other plans for your future, even from the first.'

'You will have to take my word for it. I was smitten. I still am.' He grinned. 'And I had other plans. I still do.'

'What are they?' she asked.

'To teach our son that horses are not to be feared. To live out the rest of my life quietly at Wiscombe Chase, surrounded by my loving family.' Then he looked down at her, mischief in his eyes. 'But first, I mean to bed my wife.'

Before she could answer, he had scooped her up, tossed her over his shoulder and was carrying her up the stairs to their room.

\* \* \* \* \*

# LADY PRISCILLA'S
# SHAMEFUL SECRET

To Diana Fox and the beginning of a
beautiful friendship.

# Chapter One

~~~~~~~~~~~~~~~~~~~~

Robert Magson, Duke of Reighland, treated each new ballroom like an Indian jungle set with traps not for tigers, but for unwary men. There were so many mamas and daughters in London that he would not have been surprised to see them lurking behind the furniture at White's. And they were all eager to catch his eye, even for just a moment.

It was as though they thought he could decide on a bride based on a single glance in a crowded room. He spent more time buying a horse than that. He would never lay down money without checking teeth, feeling fetlocks and enquiring of the bloodline. Surely the choice of a wife should be made with equal care.

He frowned out into the mob and watched two or three young ladies curtsy as his gaze roved over them. It was an odd feeling, this sudden deference, as though his slightest glance was the withering glare of the noon sun in a garden full of delicate blossoms. The same girls would not have looked twice at him a year ago. Then his cousin had died. And suddenly he was the catch of the Season.

He frowned harder and watched the crowd contract to give him more space. It was not as if he did not mean to marry one of them. But there were far too many who had hopes in his direction. One could not appear too welcoming, if one wanted even a moment of peace in the evenings.

To be fair, the rout tonight was surprisingly convivial. And he had no reason to suspect his host, the Earl of Folbroke, was plotting against him. The man was too young to have marriageable children and, to the best of Robert's knowledge, had no sisters.

'I hear you are thinking of offering for Benbridge's daughter,' said Folbroke from his place at Robert's side.

It surprised him that that particular bit of news had travelled so quickly. While he had been paying court to several young ladies in a halfhearted and unenthusiastic way, the matter of Benbridge's daughter had been introduced into conversation only recently. But apparently, it was already *on dit*. 'What might have given you that idea?' he asked blandly. 'I have not even met the girl, yet.'

'According to my wife, Lady Benbridge is telling everyone that your back has been broken by the parson's mousetrap.' The earl smiled. 'As far as the bit that has trapped you? It does not surprise me that you have not met her. None of us has seen her for quite some time. Of course, I would not notice, even if she were here.' Folbroke adjusted his smoked glasses.

It was a continual surprise to Robert that the earl was so casual in calling attention to his blindness. He supposed it prevented people from treating him like an invalid, when there was no reason to. Although he tended to stay at the edge of the room during events such as these, Folbroke looked no more uncomfortable than the other gentlemen that lounged against the walls to avoid the press of bodies at the centre of the floor.

Robert admired his studied casualness and sought to emulate it so that he might appear more comfortable in society than he felt. Four months after becoming Reighland it was still an effort not to turn and search the room for Gregory when someone called him by the title. He offered a silent prayer for the bright and smiling child that had been meant for this honour, just as he longed for the wise counsel of his father. Sometimes it felt that his family had not so much died as abandoned him to make his own way in a confusing world. Now, his frown deepened at the rumours swirling about him. 'Despite what Lady Benbridge might think on the matter, I wish to meet the girl before I offer for her. I might be new to the marriage mart, but not so new that I will take her sight unseen.'

Folbroke smiled in response, as he always did. He was a particularly good-humoured fellow. But Robert suspected that there was something about the situation that the earl found particularly amusing. 'In any case,' he said, 'you must meet Hendricks. He will want to welcome you to the family.' Robert hoped that Folbroke was not laughing at him for he quite liked the man and would hate to find him as false as some of the others who had been eager to offer friendship to his face while laughing behind their hands at his country manners.

'Hendricks,' Folbroke called, 'come here. There is someone you must meet.'

That was it, then, Robert thought, relaxing a little. Hendricks was Folbroke's protégé. Apparently, this event had been meant to arrange a casual introduction to his Grace, the Duke of Reighland. There was no real harm in it, he supposed. He had heard that the Hendricks fellow was damned useful to know. And when it came to navigating the subtleties of London, Robert could use all the help he could get.

A bespectacled man all but materialised out of the crowd, as though the room was a stage and he had been waiting in the wings for an entrance. It was nicely done. Though Robert had been watching closely, he'd never have suspected that Hendricks had been watching for a cue from the earl.

'You wished something, Folbroke?' Hendricks's voice was raised to be heard over the noise of the crowd, but he still managed to sound quiet and deferential. His choice of words made him seem even more like an Arabian djinn.

'Only to present you to Reighland,' Folbroke shouted back at him. 'Your Grace, John Hendricks is husband to the lovely Drusilla Roleston. Dru is the elder Benbridge daughter and sister to your fair Priscilla.' He stared in the direction of Hendricks, who was dipping his head to hear over the roar of voices. 'John, Reighland is likely to be your brother-in-law. Make nice to him.'

Hendricks's eyebrows raised in surprise before he

could master his emotion and turn to Robert with a bow. 'How do you do, your Grace?'

Robert gave him a stiff nod of response. 'Not as well as Folbroke seems to think. She is not my Priscilla, Folbroke. Despite what society claims, my intentions are not set in stone. I have not even met the girl,' he added again, wondering just what was wrong with people in London. They gossiped as though rumour was air and they could not survive without it. 'I do mean to seek an introduction to her. If there is compatibility between us…' He gave a half-shrug.

Hendricks nodded. 'If you would permit, your Grace, I would like to introduce my wife to you. She is eager for all things to do with Priss and will be glad to know you.'

'She cannot ask Priscilla herself?'

'Sadly, no.' Hendricks smiled benignly at him. 'Because of me, I'm afraid. The Earl of Benbridge did not think me good enough for his family. To my eternal good fortune, Lady Drusilla did not share his opinion, but now my poor Dru is quite cut off from associating with her sister.'

'And if I might say so, Benbridge is a fool,' Folbroke said calmly. 'You will not find better company in this room than John Hendricks, nor will you find a sharper mind.'

Robert had heard similar sentiments voiced by others. Hendricks was seen as an up and comer in political circles for his pleasant demeanour and his uncanny ability to be always in the right place at the right time. 'Is the attendance of the older sister the reason I do not see the younger here?' Robert asked, slightly annoyed by the fact. On the few times they'd spoken, the Earl of Benbridge had seemed a stiff-backed old fool who was not nearly as smart or important as he seemed to think himself. This was merely another confirmation of it. It was interesting to see that, having to choose between the company of one or the other, Folbroke would rather associate with his inferior than with Benbridge, a man of equal rank. Robert stored the information for future reference.

Hendricks nodded in answer to his question. 'Since we were invited this evening, Priscilla would not be permitted to come. It is damned unreasonable of him. My wife and I cannot forgo society just to prevent embarrassment for a family that will not welcome Dru back, no matter what she does.' He glanced at Robert and pushed his spectacles up his nose. 'If you should happen to marry Priss, you will have our felicitations, of course. But we will make no attempt to ruin the girl's wedding by expecting an invitation and upsetting her father.'

Robert found this even more annoying than the assumptions of his choice of bride. It had never occurred to him to care who was in the pews at St George's; now he had received his first refusal before the invitations had been engraved. 'This is hardly set in stone,' he repeated. 'I have spoken to Benbridge about it, of course, but I have not even met the girl.' Then a thought struck him. 'But you have, haven't you? How did you find her?'

There was a fleeting expression of caution in Hendricks's eyes, just before he spoke. Then he said heartily, 'She is a great beauty. All blonde curls, blue eyes and dimples. She will make someone a most attractive wife, I am sure. The children will be lovely.'

He'd managed to mention looks three times in as many seconds. Yet Robert was sure that the man did not like her, or her blonde curls. He had chosen the other sister. And it was obvious that he doted on her.

But that did not mean Robert might not like Priscilla, if he ever saw her. A pretty wife was better than an ugly one.

'You will have Benbridge's favour as well,' Hendricks added. 'Priscilla is his favourite.'

'The thought had crossed my mind,' Robert replied. If marriage was to be little better than a connection between powerful families, he could do much worse than an earl's daughter. If he wished to put forth any of his ideas in Parliament, it could not hurt to have an elder statesman at his back. And judging by the value Benbridge set on status and decorum, he must have drilled his daughter in the rules of good behaviour, practically from birth. She would rescue him from his tendency to social *faux pas*.

With the number of men between him and the title, he had never expected to be a duke. But Lady Priscilla had been bred to be a duchess, or at the very least a countess. She would know what was expected of her. And he would not have to give another thought to the running of his households and social life. It would be a great relief.

But it annoyed him that Hendricks could not seem to

find any word for the girl other than that she was pretty. It made him wonder if there was some secret. Hereditary madness, perhaps? Given the choice between that or weakness of character Robert almost preferred the second. While he had seen virtuous children with wanton parents, a lack of wit seemed to carry through the generations.

'Priss is the apple of his eye,' Hendricks affirmed, interrupting his musings. 'And here is mine.' The woman who was approaching them seemed sane enough. But she was neither blonde nor blue eyed. Nor did she share anything in common with Benbridge's rather florid complexion. Years of horse breeding told him that such a variety of colouring was unusual in siblings.

'Your wife is Priscilla's stepsister, did you say?' he guessed.

Hendricks gave him an odd look and Folbroke seemed more than usually impervious. 'I said no such thing, your Grace.'

Which meant that too great a knowledge of biology had just led him to question the legitimacy of the former Drusilla Roleston. He doubted that the woman had heard him above the other voices. And her husband was too eager for his patronage to rebuke him.

But it was yet another proof that he needed a keeper to muzzle him in these situations and pave over any mistakes with gracious smiles.

Hendricks appeared to have forgotten the comment already and made the introductions. In response, Robert made a proper bow and responded, 'Lady Drusilla.'

'Please, your Grace,' she said softly. 'You may address me as Mrs Hendricks.' She shot her husband a look that told the world the man had hung the stars and the moon, and there was no greater title in the world than the honour of bearing his last name.

In response, the normally composed Hendricks blushed and grinned.

Even with his time spent travelling amongst the *ton*, Robert knew that it was unusual to see a couple so obviously fond of each other. He was secretly envious. That was what he had expected, before his life had taken its recent and dramatic turn: a woman who would be happy to have him, not just angling after his title. Would that the sister shared this woman's sweet nature. 'Mrs Hendricks, then. I am honoured to make your acquaintance.'

Drusilla turned to him with a hopeful smile. 'John tells me that you have some news of my sister?'

'Only that I might make an offer for her, if she is to my liking.'

He watched as Mrs Hendricks looked back at him with equal curiosity. 'You have met with her, then? Is she well?'

'I have not, as yet, made the lady's acquaintance.' But he must soon, if only to save him from admitting his ignorance, over and over.

'You do not know her, yet you would consider an offer.' The lovely Mrs Hendricks frowned. 'I take it you have been in communication with my father on the subject.'

He gave a little nod of acknowledgement.

'I would hope, sir, that you have the lady's best interests in mind as well. I am sure my father is concerned primarily with your rank and thinks little of my sister's future happiness. My hopes for her are much more humble. I do not wish to see her bartered away from the family to a man who does not care about her.'

Robert glanced between Hendricks and Folbroke, waiting to see if either would prevent the lady from offering him further insult. Folbroke was smiling expectantly at him, as though it was a legitimate question that deserved an answer. Hendricks met his gaze as though he had been thinking much the same thing, despite his dislike for the girl they were discussing and the risk of offending a peer.

Very well, then. He would answer bluntness with bluntness. 'It is true that I know far more of trading horses than I do of marriage, Mrs Hendricks. Until my recent elevation, I had little plan for my life other than the breeding and selling of cattle. But I was known for my sound judgement on the subject. I would have no intention of closing such an important bargain without at least riding the filly in question.'

Folbroke gave a snort of suppressed mirth.

He had done it again. 'That is not to say that I wish to...' He glanced at Mrs Hendricks and then away. For if she understood the thing he had implied, but not meant to say... 'I only want to meet her,' he said at last, exasperated. 'We need to talk...to know each other...socially...before such a decision can be made. But I can assure you that, once the deal is done, I treat anything and anyone under my care with the respect and affection it deserves.'

Hendricks looked more doubtful, as though calculating just how much respect his sister-in-law was entitled to.

And the former Lady Drusilla continued to stare at him, as though trying to gauge the value of a man who might compare marriage to horse trading and admit to an interest in riding her beloved sister. 'A fair enough answer, I suppose. Knowing my father as I do, I could hardly have expected him to choose a husband for Priss based on some pre-existing bond of affection. I must trust that my husband and Lord Folbroke would not be introducing me to you if they did not think you worthy of my sister.' She gave a small sigh as though the small matter of a dukedom meant nothing to her and Robert stifled his own inadequacy. Then, she softened. 'Please, when you see Priss, inform her that I asked after her good health. And ensure her that, should she need me for any reason, she must feel free to call upon me, despite what Father might say.' There was something in the final sentence that made him think that if the mysterious Priscilla experienced unhappiness, it had best not be at his expense, or the formidable Mrs Hendricks would take swift retribution.

'Very well, then, madam. I will be happy to relay your message.' And he would do it soon, he was sure. The vague interest he'd had in the girl had been piqued to actual curiosity with this interchange. Even if he did not wish to wed her, he very much wanted to meet her and see what all the fuss was about.

## Chapter Two

'You will be pleased to know that I have chosen you a husband.' The Earl of Benbridge barely looked up from his newspaper as he casually made the announcement that might permanently alter Priscilla's life.

Did he expect her to be pleased? She frowned down at her plate. She was not. Not in the least. It felt as if her insides were being squeezed with a metal clamp. Her heart ceased to beat and her breathing ground to a halt. Her stomach clenched until the little breakfast she had taken churned weakly inside it. 'Is it someone of my acquaintance?' She kept her tone uninterested. It was always easier to start an argument with Father than to win it.

'Do you know him? Since you rarely leave the house, how likely do you think it is that you have seen him?'

'I go when I have been invited,' she said, as patiently as she could. 'And to the events that you allow me to attend.' That further limited her choices. 'If you refuse to let me be seen in the company of Drusilla, you can hardly blame me for staying home. The hostesses know that if they lose her favour, they lose the Countess of Folbroke, and possibly Anneslea as well. My sister has become quite the social butterfly since her marriage.'

'Her marriage to a nothing,' her father announced. 'And without my blessing.'

'Do not be jealous of your sister, Priscilla. It does you no credit.' Father's new wife, Veronica, seemed to think it was her place to act as a sage adviser to her stepdaughter on all womanly graces. After their brief time together, Priss found the idea that Ronnie had a store of accrued wisdom faintly ridiculous.

In any case, her statements about Dru were not so much a sign of jealousy as a simple statement of fact. Since the marriage to Hendricks, her father had forced the *ton* to choose a side. And after only a little thought, they had chosen Dru's. Priss's own scandalous behaviour, last summer, had put the last nail in the coffin of her social life and the trickle of remaining invitations had dried up almost completely. 'I am not jealous, Ronnie. I am happy that Dru has finally got the Season she deserves, even if it has come too late to get her a rich and powerful husband.'

'Bah.' It was the noise that her father often made, when confronted with the stupidity of his actions. If he had given her a Season, Dru would now be married to the man of *his* choosing. Then he would be satisfied. And poor Dru would have managed to be content, instead of as gloriously happy as rumours made her out to be.

Benbridge brightened as he dismissed all thoughts of the absent Drusilla and focused his attention on Priss. 'We will show her the error of her ways, girl. In a month or two you shall be married at St. George's and all the town shall wish for an invitation. You may pick and choose who you like and devil take the rest.'

At one time the thought of delivering slights and nods and setting pace for the fashionable world might have interested her. Now that she had been on the receiving end of it, she'd lost her taste for gossip. At the moment, there was only one person in this imaginary wedding that she really cared about. But she was almost afraid to ask about him.

'I am more interested in the groom than the guest list. Who have you chosen for me?'

'Reighland. That freshly acquired title has made him something of a nine-days' wonder. When you capture his attention, it will be a coup.'

She racked her brain, sorting through the guests at the few parties she had attended in recent months. Had she seen him? Had he been there? Had he seen her? She could find no memory of him. 'And why would he have me?'

'I have spoken to him on the subject. I need an ally in the bill that I am presenting. He is a logical choice. But he has been quite standoffish. When he expressed a half-hearted desire to marry, I informed him that I had an eligible daughter. It was the first overture in what I hope will be a long and fruitful alliance.'

When Benbridge said fruitful, he thought of nothing more than bills and laws. There was no mention of the other fruits that might result in marrying his daughter off to a stranger—nor the acts she would have to perform to achieve them. 'How nice for you,' Priscilla said weakly. 'And now, if you will excuse me, I think I shall retire to my room for the morning. I am feeling quite tired.'

'It is nearly noon, Priscilla. Too late to be asleep, and far too early to retire for the day.' Veronica was eyeing her critically.

Priss searched for an excuse that might meet with the woman's approval, yet allow her to be alone with her thoughts. 'I mean to spend an hour in prayer.'

Veronica took another sip of her coffee. 'Very well then. It is not as if your character does not need reforming. But remember, too much piety is unbecoming in a girl. I have no objections, as long as you have recovered from the effects by evening and are attired in your newest gown. We will be attending a ball at Anneslea's and you will be meeting your husband-to-be.'

Tonight, already. That left her only a few hours to find a way out of her father's plans for her. It seemed she would be praying for deliverance.

A few hours later, Lady Priscilla Roleston surveyed the ballroom and wondered if Veronica might have been right about the dangers of prayer and solitude. She felt for all the world like a girl on her first come out. Her gown was fashionable and she'd been assured that it flattered her. But the neckline, which had been acceptable when she'd ordered it, now felt exposing to the point of immodesty. People would stare.

At one time, she would have welcomed the attention that a daring dress would bring her. Now, she just wanted to be left alone.

But it seemed that was to be a hopeless wish. Her father's mind had been set on the subject of the impending introduction. No amount of feigned megrims or foot dragging had had any effect on him or his new wife.

And that was the best she could manage, really, when thinking of Ronnie. Although the woman had attempted to force Priss into calling her 'Mother' their ages were close enough to make the idea laughable. Even the word 'stepmother' was a struggle. She did not wish a female parent of any variety, though Papa had claimed that it was out of concern for her that he had married again so late in life. She needed a chaperon and wise guidance.

Perhaps he was right. At barely one and twenty, Priss expected her character was fully formed, for better or worse. But if she had wished to use her youth and good looks to capture the attentions of a foolish, old peer, she could not think of a better teacher than the new Lady Benbridge.

Since Priss heartily wished to remain unmarried, Ronnie was proving to be more hindrance than help. She must hope that the Duke of Reighland, whoever he might be, was not as willing to take a pig in a poke as her father expected.

'Straighten your shoulders, Priscilla. We cannot have you slouching tonight. You must put your best foot forwards. And smile.' Veronica prodded her in the back with her fan, trying to force her to straighten.

Priss took care to let no emotion show on her face as

they approached the knot of people in the corner of the room. Why should she bother being nice, just to please whomever Father had chosen as the latest candidate for her hand? Considering the men he had threatened her with over the years, she had very good reasons not to encourage an attraction.

But she straightened her shoulders, just a little. The continual effort of hunching, trying to seem a little less than she was, was both taxing and painful.

Veronica surveyed her appearance with a frown. 'I suppose it will have to do. Now come along. We are to be presented to the guest of honour. It is rare for an eligible peer to come to London, almost out of nowhere, right at the height of the Season.'

'Which means he will be surrounded by girls,' she said to Ronnie, trying to dash her hopes. 'There is no reason he should choose me from amongst them. Or be thinking of marriage at all. I am sure he has other things on his mind. Parliament, for example. No amount of good posture and manners on my part will make an impression.'

'Nonsense. Benbridge assures me that he is practically in awe of his own title and enjoys the attention immensely. How can he not? He never in a million years expected to be more than a gentleman farmer. Suddenly, his father, cousin and uncle are all dead in the space of a year. And here he is. It really is the most tragic thing.' But Veronica grinned as she said it, all but salivating at the thought of such an eligible, yet so naïve, a peer.

'Yes,' Priscilla said firmly. 'It is tragic. Devastating, in fact. His cousin was barely three years old. I am sure there will be another year at least for me to meet the man. He cannot intend to marry so quickly when he is still grieving for his family.' But though the new Reighland wore unrelieved black for the boy who had been his predecessor, his mourning did not extend to a complete withdrawal from society if he was attending parties all over London.

'On the contrary. Rumours say that he is on the hunt and means to return to his lands properly wed by the end of the session. He has seen the results of waiting too long to get an heir, with his uncle dying of age while the heir was still so young and vulnerable. The Reighland holdings are too remote to see much society. It makes sense to him to choose a bride while he is at market.'

'Inadequate breeding stock in the north, I suppose,' Priscilla said. There were rumours that the duke had been much better with horses than he had with people, and that his Grace's general gracelessness extended to his doings with the fair sex. But for all of that, he was still a duke and much could be forgiven—especially by one who was eager to marry.

He seemed just the sort of man her father would choose for her. One with little else to recommend him other than rank. As she glanced at him from across the room, she had to admit that there was nothing about him that she imagined would make for an easy husband. He did not need the title to intimidate her. He was an exceptionally large man with broad shoulders, bulging muscles and large hands. His thick black hair hung low over his face, which had matching heavy brows. The slight shadow on his jaw meant his valet would have to keep a razor sharp and ready more than once a day. If he would at least smile, she might have thought him jolly, but his looks were as dark as his coat.

The simpering virgins that surrounded him were dwarfed in comparison. But it was a mob and, thank the gods, she would be lost in it. Perhaps her father was wrong about the understanding they had. Priss could be just another face in the crowd. The introduction could pass out of his memory as quickly as it had entered and she could return home to her room.

'Make some effort to distinguish yourself...' Veronica prodded her again '...or I shall speak for you.'

That would be even more embarrassing than being forced upon the man by her father. 'Very well, then,' Priss said, with a grim smile. If Benbridge and Ronnie were so eager for her to make this a memorable evening, she would give them what they wanted in spades. It would be so unforgettable that they would have no choice but to remove her from town to avoid further embarrassment.

And so she was brought before the estimable Duke of Reighland, who was even larger up close than he had seemed from a distance. She was glad that this would be her only meeting with him, for prolonged contact would be quite terrifying. She kept her head bowed as she heard Ronnie speaking to the host and hostess, who then turned to their guest and offered to present Lady Benbridge and Lady Priscilla.

Reighland's voice boomed down at the top of her head. 'How do you do?'

She heard Veronica's melodious, 'Very well, thank you, your Grace.'

Priscilla made her deepest, most perfect curtsy, offered her hand and then, looking up into the face of the man, smiled and whickered like a horse.

There was a stunned silence. But she did not need words to know what Veronica was thinking. The horror emanating from her was so close to palpable that Priss was surprised she had not already turned and shouted for Father to summon the carriage. They would make a hasty retreat and she could expect the lecture to continue nonstop until such time as they had a mind to remove her from the house.

No one moved. It was as though they could not dare breathe. And now that she had created the situation, she was unsure how to get out of it. Judging by his looks, she had expected immediate outrage and an angry outburst from the duke. He might even be moved to shout at her and storm from the room.

It would not matter. She had been shouted at by experts, now that her poor sister was no longer in the house to take the brunt of Father's temper. What could this stranger possibly say that would hurt her?

But Reighland was staring at her with no change of expression and an unusual degree of focus. She felt the slightest upward tug on the hand he held to move her out of her curtsy to stand properly before him. She did not need Veronica's advice to straighten her spine for she needed every last vertebra to hold her own against the tower of manhood in front of her.

At last he spoke. 'Lady Priscilla, may I have the next waltz?'

If he wished to upbraid her for her manners, he could do it in company and not by hauling her around the dance floor and trapping her in his arms for the scolding. 'I am sorry, but I believe I am promised.'

'How unfortunate for the gentleman. When he sees that you are dancing with me, I am sure he will understand.' He cocked an ear towards the musicians. 'It seems they are beginning. We had best go to the floor. If you will excuse us, Lady Benbridge?'

And so she was headed for the dance floor with the Duke of Reighland. She had little choice in the matter, unless she wanted to have a tug of war over her own evening glove. His grip on her arm was gentle, but immovable.

And now they were dancing. He was neither good nor bad at the simple step. She did not fear that he would tread upon her toes. But neither did she feel any pleasure in the way he danced. He approached the waltz with a passionless and mechanical precision, as though it were something to be conquered more than enjoyed.

'Are you having a pleasant evening?' he asked.

'Until recently,' she said.

'Strange,' he said, staring past her. 'I'd have said just the opposite, if you had asked me. It has suddenly become most diverting compared to other recent entertainments.'

'I would not know,' she said, 'for I have not attended any.'

'I understand that,' he said. 'It is because of your

sister's recent good fortune. I met her last evening at the Folbroke rout.'

Now she had to struggle to remain blasé. *He had seen Silly.* She must remember to think of Silly as Dru, just as Drusilla's friends did. Dru had many of those now and not just a little sister to tease her with nicknames. It had been months since the last time they had been in the same room together. But then they had not spoken and stayed on opposite ends of a ballroom that might as well have been an ocean. Priss had been forced by Veronica to cut her own sister dead.

If Ronnie got wind of it, she would snap this tenuous thread of communication, even if the man offering it was a duke. Priss replied to Reighland's news with a single, 'Oh.' It hardly summed up the extent of her feelings. She wanted to pull him to the side of the floor and interrogate him until she had gleaned every last detail of his exchange with Dru and could recall them as clearly as if she had been there herself.

But the dance could not go on for ever and she did not want to give the man reason to speak. She would have to do without.

He had noticed her silence. 'It surprises me to find you so uninterested. Mrs Hendricks was most eager for any news of you. Do you find yourself jealous on her account?'

'Certainly not. It is about time that Drusilla had the chance to be happy.' She looked longingly back at the wallflowers, wishing she was amongst them. Perhaps one of them had been at the Folbrokes' party and could give her the information she craved. 'It seems I am out of practice in social settings.' She glared up at him. 'I do not remember the conversation being quite so rude, when last I waltzed.' He would let her go now. That had been a direct insult and he could hardly ignore it.

But her barbed words bounced off his thick skin as though they meant nothing. 'You must make an effort to get out more,' he replied. 'It was at my request that you were invited here. I wished to meet you. I will see to it that you receive further such invitations.' He said it without a smile. Did the man have no emotions at all?

'If you wish,' she added for him.

'Of course I wish. That is why I will do it.'

'You misunderstand me, your Grace. What I meant was that you should have finished your last sentence with the phrase "if you wish." Then it would mean that you would see to it I received further invitations and could accept them if I desired. It would imply that I had a choice.'

He ignored her lack of enthusiasm. 'If I give you a choice, I can well guess what your answer would be, although I am at a loss as to the reason for it. You seem to have taken an instant dislike of me, though you have known me for all of five minutes. I suspect that you would have formed the same opinion of me without even leaving your house, if I had given you the chance. But that would not do at all. It is time that you are brought out into the light so that a man can get a proper look at you.'

'Why would you need a proper look at me?'

'I mean to marry,' he said, as though it were not obvious. 'And you are a front runner. But no matter what your father might think, I cannot be expected to make a decision based on his word alone.'

'He could have shown you a miniature and you could have made a judgement from that,' she said. It was clear that her opinion did not matter. Of course, she supposed, since the man was a duke, her acceptance was assumed. Why would she refuse?

Other than that he had the manners of a stable hand.

'It would not have been the same,' he assured her. 'You are quite lovely and I am sure no picture would do you justice.'

'I am not so different from many others,' she insisted. 'If you wish for a pretty bride, you would be better served to make the rounds at Almack's. Everyone who is anyone is there.'

'In knee breeches,' he added. 'There is a limit to what I will go through, simply for the sake of marrying.'

'They are proper attire for evening,' she said bluntly.

'They are uncomfortable,' he said with equal bluntness. 'And they do not suit me. I will wear them at court, of course. I mean no disrespect to the Regent. But beyond that, trousers will have to do.'

'So you are willing to limit your choice of bride, based on your unwillingness to dress for evening?'

'Just as you are limiting your choice of husbands by not attending Almack's,' he said.

*Touché.* She could not explain her way out of that without admitting that she could no longer get vouchers. 'Perhaps I do not wish to marry,' she hazarded.

'Then you should go for the dancing,' he suggested. 'You are very good at it.'

'Thank you,' she said glumly.

'If we marry, I will not worry about having to hire a dancing master for you.'

She stumbled. *He knew*. Not all, perhaps. But enough. She pulled her hand from his, prepared to quit the floor.

He grabbed it back again and kept her in place. 'You will not get away from me so easily. Wait until the end of the music. Anything else will make you appear skittish.' He looked into her eyes. 'I do not tolerate skittishness.'

'And I do not care what you do or do not like,' she said.

'Then we are not likely to get on well.' He gave a thoughtful nod as though he were marking a check on the negative side of some invisible list of wifely qualities. 'Other young ladies are much more agreeable,' he said. 'One might even say that they fawned.'

'I expect so. You are a duke, after all. A marriageable miss cannot aspire higher than that.'

'Then why do you not express similar behaviours?'

'Is there anything about the title that imbues it with an amiable nature, a pleasant companion, a loving mate, or...' she struggled to find a delicate way to express her misgivings '...any kind of compatibility between us? You are young, of course.'

'Twenty-six,' he supplied.

'That might be an advantage in your favour. Barring accident, I would not have to be worried about widowhood. But I have met many men to whom I would much rather be a widow than a wife.'

His rather forbidding face split in a smile that was

as surprising as it was brilliant. Straight white teeth, full lips, which had seemed narrow as he'd frowned at her. And there was a spark in his eye. For a moment, she almost found him attractive.

Then she remembered that he was her father's choice, not hers.

'I intend to live to a ripe old age,' he affirmed. 'Do you ride?'

'I beg your pardon?'

'I said, do you ride? Horses,' he added, as though there could be any other sort of riding.

'No,' she said hurriedly, hoping that this was the correct answer to put him off. 'I am deathly afraid of horses.' In truth, she quite liked them—probably better than she liked his Grace. But one could not be expected to marry a man based on the contents of his stables.

His smile had turned to thoughtful disappointment. 'That is a pity. You do a creditable imitation of one, I notice. Although it does not suit you. This Season, I have met several young ladies from whom a snort and a neigh would not have surprised me in the least.'

The joke was not subtle. She almost upbraided him for his cruelty before he added, 'That did not bother me much, however. Looks are not everything in a woman. And I quite like horses. I breed them, you know. I have rather a lot of land devoted to the business of it. In the country, of course.'

'Then it is as I said. We would not suit at all. I cannot abide the country.' Another lie.

'You would not be there all the time, you know. Much as I do not like to be away during the prime foaling time, now that I am Duke, I will be forced to attend parliament, and all the balls, galas and entertainments that accompany the Season. I suspect you could have your fill of town were you married to me.'

And then retire for the rest of the year to a country estate, far away from the prying eyes of the *ton*. She imagined acres of soft rolling green dotted with grazing mares and their little ones nudging at them. It was tempting, when he put it that way. 'As you complained earlier, I rarely attend the events of the Season now that I am here. It is just as likely that I would be forced to socialise when I did not wish and then be forced into a solitude I did not enjoy.'

He gave her a sidelong glance. 'It sounds rather like you have taken it into your head not to be happy with anything I might offer you.'

She returned the glance. 'Is it so obvious?'

'Quite. Since you are prone to such candour, will you tell me the reason for it? If I have given you offence, as I frequently do, it would be useful to know how. I would welcome a critique of my approach, so that I do not repeat the mistake with the next young lady.'

Her lips quirked as she tried to suppress a smile. 'There. Just now. You should have said, "If I have given offence, I humbly apologise".'

'Without knowing why?'

'Definitely. That is the way to a lady's heart.'

'And if I were to begin with this apology, you would feel differently towards me?'

'No.'

He drew back a moment, as though running through

the conversation in his head. 'Then I shan't bother.' He stood in silence next to her, as though plotting his next move.

Why did he not just go away? She had been the one to give offence. And he was the one with all the power and new enough so that he hardly knew how to wield it. Did he not realise that his rank would allow him to take umbrage at the most trivial things, storm off or deny patronage? By now, he should have reported to her father that there was no way he could be leg shackled to such a thoroughly disagreeable chit and that would be that.

It would be a Pyrrhic victory, of course. There would be punishment and frigid silences awaiting her at home. But it would be one step closer to spinsterhood and the forced rustication that she craved.

Instead he seemed stubbornly attached to her. 'Now, let me see. You do not like riding, or balls, or the city, or the country. What does that leave us? Books?'

'I am not a great reader.'

'Shopping?'

'I have no wish to outfit myself in such a way that I am merely an ornament to my husband.'

'But you are most charmingly arrayed and, as previously noted, quite pretty.'

'I do not like flattery either.' But if she were totally honest with him, she would admit that she quite admired persistence.

'I suppose pleasant conversation cannot be a favourite of yours, or we would be having one now.' He gave her another sidelong glance. 'Clearly, you enjoy arguing.

And there we will find our common ground. I can argue all night, if necessary.'

'To no avail. I will never agree with you, on any point.'

'If I sought your agreement, then that would be a problem.'

'That is precisely the problem I have with you,' she snapped back, growing tired of the banter. 'No one seeks my agreement. I am to be presented with a *fait accompli* and expected to go meekly along with it, for the sake of family connections and political benefit.'

'Aha.' He was looking at her closely now. 'You are trying to avoid a favourable match because it has been presented by your father. You have someone else in mind, then? Someone not quite so rich? Or without a title?'

'Do not flatter yourself to think that I love another,' she replied. 'Perhaps I simply do not want you.'

'But that is not true either. You hardly know me. But you have formed an opinion on the Duke of Reighland, have you not? Your answer to him is a resounding no.'

'You are he.'

'Not until recently,' he informed her. 'But I am quite aware of the pressure to marry according to one's station, at the expense of one's wishes. That is the purpose of this interview and several others I have organised recently.'

She smiled in relief, sure that if he had spoken to any other girl in London, it would cement his poor opinion of her.

He smiled back and once again she was surprised

at the blinding whiteness of it. 'I must inform you that you have passed with flying colours. I look forward to calling on you, at your home, and on speaking to your father about a further acquaintance.' And with that the dance was over and he was escorting her, in stunned silence, back to her stepmother.

He liked her.

Even now, thinking of that rude whinny, he could feel his lips starting to twitch. He carefully suppressed the emotion. It was far easier to deal with people if they suspected that 'Reighland' was hovering on the edge of displeasure. They jumped to attention, in a vain attempt to keep the impossible man happy and not be the one upon whom the impending storm would break.

If he had been amiable, or, worse yet, laughed in their faces at their ridiculous behaviour towards him and offered friendship, it might be possible to dismiss him, title and all, as the unworthy upstart he sometimes felt he was. They would remember that he was the same lad they teased unmercifully at school. Robert Magson, the bear with no teeth. Once they had realised he would not fight back, it had been declared great fun to bait him. The torment had not stopped until he had gained his majority and retired to the country estate.

Now, those same men and their wives feared him, because they feared the title. If they realised that Reighland was just a thin veil over his old self, they would know how much power they still held. And it would all begin again.

So he glared and felt the crowd tremble at the possibility of his disapproval. It was better that they were kept off balance and at a distance, as they had been since his arrival in London. It meant he had made no friends, but neither had he any real enemies.

And until recently, tonight had been going according to course. Though she might sneer at his manners tomorrow, tonight the hostess was fawning over him, desperate to keep his favour. Several young ladies had been nudged into his path by their mamas, rather like birds forced from the nest into the mouth of a waiting cat. And just like those birds, they had been, to the last, wide-eyed, gawky and rather stupid. He had done the nice, of course, danced with them and fetched several glasses of lemonade, which allowed him to avoid adding his own dull wits to theirs.

Then he had spotted his supposed intended, just as he had hoped to. Hendricks had been right, the girl was a prime article. Pretty enough to put the others in the shade.

Or shadow. For there could not exactly be shade, could there, if the sun had set?

He brooded on that for a moment, then returned to the matter at hand.

The beautiful Lady Priscilla had seen through him in an instant. Apparently, she was not impressed by the farmer with the strawberry-leaf coronet.

In response, he'd been instantly attracted to her. But it was obvious that the sentiment would not be easily returned. Perhaps that was why he found her so fascinating. Of the three or four likely candidates he had found for his duchess, she might not be the prettiest in

London. Close, perhaps. He almost preferred the dark good looks of Charlotte Deveril, despite that girl's lack of a titled father.

Lady Priscilla was an earl's daughter, with connections equal to two of the other girls he favoured. And her reputation...

There were rumours. When he'd questioned friends, no one had had the nerve to speak directly of the flaw. But he was sure it existed, if her own brother-in-law could not manage unequivocal approval of her. Even without the presence of Mrs Hendricks, he'd had to give a more-than-gentle hint to tonight's hostess that he wished the presence of both Benbridge and his family. He had been informed that the new Lady Benbridge would be welcome, of course. But there had been something in the tone of the discussion that implied everyone would just as soon forget that there was a Lady Priscilla.

Perhaps it was that they knew she would misbehave in his presence. She did not offer shy and hopeful glances through her eyelashes. She did not flatter. She did not hang upon his every word, no matter how fatuous. She would not pretend one thing to his face, only to talk behind his back.

What she felt for him was plain and undisguised dislike. And it was directed to the duke and not the man inside. She refused to agree with him, in even the slightest details of his speech. She wanted no part of him and did not bother to hide it.

Therefore, she was the only one worth having. Whatever she might be, she did not bore him. And if he could win such a proud creature for himself he would know that the past was finally dead. Once Priscilla was married, whatever small scandal lay in her past would be forgotten. His wife would be beautiful, well bred and the envy of the *ton*. He would give her free rein in wardrobe and entertaining. Their house would be a show place and the feigned respect of his peers would become real.

But it was still a surprise to find that the most perfect woman in London was dead set against marrying above her station. Perhaps, a year ago, when he was a not particularly humble horse trader, she'd have courted him, just to spite her father. Or perhaps not. It would take time to find the full reason for her contrary behaviour, but he was willing to be patient.

Her distaste of riding was another problem. What was he to do with a woman who did not like horses? Granted, he had escorted two of his final four candidates down Rotten Row just this week. In the saddle, they were mediocre at best, sitting their beasts like toads on a jossing block. It had pained him to watch.

At least, when he could persuade the Benbridge girl to take to a mount, she would have no bad habits that needed to be broken. He could teach her not to fear and eventually she would enjoy it. He imagined her fighting every step of the way. The thought excited him, for sometimes it was the most spirited mare that made for the best ride.

Then he reminded himself, yet again, that women were not horses. Life would be easier if they were. He could not exactly break her spirit with a rough bit and a whip. But it would be better to have to argue and cajole for every compromise than to have a woman with no spirit to break.

The combination of riding and spirited women made him smile into his glass and take a long savouring drink. He had not expected to feel the low heat he was feeling for the woman he had met tonight. He had imagined the getting of an heir to be a momentary pleasure, surrounded by a lifetime of awkwardness and frigid courtesy. At best they would develop a fondness for each other. But suppose there could be passion as well?

Then it would be better if it were mutual desire, he reminded himself. He already knew the foolish course he was likely to take. He would do well to remember, before it was too late, that a passionate dislike from his spouse might make him long for the frosty indifference he was avoiding now.

And here was her father, eager to know how the dance had gone, but too subtle to ask directly. If Robert did not acknowledge him, the man would be hanging about all night, waiting for an opportunity to speak. 'Benbridge,' he said. 'A word, please.'

'Of course, your Grace.' The old earl looked at him speculatively and it reminded him, as always, of a stallion he'd had that would give the impression of docility, only to bite suddenly at the hand that held the apple. Reighland held precedence and they both knew it. But Benbridge thought in his heart that he was the superior and would show him that, if he could find a way.

'I have had the opportunity to speak with your daughter, and have found her to be...'

*Fractious, ungrateful, uninterested and bad tempered.*

'…quite charming. She is most lovely as well. May I have your permission to pay further visits upon her, with the object of a possible match?'

'Certainly, your Grace.' Benbridge gave only a slight lowering of the head, as though the honour were equal.

'The girl would have to be interested as well,' Robert reminded him. 'I would not wish to press my suit upon her, if she were otherwise engaged.' Despite her objections, it would make the most sense if she was pining for another.

'She is not so promised,' Benbridge said firmly. 'Even if she had plans in that direction, I would forbid all but the most appropriate match for her. After the misfortune of her sister…' There was a slight narrowing of the eyes and an even slighter twitch of the cheek to show what he thought of his other daughter's marriage. 'Priscilla will not reject you, your Grace. She would not dare.'

For a moment, Robert felt quite sorry for the girl. He wanted to pursue her, but his slightest interest was seen by her father as tantamount to an accepted offer. No wonder she refused to show him partiality.

'I must see her again, so that we might decide if we suit each other.' The earl might not care, but Robert would much prefer a wife who could at least tolerate him.

'Of course,' the earl replied, with just the slightest touch of obsequiousness. Then he stared across the room at his daughter, as though deciding on the best way to bully her into good behaviour to secure the proposal.

Silently, Robert damned him for his overconfidence. At the very least he would meet with the girl again and press the advantages of marrying a man who was not only rich and titled, but well on his way to being fond of her—and warn her of the danger of disobeying such an unaffectionate father.

## Chapter Three

'Priscilla, you have a visitor.'

No, she hadn't. For whom that she actually wished to see would be likely to make a call? Her old friends had cast her off quick enough, after her fall from grace. The sister she longed to see had been banned from the house. And she had gone out of her way to do nothing on the previous evening to warrant a call.

But rather than scolding her for her rudeness during the ride home, both her father and Veronica had seemed inordinately pleased with the turn events had taken. It was as though they'd shared some bit of information between them that she was not privy to.

*Please do not let it be the duke.* Because what would she do with the man, should he persist? 'Tell whoever it is that I am indisposed.'

Her bedroom door opened and Veronica poked in her head. 'I certainly will not. Reighland is in the sitting room, and you are going to see him.' She crossed the room, seized Priss by the arm and pulled her to her feet, brushing the wrinkles from her gown and smoothing a hand over her hair to rearrange the flattened curls.

'I am not prepared. I do not wish to see him.' *And I do not wish to marry him.* She doubted pleading with Ronnie would help, but neither would it hurt.

'You are unprepared because you spend your days hiding in bed with your Minerva novels, feigning illness to avoid company. Now come downstairs.'

'Send him away.'

'I certainly will not.' Ronnie was pushing her out into the hall and put a firm hand in her back to hurry her along. 'If you mean to put him off, you must do it yourself. And if you do, you will suffer the consequences for it. Your father will not be pleased.' She said it in a dark tone to remind her that there were worse things awaiting her than social ostracism, should she fail.

Priss gave her a mutinous look. 'Do not be so melodramatic. Father will do nothing worse to me than shout and sulk, as he has done the whole of my life. Perhaps he will banish me from the house, as he did Dru. Although how that is a punishment, I do not know. It is clear to all of London that she is the better for it.'

'It is not your father who should worry you, dear,' Ronnie replied, voice cold and venomous. 'You should know, after spending several months under the same roof with me, I will be far less forgiving. If you will not go to the duke, I will bring him to you and lock the bedroom door behind him until the matter is settled.'

The image of being so trapped with such a forbidding man made Priss a little sick, and she thanked the fates that she had not been caught *en déshabillé* today. While her father might view this as an alliance with a powerful man, she had no doubt that Ronnie would engineer her total disgrace with any man available, simply to have her out of the house. The woman was all but thrusting her through the door of the salon where her guest awaited.

But she showed no sign of following. Priss grabbed her arm, trying to pull her into the room as well. 'You are going to sit with us, of course,' she said hopefully. 'For surely a chaperon—'.

'He is a duke,' the other woman whispered. 'He does not require a chaperon.'

'It is not for him,' Priss snapped back, embarrassed that the duke could likely overhear this interchange, for he was scant feet across the room. Could they not at least pretend that she had some honour left?

'You were happy enough to escape the care of your sister, while she was still here. It makes no sense, a year later, that you are having a fit of the vapours over a few minutes alone with a man.' Her stepmother pushed harder. 'He is a duke. He wishes to speak to you alone. Benbridge said he was most specific on that point. I do not mean to be the one to argue.'

'My father is allowing this?' Priss felt another small bit of her world crumbling. She had received continual signs from Ronnie that her presence was an inconvenience. But usually Papa was more subtle with his displeasure.

'Your father thinks that Reighland is an excellent

catch. He is amenable to certain laxities if it smoothes the way for an offer.'

'But what if Reighland is not as honourable as he seems? What if he takes advantage?' Priss whispered back, directly into Veronica's ear.

The other woman's eyes narrowed and she pulled her head away. 'Do not play the sweet-and-innocent miss with me, Priscilla. If he takes advantage, then you are to do as he says and come to me afterwards. We will tell your father of it and the duke will be forced to offer with no more nonsense. But whatever you do, do not ruin the opportunity, for I doubt you will have a better one.'

Priss's heart sank. It was plain what her father expected of her. Society expected it as well. But knowing what she did, she could not imagine how she would manage it. If Reighland offered today, she would have to say no. The skies might open and hell might rain down on her if she disobeyed, but then perhaps Papa would see she was in earnest and she would have some peace. She disentangled herself from Ronnie and glanced into the mirror on the hall wall, touching her hair and straightening her skirts. Then she turned and went into the salon, where Reighland awaited her.

The footman announced her and she waved him away with a flick of her hand, trying not to flinch as she heard the door closing behind her. She focused all her attention on the man in front of her, muttering, 'Your Grace', and dropping a curtsy letting her eyes travel up from the floor until they met his face.

And it was such a long way for her gaze to travel.

He was well over six feet. She noticed the sprinkling of dark hair on the backs of his hands and up his wrists, disappearing into his shirt cuffs. It made her wonder what the rest of him would be like, without his clothes.

She quickly stifled the thought, for it only made her more frightened. There was a harmony to him, as though nature had sought to make an animal both intimidating and powerful. In the bedroom he would be just as large as he had been in the ballroom.

'Please, Lady Priscilla, if we are to be friends, let us not stand on ceremony. You must call me Robert.' His voice matched the rest of him. Deep, growling, with just a taste of a rasp that made the hairs on her neck stand to attention.

He was examining her now, top to bottom, as she had him. There was no hint of lust in it, which was just as well. If she'd thought that that was the first thing on his mind, she'd probably have run from the room in terror. This was more clinical, as though he was wondering about sound teeth, good wind and strong limbs.

But the desire that she use his first name was a very bad sign.

'Has your father explained the purpose for my visit?'

'No, your Grace,' she said, avoiding the offered intimacy. 'But I am not so dim that I cannot guess it.'

'And what say you to it?'

She searched her mind for a response that did not use the word that came most easily to mind: *trapped.* 'I thought I made it clear to you yesterday evening.'

He gave her the same blank look as he had on the previous evening. 'You merely said you would not be agreeing with me. I do not see that as an impediment to matrimony.' No talk of wooing at all. The man did like to cut to the chase.

He thought for a moment. 'You would have to agree at the altar, of course. But after that…'

Was he joking? It almost seemed that he might be. But his expression was so closed that it was impossible to tell. 'Are you sure you are quite sane?' she asked. For madness was the only other explanation.

'Is it necessary to be so?' he asked innocently. 'I was given to understand that my title was hereditary. From what I have seen of others in the peerage, you are the only one concerned with my sanity. If you mean to ask next if I am stupid, I will admit that I am not as quick as some. But in my brief stay in London, I have found many who were greater dullards.'

He was joking, then. But did he expect her to laugh? He seemed most sober. Perhaps he was seeking a mate who would be amused by him. More likely, she would be the butt of the joke, once he knew her better. His dry comments would seem innocent enough when he spoke them in public, but she would know the true meaning and would be left burning with shame.

And she could not abide a lifetime of that. 'May I be frank with you, your Grace?'

'It shall be an exciting change from the hesitant sentiments you have thus far expressed.'

'My rejection is not against you, personally,' she lied. 'It is only that I do not wish to submit easily to marrying any titled man that my father might choose.'

He gave her a sad smile. 'Then I fear you will submit with difficulty. With force, if necessary.'

Was this meant to be a threat? She would receive no help from Veronica, should he choose to make good on it. Priss felt another rising tide of panic. 'Do you mean to force me, then?'

'I shall not have to. Your father seems quite sure of your co-operation, no matter what you might say. You know better than I what he is capable of.'

Maybe it had been a warning, then. But her obvious difficulties had not bothered him enough to give him a distaste for a union with the family. 'And you would accept a wife who was so unwilling.'

'Benbridge will see you bound to someone, this Season. If you hold any choice in contempt, then you could do worse than to take me, should you be obligated to marry.'

Papa could not drag her screaming to the altar, but he was crafty, and Ronnie even more so. They had ways that she could not comprehend. The duke was right. There could well be worse choices. Her dislike of this particular man was not as instantaneous as she'd expected. But the size of him was simply too intimidating, and time was not likely to change it. 'You are no better than he is, if you care so little about how I come to you.'

'But I am hoping that you might come to think of me as the lesser of two, or more, evils,' he said, still without smiling. 'The devil you know, rather than the devil you don't. Personally, once I am set upon a course,

I do not intend to take no for an answer. And I am set on having you.'

She stared back, planning her next move. If he would not let her cry off, then she would have to work harder to give him a distaste of her. She smiled back at him, with a suddenness and brilliance he would know was false. 'I am happy to be given the opportunity for such an advantageous match.'

He snorted. 'Are you, really? You did not look it a moment ago.' He was examining her again. 'But I believe the last half of the statement. This will be an advantageous match. From your side, at least'

She bit back a furious retort. He was correct, after all. It was simply rude of him to mention the fact.

'I am recently come to the title, of course,' he said, with humbleness that was as false as her smile. 'I did not expect it. The old duke's heir died within the same year as his father, my father already having passed…'

'It matters not to me how you came to be a duke,' she said, still half-hoping her bluntness would put him off. 'It only matters that you are one at the time of offering. Beyond that, I have little interest in you.' She tried to look eager at the notion of such a prestigious match. Perhaps he would not want a title hunter.

He was staring at her again, thoughtfully. 'Considering your pedigree, it should be advantageous to the man involved as well. You are young, beautiful and well born. Why are you not married already, I wonder? For how could any man resist such a sweet and amenable nature?'

'Perhaps I was waiting for you, your Grace.' She

dropped her smile, making no effort to hide her contempt.

'Or perhaps the rumours I hear are true and you have dishonoured yourself.'

'Who...?' The word had escaped before she could marshal a denial. But she had experienced a moment's uncontrollable fear that, somewhere Dru had been that she had not, the ugly truth of it all had escaped and that now her happily married sister was laughing at her expense.

'Who told me? Why, you did, just now.' He was smiling in triumph. 'It is commonly known that the younger daughter of the Earl of Benbridge no longer goes about in society because of the presence of the elder. But I assumed there would be more to it than that. And I was correct.'

Success at last, though it came with a sick feeling in her stomach and the wish that it had come any way but this. She had finally managed to ruin everything. Father would be furious if this opportunity slipped through her fingers. It would serve him right, for pushing this upon her. 'You have guessed correctly, your Grace. And now I assume that this interview is at an end.' She gestured towards the door.

'On the contrary,' he replied. 'You have much more to tell me before I depart from here. Does the sad state of your reputation have anything to do with your family's willingness that we might meet alone?'

'There is no reason that we should not,' she replied. 'He expects that you will offer for me, not rape me on the divan in the lounge.'

If her frankness startled him, it did not show. 'And what if I did?'

'Then I would cry to my father and he would demand that you marry me.'

'As you might at any rate,' he pointed out. 'The door is closed and we are alone. Should you wish to tell tales about my behaviour, I would have no evidence to refute them.'

'Perhaps I would if I wished to trap you into marriage,' she snapped. 'It is you who have come to me and not the other way round. I never gave you any reason to think I wished a union. If your intentions are not in that direction, then, as I said before, you had best leave.'

He ignored the door and looked her up and down again, walking slowly around her, so as to view her from all angles. Then he spoke. 'Truth now. I will not tell your father, if that is what you fear. You have my word. Is there another, perhaps someone inferior to me, that you might prefer?'

'Would it matter?' she asked in exasperation. 'Between the two of you, you and my father seem to have settled the matter.'

'It might,' Reighland said, after a moment. 'And you did not answer my question.'

'If we are taking my opinions into account at this late date, then I shall tell you again: there is no other. All the same, I prefer to remain unmarried. Even if I sought marriage, it would not be with you. We do not suit. I thought I made that clear to you, when we danced.'

'I see.' He was staring at her again, appraising. 'You do not wish to leave the loving bosom of your family.'

She almost laughed at the absurdity of it. 'Of course I do. There is a dower house on the property in Cornwall that stands empty. And land further north where I might stay with my mother's sister. Perhaps I could go to Scotland. Any of those would do for a genteel spinsterhood. That is all I seek for myself.'

'Then I am sorry to disappoint you. As I said before, your father has no intention of allowing that. You will be married. If not to me, then to some other. Since you have no concrete objections, other than an illogical dislike of me, I will speak to your father. We will formalise this arrangement by the end of the month.'

Arrangement. Was that all it was to him? She had known when it came time to marry that there would be no love match. But she had not thought it would be quite so passionless as this. And so she blurted, before he could leave, 'If you mean to go ahead with this, then you had best know the whole truth, so that you do not reproach me with it on our wedding night. I am no longer innocent.' She would pay the price for her honesty, she was sure. The duke would storm out and tell her father. Then she would get a long lecture from Benbridge and his new wife about her stupidity in disobeying their orders and casting aside the only match they had been able to make for her.

But at least it would be over.

The Duke of Reighland was still standing there, giving her the same curious, up-and-down examination that he had been. Then he asked, 'Are you pregnant?'

'Certainly not!' Her cheeks heated and her palm itched to slap him for being so bold as to ask. Then a thought struck her. 'If I was, then why would I bother to tell you?'

'Why would you have told me anything?' he asked back, just as sensibly. 'If you wished to marry me, you would have kept quiet on the first point. But if you truly wished to frighten me away, you'd have lied about the second. The two statements, taken together, only make sense to me if they are true. They seem to imply that you are a most candid young lady. The truth is an admirable quality and quite rare in London. It must be cherished when it is found. I have learned all I wish to know. I will have you.' He stepped closer to her and she felt a sudden panicked scrambling desire to move away, back across the room before he would touch her.

But he did nothing more than bow before her, taking her cold hand in his and offering a kiss that was the barest touch of his lips against the skin. 'Now, with your permission, I will depart.' He rose and smiled. 'And with or without your permission, I will visit you again. While I am decided, I think we have more to discuss before an announcement can be made.'

She sat down on the couch behind her, numb with shock. He left the room and she could hear him speaking to her stepmother in the hall, arranging for another visit.

He was decided.

What had she said to him that had made the decision? She had done everything in her power to put him off. The truth, there at the end, should have been enough to send him running from the room. She was not good enough for him. Any rumours he might have heard of her elopement were true. She was ruined.

Yet he meant to come again. To persuade her. She felt a shudder rising from deep within her and tried to tell herself that it was revulsion. That was not true. But neither was it desire. She did not find him attractive. He was too large, too imposing and in all ways too blunt. She was not exactly frightened of him. That would be like fearing a mountain, or perhaps a cliff that one had no intention of standing on. It was more like awe, really.

She was not used to being in awe of anyone. The glamour of a title had been tarnished to her years ago.

And as for men?

She removed a handkerchief from her sleeve and delicately mopped her brow. Those secrets had been stripped away as well. Men were not nearly as pleasant as they appeared. She would be quite content to do without them, if only it would be permitted.

Veronica's voice, as she saw the duke to the door, was light, flirtatious and sycophantic. Whatever Priss might feel on the subject, her prospective husband was a favourite of the household and she was unlikely to escape him.

She thought of the size of him and the way he would come to her, naked, hairy as a bear, crushing her body with his weight, sweating and grunting over her as he pushed and thrust.

There was a soft rip and she noticed that she had torn the lace on the corner of the handkerchief she'd forgotten she was holding. She would need to mend it before an explanation was required of her. There had been a time when she might have lost a hundred such linens and experienced no punishment. But that was when Dru had still been in the house and there had been no Veronica, eager to find fault with her.

The duke was barely gone from the room when the doors to the salon burst open and her stepmother entered. 'Well, then?'

'He has offered,' Priss affirmed glumly.

Veronica clapped her hands together in triumph. 'Lucky for us and far better than you deserve. I will put the announcement in *The Times* immediately.'

'He does not wish to announce it yet,' she said.

'Then we will allow him to make that decision.'

'I have not said yes.'

Veronica was across the room in a moment, her hands in Priss's hair to pull her gaze up to meet her. 'Perhaps your father might permit your wilfulness, but we have seen where that led. When the time is right, you will say yes, like any sensible girl, because, my lady, in a few months there will be no space for you in this house. I will need your room for a nursery.'

'There are a dozen rooms that will suit just as well,' Priss said, glaring back at her and feeling the claws tightening against her scalp.

'But I favour the light in yours,' Veronica said with a small tight smile. 'You will be out of this house and you will be thankful that we are sending you to such a fortunate marriage and not out into the street as you deserve. But you will not be allowed to remain here, courting further disgrace. I will not let a girl who does not have the sense to keep her legs closed associate with children of mine.' She released Priss's head with a jerk that cracked her neck.

And then Veronica was smiling again. 'Come, my dear. We will go to Bond Street and buy you a trousseau.'

## Chapter Four

John Hendricks owned an unassuming house in an equally humble neighbourhood. Robert scolded himself for the assessment, remembering that he'd have thought no such thing before the title had foisted on him the various entailed properties in all their grandeur. There was nothing really wrong with this place, although he wondered what Lady Drusilla made of it, after living as Benbridge's daughter.

He knocked upon the door; when it opened, he announced himself and pushed his way past the house-keeper, tossing his gloves into his hat and giving her his most aloof ducal glare. Then he demanded to be shown to the receiving room, or whatever place was deemed best for a meeting with Mr Hendricks.

He watched the servant melt before him with a subservient curtsy. 'I will get him immediately, your Grace.'

Of course she would. It was late for an uninvited

call, of course. Not the thing to arrive at a man's house without some kind of warning. But now that he was 'his Grace' instead of plain old Mr Magson, the rules no longer applied.

Sometimes, he rather missed the rules. Dammit, he liked Hendricks. At least a lot more than he liked being Reighland and throwing his weight around. But today there would be no more pussyfooting about the truth. He wanted answers and he wanted them now, before his own native foolishness overcame good sense and he continued to press his suit on a girl who was showing every sign of being completely inappropriate. Even in his worst and least confident days, he'd had more sense than to chase after the leavings of other men when seeking a wife.

'Your Grace?' Hendricks stood in the doorway of his own home, offering an unironic bow as though it were he who had entered unexpectedly. 'How might I be of assistance?'

'You can leave off bowing at me, for one thing,' Robert muttered, unable to control the impulse. 'You might well want to bounce me out into the street when you hear why I have come. The respectful greeting will only make that more difficult.'

'Perhaps,' said Hendricks, with the faintest lift of an eyebrow. 'But we will not know until you have made your request.'

'Tell me about Benbridge's younger daughter. And not the nonsense you were spouting at the party. I want the truth this time.'

'It really is not my place—' Hendricks began.

'Yours as much as anyone else's. I will have the story in the end. She's already told me the more interesting half of it. The girl is no longer a maid.'

Hendricks sucked his breath in between his teeth in a sudden hiss, but said nothing.

'If the circumstances mitigate the truth, I should like to know it now. Who? When? Why? And who else knows of it? I heard rumours of an elopement with a dancing master. But I refuse to base my decisions based on tittle-tattle from gossiping old ladies. Any accurate information you can provide about Lady Priscilla will be welcome.'

Hendricks rose and went to the door of the sitting room, glancing into the hall to be sure that they were alone, before shutting it. 'I would rather my wife not hear what we are discussing. It is a sensitive subject in the family as you can imagine. Dru was charged with watching the girl and feels quite responsible for anything that might have happened. And I do not know the most intimate details, of course. It was several days before we caught up with the couple. The situation might not be as dire as you make it out.'

'I make nothing of it,' Robert said. 'It is Priscilla who seems sure of events. She should know them, if no one else does.'

Hendricks swallowed. 'And I can trust that, since I am speaking to the Duke of Reighland, the story will travel no further than this room.' The statement was obvious and unnecessary. Apparently, Hendricks did not trust him to keep the secret, without reminding him that he was a gentleman. It rankled.

He swallowed his pride, reminding himself that the man before him was near to Benbridge's family, no matter what the old earl might think of him. Then he responded, 'You have my word. I mean the girl no harm. But neither am I some poor gull in a country market, willing to buy a horse with bishoped teeth and piping lungs. An alliance between Benbridge and myself would be useful. But there is the succession to think of.'

'You think you might still consider her a suitable choice, after knowing the truth?' Hendricks pushed his glasses up the bridge of his nose as though seeking a better look at him.

'I am here, aren't I? Most men would be gone already.' Men smarter than himself, perhaps. But he had taken a liking to her and there was no reasoning with his first impression. He was still half-hoping that Hendricks would tell him he had misheard the girl. Or that he was the victim of some horribly unfunny joke. 'I have no real proof that Lady Priscilla will have me. Although she would be a fool to turn down the offer, she is resisting.'

'Priss is not known for her foresight,' Hendricks said drily.

'Obviously.'

'But if you mean to pursue her, then you shall have all I know of it.' Hendricks moved into the room, gesturing to a chair and offering port, before taking a seat himself. It was a decent wine and a comfortable chair. Robert appreciated the gesture, which seemed sincere, and not an effort to get on his right side for some gain later. If Hendricks was the climber he appeared to be, he was subtle and not some common sycophant.

Hendricks began. 'Late last summer, I met Lady Drusilla Roleston in a mail coach on the way to Gretna Green. She was seeking word of her sister, who had eloped with a dancing master named Gervaise. I offered my assistance. We caught the couple before they crossed the border and I dispensed with the fellow.'

'Permanently?'

Hendricks laughed. 'Hardly. He ran off with little encouragement, when he saw that he was more likely to come away with a beating than any money. Without guarantee of settlement, he had no real desire to take the girl for a wife.'

'So there was no real affection between them?'

'I cannot speak for man or girl. I can only report what I observed. Although Priss made a fuss at the time, she was over it by the next morning. It did not appear to me that either of them was broken hearted at the parting. I brought the sisters back to London safely and made my offer for Drusilla. Benbridge showed no desire to hear it. But Dru was willing, even though it meant an estrangement from her family.'

'How many days was Lady Priscilla unchaperoned?'

'At least three.'

Which probably meant that the elder sister was just as compromised as the younger had been. And willing to have Hendricks to spite her father. There was a story there, he was certain. But it was no real concern of his, since it did not figure in his bid for the other girl. 'Three days is more than enough time for mischief to be done.'

Hendricks shrugged. 'If a man is determined, three minutes in a drawing room is enough, even under the eyes of a chaperon.'

Robert gave the man a stern look. 'Not what I wished to hear from a man who had ample opportunity to be alone with my intended on the way back to London.'

'But true, none the less,' Hendricks admitted. 'Although it was unorthodox for me to be travelling with either of them, my affections were quite firmly fixed on the other sister by the time we turned back towards the city.'

'And when Priscilla returned, was it to the censure of the *ton*?'

'There were rumours, perhaps. But nothing more than that. Without Gervaise, there were no facts to back them with. It was not the disaster it might have been, had she been both imprudent and unlucky. If she is avoiding society, it is more from her own sensitivity than fear of embarrassment.'

Robert nodded in agreement. 'Disgrace can be swept under the rug, if one meets it with a bold face.' While Priscilla did not seem to be the sort to melt in the heat of society's stare, he had hardly known her long enough to make a judgement.

'Benbridge has done more to hurt the girl than she did with her own behaviour,' Hendricks added. 'The foolish feud he seeks with me makes it appear that Priscilla has some biological need to avoid society. But it has been nearly eight months since my marriage to Dru. From what I can tell, Priss looks just the same as she did on the day that I met her.'

No unwanted pregnancy, then. There had been time enough to see the results of that. 'Since that time, how has she behaved? Have you had wind of any new scandal?'

'I think it is likely that Priscilla learned a hard lesson and did not need to learn it twice. As far as I am aware, there have been no further incidents. She does not appear to be embracing rebellion. Benbridge hardly lets the girl out of his sight. Her social life was much constrained, once her sister was not there to serve as escort.'

'And now there is the new Lady Benbridge.' Robert dropped the name and waited for the reaction.

There was the faintest pursing of Hendricks' lips, as though he had no desire to think ill of a woman who was now his wife's stepmother. 'Perhaps I speak from affection. But Dru was a much steadier influence and more likely to act in the best interests of her sister, although Priss did not always see it as such.'

'Not as likely to hitch Priscilla to some ill-mannered stranger, just because he is a duke?'

Hendricks looked him up and down, then, as though appraising him. And for a moment, Robert was sure that, no matter how much the man might make of a connection himself, he would choose family over rank. 'I would think it little business of mine what the manners of the man were when he spoke to others, as long as they were good enough to suit his wife. And I would add that I wished to see Priscilla married to a man who, regardless of title, had at least a modicum of affection for her. She is far more likely to be loyal to someone who cares for her, than one who wishes to marry her father.'

'And you are wondering if I am such a man?'

'Perhaps I think it is time that someone wondered it. My wife is right. For all her faults, Priss deserves some happiness. She is unlikely to gain it if her father is left to choose a husband for her. If you wish the truth, then I will tell it to you: it matters not how you behave, or what Priscilla thinks of the matter. When Benbridge sees you, he will look no further than the title. After the coup of catching an earl, Lady Benbridge sees Priss as being little more than an inconvenience and will have her out of the house one way or another. If, after what you have learned today, you are not interested in pursuing this matter, then a rapid and strategic retreat is in order. Lady Benbridge will not be pleased that Priss has told you of her past to scare you off. She will trick you into dishonouring the girl, if she can make the match in no other way.'

'I suspected as much. It was only confirmation I sought when coming here.' Robert rose, setting his wine glass aside, and Hendricks followed him to his feet. 'Should you see her, you may tell your wife's sister that, at this time, I have no intention of retreat. I have learned nothing that has changed my intention to make a match with Lady Priscilla. But I do not intend to force an offer on a woman who does not want me. Further study of the situation is in order. And then we shall see what we shall see.'

## Chapter Five

'Priscilla, whatever am I to do with you?' Veronica was standing in the doorway to her bedroom again, shaking her head in disapproval. 'You knew to expect a caller, yet you have done nothing to ready yourself. You cannot greet a duke in such a shabby dress.'

Priss had assumed that, when given the time to reflect on what she had told him, he would see his error in courting her and sever the connection. But it appeared that he was more persistent than sensible. 'I had quite forgotten,' she lied. 'Tell him to return another day. Perhaps tomorrow I shall have enough time to prepare.' She was being childish, to the point where she bored and annoyed even herself. But when man and family would not listen to a plain refusal, she was forced to use any trick she could muster.

'I most certainly will not send him away.' Veronica came to the side of the bed and hauled her upright, spilling a half-finished game of Patience off the unmade bed. 'If you refuse to dress, then he will see you as you are now. Perhaps it will embarrass you sufficiently that we will not have this problem when he comes again tomorrow.'

They were planning for tomorrow already? Then she had just as well let him see her in a sad state today. Until she could manage to make him see that she was not appropriate, he would stay camped out in the salon and she would have no peace at all. 'Very well, then, I am justly punished for my lack of preparation. Let us go downstairs so that I may humiliate myself.'

Veronica frowned at her, as though recognising that she had been caught in her own trap. But she released Priss's arm and allowed her to proceed under her own power to the main floor. When the footman opened the door to the salon, her unwanted suitor half-turned to see her entrance, clearly interested but using his status to remind everyone that he expected to see those around him scurry to attention and not the other way round.

It annoyed her no end. She took her time with the short walk to his side, turning the last few steps into a dawdle as the doors closed behind her, leaving them alone. 'Your Grace?' She made a proper curtsy, feeling much as she had on the previous day, only perhaps a little more desperate. This meeting should not be happening. Her revelation should have put an offer well out of reach.

Which might mean he had other things than marriage on his mind. It might amuse him to keep the daughter of an earl as a mistress and would certainly tell the *ton* just how high above them he considered himself. If he made an inappropriate advance, she could do little to counter it. Her only chaperon was hiding on the other side of the house so that she would be unable to stop an indiscretion until it was far too late.

She watched him uneasily, waiting for him to speak.

'I have a gift for you.' The duke seemed almost child-ishly pleased with himself as he pulled a long thin box from under his arm and held it out to her.

She took it cautiously and lifted the lid just a crack before letting it fall closed again as her worst fears were realised. 'I cannot accept these,' she said flatly.

'Why ever not?'

'They are too intimate.'

'They are gloves.'

'Yes. I know.' Long, spotless and white. She was sure, if she touched them, they would be of the finest and most perfect kidskin and a rival to anything she might have bought for herself. She placed her hand on top of the box lid so that she could not be tempted to open it again and pushed it back towards him. 'A lady would never accept a gift of clothing and a gentleman would never offer.'

His brow furrowed, as though struggling with an unfamiliar concept. 'They are hardly indecent.'

'That is not the point. They indicate an interest in my person.'

'Of course they do,' he said, still surprised. 'Because I am interested in your person. It would make no sense to marry a woman who did not interest me in that way.'

So he was still talking about a wedding. That was some consolation, since it proved he would not spring across the room and fall upon her like a ravening beast. If she had actually wanted to marry him, she'd have been in alt. But clearly he did not understand what he must do, when making a proper offer to a lady. 'If you really wished to marry me, you'd have brought another sort of gift entirely. A book, perhaps. Or flowers.'

'Flowers will die,' he said firmly. 'That cannot send the sort of message I would wish. And as for books? It is not that I never read, but I doubt that the things I favour would hold any interest to you. What would you have said if I'd brought you a stack of stock journals, tied up with a pretty ribbon?'

'I'd have thought you mad.'

'There. You agree with me.' He pointed to the gloves. 'Those are pretty, practical and will last you longer than the average bouquet. And do not argue modesty, for they cover an extremity I can see quite plainly now.'

Which left her wishing she had changed to a more appropriate gown with full-length sleeves. He was staring at her hands, her wrists and the length of her arms in a way that felt strangely as if he was staring inappropriately at some other more personal part of her body.

She hurriedly opened the box, removed one of the gloves and slipped it on, so that he would cease ogling her.

It was a very nice glove. Though his manners were abominable, she could not fault the man's taste. The leather caressed her hands and hugged tight to her arm like a second skin. The top was finished in a carefully punched scallop, so delicate that it almost seemed like lace. Hardly thinking of what it must look like, she put on the other glove as well, then held her hands out in front of her to admire them.

'Here. Let me do up the buttons for you.' He took one of her hands and turned it over, doing up the line of mother-of-pearl buttons at the wrist.

She felt the little hitch in her breath as his large hands worked cautiously over the tiny buttons and brushed against the sensitive skin at her pulse. Then it was gone and he was holding her hands just by the fingertips, so that she could feel the heat and pressure through the thin leather that covered them.

'They are lovely on you,' he said, with little passion. 'And though I can imagine a bracelet of diamonds resting there, it is hardly necessary to improve the beauty of your wrists.'

That was more the sort of flattery she'd expected from a potential suitor. It annoyed her that she felt moved by it. And the gloves were not helping, for they made her feel both cherished and caressed. She hurried to undo the buttons and take them off again. 'They are still inappropriate. But I thank you for them.' Now that she had seen them on her hands, she did not really want to give them up. She cursed herself for the weakness, but put the gloves back in the box to set aside for later.

'You're welcome,' he responded. 'And why did you run away with your dancing master?'

'I beg your pardon, your Grace?' She dropped the box in her haste to be rid of the gloves, then looked quickly around the room, fearing that someone might have heard.

He must have seen her guilty flinch, but made no

comment on it. 'It is a simple enough question, I am sure. And one that only you know the answer to. I will repeat it more loudly, if you wish.'

'No.' It was quite possible that Veronica was listening at the door. Of all the topics of conversation she did not wish to open with her stepmother, it was the one that would lead to another rant on the foolishness of her elopement. 'You do not need to repeat yourself. I heard your question quite clearly.'

'Then I expect an answer. You must have had a reason. Or is this merely the sort of whim that you are prone to?'

'I ran because I wished to escape a tyrant.' If he'd meant to warn her of her father on the last visit, he must understand what she meant by this statement.

'You wished to trade one for another, more like,' the duke said, watching her reaction closely. 'Did you have reason to think that the man would be a kind and generous husband? If he was crafty enough to have taken you away, he had designs on your fortune.'

'Gervaise lacked any craft, I assure you. It was I who engineered the elopement. And I had no intention of marrying him. Not really. I expected to be caught before we could wed and dragged back in disgrace, which is exactly what happened. Then I would be sent with my sister to rusticate in the country.'

'You said you do not like the country.'

'Not particularly. But the city was intolerable, as long as my father was in it.'

'And you thought, if you had shamed yourself sufficiently...'

'That I could avoid a situation just like this one, where I was forced to marry a man I hardly knew.'

'You wished to avoid me.'

Because it must be about the man and his enormous self-importance. She rolled her eyes. 'I suppose now you will tell me that you are hurt. But you asked for the truth and I gave it to you.'

'Then I will give you truth as well. That seems like a surprisingly stupid and convoluted plan. Much could go wrong.'

'Much did. I was caught, as I expected to be.' And Gervaise had decided that there was no reason to wait for Scotland to assert his conjugal rights. She pushed that particular unpleasantness from her mind. 'But I did not take my sister to the country. She'd met Mr Hendricks, in the few days I'd been away.' She looked into his eyes, wondering how much he understood of her sister's life before her marriage. 'It was far worse for Drusilla here than it ever was for me. It pained me to see her constantly belittled and punished for my mistakes. And I made many, I assure you. I was a wilful child and I could not manage to control my own temper, when listening to his unreasonableness. But she bore the brunt of his anger. Her marriage got her out of this house, which was the thing I'd hoped for all along.'

'You thought, by eloping, that you would help her?'

'I thought that it might be good for both of us. I assumed that she could be chaperon to my disgrace and that we would be sent off together.' She gave a helpless shrug. 'Instead, she was happily married and I have been all but incarcerated, to prevent it happening again.'

'I see,' he said.

'I doubt you do. You are a man and can never really understand what it means to be so totally under the thumb of another human being. You have freedoms that I cannot even imagine.'

He laughed. It was an empty, bitter sound for a man so normally free of emotion. 'The freedom to walk in a dead man's shoes, you mean.'

'The shoes of a duke,' she said. 'They are hardly a hardship.'

He gave her a disgusted look. 'I came to that position because two men I loved and respected died before their time. And a baby as well. Perhaps, in your family, heartlessness and calculation are the orders of the day, but I would happily trade the title to give any one of them life. And to have my old life back as well.'

Of all the things she'd thought to feel for the man, she had not expected sympathy, or the sudden rush of kinship. She reached out and clasped his hand and felt him start in surprise. There was a moment's awkwardness as they both adjusted to the unexpected contact. Then she said, 'I am sorry for your loss. You are right. I am being selfish again. It must have been quite difficult for you.'

'You as well,' he agreed. 'Having met your father, I doubt he grieved overlong for the man who held the title before him. Now he is willing to barter you for the small advance that a connection to me might bring.'

He sighed and looked at her. 'Of course, I am not much better. I was willing to take you nearly sight unseen, if it meant the best thing for my own name.'

'Thank you for admitting it,' she said, surprised yet again by his inappropriate candour.

'But now that I've met you, it is something quite different,' he added. 'I wish to know you better and it has nothing to do with your father's name or title.'

She had been waiting a lifetime to hear someone say something just like this. Why, now, must it be this particular man? The undercurrent of fear she felt when she looked at him was still greater than any tender feelings. 'That is very flattering,' she said cautiously.

'But...' he said, placing a finger upon her lips to seal them against further words. 'I already know you so well that I can predict your next words will be an attempt to put me off. So let us stop before we get to the equivocations that I am sure will follow. Will you admit that you barely know me?' When she made an effort to speak, he added, 'A nod will be sufficient for an answer.'

She nodded.

'And will you agree that sometimes it is possible to change your initial, and might I add totally illogical negative opinion about a person, after further acquaintance?' He saw the militant glare she gave him and clarified, 'You do not need to think of any particular person. I just wish you to admit to the possibility.'

She gave another helpless nod.

He removed his finger from her mouth. 'Then will you allow me a week, or perhaps two, to dance with you, to visit with you, to spend time in your company. If I cannot persuade you in that time, I will admit defeat.'

And in that time, Veronica and Benbridge would grow more and more certain. The inevitable failure would not sit well with them and she would pay the price for it, she was sure. 'But my father—'

'Will not be part of our discussion,' he said firmly. 'In the time we are together, I will keep you safe from the intentions of others, while seeing to it that you are more regularly welcomed in society. If we must part, I will make sure there are no repercussions from your family.' He was glaring again, looking large and dark as a bear. She did not want to think what it would feel like to have that anger directed at her.

But she rather enjoyed the idea that he wished to use it in defence of her. 'What do you expect in exchange?' she asked suspiciously, for she ought to know by now that no gift was ever offered without a cost to be paid later.

'I expect a fair hearing,' he said. 'And that you wear the gift I have offered you when we dance tonight.'

'Tonight?' She shook her head. 'Where is this dancing to take place? I have no outstanding invitations.'

He gave her a grim little smile. 'You will. See to it that you answer in the affirmative. And now, if you will excuse me?' He offered her a low bow and reached for her hand, raising her fingers to his lips. She steadied herself against the kiss she was sure was coming, then relaxed in surprise as she felt the passage of nothing more than a warm breath from the kiss that he had directed to the air just above her knuckles. 'Until tonight?'

It was a question. 'Tonight,' she agreed. She was

unsure of what might happen that would make any difference in her feelings, but she was curious enough to want to see it.

# *Chapter Six*

&#10086;&#10087;&#10088;&#10089;&#10090;

Veronica proclaimed her well turned out for the evening; after admiring herself in the mirror, Priss could almost manage to agree with her. This Season, everything felt wrong. Tonight's gown, a white silk embroidered with dainty sprays of white-and-pink flowers, was complemented by a single strand of pearls and a few pink rose petals in her hair. The effect was lovely and suitable for a girl of her age. In the hazy glow of candlelight she would give an appearance of innocence, but in her heart it felt like some bad joke.

It still stung that she had not managed to procure vouchers for Almack's this Season. Her friends were dancing there tonight. The crowd here was older, married and rather staid. She would have thought it to be just the sort of party that would have Dru in her stead. It made her wonder if there was a better event occurring somewhere nearby.

She chided herself for that brief bitterness and set it

aside. This was quite enough for her, she was certain. The champagne was cold, the ballroom glittering and the music lively. And she had to admit, she was enjoying her new gloves. They matched the dress, of course. To others they might appear quite ordinary. But when worn, the soft and supple leather was like a caress from a lover's hands. They felt as she did: normal on the outside, but hiding a sinful nature.

The company did not matter so much, any more. Once the rumour got about that Reighland was interested in her, there would be few men willing to compete with him.

She should be happy, she knew. While he was not to her taste, it could have been much, much worse. He was not old, nor was he particularly unkind. Blunt, perhaps. But she had made several fatal *faux pas* in response and he had adjusted to each of them with barely a rise of his heavy black brows.

'Lady Priscilla.' Once again, the hairs on her neck stood up, as though the sound of his voice was a command to them.

She turned. She dipped her head and curtsied. 'Your Grace. I did not expect to see you there.'

'I can't imagine why not. You know it was I who saw you were invited. Asked the Hendricks to stand down for an evening, so that I might see you in candlelight.'

'I meant standing so close behind me.' And just as she'd been thinking of him. She felt a dull flush of embarrassment creeping behind her ears and stared at the floor. 'Thank you, your Grace. It was most kind of you to procure this invitation.'

He must have heard the reluctance in her voice, for he responded, 'But it was most mannerless of me to mention the fact. Sorry.'

'Apologies are not needed.' Where was her tongue? She should give him the sharp side of it, as she had before. Last year, the *ton* would have laughed along with her, thinking her impertinence to be charming. When had everything changed?

There was another awkward pause and he took a swallow of wine from the glass he held. 'If I am not in your black books, then you had best learn to look up at me when we talk. While the top of your head is very pretty, I would just as soon see your lovely face. If you can manage it, smile as well. It will be a longer evening than it already is if you mean to spend it frowning at my feet while I insult you.'

To look up would remind her of his size, and of so many other things that she preferred not to think about. But he was right. Opportunities to get out of the house were rare enough and would be rarer still should she behave strangely. She forced her chin up to meet his gaze, summoned what grace she could from deep inside herself and let it flow out in a smile that she knew to be both charming and attractive.

But no longer effortless.

It was returned, from her companion, with little more than a solemn nod. 'Very good. I was told that you were beautiful. But the word hardly does you justice.' At one time, she'd have thought it flattery and responded with a flutter of her fan. But from this man, it was such a plain statement of fact that to react to it would be like blushing at a mention of the weather.

He set his glass aside and offered a hand to lead her to the bottom of the set. 'A dance, then? I imagine we can pull together in harness, for a few simple steps at least. Of course, you will find that I am no dancing master...'

And there was the mention of her elopement again. Was it possible that he meant it as an idle comment? Or was it meant as a joke? Could he not see that her past was no laughing matter?

He either did not notice her awkwardness, or pretended not to, leading her through a few turns and placing a hand upon her back. But the jibe stuck with her as they moved clumsily together. What had Gervaise said, in those stolen moments when he had taught her to waltz? That the movements of the dance were but an echo of the act of love. And remembering how that had gone...

The man beside her, huge and oafish, was all but dragging her through the dance, his big hands on her waist as they turned together. She tried not to imagine him as a lover. On her, over her, in her, labouring over the act as he was over the movements. And the room spun in a way that had nothing to do with the pattern of the dance, tipping uneasily, as though it could throw her off. Suddenly, she was sure that if she stayed here one moment longer, she would be known as the odd girl who became sick in the middle of a crowded ballroom.

She pulled out of his grasp, touching her hand to her face, and glanced up into his shocked eyes, whispering frantically, 'Air.' Then she pulled away from him and ran for the terrace doors, not caring the embarrassment it would bring and the latest *on dit* that would be floating through the *ton* tomorrow. Lady Priscilla Roleston had left the Duke of Reighland standing open mouthed on the dance floor.

*Damn.*

He had been so eager to see her tonight, surprised to feel such pleasant anticipation at a second chance to speak to her in a single day. He had watched as she entered the room, then reminded himself that this was not meant to be a love match and that he did not exactly wish for one. The Duke of Reighland could not afford the highs and lows of hope and despair that mere mortals experienced. It was difficult to keep track of the doings in the House and at Court, and with his many tenants and properties, without wandering after some girl like a mooncalf.

There might be passion, of course. She was a damn fine-looking girl, just as he'd been told. And she was wearing the gloves he'd bought her on her slender pink arms. He could imagine himself, peeling them off again, kissing every inch of exposed skin. But that feeling could not possibly last. She was at least interesting to talk to, although she had some very odd ideas.

She did not ride, he told himself firmly, trying to quell the eagerness. He could change that in time, he hoped. But if her aversion to horses proved deeper than her aversion to him, he would have to accept failure and withdraw his offer.

But after what he had just done, she would have to hate horses near to death to equal what she must feel for him. Why had he been foolish enough to bring up the matter of the dancing master yet again? He had meant it as a joke. It was a year in the past and truly insignificant to him.

But for her it was a fresh hurt and each outing in society a foray into enemy territory. She would have to grow used to the comments, if she was ever to overcome them, just as he had. To let the taunts roll off her back, to make a joke of herself when no other way would work, and to grow tall, to grow strong...

And that advice would be quite useless. Ladies did not solve their problems on the fields of Eton, but then neither had he. He'd run for the country the first chance he'd had. If he had been a disappointment to his father, that good man had never said so, but he had been a scholar and had encouraged circumspection over foolish displays of bravado.

There would be no running from trouble now and no father to advise him. He and Priss would both have to stick it out and ignore the sidelong glances and harsh words. If the aloof Benbridge was any indication, she must have been bred to believe that others did not matter. Why could she not behave so now?

He went to the refreshment table to fetch her a lemonade. Then he thought the better of it and stepped behind a potted palm to dump half the cup away and top it off with brandy from his flask.

Next he went to the verandah, where she waited, staring morosely off into the darkness.

He pressed the cup into her hands. 'Drink.'

She took the first sip and choked. 'Whatever did you do to this? It is foul.'

'That is at least half spirits. You seemed in need of more fortification than lemonade would give.'

She took a deep breath and drank half of it down in a gulp. 'Do you mean to take advantage of me, then? For I believe we've established that alcohol will not be necessary.' She gave a harsh laugh. 'Between my loose morals, my stupidity and my father's desire that I entrap you, you might do just as you wished with me and I would welcome the indignity.'

Had other men tried? he wondered. Or had her father encouraged it? She seemed bitter and fragile, and very much alone. He chose his next words carefully. 'Do I mean to take advantage of you? You are a tempting morsel, I must admit. If the opportunity presents itself I would not turn it down. But it will not be tonight. Let us sit for a moment, then we will return to the ballroom, the best of friends.'

'Why do you bother,' she asked, 'if you think so little of me?'

'I do not think less of you. But I fear you think less of yourself. I spoke poorly, just now. But it frustrates me that you worry so about what others say, now that it is too late to change things. You are who you are. Others may take that, or leave it alone.'

'That is an utterly male way to think,' she said, as though it were some kind of fault. 'And a rich and titled male at that. They are the only sort that could walk away from past mistakes and let the world be damned for caring.'

'Perhaps,' he admitted, wishing it were true. 'I have a vague knowledge of the rules of female society. But I cannot say I care much about them. Am I being far too obtuse if I suggest that you limit your concern to the opinions of those people that truly matter?' *As though she would ever count him in that category.*

He took a breath and reminded himself that, since his accession to the title, he had no reason to worry. 'My opinion should matter, for instance. I think well of you. The others are unimportant.'

'And that is exactly what I do not understand,' she said, staring up at him. 'I need to know...why.'

'Why?' he asked.

'Why you are doing this?' She shook her head in confusion. 'The dancing and flirting, the attention to my needs. Why are you *courting* me?' Her voice dropped on the last word, as though it was something shocking or scandalous.

'Am I courting you?' he asked, with mock innocence.

'It appears that you are.'

'So my behaviour cannot be construed as kindness or friendship.'

She gave him a tired look. 'The last I checked, it is London at the height of the Season. You are an eligible duke. There is little kindness or friendship to go around.'

'Perhaps I am attracted to your refreshingly honest nature.'

'Or my father's title. I understand the reasons for

your offer. They are purely political and none of my concern.'

He thought for a moment. 'No. I do not think that is it. As you have pointed out to me, I would hardly need to waste my time on you to curry favour with him. I have but to vote as he does and that should be enough. It is he who is attempting to curry favour with me.'

'True,' she said, making a sour face as she sipped at the cup he had given her.

'And I am willing to allow it, as long as it does not impinge on my own goals or desires.'

'Which makes you sound little better than my father. It gives me no reason to think that my life will be any better than it has been. It does not explain to me why, after all I have told you, that your goals or desires include me, particularly.'

'I should think that would be obvious. You are attractive and good company.'

'I am not trying to be,' she admitted.

'And that is why I enjoy being with you.' He glanced back towards the ballroom. 'The other girls I have met in recent months try far too hard. It is clear that they give no thought at all to whether we might suit in any way other than that I am Reighland. They are willing to bend themselves into knots if it will get my attention.' He looked down at her again. 'You, at least, have spine enough to speak the truth. Further investigation is necessary.'

'So in trying to put you off, I have done the thing most likely to draw you in.'

'Exactly.'

'And I suppose I cannot suddenly turn agreeable.'

'I would think it a double blind,' he said. 'And I would continue to press my suit. Or I would assume that my charm had finally won you over and it would increase my ardour.'

She could not help herself and laughed at the idea that he might possess anything like winning charm.

He stared past her, out into the garden, and smiled in relief. 'You ask why I court you, Lady Priscilla. Then I will tell you. There are damn few people here with the courage to laugh in my presence. Even fewer who would dare to respond when I was joking at my own expense. In you? I see something. You will pretend it is not there. But you show hints of a most admirable courage. It may disappoint me that you cannot display it in your own defence, but I admire it all the same.'

'Thank you.' Her response was the barest of whispers.

'It is a lovely night, is it not?' He fell back on banal small talk to fill the awkward silence.

'Yes,' she agreed.

'Stars,' he said, making a vague gesture toward the sky.

'Yes.'

'A fresh breeze.'

She inhaled and nodded.

'And a beautiful woman.'

She faltered. Then managed another, 'Thank you.' Her voice was a little stronger, but she continued to look straight forwards, out into the darkness.

'A kiss would not be inappropriate,' he suggested. 'Between a couple on the verge of a commitment.'

'Are we on such a precipice?' she asked.

'We could be,' he admitted. He waited for the usual arguments. She did not wish to be married to anyone, least of all to him. But if they did marry, there was little point in pretending that this was anything other than inevitable. The Duke of Reighland wished it and her father had agreed. It would be done. Why must he dress it up as something that it was not: a normal courtship with moonlight, and soft sighing breezes?

If she did, he would answer that some part of him longed desperately for that pretence. He might have been an ordinary suitor, full of sweet words and flattery. He would have lured her here to steal what he was about to take by right. And she would be feeling the anticipatory fluttering inside, the excitement of a single, stolen kiss. There would be no dashed expectations, no fear, no disillusion. Just the sure belief that every moment would be as sweet as this one.

Next to him, she closed her eyes and turned towards him, waiting woodenly for the kiss that would break the spell and return them both to the truth.

He reached for her and ran the pad of his thumb over her mouth, wishing that it might be as soft as she was. He had never felt anything so delicate in his life. He brushed as lightly as he could against the firmly set lower lip, feeling it part from its mate ever so slightly. He caught his breath as he felt the tiny, almost accidental kiss on the tip of his finger. He slid it lower to rest against the line of her jaw. And then, at last, he leaned forwards and let his lips touch hers, soft, warm, just wet enough to show the life in them. Through his own barely open lips, he could taste the brandy he had given her and feel the gentlest touch of her tongue against his.

Time passed. He measured it by each breath they shared. But he dared not move. He rested against her mouth, not as an invader, but as though he were a sleeping part of her own body. It made him think of lying by her side, late at night, drifting into dream with the firm press of her against him, anchoring him like a ship that had come to harbour.

And then he drew away, slowly as he had come, closing his lips and pushing off from hers with the faintest increase of pressure, before his hand dropped away.

She opened her eyes, blinking once, as if she was trying to clear her mind of what had happened.

Somewhere in him, he felt sadness that she would be eager to forget something so utterly perfect as that moment had been.

He had kissed before.

And this was different.

It lacked the sense that all of his other kisses had, of being an immediate prelude to something else. While that type of kiss was certainly exciting, it came with the knowledge that he must keep a bit of himself apart, revelling in the physical release while leaving his heart untouched. But with Priscilla, for the first time, he had opened himself totally to another person and revealed a vulnerability that no peer could admit to having.

And she was smiling at him, as though nothing had happened. How dare she dismiss him in this way?

He readied a retort.

Then he looked into her eyes and saw that she was as shaken as he by what had happened. She might not admit it, but he had won her with a single kiss. All the rest would be formality and pretence.

He returned a smile as false as the one she gave him, for it would anger her if he revealed the triumph he felt. 'Shall we return to the ballroom, Lady Priscilla? If you allow me, I will escort you to supper. I understand that the food here is mediocre and my conversation is rumoured to be quite dull. It will be just the thing to settle your nerves.'

# Chapter Seven

That night Priss awoke in a cold sweat. She had been dreaming about the night in the inn, when everything had gone wrong. She had to get hold of herself. It was clear that these little spells of unease were growing worse and not better with the possibility of a large and virile fiancé.

She owed Reighland more of an explanation than she was giving him, that was for certain. He had done nothing to deserve her distaste of him. Since he showed no sign of ceasing his pursuit of her, she might end by fainting dead away in front of the altar if she did not tell him the truth and put an end to this.

Until his arrival, she'd at least managed to banish any demons from the daylight. But in sleep her mind always seemed to turn a situation that had been merely unpleasant into an actual nightmare. It annoyed her. It was unfair to Gervaise to twist things around to make some sort of villain out of him, when it had been she who had orchestrated the events of their elopement. She was willing to pay the price for her recklessness with well-deserved social ostracism.

But Gervaise had been no better or worse than she'd expected and she would do well to reiterate the actual events to herself to banish any nonsense.

On the first night they'd stopped, after leaving London for Gretna Green, he had taken only one room for them. She had nervously suggested that two might be better. But he had said, quite bluntly, 'You were the one who wished to run away and be married. You must have known what that would mean. Scotland is only a day or two off. In my mind, we are practically married now.'

Practically married was quite different than legally married. Still, if she wished to have any say in the matter of her own future, she must learn to stand by her decisions, even if she had begun to suspect that they were wrong. If she wanted to be stopped before the border, it would be better that they dawdled. She would be ruined no matter what went on in the bed tonight. She might as well satisfy her curiosity as to what actual ruination entailed.

'Very well, then,' she said. 'One room. And we shall share the bed.' She thought it would make him smile. He had been quite free with his humour when they'd been still in London. But now he was smiling to please himself, making no effort to put her at her ease.

Once the door was closed, he wasted little time. He kissed her. It was not like the gentle little busses he had given, when they'd stolen time together in the ballroom.

He simply put his tongue on her lips and pushed it into her mouth.

She withdrew. 'What are you doing?'

'That, Priss, is how married people kiss. I thought that you knew that, at least.'

'Oh.' She stood still and let him do it again. He was moving around in her mouth and she assumed that she was supposed to do something similar. She tried. He seemed to like it, though she could not quite seem to understand what the bother was. It was nice, she supposed. But not much more than that.

And then, with no further preamble, he had thrust a hand down her bodice and squeezed her breast. She was used to the sly touches he managed sometimes, when they danced. There had been the gentlest brushes of his hands over her bodice, under the guise of adjusting her posture when teaching a new step. Then there had been hurried and false apologies, accompanied by the blinding smile, to make sure she noticed what he had done.

Those touches had left her trembling, almost too weak in the knees to go on with her lesson. She had been sure, no matter what was likely to happen on this trip, that there would be more exciting moments such as that.

But now he was kneading her, as though she were an insensate lump of dough, and grunting with pleasure.

'Gervaise,' she said, 'more gently, please…' Or at least she tried to say. For he could not seem to let her have the use of her own tongue to speak. When he did stop the kiss long enough for her to object, he hardly looked her in the eye.

'Too rough? It's because the gown is in the way. So let's see them, then. Off with it.' He seemed most annoyed that she fumbled with the closures, for she was not accustomed to dressing without the help of a maid. At last, tired of waiting, he spun her around and did the job himself with such speed that she feared he would split a seam.

But he lied. He was no more gentle with the gown hanging about her waist than he was before. Now, he could use his teeth on her. A few minutes after that, he had pushed up her skirts and dropped the front of his breeches...

She had lain in bed afterwards, with him snoring beside her, wondering about what had just happened was worthy of song or poetry. It had been short and painful; it had hardly seemed that she was involved in it at all.

She could not even tell herself that it was the pain of the first time. When Gervaise awoke, it was much the same. It had gone on in that way for three days at each stop they'd made, until she'd managed to lock the door of the room before he could enter. He'd complained bitterly about the unfairness of it. But she'd shouted back at him that he had no right to upbraid her, that he was lucky to have had as much as he had and that, no matter what had happened, she would not marry him now if he was the last man on earth.

She had wished then that she could go back to Drusilla and demand an explanation, or at least some reassurance that it would get better with time. But when she had run away, Silly had known even less about the physical aspects of love than she did and would do no more than give her a scold and drag her back to London.

Instead, the Drusilla who'd found her had been starry eyed with love. She had seen the kisses that her older sister had shared with Mr Hendricks and known that there was poetry in love somewhere. But apparently it had not been meant for her.

Now everyone assumed that she was to belong to the Duke of Reighland. She had never met a soul more devoid of music in her life.

Until tonight's kiss, at least. He had been understanding about her flight from the dance floor. The stolen moments in the garden had been the sweetest that she had ever spent. Even now, the gentleness of the single kiss managed to quiet her heart, which was still beating hard from the exertions of the dream.

Without being able to help herself, she was drawn to Reighland. There were a hundred ways it would not work, of course. He was too close to her father. He was too powerful. He might seem gentle, but so had Gervaise, at first. Things would change the moment they were truly alone.

She rolled and punched at the pillow, trying to find some cool place where she could lay her head and rest. The Duke of Reighland might not love her, though he at least appeared to be fond of her.

But that would not overcome the very obvious fact that she did not think, no matter how gently he treated her, that she could face performing the marital act again.

If it had been bad with Gervaise, then what would it be like with this hulking stranger? Tenderness would not make him any smaller. And if he chose to be a vigorous lover?

Her palms curled in on themselves and she squeezed until she felt the pain of her nails, imagining herself clutching the bed sheet as he pummelled her, wishing the image were in any way erotic, so that she might trick herself into believing she wanted this. No matter what he would do, it would hurt her. And he would want it again and again, for the rest of her life.

Until such time as he grew bored with her, anyway. Then he would take away the pain and the pleasure as well. He would take away his gentle understanding, his dry jokes and his sweet kisses, and spend them on some other woman.

She stared at the ceiling and willed herself to sleep. Her last thought before the dreams returned was that the end of any physical pain Reighland might cause would be unequal to the agony of loss that might follow.

# Chapter Eight

*This could be yours.*

It was impossible not to think it at least once upon seeing such a house. Once she'd admitted to it, she could rest easy and think no more about it for the rest of the evening.

Priscilla surveyed the foyer of Reighland's London home, the paintings on the walls, the thickness of the hall carpet and the perfection of the ballroom, with a critical eye, exercising her covetousness like an atrophied muscle. It all could be hers, if she married him. But she did not really wish to marry any man simply to gain control of his house. If she had learned nothing in the last months of seclusion, it was her ability to do without.

He had probably hoped to inspire just such a reaction by inviting her here. She had suspicions that this rather grand event had been organised so that she would visit his home and admire his wealth. He'd made no mention of a rout when they had been alone at the ball three days ago. But the invitation had arrived the next morning with the first post. She expected he had kept some poor servants up half the night gathering guest lists and scratching out addresses to meet his impulsive demand. In response, it appeared that half of London had cleared its schedule and called for a carriage.

But now Reighland was pushing his way through the crowd towards them, holding out a welcoming hand. 'Benbridge, Lady Benbridge, welcome. And Lady Priscilla, of course.' He was favouring her with a rare smile, which did nothing to diminish his intimidating nature.

'Your Grace.' She made a polite curtsy, then let her mind wander from the exchange of greetings, talk of the weather and of politics.

Reighland broke off suddenly, as though sensing her lack of enthusiasm. 'But my talking nonsense with your father can hardly be of interest to you, Priss.'

The slight to Papa made her flinch, as did the use of her nickname. She had given him no permission to use it, but she could not very well object to it in front of Ronnie. It was clear that the rest of her party would accept any familiarities foisted upon her with enthusiasm. 'It is all right, your Grace. Pray, do not let me interrupt your conversation.'

'No, it is not. I would never forgive myself if your first visit to my home was less than enjoyable. If you will excuse me, Benbridge, I will escort your daughter around the room. I am sure that I have some delicacy here that will tempt her.'

'She would be honoured,' Veronica said firmly,

before Priss could think of a plausible objection. 'And we would be happy to relinquish her. Come, Benbridge. We must not monopolise our host.'

Father allowed himself to be led off with only a token objection, proof that he was as complicit in the illusion as Veronica. Once again, she was alone with Reighland—or as alone as one might be in a packed ballroom. But considering her precarious position in society, that sometimes felt quite alone indeed. Now Reighland was smiling down at her like a child presented with a new toy.

She returned a jaundiced stare. 'So, what are these temptations you speak of? Or was it merely a ruse to spare yourself my father's company?'

He dipped his head, as though it was possible to talk intimately with a voice that boomed as his did. 'If I made up lies to spare myself the company of everyone I find tiresome, I suspect that I would speak no truth for the rest of the evening. Come, I have prepared a treat for you.'

'Not another lemonade with brandy, I hope,' she said.

'Not unless you wish it,' he said. 'Hopefully, now that I am proving myself to be no threat to you, we will not have to resort to such fortifications.'

She glanced at the refreshment table, which was as perfectly done as the rest of the room. 'I am not interested in prawns or sweetmeats, either. Perhaps, if you had somewhere quiet that I might sit…' she gave him a firm look '…in privacy. I fear I have a bit of a megrim.'

'Really?' He gave her an equally firm look. 'Is that the best you can do to put me off? Threats of a headache will not work with me, I assure you. If you will look around, you might discover the entertainment I have provided.'

She could not think what he meant. The music was lovely, but no different than many other parties. The women were the same tiresome crowd that she saw wherever she went. And no gentleman would dare encroach on her space if she was to be perpetually set upon by Reighland.

Then the crowd parted and she saw what he must mean. Her brother-in-law was chatting amiably with a man on the other side of the room. She tried to appear unmoved while searching the room for any sign of her sister. But even a sight of Mr Hendricks was a treat so rare that she could barely contain her surprise.

Reighland, ever observant man that he was, noticed the change in her and said, taking a sip of his drink, 'John Hendricks is in attendance tonight, if you desire to speak with him. I understand you have a family connection.'

'He is family,' she admitted, 'but I am discouraged from talking to him.'

'How unfortunate,' Reighland said, giving her a curious look. 'I had hoped that you would have a chance to converse. He seemed eager to speak with you. But if you are not so disposed…'

'No,' she said hurriedly. 'I have no difficulty with him. But Father did not approve of Dru's marriage. He will be livid when he realises that they are in attendance.' She felt the skin tense at the back of her neck, as though her body was bracing for a confrontation.

'I expect he will,' Reighland said nonchalantly. 'If his opinion mattered to me, I would have given him the guest list to approve. I arranged this for your benefit. Does it please you?'

Please her? Her heart was galloping. How did he know, on such a limited acquaintance, that this visit was more precious than jewels? She stared hungrily across the room at Mr Hendricks. If she could manage it, she would have time enough to apologise to him for the first and only impression she'd been able to give. He must think her a wilful, selfish fool after the way she'd behaved on the road to Scotland.

If she could gain his attention for a few moments, before Father and Veronica realised what she was about and forced her to leave, there might be some little, precious time. 'It pleases me very much,' she said, trying not to show the extent of her elation as her mind raced to think of all the things she wished to say and to ask.

'Your sister would be here as well, but she was indisposed.'

Indisposed to see her, perhaps? Or her father. Priss's spirits fell a little. Perhaps she could get Hendricks to reveal the truth and take some message back to Silly. But the fact that she could talk to him at all would be a special treat. 'I understand.'

'There will be other opportunities to see her,' Reighland added, as though it were the most natural thing in the world to force her father to associate with the working class. 'Do not fear Benbridge's reaction. He would not dare confront me in my own home on my associations. Even if he did, I doubt it would matter. I am quite enjoying Hendricks's company. He is a dashed clever fellow and I prefer a quick wit to an old title. I fear, if you take me, you shall have to put up with my quirks on that.'

'I will?' As though it would matter to her. 'If you were expecting a scold from me, your Grace, I will disappoint you as well. I would most like to see more of Mr Hendricks.' Without meaning to, she smiled at him as though he were a favoured suitor who had rewarded her with such flattery as to be worthy of distinction.

Surprisingly, when confronted with the full force of her carefully nurtured beauty, the duke blushed. It made her colour as well. In her months of reclusion, she had forgotten how to flirt. In days past, she would have cooled his heat with a snap of her fan, perhaps catching the eye of some other swain with a fickle comment. Then she'd have led the pair of them a merry dance for the rest of the evening, playing one against the other.

Instead, she stood before a pink-faced Reighland with a silly smile on her face and they stared at each other as though there was no one else in the room. She dropped her eyes and fumbled with her reticule. He searched the room, catching Mr Hendricks's eye and signalling him to come. 'And here he is.' He looked relieved as he made the introduction. 'John, so good to see you again. Of course you know my guest of honour?'

'I do indeed, your Grace.' Mr Hendricks bowed and gave a subtle half-turn of his body that closed their little conversational circle off from the rest of the room. 'Lady Priscilla?'

She reached out and clasped his hand, feeling him

start against the sudden contact. 'It is so good to see you, Mr Hendricks. So very, very good. Tell me, my sister, is she well?'

'Unfortunately, no. She is ill this evening.' He did not glance at Benbridge, or show any disapproval of her that might demonstrate it was a lie, but then he was the most subtle of creatures. He would not have admitted to anything so rude as a harsh truth.

Reighland turned suddenly and then looked back at them with a warning smile. 'Perhaps the two of you would like to continue this conversation in the card room or in some out-of-the-way spot. I see another guest who deserves my attention.' Then he turned and said with false jollity, 'Benbridge! A moment of your time.'

Dear, sweet Robert had foreseen the problem with her father and was giving her time before action could be taken that would part her from her prize. She seized Hendricks by the arm and did her best to propel him in the opposite direction. 'A turn about the room, Mr Hendricks? I feel a sudden need for fresh air.'

'I suspect you do,' said Hendricks, regaining his calm. 'And how is your father, Lady Priscilla?'

'Much the same, sir.'

'How unfortunate for you.'

'But tell me of Silly. Drusilla, I mean,' she said, abandoning the childish nickname for her sister. 'It is nothing serious that keeps her at home, I hope.'

'A passing indisposition, I am sure.'

'Be honest with me, Mr Hendricks. Father's presence here was not the thing that upset her, was it? Or mine?' She added the last a bit more quietly, afraid of the answer.

Hendricks laid his hand on hers, in an awkward show of sympathy. 'Not at all, Lady Priscilla. She is truly ill. And very disappointed to be at home tonight. She misses you terribly.'

'And I her. Your words are a balm to me, Mr Hendricks. The house is quite empty without her.' She looked away hurriedly and fluttered her fan. 'Not that I do not wish her to be happy, sir. And she is happy with you, I am sure. She looks much better than she did at home. Softer, somehow. She smiles more. I have seen her about town, even though Veronica does not allow me to speak to her.'

'Ahh, yes. The new Countess of Benbridge,' Mr Hendricks said with a knowing smile. 'What is she like? We have not been permitted an introduction, you know.'

Priss burned with shame at being on the wrong side of this foolish argument. 'You are not missing much, sir. She is well suited to my father, I think. Grasping, ambitious and full of her own importance. And very eager to secure her place in the household, before Father comes to his senses. You can tell my sister it is probable we will have a brother before the year is out.'

'My felicitations to her,' he said. 'And to you as well.'

'Me?'

'On your impending nuptials. The *ton* can talk of nothing else.'

'If you are speaking of Reighland, it is not set in stone, just yet,' she said. 'I barely know his Grace.'

Hendricks laughed. 'He said much the same of you, only a few days ago. He is a very cautious man.'

'He does not seem so to me,' she said, risking a moment of honesty. 'He is pursuing me most shamelessly.'

'That is because he is smitten with you,' Hendricks said.

Smitten. Of all the possible reactions from a suitor chosen by her father, she had not expected that one. 'You must be mistaken.'

'On the contrary. He has spoken to me about you. I am afraid you have made a conquest.'

He had spoken to Reighland. Dear God, what secrets had they shared with each other? Between her admission to the duke, and Hendricks's knowledge of the past, she wanted to sink through the floor. 'It was never my intention to snare him. But he is most persistent.'

'And you have been honest with him,' Hendricks said, admitting his knowledge without saying another word. 'That was kind of you, I think.'

'He deserves the truth, if nothing else.'

'He is surprisingly tender-hearted, despite his rank and appearance.'

Was Hendricks warning her not to break poor Reighland's heart? The idea was so outrageous it made her laugh. 'I will do my best to let him down gently, then. I do not think we will suit.'

'You do not?' Hendricks seemed genuinely surprised. 'I am sure your father would say otherwise. Personally, I could not imagine a better catch for you.'

'But from what you know of me, given a little time, you could imagine a better catch for him, I am sure.'

'I would never—'

She cut off his objection. 'Without the family connection, you would not be so kind, sir. There are many other girls, some of them here tonight, who are my equals or superiors in birth and more proper and agreeable as well. It would content me to see him married to any of them and for Father to cease his scheming and let me retire to country spinsterhood.'

'You would not have to do that, even if the duke does not take you. There are other men, I am sure...'

'And I do not want any of them,' she said with a sigh. 'You know me. Better than you would like to, I'm sure. I am willing to admit that I am not fit to be the wife of a worthy man. There is sufficient money for me to cede the field and live quietly alone. Is it really such an unrealistic demand?'

Mr Hendricks looked worried and adjusted his spectacles, as though it might help him to see what she was seeing. 'It is a very sensible idea. And I would encourage it, if it were not my wife's sister suggesting it.' He patted her hand again. 'Dru would rather see you settled nearby. Away from your father's influence, but close enough so that you might visit.'

'Dru has always wanted more for me than I deserved,' she said simply. 'Tell her not to worry. Whatever happens, I am sure I shall be fine. If I can manage to get Father to send me away as I wish, then I shall certainly write to her often. But for now, I do not think we should risk my father's displeasure any more than is necessary.

I would hate to think that Benbridge tried to make difficulties for the two of you, because of my carelessness.'

Hendricks gave her a curious look, followed by a nod of approval. 'You must not worry on our account, Lady Priscilla. My position in society is secure, even if your father attempts to discredit it. But I thank you for your concern and will relay the message to your sister. We shall meet again soon, I am sure, and you will be able to tell her yourself. And here is Reighland again.' They had completed a circuit of the room and he was offering her arm to the duke as though she were some precious item that he had been allowed to borrow for only the briefest time.

'No, really...I would prefer...'

Hendricks shook his head. 'I think the duke wishes to speak to you again. And should your father wish to speak to you, it might be better that he have a few moments to collect his temper.'

'That is probably true,' she said with a sigh. Truly, it was not so bad to be with Reighland. He had shown unusual foresight in arranging this party for her. The least she could do was be grateful.

Robert congratulated himself on a job well done. He had arranged this meeting on little more than a hunch. But the smile Priscilla had given him when she'd spied Hendricks was of such brilliance that he could not believe there was no meaning in it. Now she was standing before him, a veritable blushing flower of devotion, looking up at him with those enormous blue eyes and saying, 'I wish there were some way to show you how much such a kindness meant to me.'

'Do you, now?' Surely, it could not be this easy.

When he had thought to marry, he had imagined it to be an arduous process of coaxing some passionless virgin out of her clothes and into his bed. But here was a girl who was not only lovely, but who had some basic understanding of what her beauty did to a man. And tonight she was smiling at him as she never had before. It seemed they had reached an understanding.

He meant to marry her, of course. What harm could there be in allowing her to express her gratitude? 'I have not shown you the house yet,' he said, doing his best to add a hidden meaning to the words. 'Would you do me the honour?' He gestured towards the door.

She gave one doubtful look in that direction, as though to acknowledge how improper it would be to go off alone in the middle of the party. But after that token of modest resistance, she gave a single, graceful nod of acquiescence.

A brief tour of his home would not hurt to sway her further in his favour. It was magnificent, with wide marble stairs running up the middle in an elegant curve and a series of hallways leading off to various receiving rooms, studies and salons. It had impressed him when he had first seen it. He'd stood in the gilt-ceilinged foyer, momentarily stunned that it was now his. While Benbridge's town house was grand, Reighland's London residence was spectacular.

How could any woman resist it?

Of course, he could barely remember to speak about it as they walked, so much was he enjoying the company he was with. He did not even notice how far they had come from the people gathered in the ballroom until he realised that he could hear the echo of his footsteps on the polished wood of the floor over the distant sound of voices.

They need go no further than this for what he had in mind. It was perfect, really. They were all alone. Her skin, which was near to flawless in the best of light, glowed like a pearl in the illumination of the single candle that had been left to make for easy passage of servants while discouraging strangers from straying.

He had never been the sort of man to be easily moved by a pretty face. Well, perhaps never was too strong a word. He had watched such girls be won by young men who were wittier, handsome and more at ease in their own skins. And he had decided that his own inevitable disappointment was not worth the brief pleasure the pursuit might bring.

But things had changed, now that he'd met Priss.

She glanced over her shoulder and the same light that had touched her skin made her curls glow gold. 'Where are you taking me?'

'I am trying to get you alone, of course,' he said, surprised that she needed to ask. 'You are almost twenty-one, are you not? By now I should think that other gentlemen have tried such tricks on you. If they have not, then London lads must be surprisingly stupid.'

She gave a weak laugh. 'Last year, perhaps. I have learned to be more circumspect with my reputation. We had best be returning, before we are missed.'

'In a little while,' he agreed. 'But first, I wish to

receive the thanks that you were offering in the ballroom.'

He tugged on her arm, pulling her through a doorway and into a darkened parlour, shutting the door behind them.

'I meant for a verbal thank you, only,' she said, with a breathless giggle.

'Or a polite note?' He was close enough so that he could smell the wine and strawberries on her breath and feel her curls tickling his chin. His body quickened in response.

'I did not mean any more than that,' she said again, placing her hands against his chest to add distance between them. But she did not push him away. Instead, she rested them there as though trying to choose between a shove or a caress.

He stayed still. If he waited, time and moonlight would tip the balance in his favour. 'And if I wanted more?'

'Then I fear you shall be disappointed.'

'A kiss?'

'I would prefer not.' It was a prim little statement, totally at odds with the soft mouth that uttered it.

'You allowed one on the verandah, when last we met,' he coaxed.

'I do not think you mean to kiss me quite in the same way,' she said, 'if you need to lure me so far from the others.'

'I think you are probably right,' he agreed, dipping his head to nuzzle her ear.

'And I think that is probably unwise,' she said again.

But she was leaning in to him as she said it, putting up the sort of token resistance that any lady would. *You do not have to be shy with me*, he thought. *Not now. Not ever.*

'Oh, yes. I should think it very unwise.' He traced the line of her jaw with his tongue and felt her tense, then relax with a sigh.

He tipped his head to the side, hesitating for a moment before his lips touched hers. This must be perfect, if nothing else in his life was. And it would be harder than he had thought, simply because he was.

Hard.

She was a sweet thing, sweeter than he had ever expected to have for himself. All the sweeter for the tartness on her tongue when she talked to him. She smelled like French lilacs after a spring rain, rich and yet subtle and full of memory. He wanted to crush her body against his face, take her into his mouth, roll in her.

There would be time for that. All the time in the world. So he counted out three of his own heartbeats before moving again, touching gently, lip to lip.

Another three beats and he ran the tip of his tongue along the seam of her lips, following the downward curve of her frown.

Not yet, then.

There was a dimple on her cheek and he focused his attention on it, brushing it with his mouth until it relaxed as she smiled.

Better.

He slipped to her ear again, breathing against it, sucking the lobe into his mouth and aching as he thought of the lips to her sex. She gasped. Was she sensitive there, or was she reading his mind? He tugged at it with his teeth and heard another gasp. Her mouth was open, then. He could take it, if he wanted.

And he did want.

Too soon, he reminded himself.

He kissed her throat, trailing down the cord in it until he had reached her shoulder blade, dipping his tongue into the hollows along the way. Then he drew back, for it would be too tempting to go lower, deeper, to lick his way down the rest of her body.

She was panting now, panting for his kiss. He pressed open mouth to open mouth breathing with her, stroking her hair with his hand. Her tongue fluttered at his lower lip. He touched it with his own.

She touched back. She licked gently at his teeth and he felt a moment's triumph. She was trying to arouse him. As if that was necessary. He caught the tip between his teeth and drew her tongue into his mouth, urging her to learn him.

Then he returned the favour. Her mouth felt ripe, kissable, and he nipped harder to brand it with his attentions. Anyone who looked at her would know what she had done and who she had been with.

She did not fight against it. Instead, she moaned and pressed her body closer to his, as though eager to be claimed by him.

The nearness of her filled him with a reckless pleasure he had longed for when Reighland was a thing on some distant horizon and no part of his life. If this goddess would have him at all, it would be for himself and not the title she disdained. When he was with her, he would be nothing more than a man and she nothing less than a woman. They would spend nights, wrapped in each other, laughing and loving. It would take the cold sting out of the days of endless duty. She would be a blessing on his life.

And he would give himself to her, give her pleasure. Give her children or jewels. Or both. He would give her anything she wanted, if only she would give of herself.

She was a fragile little thing, like a tiny bird in his hands. He must remember to be gentle. He brought one hand up to cup her breast and used the other to bend her back in his arms, half a dip, half a swoon. Then he kissed her senseless, pressing her hips to his with the firm hand that held her low along her back.

This was right. They joined where they were meant to, hip to hip, hard to soft. They could not do more. Not here.

But why not? It was his house, she would be his bride.

'Unhand me this moment, you beast,' she whispered, turning her head and pressing a hand against his throat.

He laughed. 'A beast, am I? I swear I was tame as a lamb, before kissing you. But now I will show you just how wild you have made me.'

His knees bent, taking her with him to the floor.

'No,' she said, a little desperately. But even as she refused him, a part of her seemed to revel in his attention. She was leaning backwards, away from him, as though trying to escape. But her hands were twined in the lapels of his coat drawing him down with her. 'No,' she whispered again, but she spread her legs as he lay on top of her.

'You need not worry,' he said, lowering his mouth to her breasts. 'We will be married soon enough. No one will know if you give in to me now.' He was inching her skirt upwards now, one hand on the flap of his trousers.

'No.' She struggled weakly under him. 'No. Please. Do not.'

He paused, fingers splayed on her bare hip. 'Do not pretend to hate me, Priss. I saw the way you toyed with me in the ballroom. It does not do to play the outraged virgin when you kiss like a courtesan.' He grinned at her so that she would know he was only teasing. 'I am so hard for you I can barely think. Now spread your legs for me and lie still for just a moment.'

Suddenly she was fighting for all she was worth, scratching at his face. He dodged the clawed hand just in time before her nails could lay a bloody trail on his cheek and covered her mouth with his hand to stop the scream that would bring the house down upon them. 'What the devil? Priss. Calm down.' He eased his body off hers, pulling his hand cautiously away so that it could grip her arm. She gasped, staring wild eyed at him as though she did not know him. For a moment, there was no sign of the willing woman he had kissed just moments ago. Then she took in a great breath and calm began to return.

'Talk to me, Priss,' he urged, wishing he could hold her close until the fear had fully passed. Instead he withdrew his hands from her shoulders, giving her space. 'Tell me what is the matter.'

'There is nothing the matter,' she said, pushing her skirt back down her legs. 'As long as you do not do what you were attempting, I will be fine. I cannot bear to be touched in that way.'

He rocked back on his heels, confused. 'And I can think of little else when I'm with you. We have a problem, do we not?'

She laughed bitterly. 'You say 'We' in such an easy, natural way, as though this means anything at all to you.' She wrapped her arms tight around her own body as though his touch had chilled her to the bone; the distance it created between them made him ache. 'I have not agreed to marry you, no matter what my father might have told you. Yet you think I will give myself cheaply on the parlour floor, just because I was foolish enough to do it for another.'

'I never thought that,' he argued. 'I do not want anything less for you than to be my duchess.'

'And I cannot be that for you. No matter how much I—' Her lips sealed suddenly, tight, and she watched him, frightened and stricken.

'What, Priss? Finish what you were about to say.' She had been going to say she wanted it. He was sure.

'It is nothing.'

'I do not care. Tell me any way.' For just a moment, her expression had changed, softening and sorrowful. Then she had looked away from him so that he might think her hard and unwilling. But the brief hesitation gave him reason to hope.

She took a breath and framed her words carefully, so that they might seem impersonal. 'No matter how much I enjoy your company, and how much I appreciate what you are trying to do in separating me from my father and re-acquainting me with the rest of my family, I cannot lie with you. I cannot even bear to think of the act. What kind of a wife would I be, to you or any man, if I cannot do that thing?'

'It is not me particularly that frightens you, then. Any man would have the same response?'

She gave a hesitant shake of her head.

'You are afraid of me.' He was shocked. Confused. And perhaps just the slightest bit angry. How could she be afraid of him? When had he ever done anything to deserve that? In his heart, he knew, of course. He was no longer the careless boy he had been. He had been kind to her and very careful, but she sensed the brutality in him and feared it.

But why had she kept it from him? 'When did you mean to tell me of this?' he asked sternly. 'You denied me from the first moment we met. I thought you were only being coy with me. What reason would you have, otherwise? I swear I have done no wrong to you.'

'I had hoped that you would lose interest if I gave you no encouragement,' she said.

'If you did not mean to encourage me, then why did you allow me to bring you here?'

'You were being so kind to me,' she said, clearly confused herself. 'And tonight I thought perhaps when the time came, my fondness for you would make it possible to bear the pain of the violation.'

'Pain?' He released her arms, suddenly unsure. He could not have been hurting her. When had he been less than gentle? 'It is only the first time that is painful, Priscilla. And much as I might regret it, that moment for you has passed.'

'But it was the second time and the third as well,' she insisted.

He had not wanted to think of her fall as being less than a momentary and regrettable lapse. Clearly, it had been more than that, yet she had not enjoyed it. Jealousy and sympathy warred within him. 'Did you tell your lover of the trouble?' Concern for her won out and he leaned forwards, wanting to comfort her, but seeing her shrink from his touch.

'I tried. But he said that I should lie still, spread my legs and be quiet.'

Robert swore, forgetting the company he was in and the fact that she already feared him. He took a deep breath and sought to mend the mistake. 'I apologise for my actions and my words. I behaved no better to you, using almost the same words to gain your compliance. When I meet the fellow who hurt you, I will kill him. He has taught you to think all men are animals. And I am behaving no better than one.'

'No, please.' She forgot herself and gripped his arm. 'Do not think to hurt Gervaise. He is not worth that.'

'And you are,' Robert said, enjoying the thrill it gave him to feel her leaning upon him.

'But it was all my fault,' she said, closing her eyes. He could see the sleepless shadows under them and put a tentative hand on her waist so that she might draw closer and rest her head on his shoulder. 'And again, tonight. If I had shown sense and refused to come away with you…'

She looked ready to cry. Without thinking of how it might frighten her, he pulled her close in a hug, doing his best to keep the gesture innocent. 'It is not your fault. None of this was. While I might say your charms are irresistible, you notice that I was able to master myself when you refused me. Only a clumsy and unskilled lover would have continued, knowing the lady was in pain. I promise you, with another man, it will be different. With me, for example.' He tried to keep the offer casual, lest she think he expected an immediate recommencing of activity.

For a moment, she almost seemed persuaded, relaxing in his arms and letting him support her. Then she shook her head and pulled away from him. 'It will be worse.'

'I beg your pardon.' It was a most unwelcome sentiment from a woman he cared about. And unjust as well. There had been no previous complaints about his lovemaking. But it did not seem proper to tell her so. 'Explain yourself immediately.'

'Perhaps it is because I come to you with too much knowledge,' she muttered, turning pink and clearly embarrassed to even explain the problem. 'And perhaps you are right and the fault was Gervaise's. But the thing is…' She glanced down, and hurriedly away. 'Gervaise is shorter than you. And slimmer.' She paused significantly. 'And quite probably smaller in other ways as well. If that did not work, then how…?'

He rocked back on his heels again and laughed so long and so hard that he had to reach into his pocket for a handkerchief to wipe his eyes.

The door to the room opened suddenly and John Hendricks was staring down at them in disapproval. 'What the devil are you on about, Reighland? Priscilla, come away from him immediately.'

She gave a little yelp of embarrassment and moved to rise. But before she could Robert dropped a hand heavily upon her shoulder. 'Do not move a muscle, Priss.' He gave Hendricks his iciest, most Reighland-like stare. 'As you can see, nothing untoward is occurring. We are sitting here, having a harmless conversation.' It was a bald-faced lie. He was sitting like a tailor upon the floor, with a fading erection, and his lady love was leaning back against a wall. Though her skirts were properly arranged to hide her legs, she appeared to have escaped a vigorous tumbling by the narrowest margin. If Hendricks had arrived a few moments earlier...

But he hadn't. Robert held his gaze, unwilling to admit wrongdoing.

Hendricks gave him a narrow-eyed glare. 'Then you must continue the conversation in the main room, for the sake of the lady's reputation.'

'The lady's reputation is perfectly safe with me,' Robert said, smiling. 'It is not as if you will need to force me to marry her, should someone hear of this. I will do so gladly, the minute she will have me. But there are some matters that we must settle, in private, before I return her to the party. If you would allow us a few more moments alone, I would be most grateful.'

Then he looked up at her brother-in-law, with as much contrition and sincerity as he could manage.

After taking a split second to decide, Hendricks said, 'Only a few minutes, mind. I will be loitering at the end of the hall to ensure that you are not disturbed. But I will stay close enough that I might come if I am called.' This was directed to Priscilla, who, thank the gods, made no effort to refute his story.

'Sit on the furniture and not the floor,' Hendricks added. 'There is little point in having the stuff if you don't mean to use it. I will give you five minutes. Then it is back to the dance floor for the pair of you. Have a care, Reighland. Dru will have my head if any harm comes to her sister.'

'Thank you.'

The door closed behind him.

Robert stared at her in silence for a few moments, giving Hendricks the time to retreat. Then he reached out and took her hand with a smile and helped her to a divan, taking the seat beside her. 'Your assessment of my...umm...attributes is flattering, Lady Priscilla. But while a young lady who is still quite innocent might see certain things as a detriment, most others I have been with considered them an asset.'

For all her supposed wickedness, the idea that women might find pleasure with a large member seemed to surprise her and her eyes went wide. 'If other women like that, then that is the sort you must choose, I fear. I do not think I am the best wife for you.'

'On the contrary. I think that it is more a matter of changing your mind on certain subjects than it is about adjusting my choice. I have no intention of giving you up over…an accident in biology. If you would be willing to meet with me again in private, I think, at the very least, I will be able to free you of what is likely to be a debilitating fear of the unknown.'

'Are you seriously suggesting that we…?'

'Postpone the remainder of this conversation until tomorrow,' he finished. 'Tonight, we will enjoy the food and the dancing and each other's company. You will not worry your beautiful head about what happened in the past. It is a lovely evening. It would be a shame to waste it in fear or recrimination.'

'But tomorrow?' The poor girl was still looking at him as though she expected, at any moment, he might unbutton and display his wedding tackle.

He sighed, wondering if his manners were really as rakish as all that. He had been hasty in his approach. But by his soul, he'd never expected her to be shy on this of all subjects. 'Tomorrow, you will come to my rooms and we will talk,' he said at last. 'Whatever happens, there will be no pain. No fear. I promise. Perhaps we will only use the time to discuss your future, with or without me.'

'All right,' she said, very quietly. 'We will do as you suggest.'

'Very good.' He stood then and reached out a hand to her, almost lifting her back on to her feet with his strength. Then, very gently, he wiped a stray lock of hair from her face and said, 'This is what comes from stealing kisses in dark corners. I have quite disarranged your

curls. No matter. We will make it worth the trouble.'
Then, very sweetly, he kissed her upon her closed lips.

He made sure the gesture was perfection in its innocence. She did not pull away, though she coloured for
him again. But this time it was the barest hint of pink
in the dim light, as though she had been pleasantly
surprised. He walked her from the room and handed
her to Hendricks, that he might be the one to escort her
to the lady's retiring room to recompose herself.

When he saw her later, it was to take her arm and
escort her into dinner. Later in the evening, when Charlotte Davering attempted to cut her dead, he was there
with a glass of champagne, offering an easy misdirection so that the slight failed miserably. He danced every
waltz with her, holding her at a respectful distance, all
the while making clear that he had a claim upon her.

And when it was time to part, he raised her hand to
his lips and whispered, 'Until tomorrow?'

If it had been a command, she would have run. She
would have refused and that would have been the end
of it. But he'd made sure it was a question imbued with
all the hope growing in his heart.

Only after he heard the breathless 'Yes' did he allow
himself so much as a kiss on her gloved knuckles.

# Chapter Nine

Priss walked through the marble archway of Reighland's foyer, a mixture of trepidation and relief. Father had been furious to discover Mr Hendricks at the previous evening's party, nearly angry enough to embarrass himself by snubbing the duke. But Priss had underestimated the hold that Ronnie had over him and that woman's eagerness to get an unwanted step-daughter out from under their roof. Benbridge's feathers had been smoothed, the evening had continued without incident and Mr Hendricks had made a strategic retreat, quitting the party after he'd rescued her from the embarrassing incident on the salon floor.

It had not been his place to protect her honour. She had a father and stepmother who should have been seeing to that. But that same stepmother greeted the idea of today's unchaperoned trip to Reighland's with an emotion near to glee, eager to offer what was left of her honour up so that the peer could do what he liked with it.

Reighland had promised not to hurt her, she reminded herself firmly. But she had little doubt that today's meeting would end with her on her back, as Reighland attempted to demonstrate that the marital act could be performed successfully. She meant to allow it, if only to show him the error of his ways.

It was a shame, really. Under other circumstances she might have enjoyed his company. His manners were rather odd, as were his looks. But he had a gentle soul, for all that. And he had been kind to her. His kisses so far had been both pleasant and disturbing. When she thought of them, as she had for most of the night, her emotions became a tangle of fear and pleasure, leaving her without sleep but also without nightmare. She was tired now. Tired of his courting and Ronnie's continual curiosity about it. And tired as well of the anticipation of impending disaster.

At least, after today, it would be over.

The house was even more spectacular than it had been by candlelight, though she did her best not to notice. She walked at a stately pace, looking neither here nor there at the height of the ceilings, the richness of the hangings or the art upon the walls. The lack of chaperon would be reason for the servants to gossip, without her gawking at the house as though trying to set the right price on her attentions.

She allowed herself to be shown to the same salon that she had visited the previous night. Reighland awaited her there. The servant announced her and withdrew. They were alone again.

Silence fell and she tried not to look down at the carpet to find the exact spot where they had struggled. She was a lady, after all. It was not the sort of thing that deserved acknowledgement. Though she had to admit, in daylight it was a fine rug.

Reighland was looking his usual somber self in a black coat and a pensive expression. If he was pleased to see her again, he managed to conceal it well enough. Though there was nothing lecherous or avaricious about his behaviour, she could not manage to bring herself to smile for him.

He bowed. 'Are you feeling well this morning, Lady Priscilla?'

'After my behaviour last night?' she said, embarrassed to be reminded of it.

He gave her a non-committal shrug. 'Any young lady would be given to such a display, considering the circumstances.'

'At least you did not have to force brandy upon me to calm my nerves.'

'I would do it again, if required,' he said. 'But today I am hoping that tea will suffice. The things are laid before us. Will you pour, please?' Reighland took a seat on the sofa and looked up at her.

She frowned. It was quite rude of him. He should have made sure she was seated and sent for a servant to handle the tea things. But she was so tense that she doubted she'd have taken a seat if he offered. At least preparing their cups would give her something to do with her hands other than wringing them nervously and awaiting the inevitable.

She ignored the place at his side and took a chair opposite, taking up the pot and pouring out his tea on the little table between them.

'Keeping your distance?' he asked and she saw the edge of his lips twitching in a smile.

'After last night, I think it is wise, don't you? Do you take sugar, your Grace?'

'If I were truly interested in tea, then, yes, I take sugar in it.'

She handed him the cup and looked directly into his eyes. 'And just what is it that you are interested in, your Grace?' *Come now, Reighland. Put your cards upon the table. You are making me so nervous that I can barely stand it.*

He took the cup she was offering, then set it down on the table. 'Firstly, I wish to apologise for my behaviour. I will not say it was uncalled for. If ever a mouth was made to be kissed, I am sure it is yours. But I proceeded with undue haste.'

'Your apology is accepted, of course,' she said without looking at him. 'As I said last night, it is I who should apologise to you. I was the one who went off with you, down a darkened corridor. After I'd told you of my past, what else were you to think of me?'

'You are entirely too hard on yourself,' he said, picking up the cup and taking a sip, before setting it back down again. 'Let us call it a simple misunderstanding, between friends, and leave it at that.' He patted the upholstery at his side. 'There is room enough for you here.'

She ignored it. 'I would not wish to crowd you.'

'It is what I wish,' he said, patting the seat again firmly so she would know that it was a command. 'As I explained last night, it is time that you lost your fear of me. It is groundless, I assure you.'

She sighed and rose, crossed to his side and sat. But it seemed that the nearer she was to him, the smaller she felt. She shrank against the opposite arm, putting as much distance between them on the divan as she could.

He gave her a critical look. 'Why are you so reluctant to sit beside me?'

'I merely preferred the other seat,' she said.

'And now you are lying to me. After I told you that your honesty was your most appealing characteristic, I am most disappointed in you.'

'I do not like to be touched,' she reminded him.

'As you said last night. But I am not touching you now,' he pointed out as gently as possible. 'Your continued resistance does not bode well for us. If we are to be married, I mean to touch you.'

'And I am not one of your horses, willing to submit tamely to your demands,' she snapped back.

'If you were, I'd have thrown a saddle on you by now,' he agreed. 'I am being as patient as I can manage. It is not as if I mean to practise the marital act upon you, along with my tea.'

If that was not his intention, than why was she here at all? 'You are always most adamant that we meet alone,' she reminded him. 'And everyone seems so convinced that I will disgrace myself again to cement the bargain. I am sure, even now, Veronica is hoping that you are doing just that.'

'Then damn Lady Benbridge, and her husband as well, for making this more difficult than it needs to be,' he barked with surprising vehemence. Then he looked back to her and gentled his tone. 'I have not yet taken advantage of the solitude, have I?'

'No, you have not taken advantage. In daytime, at least.' Each agreement with him felt like a lost battle. But this one at least made her smile.

A thought suddenly occurred to him. 'Perhaps it is time I started.' Before she could question him, he reached to the floor and scooped her two feet up and into his lap.

'What are you doing?' The sudden action made her tea cup rattle and she spilled a bit on the saucer. But the length of her legs maintained the distance between them and he stayed where he was, making no effort to close the gap.

'Nothing that need worry you,' he said. 'You will notice that while I am touching you, it is an extremity that keeps the maximum distance between us.'

'Stop it this instant.' She struggled, but he kept a firm grasp on her ankles.

'You do not know what I am attempting, yet.'

'But I am sure that I will not like it.'

'You are quite sure of what you like and dislike, aren't you?' he said. 'You understand that horses are not born knowing they will be ridden.'

'Yes,' she said. 'But as I informed you before, I am not a horse.'

'True. But you must understand that I would not ride a horse before I knew every inch of the animal. And that would be a sound way to treat a wife as well. You notice I am not pawing at your bodice, or forcing kisses upon you. I am only touching your feet.' He gave a tug on her ankle. 'You do not have to lock your legs together at the knee. I have no intention of reaching up your gown.'

She was working to control her unsteady breathing and gave a twitch of her skirt to make sure that her legs and ankles were properly covered. 'They are still a part of my body. And if they are so remote from the areas that interest you, I do not understand why you would bother with them.'

'They interest me because they are a part of you.' He reached out and pulled her slippers off, one by one, and tossed them over the back of the couch. She did her best to ignore the sudden shock of her feet coming in closer contact with a much more intimate portion of his anatomy. Then she stilled herself, knowing that continued struggling was likely to result in just the sort of inflammation of feeling that frightened her.

'In my experience,' he went on, as though there was nothing out of the ordinary with her taking tea with her feet in a gentleman's lap, 'feet can be quite sensitive. A light massaging might be pleasant in ways that you have not yet experienced. And you need not worry,' he added. 'I mean to limit my contact with you to areas below the ankle.' Then he stroked her insteps and laid his palm flat against the soles, measuring their length against his hand.

'You are quite mad,' she said with a nervous clearing of the throat and took a sip of tea.

'Possibly,' he muttered and traced the curves of her feet with a few firm passes of his fingers. 'But I am doing you no harm, am I?'

'That is not the problem,' she said. It wasn't painful. He was right in that, at least. But it certainly was not relaxing. Her voice sounded strange and tight, and her stays felt the same way. Though she knew the need for it, she could not seem to keep her legs still. She tried to draw her feet up under her skirt, but he kept a firm grasp on them until she relaxed again with a sigh.

'That is better,' he said softly. 'I ask no more than that you let me give you pleasure.' He ran the tip of a finger back and forth from heel to toe.

She wished he had chosen any other turn of phrase, for it made her think of the sorts of feelings that she had experienced late at night, when she was quite alone and had discovered the exquisite sensitivity of her own body. The places she felt his touch now were far away from the soles of her feet. She concentrated on the feel of the cup in her hand, smooth, hard and growing cold. It was much safer to think of that than the soft, hot, wet feelings in the rest of her body.

'Priscilla,' Reighland said her name sharply, as though trying to wake her from a doze. 'Attend me when I am talking to you.'

She opened her eyes, surprised to find that she had closed them. His touch was growing more insistent and it made her forget where she was as her mind drifted to dark, intimate places. She pressed her lower lip with her teeth to bring back some semblance of reason. 'Yes, Reighland?'

'I asked you, if you had nothing to lose by it, would you do me the honour of relaxing in my presence? Could you take pleasure in my company?'

'Yes.' It was a sigh, as though the word had been torn from her, and she was not sure if she'd meant it as answer to his question, or as a response to the movement of his hand upon her arch.

'Very good,' he responded. 'You will forgive me for saying it, but you are behaving like a skittish mare. You must learn to accept my touch, for I will not walk you down the aisle, only to find at the end of the night that you cannot bear to lie with me. I have the succession to think of. It would be beyond foolish to bind myself to a woman who could not abide my company, no matter how well placed her father is.'

A moment ago he had been promising to do nothing. Now he was talking of marriage and succession, and all the while his hands stroked her feet, leaving her hopelessly confused. 'Either you mean to have me, or you don't,' she said, shifting uneasily on the cushions. 'Decide and be done with it.'

He laughed quietly. 'You have too much experience and still no knowledge of the subject. But then, you had an extremely inept teacher. Let me put it plainly. If we are to be married, then I will have you, either before or after the ceremony. More likely it will be both. But what happens between us will happen because you wish it to be so. And it will not happen today.'

'Then stop talking about it,' she said, sagging back against the arm of the divan.

Reighland laughed as his hands circled her feet again, the thumbs rubbing firmly up and down the insteps, as though he was marking the time, waiting for some sort of answer from her. But she could think of nothing more to add, so she remained silent. If he was silent as well, then she needn't think of ways to parry his arguments. She let her head roll back against the cushions and closed her eyes again, wishing she was back in her room and these gentle touches were part of some pleasant dream. One where nothing more need come of it than to enjoy the moment, with no response on her part required. She felt the relaxation travelling up her body until it was a struggle to keep her knees tightly together.

But struggle she did, for that would be far too much like an invitation. The firm stroking felt too good and the heat was pooling in strange places throughout her body. That was what he had wanted, she was sure. He wanted her to respond.

At last she gave into it, arching her back to feel her breasts pressing against the front of her dress. He tugged at her toes, until the special place between her legs was wet and tingling. He pressed her feet down into his lap to show that he was affected as well. And the knowledge that she was cradled against his aroused body sent her tea cup clattering to the rug. 'Reighland,' she said with a gasp, sure that he would break his word, but not nearly as frightened as she had been. 'You are the very devil.'

'You think that, do you?' He pinched her little toe and she gasped again. 'You must be a wicked little sinner, then, to be so easily tempted by me.'

Then she began to feel the subtle tugging on her stockings. He was trying to pull them down her legs. In a moment, those supposedly innocent hands would begin to creep upwards to scrabble at her garters. Then there would be the sudden push that parted her knees, and the thrusting fingers that sought to soothe the way for invasion. She started upright and ready to fight against him.

The tugging stopped and she relaxed enough to realise that his hands still rested on her heels. 'Did I not tell you that it was not to be the way you fear?'

She opened her eyes, wondering if she'd spoken her thoughts aloud, still unsure of what she was to say.

'I can tell you are worried,' he said patiently, still not moving. 'I read your mind in the tension of your body, the look on your face.'

'I am sorry,' she said. 'I cannot help what I feel.'

'It must be very difficult for you,' he agreed, 'to feel so frightened.

'Not really,' she said. 'As long as I avoid such intimacies as this, it is not an issue.'

'But that would mean you would never be touched,' he said softly. 'And never loved. It will be safe, of course. But very lonely.'

God, yes. She was so lonely. When she lay down at

night, she had taken to pleasuring herself to ease the aching fear.

She could feel one of her stockings beginning to sag, as it slipped from beneath her garter. She tensed, waiting. But she felt nothing but the slow drag of the silk down the length of her leg, like a long soft kiss. Then, he began to gather it, drawing it down and off her foot.

When nothing more happened, she released a little of her fear in a sudden shudder of pleasure. He paused again and the tension in her body built. 'But if you do not mean…then…why?'

'Why this?' He pulled the stocking the rest of the way off, rolled it and tucked it into his pocket. 'To prove that I can, I suppose. And to prove to you that the world will not end if I touch your body. No harm has come to you, has it?'

She thought. 'Well, no.'

'You are experiencing no discomfort?' His fingers were now running along the bare flesh of her foot. And without meaning to, she wiggled her toes. It tickled.

He sensed her response and changed the pressure, tracing light patterns with his fingers on the sole of her foot.

She took a deep breath and dug her fingers into the upholstery to keep from touching herself. 'No, I am not experiencing discomfort.'

He began to tug on her other stocking. 'Then I shall take the other from you as well. And put them in the dresser of your room.'

She straightened and pulled away. The suddenness of her movement achieved his ends more completely than he could have, for the stocking came free and pooled in his hands. 'How dare you. You are certainly not invited to come to my room.'

He gave the final tug that freed it from her body and stuffed it in his pocket with its mate. 'Pardon me, Lady Priscilla. I meant the room which shall be yours, when I make you my duchess. You will find it is large and most generously appointed. If there is anything you wish, other than a place for your stockings, please let me know. I will be happy to provide it.'

It had been a foolish overreaction on her part, and she was almost tempted to apologise. But then she remembered that she was sitting with her feet in the lap of the Duke of Reighland as he talked of innocence and stripped the clothing from her body.

And now his fingers could touch her bare toes, separating them and stroking the tender flesh between. The slow thrusts made her forget her fear and press back against his hands and his body. Her womb clenched and, as though he could feel the change in her, the movement of his fingers increased.

'This is nonsense,' she said, as though she could dismiss the feeling.

'But you like it, do you not?' He was raising the foot very slowly and she could feel the breeze on her legs as her skirt slipped up her calf. But as she stared up at him, he made no effort to look beneath it, keeping his eyes focused on hers. And then he touched his tongue to one of her toes and bit down gently upon it.

The resulting climax took her unawares, making her whole body shake. The sensitive bud between her legs exploded with sensation. Her toes clamped together around the thickness of the thumb cradled between them. She imagined him resting snugly in her body and rode the waves of pleasure the image created.

The tremors subsided, leaving her embarrassed but sated. And she realised what she had been doing: rubbing the other foot shamelessly against his lap, trying to arouse him to break his promise.

But he was looking down at her with an expression that could best be described as bemused. 'You may act as though you know it all, my dear. But I could teach you that you are sorely mistaken.'

'That will not be necessary.' Although perhaps, if they were anything like what she had just experienced, a few lessons from him would not go amiss.

'You are sure? Because I am eager to oblige you.'

She lifted her free foot out of his lap and set it firmly on the floor. 'No, thank you.'

'Very well, then. I suppose you should be going soon or people will hear of the visit and wonder what we have been up to. But if you will allow me a farewell kiss...' His fingers circled her ankle and he lifted it to his lips, fixing them upon the little knob of bone there.

And a shock of feeling seemed to rush up her body from that point. She felt lips and tongue, and—oh, God—his teeth, rasping against it. Her nipples tightened and there was another wash of delight that left her limp and gasping on the sofa, hands clasping furiously against the cushions. Dear Lord help her, it had been twice in as many minutes. If the duke chose to press his advantage over her and take the sort of liberties she'd expected, she would be powerless to resist.

She bent her knees quickly, yanking her foot from his grasp and putting it on the floor with its mate, giving a quick snap at her skirts so they fell back into place to cover her legs. 'Give my stockings back. Immediately.'

'No.' He was smiling at her again, as though he knew exactly what had occurred. 'As I told you before, they will wait in my house until you are ready to retrieve them.'

She tucked her feet back under her skirts. 'I cannot go about without them. Someone might see.'

'Put your shoes on and be quiet about it. If you do not act as though anything is out of the ordinary, no one will notice.' He stared down at the floor. 'Although I would hardly blame a man for looking. You have a well-turned pair of ankles, I must say.'

'It is rude of you to comment on the fact.'

Now he grinned. 'Hardly the rudest thing I have done in my life. I fear you will have to bear with much, when we are married. At school, it seemed I was always saying the wrong thing at the wrong time. The other boys encouraged it and made me the butt of every joke. Of course, it was more amusing to them than it was to me.' He winced in recollection. 'Many a schoolmaster tried to cane manners into me, but as you can see, it did little good.'

He said it lightly enough, but there was something hidden, a shadow behind that carefully guarded smile that made her wonder if Mr Hendricks was right about

Reighland's tender side. 'Were you punished for fight-ing with them?'

'Lord, no.' He looked at her earnestly. 'I was broken of that bad habit long before I was sent off to school. I was always large for my age, you see. And clumsy. I tended to squash butterflies rather than catch them.' He shifted nervously. 'And there was one unfortunate incident with a little friend. All boys play rough. And I did not mean to hurt him. But it took six weeks in bed to mend his broken arm.' He said it hurriedly, as though it was a difficult moment that needed to be got through. 'I was quite young,' he added. 'You needn't fear me. I have learned to be very careful with living things. You must have noticed that I dance like a daisy-cutting horse that cannot pick up its hooves. When we wed, you will lose more than the usual amount of crockery to my accidents. But it will be no worse than that.' He was staring at her, his expression curiously vulnerable, and she could almost see the boy who had cried over his injured playmate. But then she saw the toe of one of her stockings was peeping out of his pocket.

'You have been most gentle with me,' she assured him. 'I know I have nothing to fear.' Even if she did, she would do her best to master it, for his sake.

'That is good to know,' he said, clearly relieved. 'I am sure that most of London still thinks of me as the hulking idiot whom they used to tease.'

'They would not dare to embarrass you now,' she reminded him softly.

'Because I can mask my bad manners with rank. And that does seem to be the only thing that matters to some people, does it not?' He glanced up and past her, at the door to the hall. And she wondered was he thinking of her father?

'Yes,' she said simply. 'It is.'

'But I have learned to bear it with good grace,' he said with a smile. 'Words and gossip do not hurt. And duelling and brawling over every slight would be far too dangerous for those around me.'

'Really,' she said, unsure of what to make of this latest insight into his character.

'You will take me in hand, once we are married, and smooth my rough character.' There was nothing at all guarded in the cheerful optimism she saw in him at the thought of marriage to her. Of all people. And to her surprise, she had to bite her tongue to keep from offering to take him in hand, right here in the parlour. After the pains she had taken to explain her problems, she was liable to undo it all with reckless words and a moment's overconfidence in his gentle nature.

But Reighland did not seem to notice her distress. He stood up and walked to the back of the sofa, where he had thrown her slippers. He retrieved them and came back to her, kneeling at her feet and reaching for them.

To see him there, beneath her, gave a curious tug at her insides, as though the sight of him willingly humbled should mean anything at all to her. She gingerly put a toe out from beneath the hem of her skirt.

In response, he lifted her foot again, cradling it as he slipped the shoe back on. Then he repeated it with the other. When it was through, he did not immediately get to his feet, but waited there, as though expecting some response from her.

'Thank you,' she said, biting back the urge to dismiss him like a servant. Today, his displays of devotion were making her feel more guilty than frightened. It seemed the less he asked of her, the more she felt obligated to give him.

'Will you be attending the Tremaines' ball tomorrow evening?' he asked politely.

'I think that is between you and my father. I have no say in my social schedule. But if you require my presence, I will not be permitted to refuse.'

If he was as fond of the truth as he claimed, the statement should not have bothered him. But his expression darkened and, for a moment, she expected an angry retort. Then he mastered himself, rose from the floor and took his place beside her on the sofa. 'I would prefer a wife willing to admit that she welcomed my company.'

It was petty of her to refuse him that, when it was clear to them both how she felt about him. But he had tricked her into having those feelings. It was hardly fair. 'You wished me to smooth your manners? Then you should cease upbraiding me for presenting the facts as I see them. If you and Father wish me to go to the Tremaines', then I will do as I am told. Why must you have more from me, when you are getting your way in this?'

He snorted in disgust. 'I understand why you let someone else make your decisions. You have done poorly in the past and do not wish the responsibility. But at least you might think of me as a man who means to choose for himself what is right, without the guidance of society or politics. If I decide to have you, it will be because I think we suit and not for other reasons, do you understand?'

'Not really,' she said. He was the duke again, not some soft-hearted little boy who needed her love.

'You will have to take me at my word, then. Until I can convince you, of course. And I mean to be quite persuasive.'

She swallowed nervously, trying to imagine what he might do that was any more persuasive than what he had already done.

He stood and offered her a hand, helping her to her feet. But her legs were still weak from pleasure and she tipped alarmingly in his direction.

Without a word, his arm came out to steady her, wrapping around her waist to pull her close.

She could not find it in herself to resist, but instead let her body melt easily into his. He was big and warm and solid against her, comforting and arousing all at once. She did not want to lose this feeling, to go home where everyone was cold and censorious. She wanted to stay here and be held.

But to do that would mean... 'Reighland?' she said softly.

'Yes?'

'I enjoy your company.'

'Until tomorrow night?' he asked, as though nothing unusual had just happened. But he was smiling.

She pulled away from him, straightened her gown and glanced at herself in the mirror, trying to pretend that nothing had changed for her, either. Despite the turmoil that raged within her, not a hair was out of place. And although she had never intended to be happy, her reflection told another tale. She was smiling as well.

'Until tomorrow night,' she agreed.

# Chapter Ten

*Monsieur G. has returned to London after a pro-longed absence. He will likely have a certain lady hopping to his tune, though lately she has been leading the Duke of R. on a merry dance.*

Robert fingered the bit of newsprint in his hand, then threw it into the fire. He'd seen the comment already, in the morning paper, and hardly needed a second copy, delivered anonymously by post. The purpose behind it was quite clear: someone wished to expose Priscilla to ridicule and to anger him sufficiently to part from her.

That they'd made doubly sure that he could not miss the scrap of gossip angered him almost more than the thing itself. It was not enough that they bandied his name about in the news. But it seemed they felt the need to explain the significance of it, as though he could not read for himself. They were making him feel slow and stupid, just as they always had.

But who were they? He reminded himself firmly that if he could not manage to put a name to the persons bothering him, then their opinion hardly mattered. Receiving the little notice was embarrassing, he could hardly say otherwise. But he must remember it would be far worse for Priscilla. And there was probably nothing to it. The fact that this Gervaise fellow was once more in a city of over a million meant nothing to him, nor should it mean anything to her.

Other than bad memories, of course. He understood the power that those might have. But his were little more than childhood nonsense and hers were quite different. Priss had been near to panic the first time they'd danced and again when he'd tried to make love to her. Robert was still not sure if any man her father had chosen would have received a similar reaction, or if her fear of him was out of the ordinary.

But he was quite sure that she was not attempting to frighten him away so that she could run back into the arms of her first lover. She'd given him no reason to think that she remembered Gervaise with anything less than contempt. If there was anything to this ugly little bit of news, she would certainly tell him. She had been honest enough about the subject before. It was that very honesty that had drawn him to her in the first place. And if she still wanted to lose him, there could be no quicker way than to admit that she preferred another.

He would ask her when he saw her tonight and see what she had to say on the subject. Then he'd ask her if she still 'enjoyed his company'. From any other woman he'd have thought it faint praise. But Priscilla had purred it at him, as if it had some other meaning entirely. Though he'd have preferred her to call him by his Christian name after what had gone on in the salon, she pronounced his title in a way that made him think Reighland was a very lucky fellow indeed to have won such a lady.

Robert grinned into the fire and poked the last of the paper to ashes. She was not ready to say that she loved him. But when she did, it would be the truth. And having heard her version of the elopement, he would waste no more thought on anonymous gossip. But one thing was certain: if he caught Monsieur G. in London and lost his temper, the *ton* would see how fast Gervaise could dance on two broken legs.

'There is a package for you with the post,' said her father, dropping a brown-paper bundle beside Priss's breakfast plate on the way to his own chair.

She carefully slid the packet over the corner of exposed newspaper peeking from beneath her napkin. Ronnie had waved the paper in front of her with an angry rattle of pages, then ripped out the offending page and passed it to her, before her father might see it.

Monsieur G. As if he was entitled to such a continental title. When they had been alone together, he had lost all trace of a French accent. But that had been but one small point amongst many greater disillusionments and hardly worth mentioning. Whatever his nationality, why was he back in London? And why had anyone noticed the fact?

Most importantly, what did it mean to her? She had

no desire to see him again. But the knowledge that Reighland might notice the comment and connect it to her was suddenly too much to be borne. She had warned him that she was not an acceptable choice. But now that she was beginning to suspect that, just perhaps, she might have been wrong, Gervaise was back and the old scandal would be raised again.

She quietly slipped the paper off the table, into her lap and under her napkin, rolling it into a ball and tucking it into the pocket of her gown.

'Well, what is it, then?'

'Nothing, Papa,' she said hurriedly.

'How can you be sure until you have opened it?'

The package. She had been so distracted that she'd already forgotten it. Whatever it was, the contents were a surprise for she had expected no deliveries. It was not her birthday, nor any other holiday or anniversary that she could think of that might explain a gift. But considering the shock she'd already received, she could imagine several other horrible possibilities. Had she offered Gervaise a token of some kind? And would he be foolish enough to taunt her with it now?

She tore cautiously at the corner of the paper, trying to pretend that she was not as worried as she felt to be presented with both a shock and a mystery, first thing in the morning.

Then she had a brief glimpse of the items contained within before dropping her napkin over it and slamming her hand over the top in her haste to obscure the view.

Her father and stepmother looked up from their food,

surprised. 'Do you mean to explain yourself?' her father said gruffly.

'It is from Reighland,' Priss said, swallowing to ease the sudden dryness in her throat. She had been lucky to make it home on the previous day without inciting comment about what had occurred while she was with the duke. Though in the evening, her maid had noticed the suspicious absence in her wardrobe and made no mention other than a sly smile.

'What did he send you, then?' her father said, without looking up. 'Not much of a romantic if he ships a necklace to you in the morning post. But then I do not expect much of the man.'

Her stepmother was watching her closely, with the avaricious glare of a magpie.

'It is personal,' Priss managed, her hand frozen on the top of the package as though she could squash it into invisibility.

Veronica managed to look both disappointed and curious. 'It is rather large to be a billet-doux.'

Priss seized on the idea and ran with it. 'I believe it is a book of poetry. Possibly of his own making. I will read some to you, if you wish.'

'Thank you, no.' Veronica laughed. 'I expect it is quite awful. What talent could a horse trader possibly have in such things?'

Even if her story had been true, she felt a stab of sympathy for the eagerness with which the others at the table were willing to hold the Duke of Reighland up for sport. She drew herself up to what little height she had and in her most haughty voice announced, 'It would be embarrassing for both him and myself to display such an intimate gift for the amusement of others. In fact, I suspect he thought that I would be alone when I opened this particular package. If you will excuse me, I will take it up to my room.' She stood without removing the napkin, scooped both it and the package up, and clutched them firmly to her bosom, before rising and hurrying from the room.

What had possessed Reighland to do something as foolish as this? Had he not suspected the position he might leave her in, or had he not bothered to think at all? Or had the idea of discovery not bothered him? Suppose someone had seen and enquired?

Life here was miserable enough without bringing down the further scrutiny of her father or his meddling wife. Ronnie would have found a way to turn the whole thing into some sort of inappropriate comment while complimenting her on her ingenuity. And her father would demand an immediate marriage between them.

For the thousandth time she missed her sister. Silly would have disapproved, of course, but she'd have stopped the problem before it started. Had she not, she would have been there to shield her little sister, rather than making her the butt of some cruel joke. She would have sorted out what was to be done about the item in the newspaper. Then, perhaps, she could have helped to explain the mixed feelings in her heart, whenever she thought of the duke.

Yesterday's visit had confused her. When she'd arrived at his house, she'd been frightened and wishing she could forget the invitation he had given. The night before, he had purposely suggested the visit in the presence of Veronica, knowing that the woman would not allow her to refuse. But by the end of it, Priss would have been quite content to remain longer. For ever, perhaps. It had been a struggle to get herself back through her own front door. And it'd had nothing to do with the need to walk slowly so that her bare ankles were not seen.

Now, when she was sure the door to her room was definitely closed and not even her maid was within sight, she ripped the rest of the paper from the package and dropped the wrappings into the grate. The contents had almost slithered from their bindings, draping elegantly over her hand.

Silk stockings. She'd worn them often enough, when dressing for a ball. But nothing as fine as these. These might as well have been knitted by spiders, they were so sheer and soft. They were clocked at the ankle with a delicate trail of hearts and flowers, and tied up with a blue silk ribbon was a note: *To replace that which you lost. Wear them and think of me.*

Of all the audacity. She had a good mind to go to him immediately to explain that it would be improper to think of him in any such way. And even more improper for him to suggest that she do it. But lord knew what might happen if she saw him now.

Yesterday, she had meant to keep him at arm's length, to take a single cup with him and be gone again. And in less than an hour she had been writhing in ecstasy as he nibbled her toes.

It made no sense. Other than that it must indicate a

flaw in her character, of course. She was fairly sure that she would do something far worse if he were to come upon her while she was handling the scraps of silk he had just given her.

Think of him, indeed. As though she had been able to think of anything else, for all the time they had been apart. Even now she was imagining him taking hold of her bare leg and talking some nonsense about horses while he pulled the hose up her legs, fingers lingering over the tying of garters as she moaned and climaxed. She had never in her life given herself over so completely into the hands of another, nor been so rewarded for her trust. With a few touches, he had reduced her to putty and watched dispassionately as she'd cried out, shuddered and collapsed. And then, just as he had promised, it had been over. She'd lost nothing more than her stockings and her self-control.

Considering the extent of the pleasure, it had been a small price to pay. She allowed herself one wicked and self-indulgent smile before turning her attention to the gift in her hand. Even holding the things in her hand made her legs tingle as though she were wearing them. And the way he had held her ankles and tugged at the stockings, making them shift on her leg and stroke every inch?

She shivered and then smiled again. For all his rough talk and awkwardness, he was as subtle as a serpent. Did he use such misdirection to get his way in the House of Lords? Or did he save it for getting around the ladies?

That idea bothered her, just a little. While she should probably disapprove of what he was doing with her, she did not want to think that he bought stockings and gloves by the hundredweight to seduce any girl he fancied. She hoped that he meant something special by it.

Which meant that it was impossible to deny how much his good opinion had come to matter. The thought of marrying him still terrified her. But he had revealed his own fears as well. He worried that he might hurt others through carelessness, even as he cared little about their good opinions.

That made it all the more horrifying to think that he might have read the few lines in the paper and thought less of her because of it. Perhaps even now he was coming to understand that the taint of her scandal would be transferred to whichever man married her.

She had grown to like the attention he was giving her and would be sad to lose it. Perhaps it was just that she was the favourite of a duke. Any girl would be pleased to have such a feather in her cap.

But how many had found themselves flushed and trembling on a sofa in broad daylight, as said member of the peerage offered assurance that he sought nothing more than her trust? She remembered the soft kiss on the verandah, the reassuring hand on her elbow and the sharp taste of brandy in her lemonade, the heated kisses he had given her in a darkened room and the speed with which he had retreated when he'd realised she was not ready for them. He had done everything he could to prove that while his words might be blunt, his feelings towards her were tender.

If his object had been casual seduction, he'd have lost interest on the first night or taken what he wanted despite her resistance. But if it was the challenge that drew him, he need not be so plain to all who would listen of his intention to marry her.

She poked at the brown-paper wrapping in the fire and added the scrap of paper in her pocket, watching that burn as well. She would think no more of Gervaise. If she did not seek out the dancing master, than he could do her no further harm.

She had told Reighland everything he needed to know on the subject and he had already forgiven her. The stockings in her hand were proof enough of that. Yesterday, he had been quite open about the bedroom waiting for her in his home. She had nothing to fear.

She placed them in a drawer with the rest of her undergarments. But she held the note in her hand for a moment. It seemed wrong to throw it away. She fingered the paper, scanning the room for a safe place to keep it. Then she went to the jewel box on her dressing table that held a neat pile of letters, tied in a hair ribbon. They were gifts from last Season's suitors and really nothing more than foolishness. To see them now embarrassed her, both for the excessive things the men had said and for her own extreme reaction to them. She had wasted many an afternoon reading them over and over.

Since returning from Scotland, they felt as distant as if they had been written to another person. With no more thought, she scooped them up and tossed them on the fire to burn beside the wrappings. Then she placed the single line that Reighland had penned in place of honour, alone in the satin-lined case, and closed the lid.

## *Chapter Eleven*

When next she saw Reighland, on the other side of the Tremaine ballroom, it was just as she'd feared it would be. Her heart beat faster, her cheeks flushed and it was all she could do to keep from running to his side. There was no point in pretending otherwise. Something had changed within her. Tonight, given the chance, she would make a cake of herself over the duke, acting just as silly as every other girl in London.

She had caught herself preparing for this evening with extra care, choosing a gown of blue muslin trimmed with silver that matched sweetly with her colouring, while sporting a neckline that was near to indecent. With it, she wore the gloves and the stockings. And all the while she dressed, she could think of nothing but Reighland's reaction when he saw her. She had actually caught herself turning in the mirror and practising the cautious display of ankle that might best show the stocking.

Now she was standing at her father's side, barely listening to the greetings of the host and hostess, while scanning the crowd for the only guest that mattered to her. She turned, trying to pretend that she was not looking for him, and glanced in his direction.

He looked back at her and smiled. There was the briefest flick of his eyes towards her ankles, but he made no further effort to look. It was as though he'd ascertained all he needed from the look in her eyes.

Apparently he was not as preoccupied by the silk on her legs as she was. She felt the way her thighs slipped against each other, as her little group worked its way through the crowd. Her limbs felt smooth and wonderful. It was a pity that skirts went all the way to the floor. These stockings were made to be admired.

She glanced across the room at Reighland again and felt heat rising, on her face, in her breasts and lower, between her silk-clad legs. He would want to look at them, if she allowed it. She imagined raising her petticoats for him as far as her knees, perhaps just enough to reveal the hem of her chemise.

She could imagine the feel of his hand on her calf, the other on the heel of her slipper, pulling it free...

'Priscilla!'

'I beg your pardon...' She had bumped into Ronnie, who had stopped suddenly in front of her.

'If you are not careful, you are going to spill your wine. The glass is tipping. And do stop ogling Reighland. If the match is not fully formed, you are hardly entitled to stare at him in public.'

'Yes, Veronica.'

Across the room, Reighland was chuckling as though he had just heard the most diverting story, even though he had been standing alone.

In response, she touched her skirt and gave it a twitch.

His eyes drooped immediately to the hemline, trying to spy her ankle, and then back to her face. There was a mischievous twinkle in his eye and he raised his glass ever so slightly as though offering a toast in her direction.

For a moment, she felt quite like her old self. Last Season sometimes felt like a hundred years ago. She had flirted and been flirted with, and had a throng of suitors vying for her attention. Tonight the magic had returned. She had captivated a man. And as it should have been, it was the most eligible man in the room.

But, more unusual, he had captivated her. Though she still wished it could have been any other man than the one her father had chosen for her, it did not matter quite so much, as long as it was Reighland. She was not accustomed to feeling any answering tug when making a conquest. His note had suggested she think of him. She was happy to comply.

She turned hurriedly away from him, remembering what Veronica had said. He would think she was agreeing to his offer, if she preened at him in public. And she was not sure she was ready for that.

Would it really be so bad to marry him? It would get her out of her father's house and away from Ronnie's continual meddling. He would make her a duchess. She would have access to all the wealth, power, jewels and houses that she could hope for. If they did not suit, then there would be much space in which to withdraw from each other. Even in isolation, she would live in comfort for the rest of her life.

But she did not want a husband to withdraw from. She wanted a soulmate. And after Gervaise, she doubted that was even possible. The pain had not been the worst of it. It had been the loss of control that had frightened her. The feeling of smothering. The demands upon her body that, once she was married, she would have no right to refuse.

She felt the dizzying panic rising again and looked back over her shoulder in his direction. Even if she wished to, how could she bring herself to submit to him? And then she remembered how easy it had been, when they had been alone together.

He was watching with what appeared to be innocent curiosity until she remembered that he had worn a similar expression on their last meeting. Then she had lost her precious control; it had been so wonderful that she would happily do it again for him, if he wished.

She covered her own face with her fan, fluttering it hurriedly. Last Season, she'd have flashed him some secret message with it, demonstrating her interest and agreeing to a meeting on a balcony, or in some quiet corner of the room. Tonight, her fingers felt numb against the ivory. She had never cared if her signalling to some man or other had been met with a discreet shake of the head. But if Reighland resisted, she did not know what she would do.

It probably did not matter, for it seemed he could not

read it in any case. He looked at her and not the fluttering silk, walking across the room slowly until he stood at her side. 'A lovely evening, is it not?'

'Yes.' She looked down at the floor.

'And all the lovelier, now that you are here.'

'Do you seek to flatter me now?'

'As always, I speak the truth. But it seems even that does not please you. You are frowning. Is it that I am calling attention to how desirable you are? Or is it that the comment comes from my lips and not another's?'

'How many times must I tell you, there is no other?' she said, a little too sharply.

'That is not what the paper says.'

He had read it. She saw the darkness in his eyes, just behind the smile, and moved to stand just in front of him, close enough so that her answer could not be overheard. 'So you have seen it, then.' Then she pretended to admire the dancing, as though they were speaking of nothing important.

He nodded. 'I expect half of London has as well. Is there any meaning in it?'

He doubted her. If she asked him, he would swear it wasn't so, but the few lines of text worried him more than he cared to admit. She should not have been surprised. If her father and stepmother did not trust her, then why should this man, a virtual stranger to her, be any different?

It hurt.

She took a breath. 'Of course not. I have not seen him. And if I do, I do not mean to seek him out. But I suppose it is possible that someone saw us in the same place at the same time and assumed the worst. Or it could simply be a lie meant to upset me.' And him as well.

'Very well, then.' She felt a little of the tension go out of him with the breath at her ear. 'If you tell me that it is nothing, we will speak no more about it. I trust you.'

It was an honour to have that trust. But it made her no more comfortable, for it was a great responsibility. 'I fear I will be a disappointment to you,' she said through a bland smile, afraid to turn and look at him. 'I will not be able to control what people say about me. The gossip made mention of you as well.'

He touched her arm. 'While your desire to protect me from my own worst impulses is a noble one, you must let me decide what it is that will make me happy. And I am beginning to suspect that the only thing likely to make me happy is you.'

He said it casually, as he said everything else. And that nonchalance made it seem all the more important. This was not some florid compliment, meant to turn her head. She was the font of someone's future happiness. He truly felt that the room was a more beautiful place for her presence in it. She felt the last resistance in her cracking and breaking from the gentle pressure in a way that a full onslaught would never have achieved.

'Thank you,' she said, with equal neglect, smiling into the room and wishing she could turn and sink into his arms. 'But I would think my family could have told you by now that, for all you might gain by marrying me, I am unlikely to bring you any real joy. They all tell me that I am an endless source of trouble.'

'To them perhaps you are. But I doubt they will understand you as well as I mean to.'

'You offer me understanding?' If he was not careful, he would make her lose her composure and spill the contents of her heart, right here in a crowded ballroom. She wanted to tell him how tired she was of London and of the people in it. And how life only seemed more frightening, the more she learned about it.

Instead, she gave what she hoped was a sophisticated nod. 'An interesting gift. And it has the advantage of being inexpensive as well.'

'Unlike the other presents I've given you, which set me back a pretty penny.' He was leaning forwards just enough so that he could speak into her ear without arousing the attention of the other guests. To them it might look as though he were commenting about the dancing, or the other guests. 'You are wearing them tonight, are you not? I can see the gloves. But I can hardly request that you lift your skirts so that I might examine your legs.'

'I will set your mind at rest, then. The stockings are where you would expect them to be. That was your intention in giving them to me, was it not? That they be worn together.' She smiled, fumbled with her fan for a moment and dropped it upon the floor at her feet. Then said rather loudly, 'How careless of me.'

'Allow me to get that for you.' As he stooped to retrieve the fan, she swayed in time to the music and raised her skirt just enough so that he might see her ankle. Then she let it fall into place again and he rose and handed her the fan.

There was a trace of a sly grin on his face, in place of his usual guarded expression.

'Satisfied?' she asked and smiled back, feeling as wicked as ever she had.

'Not by half. But I hope, soon, to change that.' His voice was a low rumble in her ear that made her nerves dance. And this time it was not with fear, but with the playful excitement that she had felt on the previous day.

'Do not forget where we are,' she said, more to herself than to him. 'This is a rather public place to be having such a discussion.'

'Whatever do you mean?' he countered, all innocence.

'You know perfectly well,' she said.

'Then I suppose you will disapprove when I remind you that the things I have given you be worn next to your skin,' he said, absently. 'Jewellery is far too cold to symbolise what I think, when I look at you.'

It had not occurred to her, before this. She had thought the impropriety came from a lack of manners, but he had known exactly what he was doing from the first moment. Her arms and legs were encased in his gifts to her, a continual and intimate touch. He might be offering marriage, but he was trying to seduce her as well.

'It is not enough that my gifts touch your body,' he said. 'I want each one to be a caress. Perhaps I shall purchase a silk ribbon to wear at your throat. Or a fur muff, to warm your hands in winter. But first, a chemise.'

There was nothing awkward about his suggestions

tonight, nor were they meant as jokes. He was speaking truth into her ear. The fact that they were surrounded by people made it all the more erotic. She felt a tingle down the length of her spine, as though he had passed a hand along her skin.

'What do you favour?' he asked. 'Linen? Lawn? Or the smoothest China silk, caressing the most intimate parts of your body.'

Then he laughed to cover the sound she made, which was close to a moan of suppressed desire. She glanced around hurriedly and was relieved to see that the people nearest to them were too caught up in the music to notice her behaviour.

'Perhaps I shall give you all three,' he continued. 'We shall experiment, to see which you prefer.'

'Stop doing this to me.' She could feel the same trembling in her legs that she'd felt in the salon, after he'd stolen her stockings.

'I? I am doing nothing, Lady Priscilla. You said that you were afraid of my touch. And I am barely doing that, you must admit. My hand is on your arm. That is all.' His fingers rested gently on the few inches of bare skin between glove and sleeve. It was hardly intimate.

He must know that she was burning for him. Her knees were weak and her thighs were wet. 'Reighland,' she said in warning, 'I will not even allow you my arm if you do not stop this instant.'

'Very well, then,' he said and his hand dropped to his side. 'Now, back to the subject of your new chemise. I would hope that you select something that is not the least bit practical. I would replace it, of course, if, for some reason, it were to be torn.'

Was he suggesting what she thought he was? It hardly mattered. She could imagine the torment of being rubbed to arousal by silk and picture him putting gentleness aside and ripping some sheer nothing from her body before taking her to bed. She had a brief, fearful memory of what the past had been, then rejected it. Awful though that might have been, right now, every inch of her being ached with the need to be closer to Robert.

'Please.' She turned her head and said it so quietly that no one else but he could hear the need in her voice.

'What, darling?'

'I can no longer fight you. Nor do I wish to. If it is possible to give myself to anyone, then I am yours, body and soul. You may have whatever you want from me. But please, do it quickly, and give me some relief. Do not torment me in public.' Even now, she felt on the verge of the sort of very physical reaction that she had never felt outside her own solitary bed. Never except for her time with the Duke of Reighland.

'Very well, then.' He took her hand and she trembled at the thought of the contact, even through the protection of the delicate leather. 'I doubt that all the guests will be happy with this revelation. But at least we will be sure that the papers will talk of nothing else tomorrow.' As he looked into her eyes, he reached into his pocket and she felt the suddenly increased heaviness of her hand as a ring was slipped on to her finger.

'What is this?' she said, confused.

'The Reighland betrothal ring. You said I could do what I wanted, as long as I did it quickly. And this is it.'

She was shocked and perhaps a little disappointed. When she spoke, her voice was too loud and she could not manage to care if anyone heard. 'I assumed that you meant to pull me into an alcove and ravish me.'

He touched her gloved fingers to his lips. 'First things first. Now that I know I have your co-operation. I wish to formalise our relationship in the eyes of the *ton*.'

'Marriage.'

'Engagement, at least.' He smiled and put a hand on her shoulder. 'It is what couples normally do before attempting congress.'

People who did not include her, she supposed. She hoped that this was not meant as a rebuke to her morals. But it did not seem to be, for he was smiling at her. And he had offered to marry her.

'It is not as if I do not wish to pull you into the musicians' gallery and have my wicked way with you,' he consoled. 'Just not tonight. Mrs Tremaine will be in alt that her ballroom is the location that I make the announcement. It is a social coup. But I doubt her hospitality will extend to allow sporting in dark corners. She was a vicar's daughter, after all. Now, come, let us make the announcement.'

'Announcement?' she said, still trembling from excitement, but going rapidly numb at the sudden change things that taken.

Robert was leading her towards the front of the room and paused to whisper a few words to Rosalind

Tremaine, who clapped her hands together in elation and signalled for the musicians to pause.

All heads turned in their direction. Robert explained, politely, and briefly, that Lady Priscilla had just done him the honour...

She had been trapped, although she was not quite sure how it had happened. He had not showered her with gifts, since two was hardly a shower. Nor had he given her his undivided attention for months on end. Although, in the brief times they had been together, she had felt she had it.

And he had certainly not smothered her with his lovemaking. During the aborted attempt on the floor in his house, she had been quite terrified. But beyond that he had kissed her lips only once. And he'd kissed her ankle, of all places. That was at the same time most improper and hardly improper at all.

And yet she could not help thinking that they had been together for ages. How else had she become so totally aroused by the thought of the man? Although she had sworn she never would, she was eagerly doing what her father had wanted all along.

It galled her. But it was almost worth it to see the shocked looks on the faces of the other girls. Char Deveril was there in the crowd, looking as though she had just swallowed a toad. Apparently she'd had designs on Reighland, just as everyone else had. But considering the speed with which Char had turned on her last Season, holding her up for ridicule and cutting her when they met on the street, Priss was not the least bit sorry for her.

Her feelings were much more confused when she saw her father. Benbridge looked as she remembered him from before Ronnie, and even before her elopement. For the first time in ages, he was truly smiling at her. He was accepting the congratulations of other guests as though the good fortune was entirely his. Veronica was a portrait of icy triumph, ready to use this new connection to cement her place in society. And when her father looked at her, it was with all the pride and approval he had used so many months ago, when she had still been his favourite.

For a moment, Priss was almost happy. That time had been easier, for her at least. Her sister had suffered, but she had been happy, in her own selfish fashion. She had not realised how quickly favour might be lost.

'Dance with me,' Reighland demanded. The suggestion was ordinary and, as usual, ever so slightly rude. He should have said 'please'. But it pulled her out of her reverie and back to his side. His words were full of invitation and hidden meaning, just as they always seemed to be. Out loud he had demanded a waltz. But in her mind, he had suggested something quite different. *Love me. Make love to me and with me. Let me please you.*

She sensed no conditions upon them. Reighland was as unchangeable as a mountain. He would be her rock. As he led her out on to the dance floor, she leaned upon his arm and smiled.

He leaned forwards to speak into her ear. 'It is not so bad, is it? Marrying me, that is.'

'I am getting used to it,' she admitted, a little breathlessly, squeezing his shoulder where her hand rested and feeling the ring tighten against her fingers.

'Good. Very good. I will still ravish you, of course. You need have no fear that I am uninterested on that front.'

'Oh.' What had she agreed to? The waves of passion that had caused her to agree to him were subsiding, as were the feelings of comfort. And like any ebbing tide, they were likely to uncover things she did not particularly want to think about.

'Tomorrow, perhaps?' he murmured. 'I will be visiting one of my properties not far from London, not even a day's ride. It is in the country, of course. Perhaps it is more rustic than you wish. Not one of Reighland's fine houses, but a place I bought some years back. Still, it will be your home as well, once we are married. But it needs a lady's touch. I would like to know what you think of it. We will be back by evening. Perhaps I can persuade your stepmother to allow an unchaperond trip, now that I have publicly declared my intentions.'

Even with the engagement, she should definitely refuse him. It was quite risky enough to have the little meetings they'd had. If she was gone from home the whole of the day, travelling in a closed carriage with him, anything might happen.

But what might happen would not matter to her father, any more than her indiscretions had mattered before Dru left. They had been hidden and that had been enough to please him. Now, she had accepted an offer of marriage from a duke. And to Benbridge, she might as well have been washed in snow. As long as the end result was her becoming Duchess of Reighland, her father would not give a fig for maintaining appearances. Her stepmother would not love her in any case. Priss sighed. 'I will tell Ronnie that you wish me to have the house measured for furniture and new hangings. She will approve of my spending your money, I am sure.'

'I will arrange it, then,' Reighland said. 'But do not tell her that we will be doing the bedrooms first.' He smiled at her in a way that made her heart flutter, but whether it was excitement or fear she felt, she was not sure.

# *Chapter Twelve*

Priscilla held her breath as the carriage drove round the bend and she caught her first sight of their destination. For all his talk of being a humble farmer, Robert Magson must have done quite well for himself, even before gaining the title. The simple country home that Reighland had described was larger than Benbridge Manor, with acres of parkland, riding trails, a grand house and many outbuildings. She could see the beginnings of gardens that would supply this house and the London property with fresh vegetables and herbs, and orchards blossoming that would be heavy with fruit come late summer and autumn.

But this bounty was not the pride of the property. The fields surrounding the gardens were carefully fenced and the enclosed fields were dotted with horses: glossy blacks, chestnuts, dapple greys and rowans grazing peacefully, some of them great with foal.

As they rode up the curved drive, she could see

behind the house that construction of a larger stable was in progress. 'I have only a small portion of the breeding stock here,' Reighland said, glancing out into the field. 'Most are still in the north. But it was too great a sacrifice to take on this supposed honour as Reighland and part myself from everything that gave me pleasure.'

He was smiling down at the barns in a way that he never did while in town. Not even at her, she reminded herself. Most of their interactions seemed controlled and distant, compared to the man she saw today, who laughed more easily as he allowed himself to relax in her presence. He seemed larger as well, as though being in the city was a continual restraint on his character. Perhaps that was why he had been drawn to horses. They were large animals that did not require unusual tenderness on his part. He could be himself around them.

The idea no longer bothered her. When the time came, she was sure he would take care with her. But it seemed that time had not yet arrived. If she'd expected the whole trip would be spent in amorous play, so far she'd been sorely mistaken. The two-hour journey had been quietly accomplished and their conversation a polite and rather banal rehashing of the previous evening's events. A careful reading of the morning's paper revealed no further gossip about a return of Gervaise. But Reighland had passed her a page with their engagement prominently displayed and assured her that it would settle much speculation and put an end to the rumours about her. 'Do not let them see that you were bothered by the first notice,' he said firmly. 'I was not.'

But he had asked her about it. If it had meant nothing to him, then why did he refer to it now? 'Of course, Reighland,' she said and willed herself to question him no further on the subject and trust that it was closed. Now that they were no longer sparring with each other, it was possible to view the sudden silence that fell between them as a comfortable thing. She need have no fear of what he might think during it.

And it did seem that, if he thought of anything, it was of horses. The lulls in their conversation were filled with unusually detailed descriptions of his animals, their bloodlines and the sires of their expected offspring.

Then he broke off suddenly and cast an apologetic look in her direction. 'I am sorry if I am boring you more than I usually do. But I do tend to lose track of time when I am talking of cattle.'

She laughed, relaxing a little. 'Some wives might worry about their husbands squandering time at gaming hells, or running up endless tailor bills. But if I need to find you, I shall check Tattersalls.' Of course, some women would assume that their husbands passed the days with a mistress. She would not deny him, if he found her unsatisfactory in that respect. But she did not wish to think of that today. She much preferred to think of him sneaking off to a horse auction rather than leaving her alone.

And riding was a pastime that they might share, if he was not overly protective of his privacy. If the day went well, perhaps she would ask him about purchasing a team and carriage for her use.

Then she reminded herself of the true reason for their visit and fiddled nervously with her reticule. She had come prepared to spend the better part of the day in a bedroom somewhere in the house, not discussing bloodstock in the barn. She had lain awake most of the night, her mind in turmoil. The sudden alteration of plans left her both confused and disappointed.

But Reighland did not seem to notice her mood. When the carriage drew to a stop, he bounded from it in his eagerness to see the progress made at the stables. He smiled back at her. 'I must speak to the builders, if you can spare me for a time. You needn't bother yourself with coming after me, if you do not wish to be around the animals. I will be done quickly, then we will pass the rest of the day together.'

He appeared to be dismissing her. She had to remind herself that it was quite reasonable of him to put business before pleasure. The animals had been more than a hobby to him for some time and he was concerned for their care and welfare. It would be childish of her to stamp her foot and demand to be entertained every minute of the day. 'Of course,' she said with more grace than she felt. 'I will acquaint myself with the house and the grounds.'

He smiled in relief. 'I have warned the servants to expect you and that they must attend to your every wish. Treat the property as your own. That is what it shall be, in a few short weeks.'

It was a generous sentiment, but not totally accurate. If this land was not part of the entail, it belonged to

Robert more than Reighland Court did. But that did not make it hers.

'Perhaps, later, we shall have a picnic,' he said, as though he sensed her pique. But as he did so, he was staring past her shoulder, probably at a horse.

'That would be nice,' she said quietly.

'Very good.' He gave her a short and familiar kiss upon the cheek, then hurried off, leaving her alone.

She looked after him with disgust. It was no less than she should have expected from him, really. He could have at least assembled the servants and introduced her properly, at the house, before running off to inspect the new buildings.

But she could not say she was surprised. It was what she had expected her married life to be like. She just had not expected it from Reighland, nor had she expected it so soon. But there would be time enough for formalities, once they married. For measuring the bedrooms as well. And at least in some small way, all this would be hers. She would be mistress of both of them and other homes besides—but only because she was marrying their master.

She pushed her bitterness aside. She was to be a duchess. That would be consolation enough. It was a role she had been trained to take, almost from the first moment she could remember. She had always assumed that she would be a wife to some lord or other, managing households and servants, arranging for social gatherings, bearing and rearing children. But she had been imagining something along the scale of her father's wealth. Clearly, this was much different. Everything would be done on a grander scale and with a larger budget.

She smiled to herself as a streak of pure avarice appeared to counter any remaining resistance to the match. She would have to tell Robert of it, when she could find him. It would probably amuse him.

At least her husband would have a sense of humour, she reminded herself. Robert was really quite funny. Understanding, as well. He cared for her and had proven it on several occasions. And now she was standing on as pretty a piece of property as she had ever seen, free to do as she liked.

Freedom.

That was what she had wanted, all along, but she had never believed it would come to her. Now it was finally here. The thought left her trembling with excitement. It was as though she had all the energy in the world and no idea how to expend it. Robert had said she could do as she liked. And he truly meant it.

She walked towards the house, then turned away. It would not be that much different from other houses she had seen. Any tour of it was likely to turn into a list of duties for her: hangings to change, furniture to purchase and a critique of the menus and the servants. It would be much nicer to see the grounds, where there was much to be pleased with and no responsibilities.

In the rose bower, a gardener presented her with a flower. She tasted strawberries behind the glasshouse and found them delicious. She followed a path from there down to the old stables, which were well kept and held an assortment of snorting, stamping beasts.

'Excuse me?' She looked to the first groom she could find, who gave her a quick bow. 'I think I should like to ride for a while to look at the rest of the grounds. Can you direct me to a suitable animal?'

He walked her down the row of stalls to a mare that looked not merely docile, but half-asleep. She touched the animal on the flank with a gloved hand and it barely raised the energy to switch its tail.

She turned back to the groom. 'Is there something with a bit more spirit? A jumper, perhaps?'

'Are you sure, your ladyship?' The groom looked back at her doubtfully. 'The duke'll have my head if I put you up on a hunter and see you tossed into a hedge.'

'You have nothing to fear there.' She pointed to a brute of a horse several stalls down that was stomping at the straw, clearly eager to be ridden. 'How about this fellow? He looks to be needing some exercise.'

The man seemed even more surprised by this. 'We was told that the new lady was not much for horses.'

'Where did you get that idea?' she said, surprised.

'From his Grace. He is off at the other end of the building right now, instructing the others not to frighten you by exercising the stallions.'

'Is he, now?' Then she laughed, remembering the outrageous lies she'd told on the first night. 'The duke was mistaken. I assure you, I am a competent horse-woman. There will be no trouble.' She glanced down at her dress. 'This is not a habit, of course. But I do not care if it is ruined. And I doubt Robert will mind if I do not look my London best while visiting a farm.'

She negotiated with the stable boys for a time and

they settled on a chestnut gelding, a bit smaller than her first choice, that danced a little as the side saddle was thrown on his back.

She patted his neck and talked softly to him, leaning her cheek against his mane. She could have a horse of her own. Several, she was sure. And although he had never spoken of them, she suspected Reighland had carriages as well and would not mind her having a curricle and team.

But for now, she would ride. She set out on the path that the groom had recommended, which was sedate at first, but angled downhill, further away from the house, towards a little stream and a cluster of oaks. *Freedom.* The word seemed to echo in the beat of the horse's hooves. The wind was rushing through her hair and she urged him to a gallop, hanging on to the pommel between her legs for dear life. Her sister would have told her to use sense, frightened her by talking of falls and reminded her firmly that ladies did not jump.

But her sister was not here. And Robert need not know as long as she was careful. She pushed the horse towards the fallen log at the end of the field, sure that they could clear it together, and willed her mount to leap. They sailed up, over and down to earth again, in a perfect thump-thump-thump of hooves. She reined in; as she did so, she heard the sound of pursuit and a man's angry shout.

*Robert.* He had said she might treat the property as her own. But they had not discussed her sneaking down to his stables, or taking any of the horses. While he might be all right with her re-arranging the furniture, he might think something else entirely of her meddling with his livelihood.

It had been a shame, because she had been so happy. She turned her horse and waited for the scolding.

'Priscilla. What the devil?' He was beside her now, reaching for the reins, staring at her crooked bonnet, her windblown hair and her flushed face. 'You ride?'

'Well...' She wondered if an apology for the deception was necessary and then decided to brazen it out. 'Yes, I ride. Does that displease you?'

'You scared the devil out of me.' He pointed to the gelding. 'I thought he had got away from you. When you took the jump, my heart was in my throat.'

'It was very foolish of me,' she admitted. 'It has been some time. And I am not properly attired. But the groom said this was a familiar path and the horse did not seem to mind.' She offered the reins to him, preparing to be led like a child back to the stables.

'You ride' he said it again, dumbfounded, and pushed the leather back into her hands. Then he pointed. 'There. Take the path that leads into the copse of trees. Canter. Stop when you reach the glade and wait for me. I wish to watch your seat.'

She shrugged and turned the chestnut, kicking it up to the gait he requested. It rode like a dream and she remembered, if he was not too angry at her for this deception, that she might ride often, with the duke for a husband. By the time she reached the break in the trees, she could hear him, galloping to catch up. He swung out of the saddle easily and held out his arms to her, demanding that she dismount as well.

'You ride.' He was breathless, shaking his head in amazement.

'I lied when I said I was afraid of horses,' she admitted. 'In truth, I quite like them.'

He groaned and pulled her against him, all pretence of gentleness forgotten, burying his face in her throat. 'You are perfect, you know that? The sight of you, on a spirited horse…' He groaned again and pushed her to the ground.

'You are not angry?'

He fell on top of her, his mouth on hers, his hands on her waist, kissing her as though it were the only way he could tell her his mind. It was rough with happiness and surprise, and as exhilarating as the ride had been. His tongue thrust into her mouth and she submitted weakly, moulding herself to his body, absorbing the solid strength of him.

When he withdrew, he pushed himself up on an elbow to smile down at her. 'I am overcome.'

He was more than that. She could feel him large and hard through the fabric of her skirt. She felt her mouth go dry and reached up to finger the cloth of his shirt. 'I know that I might have been hurt. But it had been so long… And you said I must treat the place as my own.'

'That horse is the very devil. But you handled him well.' He pushed open the spencer she wore and rested his hand on her heart. 'And there is barely a quiver here. You fearless creature.' He gave a low dark smile and let his hand slip to the side to cover a breast, massaging. 'Let us see if I can raise your pulse for you.'

'Your Grace…' She grabbed at his wrist, but it was

too late to hide her reaction. Her nipples had pebbled at his first touch.

He paused. 'Can you not call me Robert? And as you do it, remember that I have promised not to hurt you.'

'Robert.' She sighed, remembering that she sometimes thought of him as her Robert. She had nothing to be afraid of. With a little effort, she might lose herself in the moment, for what he was doing felt quite nice. He was right. It made her heart skip and her breath catch in her throat to feel his hand resting against her breast.

'My dear?' He was asking for permission to continue.

She released his hand and tugged at the ribbon that gathered the neck of her gown, loosening it for him. Then she closed her eyes. She felt her clothing pushed down and out of the way, then the rasp of his gloved finger against her nipples. It was the barest touch, like his first kisses had been, maddening in its subtlety.

She arched her back and pressed upwards against his hand, only to have him draw further away and continue the gentle torture of it until she whispered, 'More, please.'

'As you command.' He murmured the words into her skin, replacing the dry touch of leather with the wetness of his tongue, circling, laving, teeth nipping, mouth sucking, his hair brushing gently against her chin and his whiskers scratching against the fabric of clothing that had fallen about her waist. He was slow and methodical with his kisses, not sparing an inch of her, even though she had buried her fingers in his hair to urge him on.

And just as she felt the first flutter of orgasm, he

pulled away. 'Robert,' she said, more urgently, opening her eyes.

He was reaching for her skirt, tugging it up to free her legs of the excess cloth. 'It is time that our lessons progressed beyond a walk. After what I have just seen, I am sure you are ready for a gallop.' He drew a finger up the inside of her leg and she felt a little frightened, until she reminded herself that he was only touching stocking. They were not even the flimsy nothings he had bought for her in London, but sensible wool hose to protect her legs.

Still, the pressure of his hand against them burned her skin. The leather of his glove was on her bare leg and now it was resting on the place where her legs met. She gasped as he wagged his finger from side to side against her body just as he had done on her breasts. 'Did you lie to me when you said you were afraid of this?'

'Yes. I mean... No.' She had been afraid of something very different than what she was feeling now. This felt more like a reward than a punishment. A flood of sensations was building in her and she fisted her hands in the grass at her sides.

He paused, pressing lightly down upon her. 'I was able to be patient with you, to wait unfulfilled, because I had doubts that we would suit. You did not ride. How could I marry a woman that could not share my one joy with me?'

'You could keep me at home and pay your mistress in matched bays and silver fittings for her saddle.' She was gasping as she said it, but the image in her mind of Robert rolling in the sheets with another was unpleasant. She worked to focus on the feeling the tip of his gloved finger was creating, which was most extraordinary. She circled her hips against it, trying to push herself over the last boundaries of satisfaction.

'Or I could take you in a field of wild flowers, as I mean to do now.' He took his hand away for a moment and ripped a handful of bluebells and showered them upon her face.

'And how do you know I will allow it?' But the thought did not frighten her nearly as much as it once had.

'I can give you no choice,' he said. 'After the sight of your sweet bottom in a saddle, I am hard as stone and desperate for relief. I cannot ride in this condition, my love. And you have led me miles from the house. I doubt I could walk, if I tried.'

'Then it would be churlish of me to refuse you,' she said. Especially as he had been so patient with her. And he had called her his love, just now. Had he ever done it before? She could not remember.

Perhaps he had felt that same rush of emotion, just as she had on realising that her one true dream was realised. 'I seem to be in some distress as well,' she admitted. 'I expect it is what you are doing with your fingers.'

'Bothers you, does it?' His finger returned and he drew another slow circle against her. 'Do you wish me to stop? Or does it leave you wanting more?' He stroked relentlessly against her, making her body feel like a hot, wet void.

'More,' she whispered. 'Perhaps, if you were to use your hand, inside of me...'

'No,' he said, with a small smile. 'If I am without release, you can hardly expect me to oblige you. But if you need filling, I have just the thing for you.' With a last flick of his finger, he did something. She was not sure what, but it was as if her body was a hand that had given a single great grasp, only to come away empty.

He rolled off her on to his back and undid the front of his trousers. Then he turned his head to her, where she lay at his side. 'If you wish further satisfaction, I would be happy to help. Do as you will with me.'

She rolled towards him and leaned on her elbow to look, preparing to be frightened. But her body was telling her otherwise. If there was a problem in the previous experience, she was sure it must have been that Gervaise was inadequate, and surprisingly graceless, for a dancer. Robert was—dear God—Robert was just what she needed. She pulled off her gloves and reached to circle him with her fingers.

His member twitched against her hand and he sucked in a breath. She felt an answering twitch inside of herself, just as the moisture of her body was echoed with a single drop from him. She rose to her knees and touched him more boldly, taking him in her palm and stroking him, watching his fingers spread wide, digging into the earth to keep from grabbing her. 'I am not hurting you, am I?' Although how she could be, with such gentle petting, she was not sure.

'Of course you are, darling,' he said, through clenched teeth. He searched for her with his hand again, brushing against the same tender spot. 'You must be familiar with the agony of knowing that pleasure is so close.' He gave a tortured laugh as she ran a finger over the tip of him.

He responded with a touch that made her gasp. He was right. It did almost hurt to know that something wonderful was so very close. She was nearly as distressed as he was and definitely feeling incomplete.

So she sat up, took a breath to steady her nerves, then spread her legs and straddled him, letting her skirts form a curtain and then reaching beneath them. If she could not see, it might be easier. Or perhaps more difficult. For if he did not mean to help her, how would she know what to do? But when she touched him to her body, she was suddenly quite sure what she wished to do. She wanted to use him shamelessly, to sooth the place that he had touched with his finger. It was what he was made for, surely. Silky flesh, slipping against her own, sending spirals of pleasure through her body, raising the heat inside.

Inside. Perhaps, just a little. But a little was so good, she was sure that a lot would be even better. And before she knew it, she had pulled herself forwards, up and on to him. She felt a moment's difficulty, a stretching of her body and a fullness that seemed to go on and on to the very centre of her being. She squeezed his hips with her thighs, riding him, feeling the slip and pull of their bodies and pressing her palms flat against his chest to hold him still so she could do what she wanted, moving harder and faster, falling forwards on to his mouth, tongue to tongue in time to the rise and fall of her hips. She found she could tighten her muscles and control his response, making him groan under her. And then he clutched her hips and thrust upwards, hard, and something broke inside her until she was shaking as violently as he was, inside and out. Slowly, the insanity that had gripped her subsided and she relaxed and lay still on top of him, feeling his arms stealing around her to hold her close.

He sighed, smiling and untying the ribbon of her bonnet that had slipped uselessly down her back. 'I do not know why men are so enamoured of virgins. Sometimes, a small amount of experience...'

'For their heirs, silly,' she whispered in his ear. Perhaps he had forgotten that fact. When she raised her head to look at him, he was staring up at the sky as though he was not quite sure what had happened to him. 'They fear a woman who has strayed once will make a habit of it.'

'Or they fear they will suffer from comparison,' he admitted, with unusual candour.

'That need not be your fear,' she said, blushing. 'If what has just happened is any indication, you will be first and only in all ways that matter to me. You are magnificent, Reighland.'

He stroked her back. 'And I will not be searching for a mistress to share my rides. I am imaging some long and very interesting picnics taken at various places about my properties.'

'That sounds pleasant,' she said. 'You did promise me a picnic, you know. And riding makes me hungry.' She gave an experimental flex of her muscles.

'Apparently, riding makes you insatiable.'

'It makes you peckish as well.' She could feel him rousing within her.

He was laughing now, kissing her, pressing his face into her neck. 'Never mind your father, and the *ton* and titles and propriety. Marry me, Priscilla. Do it because you want to.'

'Yes,' she said with a smile. 'I think I should like it very much.' He was moving under her in a way that made her forget that she had ever been frightened of him. He was large, but he was gentle when he needed to be. And she was having the most unusual and inappropriate thoughts about the anatomy of a man who would be her husband, and was already a peer of the realm. It felt deliciously wicked, in a way that she had not felt since she was young and foolish, daring and unafraid of being hurt. No matter what might happen, she was quite sure that Robert would not harm her.

'What is it, wench?' he growled. 'Are you laughing at me?'

'Not at you, precisely, your Grace.' But she was laughing, thinking of all the shocking things they were likely to do together.

'Then stop it immediately. The succession is very serious business.' He reached under her skirt and gave her a playful swat upon the bottom, then surged up into her again with a groan of pleasure.

'We cannot be seeing to that, now,' she murmured against his lips. 'You have not married me yet. Perhaps we should stop this, lest we create a by-blow and not a little duke.'

'Stop?' He rolled with her until her body was trapped beneath his, then redoubled his thrusts. 'In a while, perhaps. Long enough to get a special licence and drag you before a vicar.'

'A bishop,' she said breathlessly. 'You are a duke, after all. I want a bishop at St George's.'

'I will marry you before a druid in the woods, if that is what you wish,' he grunted. 'After that, I will lock our bedroom door and you will not wear a thing more than my ring for at least a week. Perhaps two. Dear God, you are sweet. I am undone when I am with you.' To prove the fact, he spilled into her with a sigh and a shudder of pleasure.

'And suppose that is not to my liking?' she whispered.

'Then I will give you what you want. Whatever you want, to make you happy. To make you love me.' He kissed her, fervently, ardently, with all the desperation of a lovesick youth. 'No more games, Priss. Say you'll have me. You'll not regret it, I swear.' His voice was soft, urgent and totally sincere.

She pushed a hand between them and ran a finger down his chest, worming it through gaps in waistcoat and shirt until she could touch the hair on his chest. 'I want a horse.'

'Done.'

'Two, then. A curricle and team of matched Yorkshire Trotters. And a high-perch phaeton to drive in Hyde Park.'

'Yours. All yours.'

She smiled up at him. 'And I would trade them all to hear you say that you love me.'

'I think that I do.' He seemed as surprised as she was. 'I am sure of it, as a matter of fact. I love you, Lady Priscilla.'

It was the strangest feeling, being close to him like this, smelling flowers and hearing his breathing in her ear and the soft sounds of nature, all around them. She was happy and at peace as well. 'And I love you, Robert.' She smiled and said it again. 'I love you.' She raised her head and kissed him again. They belonged together. He had been right all along. And of all the mistakes she had made in her short life, being wrong about Reighland was the one that she was most glad of.

## Chapter Thirteen

The time was passing in a whirl and yet it seemed to drag on without end. The banns had been read twice. The church had been reserved, the flowers ordered and a menu chosen for the wedding breakfast.

The only thing Priss had not managed to achieve was an invitation for her sister. Her father would not permit it and crossed the Hendricks name off the guest list when she'd tried to add it. When Veronica had found her handwritten offer she had removed it from the outbound post and reminded Priss of her duty to uphold the family honour.

She would have to go to Reighland with it, she suspected. She was sure he saw the Folbrokes regularly. He must see Mr Hendricks, and perhaps Dru as well. It would annoy Father to no end, but he would submit to rank and let the duke have his way.

That would be the best thing about marriage, she was sure. A rich and powerful man was offering it to her with a twinkle in his eye, daring her to take advantage of his good nature and make him wield his power for her. Robert seemed like a most reasonable man, and she would have the latitude to visit where she wished and to avoid whom she pleased, even if it was her own father. The Duchess of Reighland could see Dru whenever she wanted.

Well, perhaps that would be the second-best thing about marriage.

Priss stared at her smiling reflection in the mirror, as the modiste crouched at her feet, setting pins in her wedding gown. But she could not help but smile when thinking about all the pleasant things she might do with her soon-to-be husband to reward him for his efforts on her part.

Robert had been very proper with her, since that day they had lain together in the flowers. They had not been alone at all in weeks. But when he looked at her, there was something smouldering, deep behind his eyes, that gave the lie to the propriety of his speech and actions. It said that the title and lands were as nothing compared to the winning of her. He was as eager for this marriage as she had become. Even if he'd been a boot boy, the look would still have been in his eye and he'd still have made her feel like a duchess.

Yesterday, she had received a carefully wrapped package from him containing a large and boring book, and a chemise so fine that it could be slipped unnoticed between the pages. There was another note that duplicated the last. 'Wear this, and think of me.'

And as before she could think of nothing else. She

had been a fool to have worried about Robert's dark looks and considerable size. She still thought of him as rugged rather than handsome and his manner was sometimes blunt to the point of embarrassment. But she had learned from Gervaise what a pleasant face and pretty manners were worth, once the doors were closed and friends and family far from earshot.

Now that she had joined with him, the thing that had once frightened her had become the focus of many pleasant thoughts. She wanted it. She needed it. She wore his gifts whenever she was able, even though they were exquisitely arousing. And she had taken to touching herself at night, to gain some relief. While she did it, she thought of how much better it might be, if it could be his hands moving on her body. He must know what she was doing, she was sure. It explained the note.

When they were alone again, she would tell him how she felt. Because of him, she was young and alive, for the first time in months.

One more reason she needed to talk to Dru. She was happy and in love, and longed for a confidant to share the news. She doubted that Veronica would care one way or the other. Perhaps she would not even understand the words. There was no question that Ronnie had married Benbridge for social status, power and wealth, but there was no sign that she had looked further than that.

Priss would have all those advantages with Robert as well, but it was better that there was a deeper fondness. She was eager to see him again, if only to hear his voice and to laugh at his jokes, which were never quite jokes. She wanted him to stand a little too close to her and say the wrong thing, even if he knew the right thing, just to annoy and amuse her.

They would go back to his house in the country and the horses that he was so proud of, which were better than the boring beasts her father allowed her in the city. There were miles of unexplored land to gallop over, and logs and fences in need of jumping. He would not be bothered to lecture her about the need of maintaining a safe and sedate pace so that she might display herself in the right light without mussing clothes or hair. In fact, he would make sure that she never returned from a ride in the proper condition she'd set off in.

The modiste helped her off with the nearly completed gown. And when she had been dressed again she met Ronnie in the front room of the shop, where she had been paging through *La Belle Assemblée* and sipping chocolate. They arranged for the delivery of wedding clothes and exited the shop, walking up Bond Street toward the printers, where invitations awaited her approval.

In the past, shopping with Ronnie had been an endless tedium. But today, each new errand increased Priss's happiness. Even conversation with her father's wife was enjoyable. Clearly, love was utter madness. But it was also quite delightful. Priss wondered why she had resisted it for so long.

And then she glanced up the street and saw him.

Gervaise lounged against the side of a building, watching her as she made her way towards him. Veronica was oblivious, of course. She had never met him and would not see the obvious risk. She would lead

Priss right past the man and think nothing of it. An explanation would mean stopping dead in her tracks for a series of questions and answers. It would call even more attention to the possible meeting.

She could tug on her stepmother's arm and demand to be taken across the street. But she suspected that, if Gervaise meant to make mischief, he would follow them. Far better to brazen it out and act as if he meant nothing at all to her. But as they came closer, each step was an agony. An agony that she dare not reveal.

Priss schooled herself, looking ahead and not to the side, focusing on her destination some streets ahead. It was like being trapped in one of her nightmares. The weight of a man's body seemed to press down on her chest, cutting off her breath. As they passed him, she answered some foolish question of Veronica's and heard the thinness of her own voice, as though it came from a great distance. Ronnie was too preoccupied with her shopping to notice the difference.

There. It had been hell. But they were past him and she had managed the cut indirect. Unlike Robert, Gervaise should understand the significance and leave her alone. He was making no move to follow her now.

From behind her, she heard a laugh.

# Chapter Fourteen

'Of course, rebellion in the north must be put down with all due haste. There is far too much latitude given to the working classes. And the troops in York…'

Robert did his best to ignore the long-winded rant of his future father-in-law. It would not do to provoke the man in the middle of his own house, especially not when it might further upset his fiancée at her engagement ball. But the earl was trailing him from card room to dance floor and back, and would not leave him alone.

It had not been Robert's intention to spend the whole of the night in male company. He had not seen Priss as often as he'd liked in the last weeks. Now that he could spend time with her, it was clear that the girl was suffering from wedding nerves. She looked tired and worried. But she was as beautiful as ever in a gown made of something gold and shiny, which went well with her hair. He had told her she looked like an angel, for the ribbon in her hair did rather remind him of a halo.

He had expected some sort of thanks in response. Or at least a blush. But instead she'd looked at him as though he were mad and said that all of London knew there was nothing the least bit angelic about her.

He suspected it was the nonsense that had been appearing in the papers that was bothering her. If he were to believe it—which of course he did not—his future duchess was being seen all over town in the company of her old lover. Things would settle down, once they were married and the rumour spreader realised that they had done no good with them.

There was no point in letting the words of meddling fools cause pain. The taunting would only increase, if one responded to it. Such pettiness could be endured and ignored. Soon they would be married, Parliament would be out of session and they could go back to the country and the horses, which were simpler.

Of course, horses could be false jades as well. But when he was with them, there was never a question in Robert's mind as to who was to ride and who was to be ridden.

When they were alone, he would remind Priss that peace was almost within reach, but for now he had managed to calm her as they had waltzed together, making her laugh and pulling her too close until she had slapped his arm with her fan and scolded him for being impertinent.

'I cannot help myself,' he'd whispered. 'It has been weeks since I've had you. And two weeks more to wait until I will have you again. A man has needs, you know.'

That should have resulted in a glib comment or perhaps another scold. But instead she'd looked even more worried and echoed, 'Two weeks. How will I bear it?' as though she were speaking some thought that she'd meant to keep hidden. Then her grip had tightened on his arm and she'd said, urgently, 'Let us not wait. You have the licence. We could run away tonight, if we wished, and be married first thing in the morning. It would be done then and you could have me all to yourself, as often as you liked. Please, Robert? Could we elope?'

It had been quite flattering to see her so eager for him. And strange that he had been the one to remind her of the need for pomp and circumstance, now that the invitations were on their way. She had looked so disappointed that he had suggested that perhaps a clandestine meeting might be arranged.

But she had shaken her head, refusing to leave her house, even to come to his. He must speak to Benbridge about it, if the man would ever leave off talking politics. 'Who is that man that Priscilla has been talking with?' he interrupted, finally out of patience.

'What?' Benbridge was clearly annoyed to be bothered with anything so mundane as his own guests.

'I saw a tall slender man with pale hair offering her a glass of punch just now.'

Benbridge turned his head. 'I see no such person.'

Nor did Robert, at the moment. But the man had been there earlier. He was certain of it. 'He stood up with her earlier, a while after I did. He seemed a bit of a fop.' And an excellent dancer.

Benbridge gave another cursory scan of the crowd.

'He is not here now, at any rate. But if it is a concern to you, you had best ask Priscilla to introduce you to him.'

'Perhaps I shall do that,' Robert said. Although at the moment, he could not manage to find Priss amongst the dancers either. 'If you will excuse me, I think it is time for me to speak with her.' Perhaps it was past time.

'Why are you here?' Priss demanded. It had not been bad enough that Gervaise had appeared at her engagement ball, making her worry which of the guests knew him, and which did not. That had made her nearly dizzy with panic, just as she felt each time she saw him on the street.

Now, when she had gone to search for Robert, trying to find him before the gossips did, Gervaise had been the one to follow her into the hall.

'I am here because you invited me, Priscilla, *ma chérie.*'

'Leave off with that immediately, you horrible man. I am not your *chérie*, and never was.' She glanced around her, relieved that they were alone. The solitude would not last for long; she must get him out of the house before they were discovered in a tête-à-tête. 'Do you not notice that I cut you each time you accost me? Why do you continue to follow me? It should have been clear after the first day that I do not wish to renew our acquaintance. And I certainly did not invite you to my home.'

'Of course you did.' He removed an invitation from his pocket and flashed it to her so fast that she could not see if it was an outright forgery or a genuine card that had been addressed to another and altered. Again, she felt as though she was trapped in some bad dream, one where she had been foolish enough to send a card to him, creating the problem, just as she had by eloping.

He was smiling at her, unctuous and knowing. 'Surely, we need not stand on ceremony. As I remember it, we were very close friends indeed on the road to Scotland.'

'Perhaps you do not remember how that ended,' she said with satisfaction. 'I applauded from the window of an inn while Mr Hendricks beat you into the dust. Then he put you into a coach and sent you away.' Gervaise was a man, not a nightmare. And a weak man, at that. He could be beaten.

'But when I heard of your impending nuptials, I returned to wish you well.'

'More likely your money ran out,' she said, buying none of it. 'How much did he give you to stay away? And how much more must I pay to see the last of you?'

'Not a *sou*,' Gervaise insisted. 'I merely seek an opportunity to meet the groom and congratulate him. Perhaps it is up to me to give the bride away, since we are nearly married already.'

'Do not dignify what we shared as a marriage, in body or in spirit,' she snapped. 'And do not think you will be attending my wedding, invited or not. If you are seen anywhere near the church, I swear…'

'You threaten me?' He laughed. 'Surely that is not wise. Perhaps you should show me more courtesy, lest I make your new love aware of your past.'

'Robert already knows.' Priss watched the triumphant smile fade from his face. She had done the right thing in admitting the truth, for what could he threaten her with, if not revelation?

'He cannot know all of it,' Gervaise insisted, refusing to believe.

'You should ask him yourself,' she encouraged, praying that he did not. 'I will introduce you. Of course, he is very large and intimidating. Powerful as well. I do not know if he will welcome an acquaintance with you.'

Gervaise was weakening, she could tell. And with his weakness she felt her own strength growing. If she could manage to frighten him away, the notices in the paper would stop and she would never have to experience the embarrassment of a meeting between Reighland and this unworthy nothing. No matter how many times Robert might forgive her, she would never forgive herself.

She renewed her attack. 'I could introduce you. Since Robert is much larger than Mr Hendricks, I expect, when he strikes you, it will hurt much more.' Of course Robert would not strike him. And if he did not want to resort to violence, then she would not be the one to push him to it. But it was probably better that Gervaise did not realise the fact. So she smiled at her former lover with what she hoped was evil glee from imagining his beating. 'If I were you, Gervaise, I would go back to wherever it is that I had come from. You do not want to interfere with this, Gerard. You really do not.'

'I will leave, then,' he said with a bow. 'After a goodbye kiss.'

'Certainly not.' He leaned forwards and she swatted him smartly across the cheek with her fan.

'You wilful baggage,' he snarled, with no trace of a French accent. 'I did not ask for your permission. I am taking what is my due. A kiss should be nothing to you. You allowed me far more than that, as we both know.' He lashed out quickly, seizing her arm and pulling her against him.

And she froze. It was like it had been in the inn, when things had gone so quickly and terribly wrong. He was holding her and she could not fight him. Her mouth was pinned against his and his tongue was inside her mouth. She did not even think of it as a kiss. For she had learned from Robert that kisses were sweet things to be anticipated and cherished.

This was an invasion and she could find no way to stop it. *Struggle*, she cried out to herself. *Prove that you do not want him.* But the part of her that had been so willing to fight, just a few moments ago, had withered like a plant in the desert, becoming small and dry, twisted and useless.

And then, suddenly, she was free of him. Feeling returned slowly to her body and she was aware of fingers wrapped around her gloved arm, and the warning word 'Priscilla?' spoken clearly into her ear.

'Robert.' She should have collapsed into his arms, sobbing. It would have been a clear demonstration of her true feelings. But like so many other emotions, the relief could not seem to come to her.

'May I have an introduction to your friend, please?'

Was he being ironic? She could not tell. But surely he

could see the truth of this without her having to create the scene that would draw the rest of the party goers into the room. 'Gerard Gervaise, may I present the duke of Reighland.'

'Your Grace.' Gervaise was demonstrating the shock that should have been hers. He was white and trembling, obviously terrified of the Duke's reaction.

'I see.' As usual, she could not immediately read the expression on the face of her beloved. 'Good evening, Mr Gervaise, and goodnight.' He grabbed the dancing master by the scruff of the neck and marched him down the hall past several alarmed guests, called to a footman to open the door and shoved Gervaise through it and out into the street.

Robert had never been so angry in his life. Reminding himself that there was probably an innocent explanation for this scene did nothing to calm him. The most logical one was that his fiancée had played him false. Until recently, he'd have sworn she was honesty in all things.

But tonight there had seemed something odd about her behaviour. And she had lied about her love of horses as well. At the time, he had thought it a white lie and a delightful surprise. But now it seemed nothing more than an untruth about the only things he held dear in the world.

'Priscilla, come with me.' As he walked back down the hall he caught her by the hand and pulled her into an empty receiving room, shutting the door in the face of a surprised matron.

'Robert, you should not have done that. The fact we are alone…'

'Cannot be any worse than the fact that you were seen kissing your lover at our engagement ball,' he responded.

'I did not kiss him,' she insisted. 'He kissed me. And it was horrible.' She threw herself into his arms. Almost without meaning to, he held her, stroking her hair as she muttered into his coat. 'He inserted himself into our ball with a false invitation. I did not try to be alone with him. Truly. He followed me into the hallway.'

'You had but to tell me and I'd have put a stop to it,' he said more gently.

'But you were with Father. And I did not want him to know what happened.'

The girl had a very good reason not to reveal the man in front of her volatile father. If Robert felt angry and betrayed by this embarrassing interloper, Benbridge's reaction might have been far worse. 'Very well, then. It was an unfortunate incident, but it is over now. And as long as it does not happen again.'

And how many times would he have to repeat those words to her, in the course of their marriage? He had told her his reasons for avoiding a fight and she had seemed to understand. But perhaps she saw it as a sign of weakness and meant to use it to her own advantage. She was just like so many others in his life, pretending friendship only to laugh at him later.

He felt her shoulders sag. Though she must know he waited for the immediate assurance that this was an isolated incident, she remained silent.

He pushed her away from him then, holding her at arm's length so that he might look in her eyes. 'You are hiding something from me, aren't you? You told me, when last I asked, that there was nothing to the gossip in the paper.'

'And at the time, there was not,' she insisted. 'But since then...'

'You have seen him?' His voice was louder than he'd meant it to be and he felt her cringe.

'He follows me everywhere,' she whispered. 'I cannot leave the house, even for a moment, without him turning up in the street. I ignore him. I avoid him. But it does no good. I do not know what to do.'

'You could have come to me.' He was almost shouting in frustration. He'd have told her to do just as she had, of course. But at least it would not have been a secret. They could have taken some solace in shared misery.

Rather than snapping back at him, the woman he had thought would be his guide through the confusing waters of society was melting under the burden of her own past.

'And what would you have done?' she whispered. 'Would you have challenged him?'

'Of course I would have,' he said. 'I should have done it tonight.' But that was as great a lie as any she'd told him. He'd purposely let the man escape. Because he'd learned, if he waited long enough, that such problems would go away.

'It is good that you did not,' she said, not bothered by his cowardice. 'I doubt that would have made the scandal less. He might have died for something I instigated.'

'Then what would you have me do?' he demanded. Because any answer would be better than the course he'd chosen. 'Am I to stand meekly by, as your old lover trails after you like a school boy?' *The bone is snapped clean through*, a voice whispered. *We'll have to call for a surgeon. Be more careful, Bobby. Next time, you must be careful.*

'I expect you to cast me off,' she said.

She was right. It was the quickest way to end the scandal, but it was more despicable than inaction. Even he was not so big a coward as to give up the woman he loved. 'Perhaps you should allow me to decide what is in my best interests,' he said, pulling her into him again.

'After what has been written about me, everyone knows that you are marrying a silly trollop.'

'After tonight, perhaps,' he said. And how long would it take before some wag from his school days remarked that it was just like Magson to end up in such a position? 'If you'd had the strength to come to me a week ago, we could have avoided this scene.'

'But I did not,' she said. 'After what you know of me, why does it surprise you?'

'I am not surprised. But I am disappointed. I need a woman who can rise above such things. Are you strong enough, I wonder, for the responsibilities you will face as my wife? How will you help me if you cannot help yourself?' But that was not right. He should be the strong one. He had failed to protect her. And now he was blaming her for that failure.

And she pulled away from him so suddenly that the lace of her gown ripped in his clumsy hands. 'I make mistakes, Reighland. I have told you so, from the first moment we met. And so do you. If you had listened to me then, all this could have been avoided.' Then she turned and raced from the room.

'Priscilla, come back here this instant!' He ran after her, into the hall, but she was already halfway up the stairs, trailing tears, in no condition to come down and face the guests. Was he expected to follow?

Instincts said yes, but manners clearly said no. If being alone with her in a sitting room was shocking, then leaving a party to climb the stairs and pound on her bedroom floor would be a disaster. Damn Benbridge for not allowing the Hendrickses in his house. The girl needed her sister. He must find Lady Benbridge to help her, but that harpy would be a poor substitute.

He turned back toward the ballroom and nearly ran into the Deveril girl, who dropped into a curtsy, blocking his way. 'Your Grace.'

'Please excuse me, Miss Deveril, I did not see you there.'

'It has been far too long since you have seen me at all.' She was pouting, as though he were flirting with her and not stating the obvious.

'Well, yes,' he admitted. Was he expected to apologise to every silly girl in the room for preferring another?

'It is no wonder if you hide yourself in the hall. Come, let us go back to the dancing.'

The ballroom was the first place he would have to

search for Lady Benbridge. He could think of no good way to shake off this little parasite, if they needed to go in the same direction. And so, with a frustrated glance back at the stairs, he allowed himself to be led away.

# Chapter Fifteen

'Priscilla, come back here this instant!'

Robert was shouting at her from the hall below. And if she could hear him, then half the party must know that they had argued. It would only take one person telling tales of Gervaise to guess the reason for it. By tomorrow, it would be all over London, magnified to be a thousand times worse than it was. The gossips would have her sporting with Gervaise under the very nose of her father and Reighland.

Poor Robert. He had been right to be angry. She had humiliated him in front of the guests. She should have come to him after that first day in Bond Street and explained everything. But she had not imagined that Gervaise would have been so brazen as to come back to the house.

She wiped a tear away with the back of her hand. She could hear running footsteps on the stairs and in the hall, and hurried to the door to turn the key in the lock.

'Priscilla! Come out of your room this instant. We have a house full of guests.' Ronnie's voice had begun as a shout, but ended in an angry whisper just loud enough to carry through the locked bedroom door.

'I have a megrim,' she called back. And a ruined dress. And a ruined reputation. 'Give them my apologies.'

'You little liar. You are hiding again, plain and simple. Your father will be furious. What am I tell Reighland?'

'Reighland knows,' she replied, trying not to cry.

'That he is marrying the most cloth-headed girl in all of London? I suspect he does. I will go back to the ball and see what can be salvaged of the mess you have made. But only because, in two weeks, I shall be rid of you. After that, it will be Reighland's job to deal with your tantrums and foolishness.'

Priss could hear Ronnie retreating with an angry rustle of taffeta, leaving her alone again. Apparently, she was still ignorant of the extent of the disgrace. Reighland would set her straight on that, soon enough. And tomorrow she could explain that Ronnie and Father would have her on their hands for much longer than a fortnight.

It was not as if she hadn't warned Robert, from the very first. But he'd almost convinced her that she might manage to escape the past. And then, in a few minutes, it had all been ruined. She could not risk Gervaise showing up again at the wedding, or the christening of her first child. And she could not survive the angry scenes that were likely to occur each time and the fresh gossip in the papers.

And what if he caught her alone, as he had tonight? At the memory of the kiss he had forced upon her in the hall, a new wave of shame and revulsion all but overcame her and she had to sit for a moment, eyes closed and breathing slowly to keep from being sick. If she could not manage to control herself around a worthless dancing master, then how could she be a duchess?

She did not want to let Robert go. Even as she gathered pen and ink, her soul wept at the unfairness of it. She wished that he had never shown an interest, or that he had listened any of the many times she had tried to explain the problems there might be.

He had no right, now that he had made her love him, to notice that her past was a difficulty. And to tell her that she must learn to manage it, as though it was a simple thing? As though there was some way to erase what she had done?

The tip of the pen snapped as she touched it to paper, requiring her to sharpen it again before proceeding. As she did, she thought of the words she would choose. Was there any point to call him her darling Robert, when she knew how the letter must end? She would always think of him as such. But for the purposes of a final farewell, he had best be 'His Grace the Duke'.

She added a paragraph about esteeming his acquaintance. It was by far the most inadequate thing she had ever written. But her true feelings for him frightened her too much to put them to paper. How could she admit that he had offered her a miracle, but that that in light of recent events she had decided to refuse it? She settled for a few non-committal words.

After reflecting on our most recent conversation, I find myself unable to continue our association. You must agree that the situation between us has grown impossible. Since I mean you no harm, I cannot hold you to your generous offer of marriage.
I wish you all the best...

In truth, she would rather die than see him happily married to another. Since he so prized her honesty, it went against the grain to lie to him now. But the truth would have him back at her door, arguing that all was forgiven. And she simply could not bear another round of hope followed by inevitable disappointment.

...in finding a woman worthy to be your duchess. But I fear I can never be that woman. And so, farewell.

She slipped off the betrothal ring, folded it up inside the paper and sealed it quickly. Then, before she could change her mind, she called a footman to carry it downstairs for her.

# *Chapter Sixteen*

⁂

Priss passed a quiet night, with surprisingly dreamless sleep. It proved that admitting defeat was the quickest way to gain a peaceful soul. And a few hours of rest made the longing for Robert less painful. She had heard the faint sounds of the ball continuing until the wee hours, proving that there was no problem, not even the disappearance of another daughter, that Father could not manage to pave over.

Had Reighland left after reading her letter? She rather hoped so. The thought of him continuing to drink and dance without her, in her own house, was particularly painful. But it had been her decision to break with him in the middle of a ball. She had no right to dictate his actions after.

More worrying was the unearthly silence that had fallen over the house, afterwards. It was normal that the family would sleep late after so hectic a night. But it was well past luncheon before Veronica knocked on the bedroom door. 'You are wanted immediately in your father's study.' When Priss opened for her, Veronica was white faced, her lips set in a tight angry line, and yet she smiled.

Clearly, an understanding had been reached. She had been tried *in absentia* and now there would be hell to pay. But as yet Priss was unsure which action on her part had been the one to do the job. In the strange state of detachment that had arisen since last night's fiasco, she found that she no longer cared. Robert was lost. Father was angry. Beyond that, there was nothing more to say.

She rose without a word and walked through her door, down the stairs, down the hall, relieved that she no longer felt fear, or even the anger at injustice that had so often led her to rebel. There would be shouting, then it would be over and she could go back to her room.

She went to stand at the place before her father's desk, wondering that there was not a worn spot in the carpet from all the lectures she and her sister before her had received here. This would likely be the last of them, for she doubted she would be living much longer in this house. At least in Scotland, or wherever he was likely to send her, she would no longer be able to hear him shout.

Without preamble, her father slammed his newspaper down on the desk between them and stabbed a finger at an article.

She leaned closer to read.

It was widely suspected that a certain Lady P. took a surprise trip to Scotland last Season with her dancing master. Last night, she was caught at her own engagement ball seeking private lessons from him. R. is discovering that London thoroughbreds are hard to train.

'Explain this,' her father said, as though he did not understand exactly what it meant.

'I think it is quite obvious what is intended,' she replied. It is about me. And Gervaise. The R. is Reighland, of course.'

Her father's eyes narrowed. 'And how did this come to pass?'

'I cannot say,' she admitted. 'Gervaise was at the ball, but I did not invite him. Robert found us together.' She would not repeat the particulars of the conversation that followed. They were no one's business but her own, though she suspected that Father had heard them already, if he'd talked to Robert.

But now he was shaking his head in disgust. 'I have allowed you much freedom of late, assuming that Reighland had you well in hand. But I should have known that you would abuse it and seek out your lover.'

'I did not seek out the company of Gervaise,' she said. 'Though we quarrelled—even Robert would tell you that. Anyone who says otherwise is lying.'

'You should know how to recognise a lie, Priscilla. You have told enough of them over the years. You have wrapped me round your finger and given me nothing but grief.' Benbridge smiled. 'But that is at an end. I had hoped, with your marriage to Reighland, that at the very least you would be his problem and not mine. If you have jeopardised that, do not come weeping to me for another chance.'

He did not know? That made no sense. Robert must have chosen to conceal the contents of her letter for a day or two, to keep the evening from becoming even more newsworthy.

But there would be no better time to speak the truth to her father. It was likely to gain her what she had wanted all along. It would save her a second scolding when the story of the break appeared in the papers.

But why, now that the moment was upon her, did she want nothing more than to run to Robert, to climb into his lap and be held by him, burying her face in his shoulder and hiding from the embarrassment of this latest disgrace? She imagined him whispering soothing words in her hair, offering her his flask, making some quiet dry joke about her popularity with the press, then easing her back on to a bed and chasing the memory out of her mind.

But that Robert was gone, as much a fantasy as her fears of him had been. She was alone and it was time to prove to her father that she was quite capable of truth when it suited her. 'I know better than to expect another chance, Father. And I understand that Reighland was the best match you would ever make for me. But after the embarrassment I put him through last night, I could not justify holding him to our agreement. Therefore I have released him from our engagement and returned his ring.'

'You did what?' It was not the shout she had expected. Really, it was little more than a whisper. But she had no trouble hearing it—she could swear that the whole house went as silent as air before a storm.

'I ended the engagement,' she repeated, resisting the urge to brace herself against an impending gale. 'I cannot put him through the shame of seeing his wife as a topic for gossip, of the *ton* questioning the paternity of his children. When I was forthcoming about my past, Reighland graciously agreed to overlook it. I hoped to live honourably with him and to overcome any scandal. But it seems that there will be no escaping from what I've already done. Nearly a year has passed and people talk more about it than they did right after it happened.'

'He knows?' Her father's eyes were bright with malice. 'And why, pray tell, does he know anything about your past?'

'I told him all,' she admitted. 'From the very first. It was only right that he know the truth.'

'Only right,' mocked her father in a high-pitched voice. 'I will tell you what is right. And that is keeping those in the dark who deserve to remain so.'

'He said it did not matter,' she argued.

'Then he is a bigger dolt than I thought. Now you are the subject of *ton* tattle, no other man in London will have you.'

She lifted her head. The worst would be over, soon enough. She would put forth her proposal and he would put her on the first coach out of London. She need never think of any of it again. At the very least, she would not have to deal with the immediate repercussions of her refusal. 'If Gervaise means to reappear each time I re-enter society, then perhaps it is best if I make a permanent withdrawal to the country, for your sake as well as mine.'

'You stupid, stupid girl. What this Gervaise fellow does means nothing. If you could not manage to keep away from the worthless lout who soiled you, than the least you could have done was refused to give Reighland his walking papers. You had a duke well and truly on the hook. And you let him go over something so foolish as your honour.'

'And his,' she insisted faintly.

Her father laughed. 'Do not try to make me believe that this was over anything more than your desire to spite me. For twenty years, you have cared for nothing more than your own wants and needs. You have used whatever tools that came to hand to make yourself tiresome and difficult until you got your way. This is no different than that.'

But it was. Still, she could not fault his argument. Nor was it difficult to see why he might doubt a change in her character. 'I cannot marry him,' she said, hoping that a repetition would be enough.

'And I cannot do better for you. Nor do I wish to see my own character dragged through the mud with my efforts to give you a place.'

She breathed a small sigh of relief. He finally meant to send her from town. He would deliver sentence, sounding no different than he did at Benbridge when acting as magistrate over his tenants.

Now her father stood and came around the desk to stand at her side. She had not thought of him as tall until this moment. He was several inches shorter than

Robert, but today he towered over her, so large was the anger he carried with him. Then he took her by the elbow and walked her out of the study and into the hall. 'I suppose you are now thinking that I will foist you off on to some other poor relative, in another failed attempt to expunge the stain on your character with time and distance.' He sounded gentle, almost sympathetic. It was her first warning that something was terribly wrong. 'It is hardly necessary, you know. I have a new wife now. And Veronica has more sense than your faithless mother ever had. I will have a new family. In a few months, there might be a son who will cause less trouble in my life than two daughters ever did. In this last act as your father, I will not be manipulated into giving you exactly what you want.'

Last act? Did he mean to kill her? 'Father…I do not understand.'

'Understand this.' He hurried her the last few steps through the hall and opened the front door; they stood on the threshold together, looking out into a steady drizzle. 'I no longer need you. Since you seem so set upon making your own decisions without consulting me, I free you from any obligation to listen to me at all. And by doing so, I free myself. Let us see how you like it, you wilful strumpet.' Then he pushed her through the doorway and closed the door behind her.

She stood for a moment, trying to process the meaning of this. She was still in a day gown, had no bonnet, gloves or shawl and had been left standing on her own front step in the rain. She grabbed the knocker and let it fall. 'Father? I am sorry I've upset you. But if you would give me a moment to explain.' He would see that this action was not wilfulness on her part, but a carefully considered decision.

There was no response, so she knocked again. Twice. And louder. 'Father!' Perhaps she had been wrong to be so sudden. She could send another letter to Robert and he could be the one to explain the situation to Benbridge. Surely fading quietly from memory was better than another scandalous and sudden parting from a daughter.

'Father!' She pounded on the door until her hand hurt, knowing all the while that it would do no good. Even if the servants wanted to, they would not open. She was sure that Benbridge stood just on the other side to prevent it. He meant to teach her a lesson, leaving her to soak to the skin before he considered allowing her back into the house. If then. It was possible she would spend the night, pacing the street in front of her own home.

Unless he truly meant to send her away for good.

She had imagined a hurried carriage ride from London and a forced visit to some aunt or other. Eventually, she would be forgotten and that would be that.

But if he locked the doors and refused her entrance, where was she to go? She had no reticule, no money to buy a ticket on the coach, no letter of explanation or introduction. She did not even have a cloak to keep off the rain. And it was growing dark.

She knew the direction to Reighland's house, of course, but she could hardly appeal to him for aid. With her ruined reputation and their broken engagement, there could be only one type of help he could offer.

For a moment, she considered it. She could be his mistress, if he was willing. He still wanted her body, she was sure. His anger on seeing Gervaise had been quite beyond what she would have considered appropriate for damaged pride. He was jealous. And she could use that to her advantage.

If she could stand to part with him again…which she could not. It had been quite hard enough, setting him free. But to be taken into his protection, only to watch him tire of her and release her again?

She shuddered from the cold and the rain and the misery of it, then began to walk.

# *Chapter Seventeen*

$\mathcal{G}\!\!\!\!\!\sim\!\!\!\!\!\infty$

The trip had been awful. It could have been worse, she supposed, if the neighbourhood she sought had not been a proper one. Even so, on the way to it she had been forced to endure the offers of help from several 'gentlemen' who were not gentlemen at all. What could she expect, really, wandering the streets dressed as she was, with a muslin gown soaking to transparency? They had thought her a soiled dove, with her wet skirts clinging to her legs and no sign of escort.

She had sent them away with fleas in their ears, using her best drawing-room glare. But there was little consolation in having pride when one was footsore and drenched to the skin. It encouraged the fear that when she reached the end of this evening's long journey, she would find that door barred to her as well.

She stood on the front step, letting the rain drip from her gown, and waited. A housekeeper opened the door and said, 'Oh, dearie', before catching herself in a familiarity and dropping a curtsy. Then she ushered her in properly, calling for a footman to find the mistress.

It was a small house, Priss noted, but it was nicely kept. Warm and comfortable. And just the sort of place she suspected would have a warm drink for a stranger, even if she was arriving unexpectedly, and possibly unwelcome. If they would let her stay the night, perhaps tomorrow she would have some idea of what to do.

'Priss!' Without warning, she was crushed in a hug.

'I know it is past time to be calling. And certainly, I have no invitation…' she muttered into Drusilla's sleeve. It was a more fashionable sleeve than she was used to seeing on her sister's arm. And the familiar smell of her sister's Castile soap was overlaid by unfamiliar cologne. But the feeling of loving arms was just as she remembered it.

'You are talking nonsense, Priss.' At least Dru still sounded like Dru. 'What are you doing washed up on my doorstep like a drowned rat? You poor thing.'

'Father,' she managed, weak with relief at the feeling of being taken in hand by her much stronger, older sister.

'Not another word,' said her sister. 'Not until we have you warm and dry again.' Her arm around Priss's shoulders, she led her towards a sitting room, calling for a toddy and a wrapper.

'I will wet it clean through…' Priss sniffled at the water dripping down her nose from her hair '—and your upholstery and rugs as well.'

'Never mind them. Come up to my room instead; we

will get you into a hot bath and one of my nightgowns. And as we do, you will tell me all about it.'

It felt wonderful to be held close and to not have to think any more. Dru had always been so good about organising things, knowing what was needed and procuring it without fuss. Now she was leading Priss up a flight of stairs to a large and comfortable bedroom on the first floor. Priss glanced around her as the footman brought the tub and the maid and housekeeper began filling it with steaming water.

There were men's things in the room. Apparently, Mr Hendricks shared the space with his wife. The cramped quarters did not seem to bother Dru in the slightest, but it reminded Priss that there was another who might have objections to seeing his house turned into a refuge. 'Are you sure that it is all right? Will Mr Hendricks mind?'

'That I have taken in my own sister?' Dru laughed. 'I will see to it that he does not.' There was something about the merry smile that hinted at secrets she would not have expected Dru to have. Priss remembered the perfume scenting her sister's sleeve. She'd have described it as lush and seductive, had she smelled it on another. Apparently, the time away from home had changed Dru more than she'd realised.

'Tell your husband I am sorry.' Priss sniffled again, then sneezed. 'But I could think of nowhere else to go. Father put me out. I never thought he would, but he was angry. Now that he has married Veronica, he says there will be a son. He doesn't need me any more, nor does he wish to give another thought to his troublesome daughters.'

'And we will not think of him, either,' Dru assured her. 'Now that you are engaged, you needn't ever go back. We will take you in until after the wedding.'

'No,' Priss said in a whisper, suddenly afraid that the sniffling might be the beginnings of tears and not illness. 'There will be no wedding. Ever. Gervaise has returned. There have been items in the paper. They did not use my name, but it was obvious. Everyone knows.' The tears began to fall again and she wiped them away with her damp sleeve. 'And it is all my fault. I could not put Robert through that. People will think he is marrying a common whore.'

She waited for the stern lecture that she knew was coming. Silly had been after her for years to mind her reputation and to mind society, begging her to just once exercise some care before acting. She had not listened. Now she was in the soup for certain.

Instead her sister pulled her down on to a couch by the window and stroked her hair, offering her a handkerchief.

Priss took it and blew her nose. 'I have caused so much trouble for everyone. Now I must pay the price for it.'

'You tried to do what was right,' Dru assured her. 'And Father was horrible to you. Reighland is horrible as well, if he will not stand by you in a time of crisis.'

'It is not his fault at all,' Priss argued. 'I could not force Robert into the shame of marrying me, so I released him from his obligation.'

There was a hesitation, then Dru's grip on her tightened. 'That was very noble of you.'

'Father does not think so. He says I am a stupid girl: Reighland was trapped and rightly so, and that all I had to do was keep my mouth shut and go to the altar. Father says he will never unload me now, so he will have no more of me.'

'You are not stupid. You are right not to want a husband who feels he has been trapped. I do not think it would make for a very happy marriage. But if there has been some event that compromised you...' Dru proceeded hesitantly. 'I can still send John to the duke and insist that he have you. It is wrong of him to turn his back on you, just when you need him. And even worse to leave you at the mercy of the gossips, in part because of his behaviour.'

Priss gave a wet laugh. 'I never expected to have a happy marriage until just recently. Now that I have ruined my chances for one, I do not think I could abide another kind. It was stupid of me to run away with Gervaise. Thank heaven you caught me before Gretna Green, or I would be legshackled to him.'

Surprisingly, Dru had found tact. A year ago, she would have agreed and ended with some pious platitude. But now, though she did not rush to her sister's defence, she allowed, 'You had your reasons for leaving our home. They led you to do things that were unwise. I think you were smarter than you let on when you told me, all those months ago, that you had no freedom.'

'I found, once I was with him, that I could not stand the thought of marriage to him, either. He was horrible to me.' That was as close as she could come to admitting the truth to her sister. 'But I thought if I were ruined, then maybe Father would leave me alone. And we could be spinsters together.'

'I…I didn't think you wished my company.' Dru seemed surprised.

'Of course I did. You are my sister. Why would I not wish to be with you? But I did not think you would ever marry. Even if you were often cross with me, I did not want you to be alone with Father.'

'And I spoiled your plans and ran off myself,' Dru said. 'I left you alone instead.'

'It almost didn't matter. I'd have been gone, soon enough, if I'd married. But it has been awful, having to listen to him and not being able to see you, even at parties. You looked happy. You are, are you not?' she clutched eagerly at her sister's hand and felt an answering grasp.

'Very much so.' Dru almost grinned. 'I have a husband who adores me. And friends. And now I have you again. If worse comes to worst, you shall stay here, in my household, as a doting aunt.'

'You are increasing?'

Dru smiled. 'I think I might be. It is about time, is it not? I wanted so much to see you the other night. But I could not manage to keep my dinner down. The thought of prawns and champagne…' She gave a shudder of revulsion. 'I was likely to shame myself in the middle of the dance floor, before I even got to say hello to you.'

Priss gave a relieved sigh and turned to hug her sister again. 'Then it shall be my turn to take care of you. Burnt toast and tea, until you are feeling yourself again.'

'Dru...' Mr Hendricks had stopped in the doorway and was staring at her where she sat on the couch. A look passed between husband and wife. Suddenly Priss was quite sure that, while Silly might extend the invitation of shelter, her husband would not be completely pleased by it.

'Father has turned her out. The engagement is off. And Gervaise is back.'

Mr Hendricks seemed to grow larger at the mention of the name. 'I told him what would happen if he returned. I will take care of it.' He turned to go.

'No!' Priss took a deep breath, then said in a softer, calmer voice, 'I do not wish you to risk harm on my account. If anything happened to you, even a scratch... and it was because of my foolishness... I could not do that to my sister.'

Mr Hendricks seemed surprised by this and shot his wife a quick glance before saying, 'Reighland, then. I will call on him and explain the situation. He shall take care of it.'

'Even worse,' Priss moaned, for that brought forth another picture of Mr Hendricks, who knew most of the story, speaking with the only man that knew the rest.

Another quick look passed between the couple. Then Mr Hendricks said, 'Very well. For the moment, I will do nothing, as long as you promise to get hold of yourself. Because if you are distressed by this man, I will be forced to take action. For now, I will send Folbroke to Benbridge and he will see what is to be done to mend this breach. But do not fear, Lady Priscilla, you are safe and welcome for as long as you need a home.'

'Thank you, Mr Hendricks.' She remembered when she'd first met him, barking his name and ordering him about. And God forbid, she had kissed him to make her sister jealous. She looked at him, praying that he did not remember any of it, but sure that he did. Then she said, 'I am sorry. For everything. And especially for involving you in yet another of my many embarrassments.'

Her apology seemed to surprise him, but he smiled. 'That is all right. If not for you, I would never have met my darling Drusilla.'

Mr Hendricks departed and Dru put Priss into the tub, then washed her, dried her and dressed her in one of her own nightgowns. The fabric pooled at her feet, as did the silk of the wrapper, making Priss feel even more like a coddled child. Then Dru combed out her hair and tied the curls out of the way so she could sleep. It felt wonderful, as it had after Mama had died and her big sister had played mother to her, stepping into the role as if she'd been born to it and easing some of the loneliness.

After all was done, Dru offered her a hot drink and led her to the guest bedroom, assuring that she could stay as long as she liked.

Although how she would live here without so much as a petticoat to call her own, Priss was not sure.

The letter she sent to Veronica the next morning, requesting the right to remove some of her possessions from the house, was summarily ignored. Dru's offer to purchase a wardrobe for her was embarrassing, but she could think of no other way to go on but to accept it with promises of repayment when she found her feet again.

Priss was in no rush to do so, for that would admit what a mess she had made of things. So she had. Priss had allowed herself to succumb to the cold that had resulted from walking the London streets in a rainstorm and spent the better part of a week with her stuffed head buried in the pillows, unwilling and unable to rise and take meals with the family. When she recovered sufficiently to rouse herself, she restated her thanks and apologies to Mr Hendricks.

He gave her an arch look from the end of the table, where she had interrupted his reading of the morning's *Times*. 'Please, Priscilla, do not trouble yourself further on the subject. It is quite apparent that you are considerably altered since we first met. While I welcome the improvement in your character, I am sorry that it was a result of the cold manners of your father and stepmother. Let us hear no more of you begging your way back into the house. I could not in good conscience let you go.'

'But whatever will I do to repay you?'

'For a beginning, you can promise not to kiss me, as you did the first time I rescued you.'

'Certainly not, Mr Hendricks.' The awful memory was being casually thrown back in her face and she took a deep breath to prepare further denials as she would have, had she been talking to her father.

Then she noticed that both he and her sister were smiling at her. 'Very well, then,' she said, with more composure. 'I will try to restrain myself.'

'Then you must allow me to tell Reighland of your whereabouts.'

'I will not see him,' she said, firmly.

'He was likely concerned by your letter, followed by your sudden disappearance. Even if you do not see him, I could seek a short interview with him and make your explanations for you.' As always, Hendricks was the soul of diplomacy. Priss suspected that it was something he wished to do, but he would not proceed without her consent.

'Very well, then,' she said. 'You are bound to see him at some point or other, although I should be able to avoid him.' It was just what she planned to do, unless there was some result from the time they had spent together at the farm. But three days with Gervaise had amounted to nothing. She must pray that she was lucky again. 'Send my apologies for wasting his time, and for embarrassing him with my behaviour. If he is angry, then I can certainly understand it. But I do not think that I can bear another scold on the subject.'

Even the thought of their last meeting made the tears well up in her eyes again. She filled the awkward silence with enthusiastic application of marmalade to toast, hoping that her host and hostess did not notice.

'As you wish,' said Hendricks, pretending to go back to his reading. 'I shall take care of it for you. Do not trouble yourself further.'

She felt none of the relief she'd hoped she would, after his assurance. It only reminded her of the times that Robert had wondered whether she was strong enough to be his duchess. If nothing else did, this would prove to him that the answer was a resounding 'no'.

## Chapter Eighteen

Robert reached into his pocket and crumpled the paper it held, which was still twisted around his ring. When he'd first read it, he'd almost shouted to all the people in the room that they must go home immediately. There was no cause for celebration. He had been jilted in front of the cream of society and they could all laugh as he knew they wished to.

But then he had remembered that this was not his house, nor were these his guests. A revelation of the note would mean alerting Benbridge to some of the more sordid details of the last few minutes.

It had been difficult enough holding up his head while people around him whispered that his fiancée had run crying to her room, and that he had been seen forcibly ejecting someone from the house. Benbridge would want to know the man's name, the reason that Priss had been alone with him, and why she was protecting the bounder when he clearly needed a sound beating for taking liberties with another man's betrothed.

Then there was the matter of the letter. And the ring. And the fact that, if the girl did not want him, did he have any more say in the matter? Did he even have the right to be here? A decent father would take one look at the letter and put him out of the house as well.

But he was dealing with Benbridge. If he pressed the issue, Priss would be hauled bodily down the stairs and forced to dance with tears still wet on her cheeks.

So he had said nothing to anyone, folded the paper up again, stuffed it into his pocket and danced and made merry as if his life depended upon it, leaving the house at dawn just as he had planned to, and telling host and hostess that he hoped Lady Priscilla would be feeling better after a good night's rest.

Almost a week had passed since the receipt of the damned letter; he had received no further word and no apologies for her hasty actions at the party or her silence afterwards. The silly girl seemed to think that she could hand the Duke of Reighland his walking papers and disappear into the night, like some sort of Bedouin.

This farce had gone on long enough. She would not be permitted to upend his life and turn what should have been a simple business arrangement into a Cheltenham tragedy. He had never intended a love match. But for a moment, he thought he'd found one, only to see it evaporate in the heat of the first argument. It was not to be tolerated.

Since she had not come to him, as he had expected her to, he must seek her out. But it was proving difficult. Benbridge had compounded her insult with his unwillingness to give a straight answer on the subject of the girl's whereabouts. When he'd called, the earl was unavailable, as was the countess. The butler had been unable to give him more information on the subject, other than that Lady Priscilla no longer resided in the house and would not be returning. When he had at last cornered the earl and demanded to know Priscilla's whereabouts, the man had looked through him and announced, 'I have no daughter' in sonorous tones, as though he could erase members of his family by sheer force of will.

The whole lot of them were clearly mad.

If she was not at home, he could think of only one other place in London she might have gone. Two other places, actually. There was always the chance that his worst fear was true: he had totally misjudged her and she had run off with the dancing master again. Although he had reminded himself repeatedly that he had no logical reason to wish marriage with someone who preferred another, the idea made him wish to tear down the roads to Scotland, locate the couple and shake Gervaise until his dancing pumps fell off.

But it was far more likely that she had gone to her sister. At the very least, the woman should know of all the properties Benbridge might have secluded her in. He would come away with a list and visit each of them until he found her.

So Robert had come to beard Hendricks in his den. He ignored the protestations of the housekeeper that the master was not at home and pushed his way past her into the man's study. To be turned away repeatedly at the door of an earl was an insult. He would not stand it from Hendricks.

'I was just about to write to you,' Hendricks said, as though there was nothing unusual about being discovered at his desk when the prospective guest had just been informed that 'the master was out'.

'Really? You could have simply spoken to me at the club, at dinner, or anywhere else in London. I see you often enough. In truth, you have been constantly underfoot, trying to win my approval. Until this week, of course.' Robert gave the man a dark glare that did credit to previous iterations of Reighland. 'Suddenly you are as elusive as Benbridge. I demand an explanation.'

'I have been unexpectedly busy,' Hendricks admitted, without turning a hair. The man's calm was maddening.

'Would this increased activity have anything to do with the sudden disappearance of my fiancée?'

'I was given to understand that the engagement was at an end,' Hendricks replied.

'Not from me you weren't,' Robert replied. 'The engagement will be over when I post an announcement in *The Times* and not before.'

'Normally, it is the young lady involved who makes such a decision,' Hendricks informed him placidly.

'This young lady should not be allowed to make decisions, since she clearly lacks the sense to know what is good for her. She will not wish to end the engagement once I have talked to her again. And I will do it over the dead body of her precious dancing master, if that is necessary. I assume that Benbridge has packed her off to the country, just as she always wanted. Or is she hiding here?' Reighland squared his shoulders and gave Hendricks a look that should have sent the man scurrying to fetch her, while the Robert Magson that still quavered inside him crossed his fingers that the answer would bring him closer to the truth.

'She does not wish to see you.' It was not the same thing as affirmation, but he suspected that Hendricks would have told him flat out if he did not know the girl's location.

'I wish to see her,' he said firmly. 'She sent me this. Now she must explain it.' He pulled the letter from his pocket, embarrassed that it showed obvious signs of agitated and frequent reading.

Hendricks ignored the crumples in the paper and gave it a cursory examination. 'It seems plain enough to me. She has cast you off.'

'But I never meant for that,' Robert argued.

'Did you do something that might lead her to write this?'

'I lost my temper with her,' he admitted, thinking of the stricken look on her face as he had scolded her.

'And both the girls have seen enough of that to last a lifetime.'

As if that had not been plain to him already. The annoying prickling of guilt that he'd felt after parting with her had grown into a continual chafing, as though his heart was full of sand. 'She does not complain of it here,' He rattled the paper of the letter, trying to shift the blame and feeling all the worse for it. 'The letter is full of nonsense about protecting me from the shame of association with her.'

Hendricks nodded. 'She would not blame you for your arrogance, of course. Benbridge may not have trained his daughters well, but he has done it thoroughly. Dru was told, practically from birth, that all problems were her own fault. I suspect, once she left, that the role of family scapegoat fell to her sister. Circumspection and humility have come late to Priss. In the past she'd got her way in all things. It has not been a kindness to her character.'

'There is nothing all that wrong with her character,' Robert snapped back, 'other than that it is damned hard to read.' Not that he had ever been good at understanding other humans. 'I thought she had more spirit in her,' he admitted. 'She did nothing but fight me for the first weeks of our acquaintance. And just when I thought matters between us had been settled, she changed.' He stared at the letter in his hand. 'I was not particularly surprised at her threatening to break the engagement, but I did not expect she would actually do it. And in such a weak and spineless way as this.'

'And do you think this speaks her true feelings?' Hendricks prompted.

'Yes,' Robert admitted glumly. 'If she has decided she is not worthy, then it is what she truly feels. But she cannot be further than the truth. It is I who am unworthy.' It was only when he saw the surprise on Hendricks's face that he remembered that Reighland would not think thus.

'She has told me she does not want to see you,' Hendricks said, watching him closely. 'She insists it is for your own good. I will not force her to, for there has been too much of that used already.'

Robert debated for a moment, applying the weight of his forgotten title to the situation. Hendricks talked as if the girl was hiding above stairs. If Reighland had pushed his way this far into the house, what was a few more feet? But Robert Magson shrank from a confrontation that might display his inadequacies before the girl's family. If she could not be persuaded to come back, it would gain him nothing.

'Going to let her go, are you?' Hendricks gave him a curiously neutral look.

'She wishes it,' he said, despising himself for having no better answer. 'She has sent back the ring as well. It might be over, but for the announcement. But if I end it, what is likely to become of her? Will her father find her another match?'

'He has put her out of the house and cut her from the family, just as he did her sister,' Hendricks said. 'In the rain,' he added.

'The bastard!'

'Indeed,' Hendricks agreed. 'She came here with the clothes on her back and nothing more. We cannot get so much as a hair ribbon out of him. She can stay here as long as she needs to, though I will admit that our funds are limited. It will not be what she is accustomed to.'

'She can hardly marry Gervaise in my stead.'

Hendricks was still watching him closely. 'It should be no business of yours whether she does or not.'

'It is my business because...I have feelings for her,' he said, not wanting to sound as miserable as he felt at the idea of her returning to the dancing master. 'Gervaise used her abominably during their supposed elopement and has been dogging her every step for weeks, trying to make mischief between us. He deserves horse whipping, at the very least. But she did not wish me to challenge him,' he added, feeling all the worse that he had not done it before now, despite his reservations.

'She does not wish me to act, either,' Hendricks said, with an ironic smile. 'She was uncharacteristically sure of that fact. It surprised me. Six months ago, I swear she'd have wanted the two of us brawling in the street for her amusement. It seems our Priscilla has developed a heart—due to her association with you, perhaps. But the real question still remains: why Gervaise has returned, after all this time, and why is he eager to renew the acquaintance? The man should not be here. I threatened his life.' Hendricks sighed. 'If I find him, I shall have to call in that particular marker, no matter what Priscilla wishes.'

One such as Hendricks did not say to a duke, 'Stand up for your woman and your honour, or I shall have to do it for you.' But there it was. Robert transferred the onus back to the other man. 'Your threat must not have been very convincing, if he was willing to disregard it and come back to London.'

'Very effective at the time, I assure you,' Hendricks said, indignantly. 'I punched him repeatedly on the nose. And I told him there would be no money, which was the only thing he truly cared about. I suspect that someone else has tracked him down and offered a sum that outweighed the risk.'

'And who might do that?' Robert said, with a half-smile.

'The same sort of person that would share his presence with the papers to destroy a lady's chances with a powerful peer.'

'I could think of several that might consider it.' Three, actually. Of the young ladies he had given his specific attentions to before he had met Priscilla, one had already announced an engagement. The second did not seem mean spirited enough, nor fixed in her affections upon him. 'My money would be on Char Deveril's family.'

Hendricks gave a laugh of surprise. 'You would win the bet, I am sure. Some day, when I am in my cups, I must tell you the connection I have with Miss Deveril. If she knows the full story, she has more than one reason to thwart the future of Lady Priscilla. But freeing up a fat pigeon such as yourself would be more than enough.' Hendricks thought for a moment, and added, 'Your Grace.'

Robert waved it off. 'The title hardly fits. There is nothing graceful about the way I handled this. My only excuse is that my blood was up, at the thought of her with that...' He still could not think clearly on the subject. 'I am not usually so passionate about such things. I certainly had not meant to be. A decision about who to take to wife should not be based on such strong emotions.'

'There are many who would tell you just the opposite.'

'Then they would be blockheads. I acted no better than she did when I saw her with Gervaise. I hurt her. This letter is because she thought I wished to cast her off. She was saving herself some pride by taking the lead, and, strangely enough, it has rebounded upon me. She's admitted her lack of virtue and proven that she is unable to behave properly or manage the scandal attached to her name. She has given me a perfectly legitimate way to avoid an inappropriate match, yet I feel even worse than I did before.'

Hendricks nodded. 'Perhaps you were right about a surfeit of emotion. It would be very difficult for her to be married to a man who so dwelt upon her past mistakes that he was willing to throw them unexpectedly back in her face and doubt her after she had pledged herself to him.'

Damn the man for agreeing with him. He'd found a way to turn subservience into a knife in the back and to twist the blade in the wound. 'But I would not be that man,' he insisted. 'I know well enough how hard it is to live down one's past. I was thought to be a bit of a blockhead in school; boys being what they are, the fellows around me used every chance to remind me of it. When I came of age, I was only too happy to walk away from the lot of them. But now?' Now he was back in the thick of his old enemies and would have to be so for the rest of his life. And much as he might try to pretend it didn't matter, each session of Parliament would bring back all the old memories even if he did prove that he was no longer a weeping schoolboy.

None of which he needed to share with Hendricks. He froze those thoughts in their place, pushing them back, out of the way. 'Let us just say that I understand Priscilla better than most. I would tell her so.' He gave Hendricks a piercing Reighland look. 'If only I knew of some way to contact her.'

Hendricks frowned. 'She will not see you, nor anyone else. I have her permission to offer all explanations that needed making, or I would not have spoken as much as I have. If you wish to send a message, I will attempt to relay it. But I will not guarantee that she will listen. Nor I will not let you speak directly with her. I suspect that pretty words would merely upset her and I will not have that.' Hendricks was looking at him now, with none of the subtlety he usually saved for his betters. It was a clear challenge to someone he deemed a threat to his wife's family.

'Perhaps you are thinking of another man, Hendricks. I have never been known to have a surfeit of pretty speeches.' But much as he had always relied upon them, silence and denial had proven worthless. 'In a case like this, actions are necessary. But she will not know of them, if she thinks to hide in her room.' He thought for a moment, then said, 'If you could persuade her to attend the gathering at the Deverils' house, as she planned to before this hubbub, I will see to it that it is a most diverting evening.'

# Chapter Nineteen

'Get up off that bed this instant, Priscilla, and stop being ridiculous. It is nothing more than a little party. And in the home of one of your oldest friends.' It was strange that several weeks had changed little more than the person standing in the doorway to scold her. Comparing the two, Priss much preferred Dru to Ronnie. There was an undercurrent of love in her sister's commands that had been absent from her stepmother's.

Priscilla stared at the ceiling of her borrowed bedroom without moving. 'Charlotte Deveril is no friend of mine.' She was almost sure of the fact. 'Char was watching in the hall when I ran from Reighland. What better reason for that than that she orchestrated the whole thing?'

'But why would she want to do anything so terrible?' Dru asked, proving that marriage had left her surprisingly naïve to the ways of society.

'Because she wished to discredit me with Reighland.

The moment I gave it back, she was probably searching his pockets for my betrothal ring.' She should have not used a possessive, when speaking of it. It did not even truly belong to Robert. But for the two weeks she had worn it, she had never owned a piece of jewellery that felt so rightly hers. 'If Char still wishes me to come to her house, it is merely to gloat over the fact that she has snared him and to laugh when I embarrass myself again.'

Dru nodded. 'It is good to see that you have become wiser in the months that we have been apart. Char was never a friend to you and tonight she will most assuredly make mischief.'

Priss tossed on the bed, flopping on to her stomach like a rag doll, and moaned into the pillow. 'Then you can see why I do not wish to go.'

'On the contrary, that is exactly why you must go. How else will you prove to her that she cannot affect you? You are worth two of her and are the daughter of an earl as well.' Drusilla sounded quite like the martinet she used to be.

Then Dru paused and bit her lip. 'And if she is angry at you? There is a chance that I had something to do with it. Mr Hendricks and I met her on the road to Scotland. It is rather a long story, but it ended with her kissing Mr Hendricks and me stealing her purse.'

'You did not,' Priss said, eyes wide with surprise.

'I am sorry if I created a problem for you,' Dru said. 'But please do not tell me that you mean to let that horrible girl get the better of us. Now get up off your bed and finish dressing. I will give you no choice in the matter.'

'Do you mean to sit in the corner, as you always used to, to make sure that I do not spoil the evening?' When they had gone about together before she married, Dru had been a steadfast but disapproving companion. However, to be honest, Priss had given her many reasons to disapprove.

Today, when she smiled, the old Silly was gone, replaced by the fashionable Mrs Hendricks. 'Of course not. I mean to dance and leave you to settle your own affairs. Like it or not, Priss, you are a woman now and must learn to find your own way. If you cannot have Reighland, then you must at least see that she does not. The Benbridge family honour is at stake.'

'But mightn't my appearance there cause trouble for Mr Hendricks? I have become a public joke, Dru. I will be an embarrassment for him.'

'Whether you come with us or not, people will ask after you. And I do not mean to hide in my house on a night when my stomach is settled enough to go out. You were merely silly when you were younger,' Dru reminded her. 'Now?' She shrugged. 'You are a notorious fallen woman.'

Priss thought for a moment, then said, 'I believe you are right. I have taken a lover, jilted a duke and been disowned by my father. Short of becoming an opera dancer, there is not much lower to fall.'

'And to my knowledge, Char has not rescinded your invitation to this ball, nor have you sent regrets. It might be quite embarrassing for her to see you.'

'Embarrassing for her?' Priss gave a laugh that was more confident than she felt. 'She is nothing more than a common gossip. And have you ever seen her ride? Reighland could never marry her. He would be miserable.'

'Then you had best go to the Deverils' to tell him so,' Dru agreed. 'At the very least, we shall laugh at his impending misfortune. Now come to my wardrobe and let us choose a gown.' Dru searched through her gowns and held out a pale-rose cambric. 'This has never flattered me, but will do for you if we pin up the hem.'

Priss pushed it out of the way and pointed. 'Let us try that one instead. Crimson satin and far too old for me.'

Dru smiled in approval. 'It is scandalously low as well. And here is proof of what a horrible chaperon I was, for I think it will suit you perfectly.'

'I agree. If I am destined to be notorious, It is high time that I started looking the part.'

Priss entered the ballroom a few polite steps behind her sister and Mr Hendricks, to receive the cool welcome of Mrs Deveril and her aunt, who was a dowager countess. The sweeping glance she received through the elderly lady's lorgnette said it all. She was not so much a guest here as a curiosity to be gawked at.

She responded with the chilly smile her father would have used on such an occasion and turned away to survey the crowd. She saw Reighland across the room, surrounded as he always had been with eager mamas and pretty young ladies forced into introductions. He stood a head taller than anyone in his crowd, looking as always like some great bull mastiff surrounded by a tumble of puppies.

He was magnificent. How could she not have noticed it from the first? She still could not lie to herself enough to call him handsome. But he was powerful: socially, politically and, Lord help her, physically. She could still remember the way it had felt to have him inside of her.

Even now, she could feel the vitality of him calling to her. It gave her a strange ache that was both sweet and sad, when she thought of him. It was like grieving. But while the loss might be irrevocable, she could not imagine trading the brief and intense pleasure of their acquaintance for an end to her current pain.

*I will always love you, Robert.* The thought came to her, pure and simple like a single monument in a barren field. No matter what might become of her, no matter what great destiny awaited him, she could look back on their few weeks together as a bright, shining moment in her past, where her life had seemed truly right and proper.

Judging by his sudden start and hurried attention to anywhere but the door of the ballroom, he had seen her as well. He might pretend not to notice, but he was aware of her presence, she was sure. She wondered if he felt the same, or if he was already tucking away the memories of her, like toys that had lost their glitter.

She turned away, vowing that she would not go to him, though she wanted to stumble across the room like a lovesick girl and take her place in the mob that pressed in upon him. Her recent actions had permanently closed the doors of the marriage mart for her. She was infamous. And while many opinions might be formed about her, no one would think of her as an innocent, or a girl.

Then she watched the crowd part around her. Though the crush was quite overwhelming, it seemed that she was to be allowed space, as though the other ladies were afraid of coming too close. She was tempted to announce that, despite what they might think, dishonour was not a contagious condition, but then she saw the reason for it. Although it would have been nearly impossible to force her way across the room to Robert, there was an open corridor in the crowd that, if she followed it, would lead straight to Gerard Gervaise.

The usual wave of nervous nausea she felt when she looked at him was replaced with righteous anger. It did not particularly surprise her that Char Deveril would drag her own honour through the mud by inviting him here, if it meant there would be another chance to laugh at Priss's expense. But it was unfair to involve Robert in it. She was meant to be trotted out like a puppet and forced into Gervaise's company, while the *ton* reminded the Duke of Reighland of the dangers of choosing an unsuitable wife who would shame him at any opportunity.

But she had nothing left to lose and did not need to play those games any longer. She would not stand by and let Robert be hurt by this scene. Not tonight. Not ever. She turned without a word and went down the hall to the retiring rooms. That way would lead to the library, and the door opposite would take her to the front hall and out the door. She would find the Hendricks carriage, if she could, and sit in it until her sister was ready to depart. And if not? She would walk the distance to their house. She had done it once and would do it again, even if it was a hundred miles.

Her exit would be as grand as her entrance had been. She gave a single look of disgust in the direction of her old dancing master, turned with a swish of skirts and marched from the ballroom. She did not hurry. Hurrying was unseemly, at least until she was sure that no one would see it. Then she would be gone from this place, back to her bedroom where she could cry in peace.

'Running?'

'Robert!' He moved quietly for one so large. She had not heard him approach. But he must have moved with some speed to be able to cross the room and be ahead of her already. If her exit had gone unnoticed, his most surely had caused a scene. He stepped in front of her, ending all hopes of escape.

'Your Grace,' she corrected, giving him the respect due a peer. The days of thinking of him as her darling Robert were firmly at an end. She could not allow his sudden appearance to fluster her into rudeness.

He bowed in response, just as formal, while swallowing the hitch in his breath from what must have been a full-speed tilt across a crowded room. 'Lady Priscilla.' But he made no move to step out of her way, seeming to block the whole of the corridor between her and the front door.

Now that she was facing him, she could not find a single word to say. What thought could she express that would not result in immediate and very public tears?

She stood there, open mouthed, staring beyond him at the sliver of view still left.

'I asked if you were running away,' he said again. His voice was pitched low, yet it still seemed unusually loud.

'Just seeking air,' she said, staring at his feet. 'I feel… unwell.' That was perfectly true, at least. 'And now, if you will excuse me…' She made to go past him.

'No, I will not.' His fingers closed on her gloved wrist. He glanced down at the hand, rubbing his thumb gently against the inside of her arm. 'You are not wearing the gloves that I sent you.'

'They are in my father's house,' she said, 'and therefore lost to me. I expect he has burned them by now, along with the rest of my clothes. I proved a great disappointment to him.'

'I will buy you another pair.'

'And I will not accept them. It would not be proper.' *Buy them for Char, you idiot*, she wanted to scream, *but leave off tormenting me.*

'Then I will not.' He smiled. 'As you know, I would not wish to do anything improper. But neither will I allow you to leave.'

'Do you wish me to stay and be tortured for your amusement? I have let you go. Isn't that enough?'

'No. I find that it is not.' He looked sad and his grasp slipped down her hand until they were touching only fingertip to fingertip. 'Have you thought, even for a moment, that perhaps I am torturing myself? It is quite a blow to my pride to see the two of you together. He is a most insubstantial fellow.'

'Do you not understand the embarrassment that awaits us both if I stay? Please allow me to leave so that you do not have to witness a meeting I did not arrange.'

'But that will spoil your fun,' he said, stubbornly.

'There is nothing enjoyable about this, because there is nothing between Gervaise and myself,' she said firmly. 'You wanted me to manage the scandal when last we talked. And I am avoiding his company, just as a lady ought. You can hardly expect me to be responsible for wounds to your pride.'

'This has nothing to do with your responsibility for my feelings. I simply wished you to know of them.' He stepped closer to her, until she was convinced that she could feel the heat of his body. 'But I want you to know that the sight of you in the same room with him drives me mad with jealousy.' He put his hand upon her shoulder; she felt the palm burning hot against her skin.

'You have no reason to be,' she said, trying not to look into his eyes.

'It would be so with any man,' he said. 'Whenever you dance with another, I want to snatch you out of the arms of your partner, spirit you away and keep you for myself.' His tone was different, not the ironic detached man she was accustomed to, but that of a passionate lover. At one time, she'd have enjoyed toying with him, trying to inflame him to more and more ludicrous declarations of devotion, but now she laid a comforting hand against his cheek.

'But Gervaise is the worst,' he admitted, cradling the hand she offered, stroking it and whispering the words into her palm. 'That he ever touched you? I ache with the thought. And that he hurt you?' The hand on her shoulder tightened ever so slightly to draw her even nearer. 'It would be easier if he had made you happy. But tonight, I would die if I could erase the hurt from your mind. Or he should. I would gladly kill him.'

'You do not fight. You said so yourself.'

'But I will if you wish me to.'

'Do not.' She wrapped her other arm around one of his and buried her face against the lapel of his coat, not caring who might see them.

'Because you care for him?'

'I care for you. For your safety. And for your reputation. I beg you again, do not take that risk on my account.'

He dipped his head. 'Very well, then. As you command.'

'And that is why I will not marry you, you know.' She gave a small bitter laugh and pulled away from him as he kissed the top of her head. 'Because I care for you. You do not need to be saddled with my disgrace.'

'It is no burden,' he said.

'You say that now, but admit the truth to me. When you saw me with Gervaise, you doubted. And that was just the first time. Now that she has found him, I expect Char Deveril to keep trotting out Gervaise for the express purpose of embarrassing me. In the future, your doubts and embarrassment are likely to grow. It is better to end this now, I think, while we can still remember the happiness.'

'I doubted,' he said grudgingly, 'but I did not ask for my freedom. I needed time.'

'Says the man who must rush through everything,' she said with a laugh.

'Just as you will run away at the first sign of trouble,' he accused. 'I could have accepted it, if you'd told me to go hang for my lack of faith in you. I certainly deserved it. I was despicable. Instead, you sent me that mewling note, full of self-pity and cowardice. You took all the blame for what has happened upon yourself.'

'Because it is all my fault,' she argued.

'It is not,' he said firmly. 'But it appears so, because you keep apologising.'

'I'm sorry,' she said, then hurriedly snapped her mouth shut, surprised at how quickly she had affirmed his argument.

His eyes narrowed, clearly angry. And so close, it was a daunting sight. But she knew no real harm would come to her. It was all frustration, and some of it was for her own benefit. 'Perhaps, in the end, you will run from me. But I will not let you run from this.' He reached out and touched her gently on the arm. She remembered every touch he had ever given her and a sweet, sad longing rose inside her.

'The elopement was a scandal of your own making,' he said softly.

'Because I was young and foolish,' she agreed.

'But you are older and wiser now,' he said firmly. 'What happened when you were with Gervaise was proof that he was no gentleman. He should have treated you with kindness. He could have cherished you, like the treasure that you are.'

*As you have done.* She felt a wave of gratitude towards the man who stood before her. What had happened on the road to Scotland could have been wonderful. It could have been a wicked, but cherished memory. It could have been like her stolen moments with Robert.

And it was not. When she thought of Gervaise, she felt nothing but pain and embarrassment and shame. Yet she had performed the same act and more with Robert. And she would gladly do it again, married or not, without a care to who knew of it.

'It will follow you for the rest of your life, if you let it. Or it can end tonight.' As always, his words were seductive.

Her heart was as eager as ever to give in to him. 'And just how do I make it stop?'

'Silence will not be enough and I was wrong to encourage it in you. You must do something to prove that you are not bothered by this. Only then will people stop taking notice.'

She did not want to waste time in the ballroom with Gervaise, or anyone else. She swayed to be closer to him, barely able to concentrate. 'They will cut me from their social circles.'

'They were doing that already. Better to have it based on fact rather than on rumours. Do you prefer to be a disgraced coward, or brave but unwise? Tonight, you must choose.' He let go of her hand. And despicable as he was being, he was right.

She remembered all the times he had wondered about

her strength of character. And how, each time he had, she had run. Then, after giving herself to him, and promising him her life, she had run again.

Yet, here he was. Warm. Stable. And offering her yet one more chance, if she were brave enough to take it. 'Will you escort me back into the ballroom, then?'

'With our engagement broken, are you not afraid it will give the wrong impression?' He was not taking her back so easily as that. She did not think she would have to beg for her place at his side. But her heart still cringed a little at the memory of how it had been the last time they'd been together.

'You are probably right.' She glanced down at herself. 'Considering the gown I have chosen, perhaps people will think you are taking a mistress.'

'That is a capital idea. I have been spurned recently. My heart is still tender from it. Perhaps I should take a lover.'

She gave him a sidelong glance, as unsure as ever as to whether he joked or was serious. 'We will discuss it later. But for now, do you still have the flask of brandy in your pocket? If I mean to have courage, I had best get it from somewhere.'

His expression hadn't changed. But she had the impression he was smiling at her as he reached into his pocket and offered her a drink.

She took it, letting it burn into her, and wondering what the world would think if it got close enough to smell spirits on her breath. She handed it back to Robert. 'Very well, then.' She glanced into the mirror on the wall of the hallway, staring down the reflection until the young lady there found her composure. 'Back to the ballroom it is.' She glanced back at the duke, low and through her lashes in a way that she was sure he would like. 'If you are lucky, Robert, perhaps I shall save you a dance.' Then she turned and swept down the hallway, as though she could chase all hindrances away with a flip of her skirt.

# *Chapter Twenty*

Priss re-entered the ballroom, as though nothing had happened. If Reighland had followed, she did not know. Though he had walked arm in arm with her for the first few steps on the return journey, at some point he had released her, like a boy sailing a toy boat out on to a troubled pond. He meant to watch her, she was sure, to see how she might do without him.

He was right. For all her grand thoughts about being a woman and not a girl, she had shown no real courage of her own. While it might be nice to think that a powerful marriage could set everything to rights again, she would need to play some part in the rebuilding of her own reputation. If she wished to be his wife, or any other man's, it would be better if she brought some backbone to the marriage.

As she stepped forwards, once again she felt the other ladies withdraw. Inside her, the girl that she had been recoiled as well.

And once again she remembered her father. His plan in any situation, whether social or political, was to attack first and hit hard. Because of this, society feared him all out of proportion to his actual worth. She thought of the mud in her slippers, the ruined gown and the miserable head cold that had come along with the shame of banishment. She had learned a hard lesson on her worth in the family and the danger of challenging him.

Now she could teach a similar lesson to those who threatened her. She glanced around the room, choosing her targets with care. The brandy warmed her blood, making her reckless. Or perhaps that was the warmth she felt from the eyes of the only man she truly cared about, watching her from somewhere in the room.

*No one else matters*, she repeated to herself. What could they possibly do that would be worse than losing Robert? Everything that he had said and done from the very beginning proved to her that once she had it, she would not lose his love.

But only if she was brave enough to accept it.

'Lady Priscilla, may I have the next dance?' The Earl of Folbroke was standing just beside her, smiling pleasantly.

'Are you sure you are speaking to the right person, my lord? Your choice in me for a partner does not seem to be a wise one.'

He adjusted his gaze carefully, following the sound of her voice so that he might appear to be looking directly at her. 'If there is some problem with it, I cannot tell what it might be.' Then he pretended to look around the room for the source of her concern. 'I see nothing amiss.'

She could not help it. She giggled. 'Thank you, my lord, for coming to put me in a good humour again. I feel distinctly unwelcome this evening.'

'But you will always have true friends,' he assured her. 'Myself. My wife. And your sister and her husband, of course.'

'I worry that I am a burden upon Mr Hendricks,' she admitted. 'He has ambitions, after all. Such an association might be difficult for him.'

'You will find that his sense of justice far outweighs his aspirations. He will not abandon you. And now, the dance I requested?'

'Of course, my lord.'

He gave her a series of *sotto voce* instructions on how best to help him, so that he might lead her through the set without bumping in to the other dancers. They proceeded, nearly without incident. When his blindness caused a difficulty, he took it in good humour, and made apologies so self-deprecating that the other parties could not possibly be annoyed. As the music ended, she whispered directions to him so that they might end where she most needed to be: in the place where she might do the most damage. And then she thanked him, 'I swear, my lord, you are quite the best partner I have had in some time.'

'Even better than Gerard Gervaise? He is here this evening, you know. Or did you arrive together?' Charlotte Deveril inserted herself into the conversation without invitation, just as Priss had known she would. She was smiling, as though whatever response Priss might give would be a welcome treat.

'Gervaise? Here?' She turned to Char and blinked her eyes in a way that would make them seem larger, bluer and more guileless than she had managed in quite some time. 'For the sake of his future partners, I would hope not. I already know him better than I wish to. And I must say, in all confidence, he is not much of a dancer.'

That had done the trick. She heard a snicker from a nearby widow and felt the mob shift as someone went off to tell someone else of Gervaise's inadequacy. Char's expression turned so bitter that her lips nearly sucked back into her head. 'You are shameless, you know that, don't you? To come into my parents' home and make light of your disgrace.'

'Why, Char, I have no idea what you mean,' she said, still playing the innocent. 'I was invited into your house. Apparently, so was Gervaise. Although I cannot think, for the life of me, why you or your mother would allow such a disreputable fellow to come here. Has he been giving you lessons as well?'

'Certainly not,' Char said, her cheeks reddening more with anger than embarrassment. 'You notice I have invited Reighland as well. After his recent unfortunate mistake, he is once again the most eligible bachelor in London.'

'Is that the meaning of this?' Priss gave a merry laugh. 'I suppose you think, after our recent contretemps, he is fair game. It is too soon to count your chickens, dear Charlotte. There has been no notice in

*The Times* to mark the end of our engagement. Until you see one, poor Reighland is quite under my thumb.'

Folbroke let out a laugh, but the noise Char was making reminded Priss of nothing less than a spitting cat. When she could find words again she said under her breath, 'We shall see, at the end of the evening, whether you are so confident of your place in society. Gervaise will dog your every step from here until the last trump. It will be quite embarrassing, should he arrive at the church with an impediment, will it not?'

'And just how did Gervaise find the nerve to come back to London?' Priss said, with a smile. 'Could he have had help?'

There was a slight, nervous flicker in Char's eyes. 'I have no idea what you mean.'

'And I have no idea why I ever called you friend,' Priss said, shaking her head. 'I must apologise to my sister for being such a ninny. It must have pained her greatly to put up with you. But I must put your mind at rest on one thing. Gervaise would have no reason to offer impediment to any marriage. It is not as if he can cry bigamy, for we never managed to cross the border.'

Char was quite without speech now, managing nothing more than an unladylike shriek of fury.

Priss gave a casual brush to her skirts. 'You poor thing. You sound quite undone. Perhaps you should attend to your other guests. I would not want to keep you from them.'

As her hostess stalked off, Folbroke whispered, 'Masterfully done, my dear.'

'Do you really think so?' In truth, the last battle had

made her want to sink through the floor and it was just the first of many she would have to fight. 'This was all much easier last Season, when I was merely playing at being wicked. The stakes are much higher now.'

'But, Lady Priscilla, if one has fallen from grace, the *ton* is equally fascinated by one's resurrection.' He looked off into the distance for a moment, then said, 'While I have your most charming attention, there is one other matter with which you might help me.'

'Anything, my lord.'

'I have come into possession of a misplaced piece of jewellery that must be returned to its rightful owner. I am sure some lady is distraught at the loss of it. Perhaps you can help me reunite the two.' He fished in his pocket for a moment and offered an open palm.

The Reighland betrothal ring.

It might have been possible that Robert had lost it, only to have it found and pocketed by a blind man. But it was far more likely that he had given it to a friend so that it might be returned discreetly, before anyone commented on the absence.

Priss closed her open mouth and favoured Folbroke with a smile that was wasted on him and a coo of delight that was easily overheard by everyone around them. 'Thank you, my lord. It is my ring and a gift from Robert.' She touched his wrist so that he might find her hand and slip it on over her glove. 'It is rather large, you see. And sometimes it falls from its place without my noticing.'

'You had best be more careful with it in the future. Tell Reighland to get it properly sized for you and I will say nothing of how I found it.' For a man who wished to say nothing, he was saying it rather loudly, and a nearby matron was all but taking notes on the story. It was quite likely that tomorrow's paper would have a carefully coded account of a future duchess's lost-and-found jewelry.

'And now,' he said, 'if you might direct me toward my wife, it is almost time to go into dinner.' She gave him a touch on the arm and a gentle direction.

Dinner. How had she not thought of that? She glanced around hurriedly to see if Robert was nearby, that he might escort her into the dining room. But though she was once again wearing his ring, he was standing at the side of Charlotte, in close conversation with her.

Was this some final slight on his part, to pay her back for her carelessness? She held her breath and waited. And watched as he turned rather suddenly and spoke to Char's aunt, offering his arm to the dowager with a courtly bow. Char was left standing alone, clearly piqued. To hide her confusion, she grabbed the arm of a rather confused young man who could not manage to get out of the way quickly enough.

'Eet seems we are thrown together again. Clearly eet eez a sign that fate favours mee. May I offer you my arm, Priscilla?'

Dear Lord, it was Gervaise again. And if possible, his French accent had grown worse with the passage of time. How was she to get rid of him without being rude? But that had been her problem at the last ball. A desire to avoid a scene had resulted in her going off with a person she loathed and creating an even greater scandal.

Tonight, she turned to him and gave him one final scathing glance. 'No, Gervaise, I think not. That would require me to touch you. And I am recently bathed and have no wish to spoil the feeling of cleanliness with such contact. In fact, on looking at you tonight, I cannot imagine what possessed me to share intimacy with you in the first place.'

'But you must,' he said, looking at her in surprise, then at the dining-room door. 'Azz you can see, there are no other gentlemen willing to have you.'

Looking around, it did appear that the few men she knew who might give her aid had already disappeared from the room. She was left with the choice of Gervaise or nothing.

'Then I shall have to go alone,' she said, and before she lost her nerve she proceeded through the doors of the dining room, unescorted, to search out her seat.

Out of the corner of his eye, Robert saw Priscilla's look of horror at the approach of her old lover and had to force himself not to rush to her rescue. She would never learn to manage if he saved her from every embarrassment. Still, it felt as if he had thrown her into deep water, only to see if she could swim.

And hadn't it been she who was meant to rescue him from drowning? When had things reversed so completely? He held his breath. After what seemed like an eternity, she raised an eyebrow, said something that must have been cutting, judging by the shock that had replaced the smugness on the face of the dancing master. Then she swept past him, and past Robert as well, to find her own way to her seat about halfway down the table.

She had been a pretty girl when he had met her, with a pedigree as fine as he could have hoped for, despite her lack of virtue. But as a woman, she was magnificent. Between the red of her gown and the perfect hauteur, she seemed to glow with a fearless grace that made Charlotte Deveril look like a scheming child in comparison. In response to her entrance men all around the room pricked to awareness like stallions in rut.

And he was one of them. Not just one. He was the strongest, the largest, the most important, the leader of the herd and the only one worthy of such a woman. For the first time in his life he was glad to be Reighland. It would make the winning of her an easy thing.

When he had thought of himself as just plain Robert, he had hoped she would be the making of him, with her family name and her careful breeding. But she was still young, almost painfully so, and barely formed in mind or body. It had been too a heavy burden to place all his hopes on her. But tonight, before his eyes, she was becoming the woman he needed, with grace, power and the quick wit to navigate the deep waters they would inhabit.

He found his seat near the head of the table, as precedence dictated, and stared down the table until he'd caught her eye. She looked startled, as though her nerve was failing. But she was wearing his ring again. He glanced at her hand resting on the stem of a goblet and gave a nod of approval. He wished himself at her side, leaning close to speak to her so that she would know that all the trouble between them was over. Instead, he would spend Lord knew how many courses wedged between the hostess and the dowager in awkward conversation.

But it seemed that dinner would be interesting after all. The dancing master was taking a seat across the table from him. To explain the honour, Mrs Deveril made some excuse about an old French title in the house of Gervaise, but all present knew that it was nothing more than a sick joke to seat them together. Gervaise should not be at the party at all. If he was suffered there, he belonged at the foot of the table, or perhaps in the kitchen with the rest of the help. His presence was yet another attempt to humiliate Priscilla and to make Robert not so subtly aware that the rumours had truth in them. His future wife had been another man's plaything. If he did not wish to acknowledge it, society meant to continually rub it in his face until he was forced to cry off.

Down the table, Priss saw what was happening and poked the meat around her plate, waiting for the inevitable misstep by Gervaise that would raise Robert's temper. She took a bite and chewed methodically, clearly tasting none of the food. She meant to ignore the slight, even if it meant that she choked to death on her dinner.

Which meant that he was expected to make conversation with his neighbours, while the whole table hung on every banal word, hoping for a disaster to enliven the evening. Now, of all times, he should not let his composure slip.

Cold fury flooded through him, the desire to strike out blindly at his enemies. And as always, it was followed by impotent rage and the patient voice of his father reminding him that he must control himself, at all costs. What was the good of being large enough to hurt someone, if one never dared use that strength?

But now he was not simply large—his reach as Reighland was longer than any corporeal arm. The strength of the title was greater than mere muscle. And as he thought about the unfamiliar power that had been given to him, he felt the first real understandings of its use. He had been but playing before, Robert Magson acting as he thought a duke should behave. But the truth was suddenly plain to him.

He was Reighland. He sat in a place of honour at another man's table; the places where he would not be given the best seat numbered on less than two hands. Here, he could and would do just as he wished and the people around him could like it or be damned.

He smiled. It would be a shame to send the crowd home without a show.

Then he applied himself to the plate before him, cutting an oversized chunk of meat and stuffing it into his mouth, taking it down with big gulps of his wine. Let him be every bit the country farmer that people thought him. 'So, Mr Gervaise, what do you do to occupy yourself?' He interrupted the dancing master's conversation with his neighbour and said the question overly loud, pointing his knife in the man's direction.

For a moment, Gervaise remembered their last meeting and his eyes rolled white. Then he wet his lips with a sip of wine. 'Since the fall of *ma belle* France, I have been forced to take employment educating the young ladies in the terpiscorial arts.'

'Terpsicory?' Robert grinned at him, showing his fangs. 'And what is that, then? Some sort of gardening, I'll wager. Cutting the shrubs to look like sheep and what not? I would think they'd have servants for that.'

'No, your Grace,' Gervaise said with a smirk. 'I teach zem to dance.'

'Oh,' Robert said, giving a small laugh at his own expense. 'My mistake. What is it your people say? "Love teaches even asses to dance".'

He'd said it quickly and in what he had been assured was perfectly accented French. Perhaps these nothings assumed that he had spent a lifetime mucking stalls. But before the war, he had managed the Grand Tour, just as the rest of them had. All down the table, people seized their napkins and covered their mouths to hide the laughter. But Gervaise remained totally blank, for he had not understood a word.

Priss shifted nervously in her chair. A few looks in her direction showed that the guests were questioning whether all the barbs in that proverb had been directed at Gervaise alone. They were wondering—did he know about her past? And what did he think of it, if he did?

He would show them soon enough.

'Do not worry about your diminished position,' he said to Gervaise, with a conspiratorial grin. 'Before I began with running the country, I had a farm. And look at me now.' He spread his arms wide to prove that he ruled the world, nearly knocking over his water glass.

'How interesting, your Grace.' Gervaise had the nerve to shoot Priss a sympathetic smile. 'And what did you raise on zees farm of yours?'

'Horses, mostly. But there were the usual number of problems that one might expect on a farm. There was always something breeding. The dogs, for example.' Reighland dropped his voice to a whisper. 'Did you know that some men, when presented with an unwanted litter of pups, will simply bag them up and toss them in the river?'

A few of the ladies at the table gave low gasps of disapproval at his topic of conversation.

'Do not fear,' he said, grinning down the table at them, wagging his finger. 'I am quite fond of dogs. I would never drown some insolent puppy for being a bother. What can they do, after all, but bark mindlessly and gnaw at my boots with their little milk teeth, trying to annoy?'

Eyes went round all around the table. And Gervaise still appeared to be a step behind.

'But vermin? They are quite another manner.' And this he delivered straight into Gervaise's blank face. 'I do not like vermin. They make no end of destruction. They threaten my comfort, my property and my family,' He lost his smile and all trace of the hearty and genial farmer disappeared. 'Vermin, Mr Gervaise, are not to be tolerated. When I find them, I exterminate them. Utterly. When I am through with them, Mr Gervaise, it is as if they never existed.' He brought his knife down so suddenly on his plate that the whole table jumped and he had to glance himself to make sure he had not damaged the Deveril china. Then he brought the blade forwards in a swift stroke, cutting a particularly bloody bite of roast beef, and chewing slowly as though he could feel the flesh of his enemy between his teeth.

Gervaise had gone as white as a parsnip. Apparently, the message was received and understood.

Robert swallowed and looked down the table at his fellows. 'I should be little better, if I were to find that my neighbours had set the rats in the grain bin to do me mischief. Where there should be brotherhood, it would pain me to find betrayal. And I would treat my enemies much the same as I would the rats they released, grinding them into the dirt and sweeping them from my path.'

He took another bite of meat, chewed, swallowed and made another sweeping gesture with his knife that made the people around him flinch.

'There are so many paths available to me I hardly know which way to choose. Duelling, of course, would be deeply satisfying, should I feel someone was threatening me or mine. But that is a rather antiquated way of solving problems, when there are so many subtle courses open to a man of rank and means.' He looked dreamily off into space for a moment, as though imagining some interesting form of revenge. Then he focused on the crowd again. 'But I should certainly not sit quietly while those around me made sport at my expense. Nor would I wish to see other, more vulnerable creatures so harassed. A lady, for instance. I am sure I would come to the rescue of the woman I love and hold her honour as dear as my own.'

When he looked at Priscilla, her hands were shaking so much that she almost spilled her wine. He willed strength back to her and she stilled, raised her glass and drank, giving him a look that raised the temperature of his blood. He had not told the whole room he loved her, but the lot of them would have to be as blind as Folbroke to have missed the fact.

And then he let his eyes rove around the table, to his host, his hostess and their repellant, conniving daughter. 'But one thing I will not do is waste another moment of my time playing games, held up as a country novelty for the entertainment of the common crowd. I lack the talent to hide my intentions behind false smiles, as some of you do, so allow me to speak plainly. I am young yet, new to London and to my title. But unlike my predecessors, I mean to live a good long time.

'Those who are my friends will see the benefits of my patronage. Those who think to slight me now will have years to suffer the consequences of their mistakes. Now, if you will excuse me, I must take my leave and attend to other matters.' He reached into his lap and dropped his napkin on his plate, then stood and left the room without another word.

He walked towards the front door, in a flurry of servants. But before they could attempt to disentangle his carriage from the host of others waiting outside, he held up a hand to stay them. One of his grooms was summoned and he offered a few hushed instructions before heading off on foot towards his next destination, which was barely a mile away.

The servants of the Benbridge household opened for him, but offered some weak excuse about the master being absent, which was utter nonsense. Where else could he be, other than sulking in his own home?

'Then I shall wait,' he said. 'Direct me to a sitting room and tell Benbridge and his lady of my presence so that they might wait upon me when they return.'

He was left to cool his heels for the better part of an hour, as servants scampered up and down the stairs like mice, relaying his message to the master and mistress, and assuring them of the duke's unwillingness to quit the premises. Then a decision had to be made as to whether it was necessary to dress so as to appear to be returning to maintain the charade.

When at last he saw Benbridge and his loathsome wife, the earl greeted him in normal dinner clothes with a shallow bow and a patently false apology for being away from home.

'You hardly could have been expected to wait upon me tonight. I assume there was some gathering or other that I have missed?' He looked hopefully at Lady Benbridge, who automatically supplied, 'There was a ball held by the Deverils this evening.'

'Really.' He feigned surprise. 'I did not think it likely that you would be there. Both of your daughters attended, and you do not seem inclined to speak to either of them.'

'I have no daughters,' the earl erupted with such heat and force that the words might as well have been lava.

'On the contrary. You have two daughters. I have met them both,' Robert corrected. 'I am going to marry one of them.'

'You still intend, after all the news of her, to wed that little fool?' Benbridge's response was half-surprise and half-hope, as though, at this late date, he could retract his bad behaviour towards his younger child.

'Mind your tongue, old man. You are talking about my future wife,' Robert said, finally out of patience. 'I have had enough with your family intrigues. They end tonight. The wedding will continue, exactly as planned, and you will attend it, as will John and Drusilla Hendricks.'

'I beg your pardon?' Benbridge held a hand to his ear, as though pretending he had not heard.

'Let me speak more clearly,' Robert answered. 'It is one thing to politely avoid the company of a person we do not like. That is what I plan to do with you in the future. But it is quite another to make embarrassing public displays of animosity in some pathetic effort to call attention to your own importance.' He glanced in the general direction of the witch that Benbridge had married. 'Just as it is one thing to refuse an invitation and another to have no invitations to refuse. If you wish to play these silly games, I will play them as well and see to it you are cut from guest lists all over London. In the end, I will come out on top of any argument we might have.'

'Are you threatening me, sir?' the old earl all but crowed in outrage.

'Yes, I believe I am,' Robert said, with a pleasant smile. 'Either we will manage to maintain a cordial dislike and you will treat both your daughters with civility, if not with warmth, or I will go out of my way to crush your hopes and thwart your goals. Your choice, Benbridge. Entirely your choice. And now, I must go. It has been an interesting evening thus far, but for me, it is far from over. We look forward to seeing you in church.'

When he exited Benbridge's house, the Reighland carriage was waiting in the street, just as he'd assumed it would be. The groom helped him into his seat and he gave a benevolent smile to the man on the opposite bench who was trussed like a Christmas goose.

'Gervaise. So kind of you to join me this evening. I will require just a few moments of your time.' He reached across and removed the gag from the man's mouth. At one time, he might have shouted at the man to ensure his fear, but tonight he needed to be nothing more than icily polite. It was clearly effective for the dancing master looked ready to wet himself.

'I did not join you. I was set upon by ruffians,' he stammered.

'Only because I was too busy to wait for you myself. So I arranged for your kidnapping,' Robert said. 'I did not have to lift a finger.' Which ought to satisfy both Priss and the memory of his father.

'Where are you taking me?' Gervaise's gaze darted towards the covered window.

'To a place where you will never be able to disrespect me or my duchess ever again.'

'You mean to kill me. Exterminate me, as you said at dinner.' Gervaise's voice was shrill and there was no trace left of the false French accent he had attempted.

'You admit you are vermin, then?' Robert gave him an encouraging nod.

'Yes,' Gervaise whined.

'Very good. We are in agreement. But now let us set the matter straight. I do not mean to kill you. I wish to kill you. But those are two quite different things.'

'Please, don't.'

'That should be "please don't, your Grace".'

'Your Grace,' Gervaise sputtered.

'You would do well to remember that. As I said, I am not going to kill you. I made a promise to Lady Priscilla not to hurt you, but my vow can hardly be expected to extend to my servants. It appears that they were over-zealous in collecting you. I apologise, of course. But I will admit, it does not bother me over much.'

He leaned across the space between them so that he might speak directly into the man's face. 'You would be wise to thank God for the lady's charity and for my sudden decision to value my word of honour over my personal desire to maim you. After what you have done, you are lucky to be so small and pale and worthless. If I were not so sure that I could snap you in half without exertion, you would die for what you have done.'

'What I have done?' Gervaise squeaked with outrage, making him sound even more like the rat he was.

'My intended has told me how you treated her on your aborted elopement. What she describes was little better than rape.'

'She was willing,' he argued.

'She was alone,' Robert shouted and the man quailed back into the cushions of the seat. 'And you hurt her. More than once.' For a moment, Robert forgot his promise and saw nothing but blood. He regained enough control to limit himself to a single, satisfying slap across Gervaise's face, but it was enough to loosen several teeth and would raise a welt that would be purple for a week. The dancer sagged from the seat in a dazed heap on the floor of the carriage. Then Robert remembered all he had been taught: physical violence was no answer, nor was it necessary. Especially not now that he was Reighland. He took a moment to calm himself and then continued the speech he had planned.

'As I said, you may retain your worthless life because I would find no sport in ending you. But you will not be given the opportunity to bother Priscilla again.' The carriage has stopped and the door opened. He grabbed the other man by the collar, pulled him forwards and dropped him to the ground. 'I have brought you to the docks because, I think, in the interests of your health, a sea voyage is in order. I do not really care where you go, as long as you do not return.' He grinned down at Gervaise, then scooped the man up, set him on his feet and brushed the dirt from his coat. 'So which is it to be? Australia? The Americas? Or do you favour a career in the Navy? The choice is yours. But think quickly, before I drop you into the river and let you drown with the rest of the rats.'

Gervaise was struggling in his grasp, eager to be on his way. 'Whatever boat is nearest.'

Robert smiled. 'The Navy it is, then. And a word of advice, Gervaise. The thing in front of you is called a ship. Off you go, then. *Bon voyage.*' He directed the driver and groom to see to it that Mr Gervaise found his way to the captain and climbed back into the carriage to wait.

It was almost dawn before he reached his next destination. He yawned and wondered if he would ever adjust to London hours. It seemed the streets were never empty, no matter when he was on them. In his opinion, decent people should be asleep, rather than just coming home.

Then he smiled. He might be thoroughly done up, but there was at least one who was still awake and hoping that he would visit. While a few hours' sleep might be welcome, he had wasted too much time away from her already.

# Chapter Twenty-One

'Did you have a good evening, dear?' Dru yawned as she pulled off her gloves and shrugged her evening cloak into her husband's waiting arms.

Priscilla gave her sister an arch look, then smiled. 'You know I did. I hope that my behaviour was not too trying.'

Drusilla smiled back at her. 'Now that it does not affect my prospects for marriage, I find it most entertaining. Of course, if Father hears of it, he will be furious.'

'We have no father,' Priss said, pulling a face that she hoped was a creditable imitation of Benbridge when he was angry.

'We will see how long that lasts, once you become the notorious Duchess of Reighland.' Dru glanced at her husband. 'John, will you help her Grace with her cloak? We want her to remember her humble family with kindness after her marriage.'

'Do you really think so?' Priss asked hopefully. 'He left before dinner was even completed. And he said hardly a word to me. He did not even ask me to dance.'

'You are wearing his ring again, aren't you?'

'Well, yes…but he did not give it to me. It was passed to me by Folbroke.'

'If Reighland did not wish for you to have it, it would still be in Folbroke's pocket,' Mr Hendricks assured her.

'And the way he behaved at dinner did seem significant, didn't it?' Priss sighed as she thought of her Robert handling the cream of London society as though he was whipping show ponies around a ring. Why had she ever thought him coarse or common?

'Does that mean the next time he calls, you will be at home to him?' Hendricks asked.

'You had better be,' Dru reminded her, returning to her old dictatorial ways. 'After tonight, I will not let you mope in your room another moment. It is clear that those hostesses who slight you will do so at their peril. I expect to see a flood of invitations in tomorrow's post. And if we do not see a renewed offer from Reighland soon, he shall likely have to fight for your hand.'

Priss twirled once, then dropped on to the sitting-room sofa. 'There will be no others, Dru. If I cannot have Reighland, then I shall have no one at all.'

'Do not be foolish, Priss. You cannot discount all of London without a fair hearing. You had other favourites last year. I know for a fact that several of them are still single.'

Priss reached out and caught her sister's hand, looking seriously up at her. 'This is not caprice, Drusilla. I am quite serious. If I cannot have Reighland…I simply do not know what I will do.'

Her sister squeezed her fingers, then patted her firmly on the shoulder. 'You do not need to think of that tonight, my love.'

Hendricks pulled aside the curtain and looked out on to the street. 'It is morning, dearest. And it seems she will have to think of it after all. We have a visitor.'

Before they had even heard a knock on the door, Hendricks was out in the hall and opening with a deferential, 'How may I be of service to you, your Grace?'

'You can leave off with bowing and explain to me how you were waiting at the door to let me in. Your foresight is quite uncanny, Hendricks.'

'A coincidence, your Grace, nothing more.'

'Robert!' She could not help it, but she sprang to her feet and ran to the hall, pelting into him and throwing her arms around his body before he had even managed to remove his coat.

In response she felt his arms tighten around her and his body slump gratefully into hers. 'Hendricks, Mrs Hendricks, might I have permission to speak to my betrothed alone for a time?'

'Is that what she is again?' Hendricks asked. 'The *ton* is buzzing with rumours as to whether you will marry or not. Considering the recent scandal and the incidents of tonight, circumspection might be wise.'

'Oh, John, do not be difficult.' To Priss's surprise, the last came from her sister, who had twined her arms about her husband's neck and was murmuring sleepily into his lapel. 'I swear, I am so exhausted that you must put me to bed.' She looked up long enough to give Reighland a sloe-eyed stare. 'We must trust you to treat my sister properly, your Grace. Perhaps tomorrow a special licence might be procured.'

'Unfortunately, not,' Reighland replied and Priss loosened her grip on him, afraid that she had misunderstood everything that had happened in the last few hours. 'We will be married in St George's on the day we reserved it. There will be a bishop at the altar and the Prince Regent shall sit in the first pew. There will be so much pomp and ceremony that all of London will take notice.' He gave Priss a tired smile. 'I am sure I will find it quite unbearable. But when it is through there will be no question that you are my duchess.'

'Father will want to know of it,' Priss said, trying not to sound disappointed by the fact.

'He has already been informed that his presence is required,' Robert said. 'And I assume you will want your sister and Mr Hendricks to stand witness.'

'I did not think it would be possible,' she whispered.

'If it will make you happy, then I insist upon it,' Robert said, looking and sounding less like an irritable bear and more like a sleepy lion who assumed his wishes would be attended to with no further growling.

'It is clear that my sister is in good hands, Your Grace.' Dru whispered something in her husband's ear and tugged upon his arm, leading him towards the stairs. Then she glanced back over her shoulder. 'When you are finished talking, please let yourself out. Priscilla, we will see you at breakfast.'

Priss burrowed a little further into Reighland's coat

and listened to the retreating footsteps, wondering if she had actually heard the irony in her sister's voice at the idea that all they would do was talk. Then she pulled Robert back with her towards the couch in the sitting room. 'We have been left unchaperond again, Reighland,' she said.

'Considering how I feel about you, that is probably unwise,' he rumbled. 'But then, when have either of us ever bowed to convention?'

'True enough.'

'This evening, your behaviour was quite scandalous.' He collapsed on to the seat with her and pulled her close until she was practically sitting in his lap.

'I am sorry I have shamed you.'

'On the contrary. You were most diverting. Is it true that you called Gervaise an inadequate lover?'

'Merely a rumour,' she said.

'Then of course I shall ignore it.'

'But there is some truth in the statement,' she admitted. 'He was most unsatisfactory.' The description made her smile. 'Most unsatisfactory indeed.'

'And he deserved to be punished for it,' Robert agreed. 'I have sent him away again, more permanently this time. I drove him down to the docks and put him on the nearest ship. He will be gone with the morning tide. But now to less insignificant matters. What do the gossips say of your other lovers?'

She smiled. 'That I had one of the most powerful men in England at my feet.'

'And you do again,' he said, sliding off the sofa and on to his knees before her. 'Of course, in that dress, you could bring any man to his knees. You look positively indecent in it.'

'Do you really think so?' A few weeks ago, the comment would have embarrassed her, but now, coming from Reighland, it seemed the most natural compliment in the world.

'Allow me to show you.' He crooked a finger to coax her closer, as though he were about to whisper a secret. But as she leaned forwards, her bodice gaped and he hooked his finger in it and tugged it down to free her breasts. 'Shocking,' he muttered, then buried his face in them.

'Reighland,' she whispered, tugging at his hair, 'does this mean I am forgiven?'

'There is nothing to forgive,' he muttered. And then he paused and looked up, smiling. 'Unless it is I who need forgiving. I left you alone when you needed me. I did not help you, when you were afraid. And I shouted at you, the night we argued. But I mean to make up for that now.' He reached for her slipper, pulled it off and threw it behind him.

She gasped.

'Am I to be treated to such a reaction each time we remove your shoes?'

'Only because I remember what happened the last time,' she said. 'And you cannot be throwing clothing all over my sister's sitting room. It is not proper.'

'Very well, then. Only the one shoe tonight. I will save your full unveiling until after the wedding.'

'That is good,' she said, a little disappointed that it had been so easy to persuade him to behave.

Then he lowered his mouth to her breasts again, taking a nipple deep into his mouth and pulling upon it until she thought she might scream from the excitement. He sensed her agitation and looked up. 'Do you want me to stop?'

'It is almost dawn,' she said. 'The servants will be up soon.' She thought for a moment of the sorry state she was in and the feeling of his kiss drying on her breast. 'I want you to hurry.'

'But I meant to take my time,' he said, kissing slowly upwards in a trail of nips. 'I would not wish to be thought inadequate. I have a reputation to maintain, after all.' He found her mouth and ravished it, his hand cupping the back of her neck so that she had to struggle to escape him.

'Reighland!' she whispered.

He sighed. 'Very well, then. As my lady wishes, we shall do this quickly.' And he flipped her skirt up and buried his face between her legs.

'What...?' It was the last thought she managed before he found the core of her and sucked it into his mouth, working it mercilessly with his tongue. In seconds she was fully aroused, and in less than a minute she was begging him. By the first shudder he had undone his trousers and yanked her out of her seat, on to her knees and on to him, pinning her against the furniture and taking her in short hard thrusts. She kissed him to stifle his groans and her own, digging her hands into his shoulders and letting go of everything else in the world as he lost himself in a rush that swept her along with him.

He relaxed back on his haunches, holding her to him with one hand and tugging her bodice up with the other. Then he whispered, 'Was that as you wished it?'

'That was amazing,' she replied.

'Six days,' he said, 'until we are married. If I do not mean to spend it here on the floor with you, I had best be going.'

'On the contrary,' she whispered, 'I think you must stay for breakfast.'

'Think of your reputation,' he said with no real enthusiasm.

'I am,' she said with a smile. 'If I do not do something scandalous at least once a day, whatever shall they write in the papers?'

\* \* \* \* \*

# MILLS & BOON

## HISTORICAL

### Awaken the romance of the past

Escape with historical heroes from time gone by. Whether your passion is for wicked Regency Rakes, muscled Viking warriors or rugged Highlanders, indulge your fantasies and awaken the romance of the past.

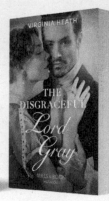